Other *Leisure* books by Stephen Laws:

DARKFALL

THE HIDEOUS VISION

Then Karen saw the corpse.

It was hanging by the neck from the gallows like a bag of rags and bones. She could see bare ribs beneath the ripped fabric of an old coat. A bloated tongue was sticking out of the body's mouth, blood was dripping to the ground. The wild, white eyes were staring in agony as the body swung in time to the creaking of the gibbet. The corpse's neck had been horribly stretched by the rope like scarred white rubber. Stark, clawlike hands jutted away from the hanged man's body.

And then the rope snapped.

The corpse dropped to the ground like a sack of old bones.

But now the corpse was more than just a lifeless body.

It began to crawl in the dark.

Karen wanted to turn and run away, but she could not move as the creeping, fumbling thing began crawling towards her. She could see the moon-glinting of its eyes as it came. It was smiling, but the eyes still held agony. It rose slowly and awkwardly to its feet. And now Karen could see that in one of its claw hands it was holding the noose which had been around its neck, swinging it from side to side. It spoke in a voice that gargled words. . . .

STEPHEN LAWS

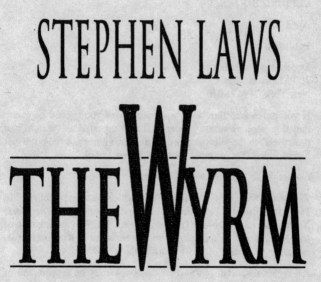

THE WYRM

LEISURE BOOKS **NEW YORK CITY**

LEISURE BOOKS ®

April 2004

Published by

Dorchester Publishing Co., Inc.
200 Madison Avenue
New York, NY 10016

ISBN 0-8439-5219-9

Visit us on the web at www.dorchesterpub.com.

CONTENTS

"Whoever fights monsters should see to it that in the process he does not become a monster. And when you look long into an abyss the abyss also looks into you."
—Nietzsche, *Beyond Good and Evil*

". . . what clever people have not yet learned, some quite ordinary people have not yet entirely forgotten."
—C. M. Kornbluth, *The Mind Worm*

Prologue

"Reality is a crossroads," said the white-haired man, reaching for his drink.

There was a strange expression on his face as his hand grasped his glass: a hint of memories, unpleasant memories. And of suppressed truths, perhaps. He knew that the statement would intrigue me. I had been very persistent all afternoon, asking what I hoped were subtle questions of this strange celebrity who had always adamantly refused interviews with the media. Finally, under my cautious interrogation, it seemed that he was opening up. I was excited. Could this be the story my colleagues had hungered for?

"Tell me more," I asked, feigning nonchalance.

The man smiled. I was aware that my heart was hammering but the shame of my unprofessionalism was swamped by mounting excitement. I had to be careful. How many interviews had this guy walked out on? One wrong word . . . just one . . . and I might lose him.

"Look, I know how you feel," I continued. "You've avoided publicity for over six months now. But the publicity industry *has* to follow you around, don't you see that? How can you avoid it? Six hundred and thirty-five people are dead. Six hundred and thirty-five! How can you expect the press to leave you alone?"

And now, my big pitch. The one I'd been working up to.

"I know you can't tell me everything. I know you've taken an oath not to talk . . . a personal vow of secrecy." *Hit him with it! Hit him with it now! Go for broke!* "And I respect that. I don't want you to give me everything. I know that the gutter press have pissed you off. But believe me, I don't want it all (*yes, I do*). And I know that you want to talk. So . . . we're here . . . and I'm not hassling you, or wanting to squeeze out more than you're prepared to give. Why not talk?"

The white-haired man smiled again. A sad smile. And then he began to speak.

"As a species, we're very limited in our perception of what constitutes reality. We inhabit flesh-and-blood physical bodies consisting of flesh and blood and complex chemical interactions—machines of blood, sinew and muscle. We require proteins, liquids and oxygen to survive. Our viewpoint is based on a perception of three dimensions: height, breadth and depth. Some of our more educated men have put forward the theory that there is a fourth dimension—time itself. However, even that theory is still frowned upon by . . ." Again, the smile. The white-haired man sipped at his glass before continuing: ". . . men of science. The predominant attitude is that unless an event or happening can be proved within the parameters of our limited perceptions then it cannot be regarded as factual. It's the general attitude."

The man stared out of the window for a while. He could have been listening to some mysterious internal voice as it told him what to say next. I didn't push him. If I did, he might clam up. After what seemed to me an agonisingly long time, he began again.

"It's also a mark of supreme arrogance."

"You think we're just fooling ourselves, then? You believe we're overlooking fundamental truths by ignoring . . . well . . . (*careful*) paranormal events?" I was too eager. I prayed to God that it didn't show.

The white-haired man frowned, stroking back his hair. He wanted to tell me things—I could see it in his face— but he was holding back, choosing his words very carefully. "Yes . . . but there's much more to it than that," he said slowly. "We're in danger. Constantly endangered by our attitude and our limited perceptions. *Dreadful danger*. One day, something could happen . . . something so terrible . . ." His words trailed away.

"What kind of danger?" Another mistake. The question was too direct, and he didn't like that kind of question. I quickly retracted by asking another, less direct: "You said that reality was a crossroads?"

A pause. Had I lost him?

"This world of ours," he began again, "our reality if you like . . . is at the intersection of a crossroads. That's the best way I can describe it. But the roads I'm talking about are . . . different. They're different realities in themselves. Do you understand what I'm saying?"

I understood. His secret story had been my fascination for a long time. I had studied all the available information—which was very little—and also the textbooks (both

3

serious and demented) which dealt with the subject-matter. "A number of different roads—all different realities," I said. "All intersecting on our own reality, our world. But we're unaware of them. Limited in our perceptions, like you said. And that's . . ."

"The danger," the man finished for me. "The things of which we should be most afraid draw their power from the fact that we won't . . . that we refuse . . . to acknowledge their existence. We refuse to acknowledge their existence even though instinctively we can sense their presence. It's an instinct . . . a primitive instinct, if you like, which has been browbeaten by our intellectual powers. The more civilised we grow, the less contact we have with our inbuilt warning instinct." The man was eager now, draining his glass, pausing only to draw on his cigar. This was the moment I had been waiting for, the moment when his instinctive enthusiasm would overcome his protective caution.

I hailed the waiter. I had bribed him for just such a moment. Within seconds, he had arrived at our table with two fresh drinks. Doubles.

"Do you know what fear is?" asked the white-haired man.

No. Perhaps not. But I could sense it in his question, feel its cold breath in my face and its cold hand on my shoulder. I could see its effects in the man's prematurely white hair. No shit. Honest. It must have been eighty degrees in that bar, but I swear I felt a shiver running through my body.

"I mean . . . real . . . fear?" he asked again.

He didn't wait for an answer. Not that I could have spoken just then, anyway.

"Well, I do. God help me, I do."

He did. I believed him.

He began to talk.

4

Part One
The Sleeping

Chapter One

Michael Lambton was dead, and he felt much better for it. Not good, but better.

He watched his two German shepherd dogs, Mac and Dutch, as they chased each other over the grass in a black-and-tan flurry of fur. In a way, he envied them. They were alive and enjoying every minute of it—a simple concept which Michael could no longer grasp. He could not afford to be alive again; it was much too dangerous. Dutch began barking, just for the hell of it. The dog wanted everything within earshot to know how good it was to be living. He spun round and raced back towards the farmhouse with Mac close behind, almost on his tail. Michael watched them run.

It was warm today. He could feel the sun on his skin.
Dead skin.

He shrugged off the thought and concentrated on examining the surrounding countryside from his vantage point. He was standing by the fence on the western boundary of his property, looking across unkempt grass to the farmhouse. Its days as a working farm were long gone. The single-storied, roughly hewn stone bore testimony to its origins, but the thatched roof owed more to the twentieth century plastic and insulation industry than to turn-of-the-century crofters. Michael's dogs—the closest thing to livestock that the farm had experienced in more than twenty years—were even now bounding past the farmhouse to the ruined foundations of an ancient barn, pulled down by Michael when he had first bought the property over two years ago.

He looked past his home to the first slopes of the mountain range which surrounded the valley: coarse brush giving way to clusters of boulders as the incline steepened; then sharp, angular buttresses of rock. A rough track from the village wound its way up from the foothills into the higher reaches of the mountain range.

Dead skin.

In spite of the sun, he shuddered, and began to walk slowly towards the house. On his left, the main road out of the valley passed the farm, still known by its old working name: Split Crow Farm. On the right, the road continued down towards nearby Shillingham and then up again into the mountains. The village nestled in the cradle of the valley and was proud of its position in the Border area, right smack dab between England and Scotland and fiercely protective of its individual identity. Fringed by forested hills, the names of its roads were derived from the woods and copses; the wandering country lanes were uncongested by traffic. The first roots of Christianity in England had been planted here. Historically, the village had suffered at the hands of both the English and the Scots and it seemed that, even now, the inhabitants were unprepared to forget this fact. Under Edward I, attempts had been made to forge laws to govern relations between the two countries in the maintenance of law and justice, but Shillingham at that time had been notoriously "evill countrie," harassed alike by Scottish raiders and English looters.

Although it was still early, a heat-haze shimmered over the distant rooftops and the spire of the council buildings. *A village full of strangers*, thought Michael, and then laughed at himself. Was it a sign of emerging paranoia or a mammoth ego to assume that the inhabitants of Shillingham were the strangers and he, the relatively new and isolated intruder, was not? He was the stranger and outsider; a fact confirmed by popular opinion. And it was an arrangement he was happy to maintain. He did not want anything to do with anyone. He only wanted to be alone. If he had wanted to socialise, he would have stayed in the city. He wanted to remain . . . *a dead man* . . . an outsider. He wanted isolation. He had Dutch and Mac. They were the only company he needed, and a damn sight more trustworthy than the majority of the people he had known, particularly in the last eight years of his life. (*Before my death*, he thought again wryly.)

He looked up to see that the dogs had doubled back and were heading towards him again, Mac now in the lead. The dog did not halt in its flight, leaping up at Michael and hitting him full in the chest, a favourite trick. Michael doubled over, winded, grabbing the dog's paws so that they both staggered in a drunken dance. He laughed. It was as if the animals could sense his moods, could imagine what he was thinking and wanted to snap him out of it.

"Okay, okay . . . I get the picture. You don't want me brooding. Fair enough. Let's go and have breakfast."

9

He pushed Mac to one side, ruffled Dutch around his mane to show that there was no favouritism and carried on towards the farmhouse. He remembered how Dutch had knocked the village postman flat on his back one morning and had stood snarling over the poor fellow's prostrate form, letters and parcels scattered all over the grass. Michael had heard the screams for help and had emerged from the kitchen to find the postie staring up into the dog's fixed eyes, fur sticking up, growling low in its throat. Mac had taken advantage of the situation to begin chewing open a registered parcel for someone at the council offices. Michael had recalled the dogs and attempted to placate the postman.

"Not savage?" the dishevelled, balding sixty-year-old had replied to Michael in indignation. "Not savage? Who are you kidding, then? The bloody things are like wolves. You should keep the buggers locked up in a cage."

"You probably took them by surprise. I didn't hear you coming up . . ."

"Took them by surprise? You've got some nerve, lad! Well here's a surprise for you. There'll be no more deliveries up here at Split Crow as long as those animals are around. You can collect the stuff yourself from the post office in the village. If I wasn't such an even-tempered fella, I'd report you to Sergeant Grover for being in possession of two wild animals. Count yourself lucky I'm an animal lover, Mr. Lambton. Otherwise, the pair of them would be put down."

Dutch had not helped matters by growling low in his throat again, sensing the postman's hostility from his words. As a result of this incident, Michael now had to walk the two miles into Shillingham every other day. Even now, a year later, the staff at the post office was still rather frosty.

Walking the dogs in the village was also a thing of the past, but this was something neither he nor the animals missed: a remembrance of civilisation.

Michael reached the front door and allowed the dogs to bustle inside, looking up only fleetingly at the mountainside as he did so. He was glad that he had, otherwise he would have missed the girl walking along the rough track which bordered his property and led down to the village. As usual, she was waving. As usual, he waved back, smiling.

They had never met. But the waving ritual had been going on now for more than eight months. Today, she was wearing blue denim jeans and a white blouse. She was carrying her usual holdall, containing her work clothes, Michael presumed: the bag was too light to be a shopping bag. Her long hair was sleek and black and, even from this distance, Michael could tell that she was smiling. She always walked along this track to the village at the same time every morning and at the same time in the evening. She had begun the waving ritual, but had never crossed the short distance to the boundary fence in an attempt to be friendly. Michael was grateful to her for that. She was obviously a neighbour, probably from one of the farms on the other side of the hill, but she respected his privacy and did not intrude. The ritual was one of the high points of his day, nevertheless. He looked forward to it.

She continued on her way, swinging the holdall. Michael waved again and she responded before rounding a bend and vanishing from sight behind thick clumps of gorse. Inside the farmhouse, the dogs were barking, impatient for their food. Michael went in and closed the door behind him against the outside world.

He wondered if the girl knew that she was waving to a dead man.

11

Chapter Two

Christy reflected on the strange man who lived at Split Crow Farm as she made her way down to Shillingham. He kept very much to himself, and the only real interaction he had had with his neighbours seemed to have been the incident between his two dogs and the postman. According to the post office, they had very nearly torn the poor old boy to pieces, but Christy suspected that the story had been exaggerated. Since his arrival he had made no attempt to get to know the villagers, and this had been taken by some as an expression of hostility, which Christy felt was a little unfair. If he wanted to be alone, why not leave him to it? There was no harm being done. Popular opinion in the village ranged from the unlikely to the downright fantastic. The man was a loony, or an ex-prisoner. They knew that he was a writer of some sort, probably of pornographic books, or worse. He had often been seen frequenting that weird bookshop in End Row, owned by the ex-hippie. He had obviously trained his dogs to attack innocent bystanders. Christy had listened to the gossip circulating in the village and amongst the customers who frequented the coffee shop in Shillingham's High Street, where she worked.

The man had moved into the Split Crow place about two years ago. Prior to that the farm had fallen into disrepair, following the departure of the previous owner. The property had been quite cheap to acquire, and the local grapevine had found out (from the local labour involved) that Lambton had invested a substantial amount in renovating the house to suit his needs—which in itself seemed strange, since he could easily have bought another place in the valley which would have cost him much less to repair. Another mystery. Another suggestion of hidden motives, all adding to the village's uneasiness about him.

Christy felt sorry for him. She was sure that 90 percent of the gossip in the village was untrue. She had seen one of his books in the local supermarket with a photograph on the cover. It was a thriller of sorts, but looked a little too heavy for her. Christy did not go in for that kind of reading, but she had sneaked a look at the blurb on the cover and the critics seemed to think that his work was very good indeed. Maybe he was one of those eccentric writers who needed a quiet country retreat to get absorbed in his work. As for being a loony, well, she was certain that eccentricity was not a crime. Let the others think what they wanted. On the day she had come to that conclusion, she had waved at him as she passed Split Crow on her way to work. He had hesitated and then waved back. It had seemed an eager wave, Christy thought, and this had made her even more sympathetic towards him. Maybe he was lonely.

She knew all about loneliness.

A small van rattled away up the mountain road to her left, raising dust. She waved, not able to see that it was Mr. Johnson at the wheel, but knowing it anyway. The invisible driver angrily beeped his horn as the vehicle coughed and spluttered out of sight. Mr. Johnson owned the grocer's shop not far from the coffee shop. He was a short-tempered, short-sighted man, with large ambitions and a long memory for those who crossed him. Christy managed to irritate the hell out of him by being nice to him when, of all the people in the village, he was the last one to deserve any civility. She reached the first houses on the fringes of Shillingham and crossed the ancient stone bridge over the river which ran bright and clear down from the mountains on its way to the sea, over fifty miles away.

She paused on the bridge, braced her hands on the rough stone and watched the crystal-clear, foaming water and the riverbed beneath. *No beer cans floating there*, she thought. *No bike frames, no used condoms, no sewage*. That was one of the joys of this part of Northumberland and the Borders: it was unspoilt land—unspoilt, that is, by modern man. She raised her head, looking up along the river and higher, to its source, in the slopes surrounding Shillingham. The countryside was, by turns, stark and beautiful, idyllic and—occasionally—dangerous. When winter came, it could be a harsh and deadly mistress, with the tree-lined country lanes turned into treacherous, snow-smothered, ice-lined death traps. But now, in August, summer brought verdant greenery and kindly skies. With an unchallengeable simplicity, Christy loved the forests, the sinuous valley roads, the mountains and the grey stone buildings of Shillingham. But it . . .

. . . *isn't enough*, thought Christy. *If things were different at home, then maybe I could stay. But they're not, and I can't. I need to, need to . . .*

She needed to escape.

Sighing, she crossed the bridge. Not for the first time, she realised that she was finally coming to her own internal crossroads. A decision would have to be made.

She continued on her way, crossing Dene Row, a rough cobbled street, her mind on the rooks circling overhead. She felt strangely envious of them, but did not understand why. Reaching the village square, she paused for a while to look round. The Victorian clock in the centre of the square pointed to twenty minutes to four—a lie. The clock hands had been stuck on that time for over a month and had caused major arguments in the council chamber of the village hall. No one would accept responsibility for fixing the clock, a bequest from local landowners at the turn of the century.

Christy recalled that Mr. Johnson had written a letter to Shillingham's leading Councillor, expressing his view that the reason for the breakdown was that the clock was full of pigeon shit and that if someone would give him permission, he would bring his twelve-bore down to the market place and blast the living hell out of all the pigeons in sight. The Councillor had declined his kind offer with thanks. Mr. Johnson did not like pigeons, or "scems" as he liked to call them in his rich Northumbrian accent, spitting the word out in disgust. His motives, it was well known, had more to do with losing an allotment of young greens to scavenging birds than to any sense of civic responsibility.

Christy crossed the square and made her way up the High Street towards the coffee shop, aware of the small village coming to life around her. Shops were being opened, newspaper boys on bicycles swished past on their delivery rounds. A milk float rattled round the corner and Christy ignored the wolf whistle that accompanied it. Hearing a distant, overhead rushing of air, she shaded her eyes, threw back her long black hair and squinted into the sun. In the cloudless blue sky, a charter jet was streaking towards exotic climes. It was a faint grey speck tracing a white scratch across the sky. And on board were dozens of people, all drinking duty-free and discussing their plans for two or three weeks in another country, another world. Christy wished that she was on that aeroplane. But she would not be here forever. Her job in the coffee shop, working for Iris Wooler, was only a stepping-stone. She was taking an Open University course in Humanities. And when she had passed that (there was no doubt about that fact in her mind), then she was heading south—or north—depending on her final decision.

"You wouldn't enjoy it," said a voice from the shop doorway as Christy drew level, still watching the rapidly disappearing aeroplane.

Christy drew up abruptly, startled and lost in her thoughts. Iris was washing the front window of the coffee shop and smiling. "Greasy food, rotten sanitation, hostile natives, sunstroke. And no one speaks a word of English, you know."

"Morning, Iris. Don't you ever take a holiday?"

"Did once, while my George was alive. Didn't like it. Shillingham's the place for me. This is where I want to spend my last days."

"Not even nine o'clock and you're talking morbid again. Iris, you're a dead loss . . ."

"Coffee's nice and hot, and you don't have to pay. What better way to start the day?"

Iris swung the ragged cloth jokingly at Christy as she dived, laughing, into the shop, ducked under the serving counter and went into the small lounge hidden behind a curtain of plastic beads. In a short while she had changed into her work clothes and was behind the counter again. The shop was empty at the moment, but it was always empty at this time. In ten minutes, the locals would begin to arrive. Christy filled a cup from the coffee machine and sipped at it reflectively, watching Iris as she finished washing the window. It was not dirty, but—with Iris, it was a ritual to wash it every day.

Iris Wooler was small, about five foot three, with silvered

hair tied back behind her ears. The hair beneath the silver suggested that it might once have been as raven black as Christy's own. Iris was sixty-six years old ("pensionable age but I'm not sitting on my bum") and extraordinarily active. She had bought the coffee shop from the original owner more than six years ago ("I got it for a song. The song was 'I Ain't Got No Money.' He was in a good mood that day, I suppose.") Her husband George had died two years before that and she had spent the intervening time trying to live the quiet, restrained life of a widow. It had not agreed with her. She had finally come to the realisation that George, of all people, would not have wanted her sitting at home all day ("on her bum") doing nothing and generally moping about. Hence, the acquisition of the coffee shop.

Christy envied her. There had been bad times for Iris, but they had never affected her outlook on life. She was always the same, always so bloody cheerful; Christy wondered how she managed it. She wished she could summon up the courage . . . if that was the right word, and somehow it was . . . to ask Iris for advice about her father, the greatest source of sadness in her life. Maybe one day she would find the nerve. She looked past Iris, still busily scrubbing at the window, to the foothills beyond the village. Those foothills led up to the mountains surrounding the valley. Once again, she found herself thinking of the writer at Split Crow Farm and the enthusiastic way he always waved back.

Chapter Three

Michael switched off the record player, picked up his coffee cup from the small table beside him and moved slowly to the window. It overlooked the track bordering his property. He had been listening to Dire Straits, playing one of his favourite songs: "Tunnel of Love." Mark Knopfler's guitar had stirred memories inside him: memories of Newcastle, Dire Straits' home town, Michael's home town . . . and the fairground he had haunted as a kid. He tried to feel what it would be like if he could go back in time and tell himself, as a child of eight, how he would be feeling now as a man of thirty-nine. What steps could that eight-year-old take to avoid the situation he was in now, thirty-one years later? It was a dead-end, sterile train of thought. Michael discarded it, but still felt his sense of loss. He was amazed that dead men could still have feelings. Now he was being self-indulgent, and he knew it. He laughed at himself sarcastically and scanned the track outside. It was six-thirty. She would be passing by again soon.

He crossed the room, stepping over the prostrate form of Dutch, lying in front of the fire. Mac was sniffing around in the kitchen, wondering if the casserole presently cooking in the oven was meant for canine or human consumption. Michael finished his coffee, replacing the cup on the table. As he straightened up, his attention focused on the bookshelf in the corner. One name predominated: *The First One* by Michael Lambton, *Captive* by Michael Lambton, *Beyond Me* by Michael Lambton, and . . . Michael felt that

old, familiar spasm of uncompromising, sickening fear . . .
The Borderland by Michael Lambton. *Not again*, he
thought. *I can't handle it again just now*. His anger fought
with the fear to balance out his emotions. But the fear won,
as it always did. His stomach lurched as if some terrible
and unstoppable threat was even now hanging over his
head. He could not rationalise it. He must, as always, give
in to it. In an instant, he was transported back to the time
when his problems had first begun. The debilitating fear,
the sharp, stabbing anxiety, were as intense as the first time,
when he had been living in a luxury Jesmond flat with the
literary world at his feet. In the comfort and security of
those former surroundings, it had descended upon him:
driving him into seclusion, chasing away his friends, settling like some poisonous parasite in his soul. Eventually,
it had engulfed him.

A man on a stretcher, crying like a baby . . .

A trapdoor in his mind was opening again.

"No . . . no . . . NO! I *won't* let it!"

He heard a whimper from the carpet and turned to see
that Dutch was gazing at him. He was still lying before the
fire, but had now turned his head watchfully. The dog's
eyes were somehow deeply compassionate, reflecting the
firelight. The liquid eyes dissolved the horror inside Michael. The trapdoor, hiding a great terror, began to close.

"Sorry, Dutch. It's nothing." *That bloody dog's reading my
mind again.*

Dutch let his head fall onto his paws.

A movement of white on the track caught Michael's attention and he knew that it was time. In moments, he was
outside, casually strolling towards the ruin of the barn as
if something of interest was waiting there for him. Dutch
had followed him immediately and, as Michael turned to

see the girl rounding the bend in the track, Mac emerged, too.

She waved when she saw him, and Michael waved back. Now, as usual, the girl would continue past Split Crow, climb the track to the crest of the ridge, wave again, and vanish from sight on her way home.

Except that she was not doing that today.

She had stopped and was looking down the slope at him with that beautiful smile on her face. She seemed to be pondering. Now she was walking towards the boundary fence.

Dutch and Mac had spotted her. Before Michael could react, both dogs were racing in her direction, barking.

"Dutch! Mac!" *Oh, God, just like the bloody postman!* But the dogs were too far away and too intent on reaching the girl to obey his shouted orders. Michael began to run. "Move back from the fence! Move back . . ." He was waving his arms furiously at the girl.

The girl must have heard him; she must surely see that the dogs were making straight for her, but she continued down through the gorse, still smiling.

Michael pounded over the grass, shouting the dogs' names, calling them off. The girl had reached the boundary fence now. She was a stranger and, to Mac and Dutch, a potential intruder. Michael would never be able to reach them before they reached her. Even now, she had drawn level with the waist-high fence and was whistling to the dogs.

"Oh, God . . ."

Dutch reached the fence first but did not stop. He cleared it only three feet from where the girl stood, catapulting beyond into the bushes and whirling back towards her. Mac was there an instant later, barking and jumping at the girl.

Michael stopped in his tracks.

The girl had caught Mac's forepaws in her hands, just as he himself had done earlier that day. The dog was straining upwards and licking her face. Dutch had reached her now and was rubbing up against her legs, barking in the "laughing" tone of voice that Michael knew so well. The girl was laughing, too, as she danced with Mac, eventually letting him go and turning to stroke Dutch. Mac barked at Michael as he finally drew level with the fence. The girl looked up at him, her eyes alight.

"I don't believe it," said Michael. "I thought they were going to tear you to pieces."

"What? These two? Not a chance."

"I don't understand it. They're not like this with strangers. They took the postman for a bone . . ."

"So I heard. But the thing is, I'm not a stranger. I've often been down here when you weren't around. They know me quite well. They've been on speaking terms with me for . . . oh . . . about a year now."

"I thought you always just passed by here . . . on your way to work . . ." *Why do I feel nervous?*

"I think you're a man who treasures his privacy. You've a right to that."

"Until today, it seems." Michael was smiling, not wishing to be misunderstood.

"Yes, until today. My name's Christy Warwick." The girl with the raven-black hair and the sparkling eyes was holding out a hand. Michael took it; the flesh was cool, the skin soft.

"Michael Lambton."

21

"The writer. Yes, I know. I've seen some of your books in the supermarket."

A sudden stab of anxiety in Michael's stomach.

Dutch barked and nudged at Christy's legs. She bent and began to pat him. Mac was busy foraging in a bush for imaginary rabbits.

"You must be good with animals," said Michael.

"No," replied the girl, without looking up. "Just these animals."

"You live on one of the farms on the other side?" Michael heard himself ask, aware that he was making conversation.

"Yes, my father manages it. Not much of a place, really. Very small. It's the property on Chesapeake, just before the mountains begin."

"You work in the village, Christy?"

"Iris Wooler's coffee shop. I'm the general dogsbody. You'll have to call in."

"I'd probably put your customers off. I'm not Mr. Popularity at the moment."

"Give them a chance. They're okay. They're only being stand-offish because you're being stand-offish. Once you begin to show your face a bit more, they'll get used to you."

Michael smiled. "Thanks for the advice."

"A pleasure. I'd better be getting on. Dad's fairly strict about the time I arrive back."

"Nice to meet you, Christy. Don't be a stranger."

Christy smiled back, roughed the dogs up a little and then moved up the slope towards the track. Michael called to the dogs. They cleared the fence back onto his property.

"By the way," said Christy. Michael looked up.

"You've got first-class taste in music. I've heard your Dire Straits collection when I've passed. It makes a good start to my day."

22

"What would you like to hear tomorrow?"

" 'Sultans of Swing.' That's my favourite."

"You've got it. Eight-ten sharp."

Christy smiled again and turned to finish her climb back to the track. Somehow, Michael could feel disappointment rising inside him like a bitter tide. This was the first time that anyone in Shillingham had ever spoken civilly to him. He had built up a shell of uncaring complacency about it, but now he knew that, to a great extent, it had been a self-protective sham. He was human like anyone else . . . *even if I am a dead human* . . . he needed to speak to people, he needed pleasant conversation from time to time. His self-imposed exile provided a certain amount of security, but there were bitter side effects, too. Loneliness was the biggest of them all. He was not born to be a hermit. The girl was moving away now and he was losing the moment. Maybe she would never descend to the boundary fence again. He needed to say something, but could not find any words. She was walking away. This was his last chance.

"You can tape any of the records, if you want," he blurted . . . and was instantly ashamed that he sounded like a tongue-tied thirteen-year-old trying to impress; not a grown man of thirty-nine.

Christy turned back. There was still a smile there, but it was shadowed and Michael could see pain in her eyes.

"I'm not allowed records. Dad doesn't let me. Thanks all the same."

And now she had turned and was walking on. The moment was lost. Somehow, Michael had spoiled it, but he was damned if he knew how. Keenly disappointed, he began to walk away from the fence, the dogs galloping back towards the farmhouse.

After twenty yards, he turned back to see that Christy

had reached the bend in the track which would take her over the hill and out of sight. She turned and Michael felt something inside him kick when she waved, smiling that wonderful smile again without a hint of shadow. Not caring now whether he was behaving like a young boy, Michael waved furiously back, realising that nothing was spoiled after all. He would be mentally pacing the hours between now and eight-ten tomorrow, and the "Sultans of Swing."

Chapter Four

It slept.

But in its sleep there was no rest.

Unconscious of the present, yet aware of the many years it had been imprisoned, it recalled and revelled in all it had done while alive. It was sustained by the memories of its deeds, endlessly regurgitated, fed upon and excreted. Its excreta was the poisonous hatred of all that lived and of those responsible for its existence in limbo. It devoured its own excreta of hatred and longings for revenge, in a never-ending cycle of loathsome replenishment. And, as it slept, its hatred grew. There must be a time when the imprisonment would end and, when that time came, the revenge would begin. There was so much that it planned to do. It could wait.

It slept.

And waited.

24

Chapter Five

Michael turned the corner from the market square into End Row, passed the local history museum with its faded notice board and crossed the cobbled street towards the bookshop. He was feeling good today. Still dead, but good. His encounter with Christy yesterday, and their shouted greeting this morning, had refreshed him and there was vigour in his step. He was thinking back to his previous existence as he walked—and not with as much pain as he usually experienced. *Christy must somehow be the reason for that.* He remembered the mind-reeling pace of his city life; an existence which he now realised he had always disliked, even before the trauma, when his self-protective "shell" had cracked.

. . . all the King's horses and all the King's men, couldn't put Lambton together again . . .

Mentally he beat down that little voice and realised how glad he had been to get away from the city. So much of England was being buried beneath concrete and mortar, but here, in Shillingham, the countryside and the village itself were changeless, despite the coming and going of the seasons.

The bookshop, Zoneshifts, was situated between Johnson's grocery and a draper's shop. It was decidedly out of place in this small rural village. Its glass windows bore old cinema posters for *Conan the Barbarian*, *Nightmare on Elm Street* and *Ghostbusters*, curious in itself since there was no cinema in Shillingham; the nearest was in Hextall, fifteen miles away over bleak moorland.

Michael reached the door and opened it briskly. Overhead, a bell tinkled. The owner of the shop, Sean Jackson, had tried to fix up an electronic warning instead, a device similar to the foghorn which always sounded when anyone pressed the bell of the Addams family's front door in that old 'sixties TV series. But Sean's electronic know-how was not up to the task, and he had been forced to adopt the conventional system. Michael entered. Racks of magazines confronted him: fantasy, science fiction and horror. Books lined the walls, with a special section for American imports; the pricier editions were placed on the higher shelves, out of reach of the grubby little fingers of the schoolkids who haunted the shop, but whose pocket money limited them to the cheaper comics and magazines. There were more movie posters on the walls. *Them! Them! Them!* shrieked a garish poster from the 1950s, depicting giant ants on the rampage. A huge black-and-white poster of Lon Chaney Junior as the Mummy covered half a wall, carrying off a helpless heroine. Heavy Metal music played from an invisible tape recorder behind the comic-strewn counter. There was no sign of the owner. Michael moved forward.

"Shop?" Sean seemed to have disappeared.

Michael recoiled in alarm as the shop owner suddenly popped up from behind the counter, like a jack-in-the-box.

"Sorry," said Sean abstractedly. He was sorting through a pile of magazines, completely absorbed in them. He was small, no more than five foot five, with long, light brown hair ("mousy" as he himself described it with a kind of defiance) kept severely in place by a sweatband. He was wearing a tracksuit top. A thin tuft of moustache decorated his upper lip. His eyes were narrow but sparkling with excitement today. All in all, he reminded Michael of a small, intense Geronimo, without the latter's hostile tendencies.

"Amazing," continued Sean. He had not looked up to see who had entered the shop and could have been talking to anyone. "Abso-bloody-mazing! Fella's just been in here and sold me these for a few quid. Old guy up on the Peak. Was clearing out the farmhouse and found a pile of magazines. Thought he'd earn a few bob by bringing them to me. Have you seen them . . . ?" Sean at last looked up from his objects of adoration and saw who he was talking to. ". . . Michael . . . have you seen 'em? A half-set of *Amazing Tales*. Published in 1932, first editions, with all the genre writers in 'em. They're worth a bloody fortune! A fortune! Can you imagine? These magazines have been lying in a box in a barn for over fifty years, way out here in the Borders. Just waiting for me. Amazing!"

"Good for you . . ." began Michael.

"People think I'm a loony or something, running a specialist bookshop in a one-horse place like Shillingham. Think I'm an acid freak or something. They don't know how much specialist mail-order customers are prepared to pay for stuff like this. For these mags, they'll pay a fortune. A weirdo, that's what they think I am. Selling twopenny-halfpenny comics to the kids. Stuck out here in a wilderness. I like it here . . ."

"I know you do . . ."

". . . keeps your head cleared, out here in the country. You don't get screwed up like you do in the Big City, man. I've had my share of that Big City shit . . ."

"Yes, I'm certainly with you on that. Is there . . . ?"

". . . Best of both worlds, that's what I've got. And enough of that crinkly green stuff to keep me going . . ."

"Any new material for me? Books, magazines?"

"And what about this bloody motorway, then?" asked Sean, his mood of elation subsiding.

Michael sighed. He knew of the proposal to develop a north-south highway from Scotland to England, passing within a mile of Shillingham and with a side-route to the village. He shared the bookshop owner's concern, albeit for slightly different reasons. "They call it progress, Sean."

"Progress? Yeah, but progress for who, eh? Progress for the rich fat cats, that's who. Progress for the Big City people and the people living out here in the great Unspoiled who aspire to the Big City. If they like the idea of smog and office blocks and traffic congestion, why don't they just bugger off to the city and leave places like Shillingham alone? All that Big City crap was what I was getting away from. Now it looks as if it's following me. You know what it is, Michael . . . ?" Sean was in full flood again; Michael had seen it before. ". . . In the last month before I decided to make a break for it, I was mugged twice, the guy who called himself my best friend put my lady in the family way and my flat was burgled while I was out collecting for charity. I'm telling you, man. The Big City just chews people up and spits out the pieces . . ."

In Michael's mind, an image: *A man on a stretcher, arms securely tied, head twisting frantically from side to side. His face is contorted and he is shouting; inarticulate, hoarse, tear-filled cries of anguish. The adult veneer has been stripped away and the man's grief is unashamedly childlike. But this grief does not involve the loss of a second party—a lover or a close family member. This grief has something to do with the man's soul and something that has happened to it. He is shrieking for help. The grief has to do with the man's own loss of self-control, the loss of emotional balance*

*and sanity. The sounds are terrible in the extreme. An am-
bulanceman is trying to give words of comfort, his face set
and unemotional. But they are token words only. The man's
grief frightens him; people are only supposed to sound like
that when they have suffered some kind of terrible physical
pain. The ambulanceman's words are unheard by the man
on the stretcher as it slides into the ambulance. Now, the
outpouring of anguished and racking sobs has evened to a
keening sound of exhaustion. The man has suffered . . . is
suffering . . . a nervous breakdown. Michael sees the man's
face just before the ambulance door slides shut. The vision
is three years old. And the face that Michael sees is his own.*

Michael juddered back to the present again. Sean was still
talking and did not seem to have noticed that his mind had
been drifting. ". . . I like Shillingham. It's what I need to help
keep my head clear. It's just what you need to help you
write, Michael. I know that. I can empathise with you . . ."

*Not quite, Sean. I pray to God that you never find yourself
in my shoes.*

"What's the official line from the local traders? 'It will
bring only prosperity, growth and tourism.' Yeah, well I'll
tell you what else it's going to bring. It's going to bring Big
City people parking their fucking caravettes all over the
place, looking for junk food shops and leaving their shit all
over the countryside."

"There's a public meeting on at the village hall today,
isn't there?"

Sean looked at his watch with an overly dramatic gesture. "In fifteen minutes. That's when the 'public consul-
tation' takes place. What a laugh! The decision's already
been taken and they're just going through the motions.
Gauging public opinion? Don't make me laugh."

"I expect you'll have a few things to say, then?"

"Me? No way. Wouldn't catch me dead in there. Place'll be full of local Councillors, Department of the Environment officials, planning reps and bigwig local businessmen. As far as they're concerned, rustic and idyllic are two words that aren't in their dictionaries. The white collar brigade has got the pull. Doesn't matter what a spaced-out ex-hippie like me thinks. Or you, Michael. You're just a loony writer, as far as they're concerned. No . . . me? . . . I'm just going to take down a bottle from my shelf in there and . . ."

"Commune with Nature?" suggested Michael, with a hint of a smile on his face.

"Yeah, why not? I tell you what, Michael, one of these days Mother Nature's gonna turn on us for screwing her up. Just wait." Sean pointed melodramatically to another cinema poster on the wall, reading out the words in a mock stentorian voice: "Bloodthirsting animals . . . All out to kill mankind . . . There's no place to hide on . . . 'The Day of the Animals.' " The poster depicted a gigantic, slavering hound, baleful eyes gleaming as it reared over a crowd of desperately fleeing people. "Seen it all in the movies, Michael. Nostradamus has got nothing on Hollywood when it comes to prophesying the future. Giant ants, man-eating dogs, even saw some killer rabbits in a film, once."

The picture of the huge dog reminded Michael of Dutch and Mac . . . and the postman. Then he thought of the way the animals had reacted to Christy and he had a sudden vision of her sad, haunted face. She was far too young to have such a sad face.

"You know a girl called Christy?"

"Why, do you fancy her?"

"She's just a kid. I'm twice her age. No . . . it's just that she passes Split Crow Farm every day on her way to work."

"Christy Warwick. Frank Warwick's daughter. Works in Iris Wooler's coffee shop. She's a great lass, Michael. Great. Billy Rifkin's been trying to get inside her pants for years now."

"Who's Billy Rifkin?"

"Believe me, you don't want to know. He's an absolute maniac. Really dangerous. And Christy's got enough on her plate as it is with one maniac in the family already."

"How do you mean?"

"Frank Warwick, her father. He's pretty cuckoo. Keeps himself up on that farm and never comes out as far as I know . . ."

"You mean like me?"

"No. You're a writer. You need your privacy to work. But Frank . . . well, Frank would take a pot shot at anyone who came near the place. Worse than Johnson the grocer and his twelve-bore. Frank gives Christy a pretty hard time. Won't let her wear the clothes she wants. Won't let her go out. A real prude. How the hell she's able to keep that coffee shop job, nobody knows. Frank's dead against it. As far as I can see, it's about the only thing that she does get away with."

Another image in Michael's mind: the girl standing behind the fence, turning back to say: "I'm not allowed."

"You should go down to that public meeting, Michael. You've got a way with words. Let 'em have a soliloquy . . ."

"That's a pretty heavy word in itself."

"Right! I know you've got the same feelings as I have about Shillingham. Why don't you go?"

"Putting words down on paper is one thing, changing people's minds in public is something else. If the majority want it . . . then the majority will get it. No, I don't think I'll be going. You're right, they don't know what they've got

31

here, or how good it is. In any event, it's like you said: that decision has already been made. It's all over bar the shouting."

"Heard the latest about the gibbet down on Split Crow Lane?"

Michael had walked past the place many times since moving into Shillingham. It was the town's greatest historical artefact, a piece of local history: a seventeenth-century gallows standing at crossroads, cared for and treated over the years to prevent rot and weather damage. Just the sort of thing that the incoming flood of tourists would be interested in. It stood about half a mile from Split Crow Farm.

"No, what about it?"

"It's right in the bloody way of the new road, isn't it? A perfect argument for diverting it somewhere else. But oh no, they've managed to convince the Department of the Environment guys that it should be removed. Can you imagine? Those guys generally go rabid when anything like that's mentioned. But not this time. There's gonna be a supervised removal. The Local History Society . . . and yes, I do mean Mrs. Garvanter . . . is putting up funds to aid in a—wait for it—'supervised removal in the presence of the Department of the Environment.' Presumably, she doesn't mean all of them. Anywhere else and it couldn't happen."

"What are they going to do with it? The gibbet, I mean?"

"It's gonna be the prime exhibit in the local history museum. What else? Why do you think they're putting up the cash?"

Sean's copies of *Amazing Tales*, which would probably pay for his heating, telephone, electricity and rates for the next year, seemed forgotten as he flapped them emphatically on the counter. For the first time, Michael found himself really warming to this strange young man. Despite his protestations, he was a Big City Boy. Something about the way that he was speaking made Michael realise that Sean was vulnerable. He recognised some aspect of that vulnerability in himself. Fantasy had been Sean's mainstay, it had been his way to "avoid freaking out," to use the outdated jargon which Sean deliberately sought to cultivate—in itself a defiance against ordinary speech, and all the better since it had once been fashionable and had now been discarded. Running a fantasy bookshop was probably the perfect occupation for him. And, there was no doubt about it, selling specialist books and magazines could be a lucrative profession.

"Well, if you haven't got any material for me, I'd better be off."

"Yeah . . . right . . . wait a minute, though . . ." Michael turned back. Sean was waving his hands. His intense mental activity and outrage at the impending rape of Shillingham had momentarily thrown all other thoughts out of the window. "I'm sure I do have something for you . . . something . . . Yeah! I mean, no. We've got some special editions of *The Borderland* in, but I don't suppose you'll want to buy one of your own books, will you?"

The shop was suddenly claustrophobic. Michael felt sweat breaking out all over his body. His neck muscles spasmed into tense rigidity; pain crept like a rusted iron band across his temples. He could feel the beginnings of cramp in his stomach which always led to a violent vomiting bout. "Sorry, Sean . . ." The words tasted dead, like sour wine in his throat. "Got to rush. Parcel to collect." Michael turned sharply, grabbing at the shop door handle, unaware of Sean's look of astonishment. The bell above the door emitted a harsh jangle that made Michael grit his teeth in agony. Seconds later, he was outside on the pavement, not knowing where he was heading, so long as it was away.

Away . . . away . . . from that book. And everything that the bastard has done to me.

Inside the bookshop, Sean was carefully locking his copies of *Amazing Tales* into an ancient Chubb safe with a rusted lock. He was shaking his head sadly, as if he knew all the answers to Michael's problems. "It's the Big City, man. The Big City. It just chews them up and spits out the little bitty pieces."

Chapter Six

The anxiety attacks almost always hit Michael in the same way. Consciously unbidden, but a product of his tortured subconscious, they reared up screaming from that Freudian pit of the mind beneath his mind. As a writer of psychological fiction, he had always prided himself that he understood the secret workings of the subconscious mind. This had helped him produce four best-sellers. But it in no way equipped him to deal with the savage effects of his own tortured subconscious mind. The attacks could not be rationalised. They came without warning, producing not only mental agony but distressing physical symptoms which he could not analyse away within himself. The fates were laughing at him. He had released the monster of his own *id* within his mind and it wanted to destroy him.

He strode unsteadily but quickly away from the shop, unheeding of the alarmed looks from passers-by. He paused, putting a hand out against a rough stone wall for support. He sucked in lungfuls of air, slowly and deeply, trying to regulate the hammering of his heart. His shirt seemed to cling to his back, soaked in sweat. The unreasoning fear still gnawed hungrily at his stomach. There was only one solution. Walking briskly, he reached the side-street which he knew lay beyond. He walked under an ancient arch, feet ringing on cobblestones, and down a littered pavement until he reached the two large rubbish bins there. He was behind Iris Wooler's coffee shop. Safely out of sight behind the bins, he convulsed over a convenient gutter grating and let the fear out. It came in a surge of bile, with hardly any effort at all. He retched until his eyes streamed and he could hear singing in his ears.

"Oh, God, when will it stop? When . . . ?"

And the singing in his ears answered: *It will never stop, Michael. Never. You know what Nietzsche said—"If you look too long into the abyss, the abyss will look into you."*

"Sod Nietzsche . . ." gasped Michael.

He began to suck in lungfuls of air again, bracing himself against the brick wall beside the rubbish bins. Every once in a while, when his vigilance was off-guard, the terrible pressure of the fear which lived beneath that trapdoor in his mind would push it open again on screeching hinges. Gritting his teeth, breathing heavily, he fought back and began to push the trapdoor down again.

I'm still here, it laughed, as the trapdoor squeezed down. *I'll always be here!*

Michael staggered away from the wall and began walking. It did not matter where.

Chapter Seven

The village hall was three-quarters full when Michael entered. Two ranks of chairs had been arranged, with an aisle down the middle. As usual with such events, people were reluctant to sit at the front and the first three rows were empty. Beyond them, a trestle table had been placed. Michael recognised one of the men sitting there: George Mitchell, a recently elected Councillor. The polling booths stacked at the right bore testimony to his recent electoral victory. The counting of votes had taken place in the hall; Michael remembered seeing photographs. Mitchell himself wore a casual checked shirt with sleeves rolled up; beard and unruly hair completed the picture of a man who believed in cutting through bureaucracy and "getting results." In direct contrast, the other men wore suits and ties: presumably council officials, planners and—if Sean was to be believed—men from the Department of Environment and Department of Transport. A man in the audience was speaking as Michael entered. He was addressing his remarks to a blank-faced man in a suit, sporting a tie that looked like a dead rattlesnake. Michael had time to hear references to "the great advantages the road scheme would bring to Shillingham." The man's words were received with thunderous applause as Michael tried inconspicuously to find a seat.

He had not intended to be present at the public meeting. After his panic attack he had just kept walking, preoccupied by the feeling that somehow, something had happened . . . something *was* happening . . . which was going to change things forever. Whether for good or ill, he had no way of knowing. And despite the fact that he had tried to analyse what it was that made him feel he was part of some kind of predestiny, he was no nearer to finding the solution. Perhaps it was just another phantom train of thought from the past. He had been ill. Ill in his mind. And there had been times, under sedation, when his perception of reality had borne no resemblance to anything that was going on around him. But that had been in the bad days, when he was recovering. He had hoped beyond hope that his recovery was complete now . . . apart from his fear-block when it came to writing. Now his obsessive thoughts about predestiny were threatening to throw him off balance. He had struggled from his internal wanderings to find himself standing outside the village hall, and this only seemed to make the sense of predestiny stronger. Angered, he had not walked away. It would only make him feel worse. So he had decided to brave the lion in its den, sit in on the planning meeting and then leave quietly. Back at Split Crow, he could empty a half-bottle of whisky and forget his distressing thoughts.

Sean had been right. The "feeling" of the meeting was that the new route was to be welcomed with open arms and, perhaps, eager pockets. There was not a single word of protest; not even the token complaints of environmentalists. Michael had the impression that the DOE representatives were waiting for just such a complaint: there was an air of tension among them. Finally, when no hint of discord was forthcoming, there was a brief, whispered exchange: the prematurely grey fellow with the dead rattlesnake around his neck stood up and addressed the crowd.

"I believe that everyone has been circulated with the

Departments of Environment and Transport report about the removal of the crossroads gibbet. That report contains all the details of how and when the gibbet will be removed in association with the National Trust. We've laid particular importance on this matter as the gibbet is—without doubt—the most attractive and important piece of Shillingham's local history . . ."

Michael could see that the man's remarks appeared to be addressed directly to someone in the fifth row, on the left. He strained to look over and was in no way surprised to see the resplendent form of Mrs. Garvanter, DOE report held proudly before her, beaming with delight. She was a large woman with an ability to declare her opinions in a similarly large manner. An overlay of make-up attempted to conceal the natural rosiness of her features which, some might say, were "handsome." She was nodding as the man continued.

". . . and therefore we have paid particular attention to the problems which the removal of such an old and valued artefact might present. We certainly don't want to be strung up on that gibbet for making a mess of the operation." An obligatory ripple of indulgent laughter. "Are there any questions about the removal?" The man paused, knowing full well that Mrs. Garvanter had arranged a series of meetings at her local history museum to discuss the matter. Michael surmised that, in reality, everyone was probably sick to death of the business by now, and that the sooner the damned thing was pulled out of the ground and stored away in the museum, the better. Then they could get to work on the road scheme—the real source of interest—and the flood of traffic could begin.

After a polite pause, with no questions forthcoming, the man went on.

"Well, if anyone should think of anything, please don't hesitate to contact me . . . the telephone number is on the report. Once again, my name is Peter Elphick. I'm Senior Archaeologist. I'd just like to finish my brief summary by thanking Mrs. Garvanter . . ." Michael did not see Mrs. Garvanter's widely beaming face, but he could well imagine it. ". . . for her financial assistance. In this time of cutbacks at central government level, Mrs. Garvanter's Society's help has been . . ."

The sound of a fire door slamming on the left interrupted Elphick's eulogy. A man was shouting, the words echoing and muffled at first, but growing louder. Heads were turning as the object of the interruption strode into view.

He was a tall man, lanky even. A full head of shining black hair in disarray gave a somehow childlike impression. Faded brown trousers, grey open-neck shirt. And he was angry. Very angry. Completely disregarding the people in the audience, he strode grimly to the trestle table and crashed both hands firmly down on the edge, gripping the rim and staring at the astonished men on the other side.

"You'll leave it alone, Mr. Elphick," said the intruder. "The gibbet's been there for three hundred years and it should stay there!"

Michael saw the man with the rattlesnake tie slump back heavily in his chair, rubbing his face in annoyance.

"Please, Frank. Not again. We've had all this out before. Now . . ."

"Greed. That's what it's all about. I've got eyes to see and ears that listen. What you're doing is wrong. It's part of our heritage, part of our past. Take that damned road somewhere else. It doesn't have to come right through the crossroads. I know that. I've seen the plans . . ."

Elphick was on his feet now, staring hard at the wild man

confronting him. "Mr. Warwick, you were advised by the police the last time you tried to interrupt committee proceedings at the village hall. If you intend to disrupt the meeting again, I'm afraid that steps might have to be taken."

"Don't give me any of that stuff, Elphick! You set yourself up to me and I'll knock you on your back."

Elphick sighed dramatically, a gesture meant for the audience, and then began to whisper to one of his colleagues, who quickly stood up, marched round the table—on the other side from the intruder, of course—and away down the central aisle.

The crowd was clearly unhappy about this interruption. It seemed to Michael that they had experienced this sort of thing before.

"Sit down, Frank! For crying out loud!" said a voice from the back.

"You know very well that they're going to look after it," said another. "Come on, Frank. Give it a rest!"

The man whirled on the audience, teeth gritted. A wood panel on the table squeaked in protest as his grip intensified.

"You're greedy bastards. The whole lot of you! You don't give a damn about anything, unless it affects what goes into your pockets or your mouths. And you . . . you! Mrs. Garvanter!" The woman's rosy smile had become a mask of outrage at the intrusion. That she should be singled out for comment was an insult of the first order. "You don't give a bugger about local history or that gibbet. The only reason that you're involved is because of that great fat ego."

The word "fat" seemed to have aroused quivering waves of anger in Mrs. Garvanter's not unlarge body.

"That's enough, Mr. Warwick!" Elphick was joining in

again, but keeping a respectful distance from the man on the other side of the table. "I don't see any need for verbal abuse. It really would be easier if we could discuss the matter in less emotional circumstances. You've been given the chance to do just that, you know. We've spoken on numerous occasions . . ."

"Yes, we've spoken. And spoken. And spoken. But that's just the trouble, Elphick. Speaking doesn't do any good. Because you don't want to listen to what I say. You've all made up your bloody minds and it doesn't matter what anyone else has to say about it. Well, I've bloody well finished talking to you . . . or anyone else . . ." The man took in the whole room with one sweeping gesture. "The gibbet is staying where it is. It was meant to be there. Not rotting in some museum . . ."

"It certainly will not rot, Mr. Warwick. It will be treated with . . ."

"IT'S MEANT TO BE THERE!" thundered the man. "And if anyone tries to tamper with it, they're going to have to settle with me!"

Then, in a low, quiet voice which still seemed somehow to carry throughout the room: "I mean it. You'd better listen . . ."

Michael turned at the sudden movement on his left. A police sergeant passed him down the aisle, heading for the table. The wild man straightened up at the sergeant's approach, his face expressionless. Michael could see the visible signs of relief on the officials' faces. Councillor Mitchell, who had remained motionless and silent throughout, was standing now. Michael could sense that he had chosen his moment.

"Sergeant, I think we would all be grateful if you could remove this man."

41

The policeman advanced on the wild man.

"You, too?" asked the man as he drew near.

"You've been told before, Frank," said the sergeant quietly. "This could mean a breach of the peace charge. You know that."

"No, I don't think so," said the Councillor, and Michael knew that, as with the officials, his remarks were addressed less to the wild man or the policeman than to the audience. "We're all reasonable people here. This is a public meeting and, as such, everyone's entitled to their views, even if this gentleman is more outspoken and less polite than he should be. I don't think we'd want to arrest him. He's said his piece. But, just like that time last month in committee, Mr. Warwick hasn't come up with a single shred of evidence or even a comprehensible viewpoint which could change anyone's mind. The experts are here, the local people are here, and there has been a promise that the gibbet will be carefully removed, fully renovated and put on display. Even if there hadn't been a road scheme, Mr. Warwick, what we're going to do with the gibbet should have been done anyway. Years ago! Because it's a wonder the thing has lasted so long. Three hundred years in our weather! I'm surprised it's still standing. What we're doing for it is the right thing. Now . . . Mr. Warwick . . . can you give the people assembled here any good reason why the gibbet should not be removed?"

Even from where Michael sat, he could see the rage that boiled in the man's face. He was trembling, fighting to find words. But no words would come. The Councillor was taking a chance. Michael was convinced that the man would hurl himself at Mitchell at any moment.

"We're waiting, Mr. Warwick."

Warwick, thought Michael. *Frank Warwick. Christy's father.*

The sergeant had reached out to grasp Warwick's shoulder. The big man shrugged it off. The sergeant allowed it. And then Warwick was walking slowly down the aisle, with the sergeant following. His thoughts were elsewhere now. The rage had gone. Warwick seemed resigned.

"Perhaps, ladies and gentlemen, we can continue with our discussion in a more civilised manner?" The Councillor's words were greeted with a spontaneous round of applause. Michael sensed the rebuke to Warwick in that applause as the man passed him. There was no shame on his face, only a kind of desperation. And that look, Michael reflected, was closely related to the loneliness he had seen on Christy's face.

The outside door banged shut. Warwick and the sergeant were gone. The meeting continued with an audible murmur of relief, and with more jollity than previously. Michael had no further taste for the debate. Quietly, he slipped out of the back row.

Outside, there was no sign of Christy's father or the policeman. In the distance Michael could see the deep, mysterious green of the forest which bordered the base of the mountain range around Shillingham. Beyond that, in the west, a concrete serpent was on its way. It would cut a swathe through that greenery. Michael wondered whether, as Sean had suggested, it was time to move on. The Big City had found him, just as it had found the bookseller. Time to go, perhaps.

He made his way home, thinking of Frank Warwick. Was he drunk when he burst into the public meeting like that? He had seemed sober enough. What had Sean said about him? A loony. Perhaps. And Christy? Struggling under a burden with which Michael could sympathise. *All prisoners*, he thought as he turned down the dusty lane towards Split Crow Farm. *In our own way, we're all prisoners.*

Who has the keys?

Chapter Eight

Frank Warwick was a lucky man. Lucky that he was not being locked up. Lucky that people were so understanding, particularly people in authority. And he was also lucky to have a daughter who was prepared to put up with him. Christy was his daughter, not his charlady, meal-provider and servant. The man had responsibilities, dammit! His wife, Christine, had been dead for ten years. The accident had been hellish, and everyone was sympathetic. But it was all in the past now. Frank had to pull himself together and not rely on Christy to be at his beck and call all day and every day. She had her own life, then nobody could stop him. But Christy deserved to be in control of her destiny.

Sergeant Grover told Frank all of these things and more as he escorted him to the edge of the village and onto the path which led up Split Crow Lane and eastwards to Frank's home.

"You'd better pull yourself together, Frank. I've known you a long time . . . and I'm not sure what the hell's been eating you all these years. It's more than Christine's death, I know that. You've told me before that you don't need any specialist help and, God help me, I don't think you do. But whatever devil's biting your arse and making you do these things, for your own good, you'd better pack it in!"

Grover could cheerfully have locked Frank up for the night just to teach the daft old bugger a lesson. He would have done so, but for Christy. The poor lass had enough to put up with, never mind the humiliation that a twenty-four-hour lock-up for her father would bring.

Frank listened to all the sergeant had to say, with his head held down, face expressionless.

When Grover turned back towards the village, Frank continued on up the path, deep in thought. He had lost a vitally important battle today when Mitchell had faced him down in front of all those people; asking him the straight question about why the gibbet should not be removed. How the hell could he have answered? Who would believe what he had to say? Even if he had spoken out and told them all he knew, what could they possibly do? Why should they believe him? How on God's earth *could* they believe him?

"The loony bin," said Frank out loud. "That's where I'd end up. They'd lock me up in the bloody loony bin."

He took a half-bottle of whisky from his inside pocket, screwed off the cap and swallowed a great mouthful. It was his first of the day, even though he assumed that everyone attending the public meeting would have thought that he was drunk when he entered. He intended to remedy the situation when he got home. Recently Christy had taken to hiding the bottles, but he had one out in the cowshed, hidden behind bales of straw, that she had not found yet.

The dreams were always less bad when he was pissed. They were bad, very bad, when he was sober. But the alcohol seemed to soften their effect.

Frank addressed the sky as he walked. "Why me? Why the bloody hell does it have to be me?" But the sky had no answer. He was the Keeper of the Secret. It was his responsibility. His burden. And he had failed in his responsibility today. "Maybe I'm just round the twist," he continued aloud. "Maybe it's some sort of family . . . insanity or something. Perhaps it's all just a pack of bloody lies. Why the hell should I be responsible for this? What the hell have I done to deserve . . . Sod it!"

He flung the whisky bottle at the ground. It exploded against a rock and the alcohol soaked into the greedy earth. He stopped, knelt down on one knee and watched as the whisky drained away, leaving only a dark smear. "That's it. Go on, you greedy bastard. Drink it all up! Drink it, and stay asleep, damn you!"

In that moment, he knew that he was not mad. There was no hereditary insanity. He was the Keeper of the Secret. The lot had fallen to him and there was nothing to be done but accept that fact. He looked back at Shillingham again, wiping the sweat from his face. "You stupid bloody idiots. If you only knew what you're doing. But how the hell can I stop you? How . . . ?" Now he wished that he had not broken the whisky bottle. He stood up slowly, shaking his head, and continued on his way.

"No such thing as dead and buried in Shillingham. No such thing. No such luck."

Night was coming.

Chapter Nine

It stirred.

Something at the core of its semi-existence had reacted to an event which had just taken place in the living world; the living world of which it was only dimly aware. Like a pebble dropped into a poisonous, corrupting and bottomless well, ripples were spreading throughout its being. Still semi-comatose, it could not understand what was happening in the world beyond. But the promise of the dimly formed impression was enough to excite—albeit an excitement which could not end its sleep. It was something which it had awaited for over three hundred years.

It was the prospect of freedom.

Chapter Ten

"Can I look at the treasure again?" asked Graham.

He was giving his little-boy-lost look, but Karen was wise to that trick. Graham was only seven years old; Karen was three years older and, as such, she took her responsibility very seriously.

"We're late already. We should be getting home. You know they don't like us playing up here . . ."

"Ahhh . . . please . . ."

"Just five minutes, then. After that, we have to go."

Graham whooped and dashed back across the lane, kicking up a cloud of loose pebbles and dust. His jeans were crumpled and grass-stained from where they had been practising their forward rolls on the big grass bank just outside Shillingham. Graham always won that game. He was very good at it. Karen watched him go.

They were standing at the crossroads on Split Crow Lane. The gibbet towered from the centre of the crossroads, casting its late-afternoon shadow over Karen.

Graham reached the base of the gibbet and busied himself there with their most recent discovery. Karen remained in the shadow looking up at the gibbet. It seemed impossibly tall today, piercing the sky. They played here a lot. Graham loved it, but Karen did not like the place at all. The gibbet was old and creepy. When there was a strong wind blowing, it creaked and moved. She dreamed about that gibbet sometimes. As she stood there, forcing herself to remain in its shadow, looking up, she remembered one such dream . . .

She was standing just as she stood now, except that it was the middle of the night. The moon was sailing in the sky like a huge, bloated face, and the moonlit shadow of the gibbet was over her, just as the daytime shadow was over her now. There was a night wind. She could hear it blowing in the trees further down the lane. They made a "rushing" sound as if encouraging the gibbet, which was groaning and creaking the way it usually did. Karen knew that she was dreaming and that Graham was safe at home in bed. She wanted to be at home now, inside her daytime body. But she was paralysed in this dream, standing and waiting.

Now, she could hear the sound of someone groaning. And it was a terrifying sound. At first it seemed to be coming from beneath the ground, then it seemed to be in the air itself, maybe a part of the rushing wind. There was no pain in the voice, and this in itself made it more terrifying. Whoever or whatever was making the noise, it was doing it deliberately, just to scare her. Karen tried to look round, but every movement seemed to be impeded by some invisible force. With a great effort she turned slowly to look down the lane.

Nothing. Just the pebbled road, the broken fence and the ragged fringe of trees beyond. The bare crossroads seemed to be bathed in an unearthly light from the moon. All else was shrouded in blackness. She turned back to the gibbet . . . again painfully slowly.

Then she saw the corpse.

It was hanging by the neck from the gibbet, like a bag of rags and bones. She could see bare ribs beneath the ripped fabric of an old coat. A bloated tongue was sticking out of the body's mouth, blood was dripping to the ground. The wild, white eyes were staring in agony as the body swung in time to the creaking of the gibbet. The corpse's neck had been horribly stretched by the rope like scarred white rubber. Stark, clawlike hands jutted away from the hanged man's body.

And then the rope snapped.

The corpse dropped to the ground like a sack of old bones.

But now the corpse was more than just a lifeless body.

It began to crawl in the dark.

Karen wanted to turn and run away, but she could not move as the creeping, fumbling thing began crawling towards her. She could see the moon-glinting of its eyes as it came. It was smiling, but the eyes still held agony. It rose slowly and awkwardly to its feet. And now Karen could see that in one of its claw hands it was holding the noose which had been around its neck, swinging it from side to side. It spoke in a voice that gargled words.

"Come along, little girl. I'll make a swing for you. Up there. You can swing so high, little girl. Come along, I'll give you a push."

Its advancing shadow blotted out the grinning moon.

Slowly, agonisingly, Karen fought the immobility and began to slide to her knees, letting gravity help her. The thing was giggling now. She could see the horrible, blood-stained rope swinging like a pendulum in front of her. Desperate with fear, she raked her hands along the ground, grabbing a handful of the strange white pebbly soil which was all around the crossroads. Standing up again with even greater effort, and trying not to look at the semi-transparent, tattered body which was almost upon her, she mustered her strength and threw the handful of white pebbles and soil directly into the thing's face. It made a distressed, mewling sound, like a drowning cat, and clawed at its face, scrabbling furiously to remove the offending soil. But the panic-stricken fingers were also tearing off pieces of the corpse's rotting face in great chunks. The fingers kept on and on, scrabbling and tearing, as the head progressively caved in and fell away. Finally, with shredded hands full of bone and tufted hair, the corpse sank to its knees and was gone.

There was a change in the dream now.

Karen was still at the crossroads, still standing before the gibbet. But something else was happening. And she knew that this would be even worse than the corpse.

There was no wind, but the gibbet was still swaying and creaking, swaying and creaking. And now Karen knew what was happening.

The gibbet was alive and it was uprooting itself.

The wood groaned and cracked, the soil at the base of the gibbet split and burst open. The dead man's tree was coming alive, because it wanted Karen. It wanted her to sleep with it in a bed of soil and clay and stones, with cockroaches and worms and spiders for bedfellows. Karen tried to scream but spiders had spun threads of steel around her head and jaw. She had to watch. A writhing tree root erupted from the base of the gibbet, wriggling and bracing like some horrible, knotty leg. It heaved, and the gibbet swayed further over. The post was sliding out of the ground with a horrible sucking noise.

And that was when Karen had woken. Just before the really horrible stuff was due to begin. Dreams were sometimes like that. Now, in the warm, late afternoon sun, she stood on Split Crow Lane in the shadow of the gibbet and stared up at it.

"Come on, then," she said in a low voice. "Pull yourself out."

She was barely aware of Graham as he busied himself at the gibbet's base.

"Come on. You wanted to scare me. If you can do it, come out."

The gibbet creaked.

Karen jumped, but forced herself to stay where she was. Her bad dream could only be neutralised if she faced up to the gibbet and dared it.

"You don't scare me. You're just a dead man's tree. You think you're so scary? Then come out, now. I dare you."

This time the gibbet did not creak.

Karen walked down the length of the shadow to where Graham was playing.

"You're just dead wood," she whispered. "That's all. I won't be scared of you again."

"Who do you think leaves this stuff here?" asked Graham. He was too preoccupied to notice what Karen had been doing or saying. Karen looked down at their latest find. This time it was a tin box with two chunks of bread, a kipper (now crawling with ants) and a bottle of unidentified liquid. Two weeks ago, it had been a jar of mussels, more bread—buns this time—and a large box of matches. Every two weeks, without fail, someone left food and fuel at the base of the gibbet.

"I don't know who leaves it. Might be fairies, I suppose."

"What do you suppose is in the bottle. Beer?"

Graham began to unscrew the top.

"Don't do that!" warned Karen. "Someone might have peed in it."

"Yeeeeach!" Graham quickly replaced the bottle, wiping his hands on the grass.

"We'd better get home."

"You said five more minutes," Graham grumbled.

"That was seven minutes ago." Karen pointed authoritatively to her watch, which worked really well even though Dad had said that it had fallen off the back of a lorry. This time Graham allowed her to take his hand and pull him to his feet.

"Maybe it's magic food, then," he continued. "Do you think we should take some home? We could plant it and get a beanstalk."

"No. We'd only get bad things from it," replied Karen, as if she knew about these matters. "Best leave it where it is. We'll keep it a secret."

As they walked, she looked back over her shoulder. The gibbet was still there. It had not followed.

"Dead wood," she said.

"What?"

"Nothing. Come on."

They walked for ten minutes in silence until they reached the outskirts of the village. Then Graham spoke up again.

"Karen?"

"Yeah?"

"Do you ever hear the voice?"

"What voice?" Karen gripped his hand even tighter.

"Back there at the Dead Man's Tree."

"No. What kind of voice?"

"A funny voice. It wants me to play with it. But I can never see anyone."

"Where does it come from, then?" asked Karen, and knew the answer even before Graham spoke.

"From the ground, of course."

"You're tired, that's all. Let's go home for supper." *You'll never have him. Never. He's my brother and I love him. And you can rot there forever, tree. 'Cause I dared you and you wouldn't come out.*

Chapter Eleven

The dogs seemed troubled when Michael arrived back at the farmhouse. They were barking, not recognising his presence as they usually did. Normally, the barking held a note of welcome and expectancy. But this evening they seemed strange. When he unlocked the latch on the front door, they bounded out onto the grass and began prowling around the farmhouse, sniffing at the air, hardly pausing to welcome him home. At first, Michael wondered if they had picked up some kind of emotional reaction from him, as Dutch had done on the previous day. But no, it was somehow more than that.

Something is coming, he thought, wondering at himself. *Something is on its way. And I don't know what the hell it is.*

He could not shake off a feeling of *déjà vu* as he entered the farmhouse and began preparing a meal. The meeting with Christy. The encounter with Sean. The sudden wave of fearful nausea. The public meeting. Christy's father. He remembered telling Sean that he had no intention of going to that meeting; he remembered walking in there, telling himself that it was as if his course of action had been planned for him.

And all the time, he was aware of Dutch and Mac prowling around outside, as if something had visited the house while he had been away. He moved to the window and watched them. For the first time, he noticed that their attention seemed to be directed towards the ground; not so much as if they were picking up a scent, but as if something might be burrowing under there, or was secretly buried and they could not find the exact location. He returned to the kitchen to prepare their food. He had to call them three times before they appeared in the doorway, which in itself was unusual.

Michael deliberately ignored his bookshelf and the typewriter as he ate his meal and drank a glass of wine. His stomach had settled; not even the thought of looking at *The Borderland* threatened to ruin his appetite.

If only I could break this thing. It's more than a writer's block. I don't know what the hell it is.

And then, the little answering voice: *It's fear, Michael. Cold, undiluted fear.*

Yeah? he answered the voice sardonically, sipping at his wine. *You mean "I dared to go where no man should go?" Isn't that the old cliché?* It was a film cliché that had lasted through cinematic generations. The creation of Frankenstein's monster which would destroy peace of mind.

Yes, that's what I did exactly. My Frankenstein monster was The Borderland. *And it did destroy my peace of mind, God help me.*

After their feed, the dogs seemed to have settled down. When Mac barked amiably in a familiar sort of way, Michael looked at his watch and was not surprised to discover that it was six-thirty.

Moving quickly to the stereo, he found "Romeo and Juliet" by Dire Straits, placed it on the turntable and turned the volume up. Would she enjoy it as a follow-up to this morning's "Sultans of Swing"? The dogs were out of the door before he was, and by the time he reached the threshold, he could see them bulleting across the grass towards the fence. A familiar female figure in blue jeans, white top and flowing black hair was standing there. She waved immediately on seeing him. Grinning like a fool, but not giving a damn, Michael waved enthusiastically back. Tonight, the ritual was more perfect than before.

Christy was moving along the fence, one hand casually gripping the top rail, the other swinging her work bag. She looked happy, carefree even. And Michael could not help but think of the wild man Frank Warwick and his brusque entrance at the public meeting. He was probably at home now, waiting for her. What kind of hell might she be in for tonight? But perhaps he was exaggerating. He was basing everything about her relationship with her father on what

Sean had said earlier in the day. Just because he had been told that Christy led a hell of a life and he had seen Frank in action today, did not mean that she did not love her father or that she had a bad time. It certainly did not show in her walk and her smile and her enthusiastic waving.

Instincts, Michael, he told himself. *Remember the look in her eyes.*

Of course she was lonely, poor kid. But she was bloody brave, a damn sight braver than he was. She did not give in to it (again, that vision: . . . *a man strapped on a stretcher, crying like a baby . . .*). She fought back by forcefully staying cheerful, taking the good things, giving some of the good things back . . . and not letting it get to her. God, how he envied her that. Michael hoped that she would come over. The dogs had reached her, clearing the fence again in gigantic bounds as they had done the day before. Michael wished that the postman was here now to see them. She was good with them, spending equal time with each dog, giving equal affection to avoid any petty jealousies between the animals.

But she wasn't going to come over.

"How are you?" she shouted from the fence.

"Pretty good!" *Why don't I just walk over?*

"Been working hard?"

"Pen-pushing, you mean? No . . . not really . . ." *Go on, just walk over. Why the hell don't you do it? All you're doing is lounging in the doorway, smiling and shouting. You should be there by now.*

Mac jumped up at Christy and she playfully shoved him back to the ground. When he stood on his hind legs, he was almost as big as she was. "Do you know?" she continued, "I might just take these dogs home with me one day."

"I'm sure they wouldn't mind."

And now, Christy was smiling again. It was a shadowed smile, just like the way she'd smiled at their first proper meeting, the day before. Sean's words came to mind: of her "lunatic" father, and the hard times she endured. Suddenly, he realised what that haunted look in Christy's eyes represented. He had recognised some of that look on Sean's face; but more importantly, he had often seen it looking back at him from his own bathroom mirror. He cursed himself for an insensitive, out-of-touch fool. For a has-been writer of psychological tales, he really was a first class idiot. Sometimes the simplest and most basic emotions of all could be the most complex to recognise. That "look" had been the look of loneliness.

"What's the music selection for tomorrow?" he found himself asking.

Her laughter was bright and clear, cutting through the evening with a sharp and pure clarity. "Let's see . . . I know . . . 'Tunnel of Love.' That's a good one to start the day with."

"Eight-ten on the dot." *You'll lose her now. She's going to walk away.*

"Goodnight, Michael. Take care."

The dogs were bounding back as if they had understood her words and knew that the meeting and conversation were at an end.

They waved again. Then Christy turned the bend in the track and vanished.

Now, Michael realised, with that curious *déjà vu* that he had experienced before, why he had not walked over to her. It was not part of the ritual. It would probably have spoiled things. The more he thought about it, the more he realised that he was right. It was better like this. He felt happier, more relaxed; although he was damned if he understood why.

He called the dogs home.

Christy Warwick, he thought, *You're a remarkable young girl. If you weren't so young and I wasn't so screwed up in my mind, I might even make a play for you.*

Night fell, soft and cocooning, like a velvet blanket. It was the best, most relaxed night Michael had experienced in more than two years.

Chapter Twelve

Christy delivered the two coffees with cream to Mrs. Anderson and her crony, Miss Gavin. The old ladies ceased their conversation and appraised her with unmistakable displeasure, until she was ready to move away. Christy still managed to deliver a smile with the coffees, even if it was a trifle forced, before returning to the serving counter. She knew what they were thinking. No one had told her yesterday about Dad's latest performance in the village hall: she had found out for herself on returning home. Dad had managed to demolish about half a bottle of the gut-rot and was delivering another of his third-person speeches when she arrived. She had been able to piece together exactly what had happened. How could he have done it again? Particularly after the embarrassment caused at the committee meeting last month. She had fought the tears back again. Tears did not help, they only made matters worse. She had fed her father, put him to bed and, after cleaning up the house, had tried to read. It was one of Michael's books. But her mind was not on it; she could not concentrate. Sleep came fitfully as she anticipated the usual reaction from her friends at the coffee shop. Things had been bad after the committee business; she could just imagine how it was going to be for her tomorrow after this most recent display. At three o'clock in the morning, her father had clambered from his bed and thrown up his supper into the kitchen sink. She was glad, in a way, to have an excuse to get out of bed and clean up.

Now, in the coffee shop, she was getting her first taste of public reaction. Iris had said nothing, of course; just squeezed Christy's shoulder meaningfully, without looking at her face. Iris knew. Without her example, Christy was sure that she would not be able to keep going. She could face the Mrs. Andersons and Miss Gavins of the world, but her "friends" were another matter altogether. They would be arriving at ten o'clock as usual, and Christy dreaded it. Linda worked in the clothes shop down the road. Dennis and Bob worked on their fathers' farms, but always made a special point of calling in at Iris's coffee shop for ten o'clock.

How the hell could she be expected to lead an "ordinary" life? How could she become one of the crowd if her father continually managed to distance her from her peers by his outrageous behaviour? All she wanted to do was be like the others. Linda did not have her clothes "vetted" to see if they were too outlandish; Dennis and Bob could buy the music they wanted couldn't they?

She was beginning to brood and managed to check herself. She stood at the counter for a moment, took a deep breath and turned back as the outside door opened and the Haig kids bustled in—Karen and Graham. They were with their parents, Len and Julie. Christy enjoyed the kids, but found it difficult to relate to their parents. They were incredibly status-conscious, which was a waste of time as far as Shillingham was concerned.

"Hi, Christy." Graham swiped at Christy's rear as he dashed for their usual corner seat. His mother snapped at him.

"It's okay, really," Christy said to her, stroking Karen's hair.

"Can I have a grown-up cup today, instead of a kid's one?" asked Karen.

"Course you can."

Christy took the Haigs' order and moved back to the counter. Iris began to pour coffee and select pastries as Christy looked back at the Haigs and their kids. Len was giving a lecture to Graham on how to behave in public. She did not like the way he was doing it, but suddenly realised how much of a hypocrite she was being. Was she simply substituting Len for her father? Hadn't Dad lectured her like that when she was young?

No . . . he didn't. Not when I was young. He was loving and kind. He never raised his hand to me. It was when Mam was killed. That's what started it all, that's what started the drinking and the crying and the orders and the wild behaviour.

"Christy, can I . . . ?" Karen began to say, and was cut short by her mother. Christy could not hear what was said, but could guess. Another lecture on how to behave in public, how unladylike it was to shout across a crowded room. Christy turned from the counter and headed towards the table. Julie was a good-looking woman who was attempting to flush out the traces from her face. Enforced crow's feet from a cultured frown, tight lips holding back a voice which wanted to shout its displeasure at the way life was being conducted. Fine, natural blond hair tied back behind the head in a fierce ponytail. Julie's make-up always looked as if it had been applied carefully, sparingly and, more importantly, with an angry hand.

"Yes, darling?" asked Christy.

"Please could I have a cheese pasty?"

"Of course you can . . ."

"It'll spoil your lunch, Karen. No." Julie steadfastly refused to look up at Christy. Len sat back uncomfortably in his chair.

"Coffee ready?" he asked.

There . . . now I can see it . . . see it in Len's eyes. He's heard about yesterday, too. He doesn't want me to be nice to the kids because of Dad's outburst. He thinks that Dad's a lunatic and that, by association, I am, too.

Christy did not reply, noting Len's reluctance to look her in the eye. He was nervously stroking back thin, fine hair across his bald patch, attempting to look nonchalantly out of the window, only snapping back again to the table to slap Graham's hands away from the salt cellar when he began fiddling with it. How could such intolerant parents rear two good kids like this?

Christy returned to the counter, collected the coffees and pastries—presumably *they* would not put the parents off *their* lunch—and returned to join Iris behind the counter, washing cups and saucers.

"Watching the clock a lot this morning," said Iris without looking up from the sink.

Christy tried to think of a reply, could not find it, and then gave in to laughter. "Will you stop reading my mind? It's . . . unnerving."

Iris laughed, stroking a wisp of hair from her face with a forearm. "So they'll all come in and that little trollop Linda

61

will try to find something to say about your dad that will get you worked up. You know that. I know that. But if she does get you worked up, then she's succeeded, hasn't she? You'll have given her exactly what she wants when you lose your temper or, better still, burst into tears. Now you're not going to do that, are you?"

"No, but . . ."

"No, of course you're not. Let it . . . wash over you. They'll just be words. And, when you don't react to them, Linda might realise what an idiot she's making of herself and they can talk about something else."

"I just want to be like them, Iris. I just wish my dad . . ." *oh, no, not tears! Not now, not in front of Iris. I can't . . .*

Iris was deliberately not looking at Christy as she grabbed her round the waist in a brief but breath-squeezing bear hug. The breath that was catching in Christy's throat and threatening to bring tears was suddenly whooshed out of her.

"Mind what I say, Christy. If you show them you're upset, then Linda's won, hasn't she?"

"Thanks, Iris."

The shop doorbell rang vigorously. They were all there, as if someone had deliberately stage-managed the effect. All the people she had been worrying about. And, following up in the rear—Linda. She was trying to hide a smirk. She knew. And she was going to say something. But it did not matter now. Iris was right. Christy was wise to the trick and she was not going to let her win.

She could see Linda's intentions in her eyes as she approached the table: the superior air; the suppressed smile; the delight that she had something (she thought) which could damage Christy and at the same time make Linda look good in front of the others.

But Christy felt somehow in control. It would be a different matter if Dennis and Bob thought as Linda did, but they did not, although they could be led. She had worked out her strategy before she reached the table.

Linda looked up. The hidden smile had surfaced, presumably as rehearsed.

"Here's Daddy's girl."

Christy smiled back, placing the coffees carefully on the table.

"It's a shame we can't all make that claim."

Linda's face clouded. She had not expected a retaliation.

"What do you . . . ?"

"Going to the disco on Thursday, Christy?" asked Dennis, reaching for his cup.

In Christy's head, an argument four days old from her father: *I don't want you going there, Christy. Those mindless yobs aren't for you. You've got to keep your distance from people like that. They don't think. They don't know . . .* And then, Christy: *Well I'm going, Dad. I'm sorry . . . but I'm going. People already think I'm strange because of you. If I never go out and mix, how am I ever going to be happy, how am I ever going to get on . . . ?* Dad: *But, Christy . . . ?* Christy: *I'M GOING, DAD!*

Quietly now in reply: "Yes, Dennis. I'll be there. I'm really looking forward to it."

"Won't Daddy object?" asked Linda, grinning into her cup.

"No. Why should he?"

"Oh . . . I don't know. He just seems very protective of people . . . and things."

"That's what fathers are for, Linda. Don't you know that? Heard from your dad recently?" *This is the dad who is supposed to be working on the oil rigs, but everyone knows*

*that he ditched you and your mother over three years ago
and that he isn't coming back. So what do you want to say
now, Linda? Am I being a bitch by fighting back? Am I supposed to just stand here and take everything from you? You
started it, Linda. And even though I don't like to do it, I'm
prepared to finish it off.*

"He's expecting to be home in a couple of months. It all
depends on the weather."

"Oh, really? When *does* Hell freeze over again?"

Linda drew in her breath, ready to explode. But Christy
had delivered the *coup de grâce*. A shower of coffee from
an upturned cup sprayed into Linda's lap. Linda shrieked
in outrage, jumped back and began mopping at her mini-
skirt.

"You clumsy cow!"

"What a shame," said Christy flatly. "I'm so sorry. On your
new skirt as well . . ."

Eyes blazing, Linda turned on Christy again. But now
Dennis and Bob were laughing behind their hands; an outburst would only show her up. Instead, her hostility was
suppressed in a thin, clipped smile as Iris approached,
holding out a towel like a trainer who had been watching
from the wings.

"Why don't you pop into the ladies'," Linda?" cooed Iris,
casting a reproachful eye at Christy. "Christy'll get you another cup free of charge and I'll pay the dry-cleaning bill
if you send it to me. Okay?"

Linda swallowed hard and headed for the toilet. Christy
followed close behind, not proud of herself, but grateful
that she had managed to shut Linda up. Iris walked slowly
back and whispered to Christy over the counter as she
poured another coffee. "Words, Christy. Words speak

louder than actions. And I'm not earning money in this shop to pay dry-cleaning bills."

"Sorry, Iris. I won't do that again . . ."

The coffee shop door jolted open, quivering on its hinges, the bell above the door jangling. Christy and Iris looked round, startled, their alarm softening to badly disguised distaste when they recognised the man in the doorway.

Billy Rifkin had arrived.

"All right, everybody? The shagger's back. Anybody game?"

Billy was tall, perhaps six foot four. A stained donkey jacket, its ragged cuffs matted with sheep dip mixture, covered a well-built body. His lumberjack checked shirt lacked most of its buttons; his Wellington boots were grass-stained and caked in mud. A rough woollen cap was perched on his long, square head. He slammed the door behind him with unnecessary force, setting the bell jangling again.

"I've told you, Billy," said Iris forcefully. "If you break that door you'll pay for it."

"Oh, yeah?" Billy grinned back, moving to the counter. His too-wide smile revealed broken teeth; his thick black eyebrows were matted together in mirth over the bridge of his nose. He leaned on the counter, staring at Iris; then he blew an exaggerated kiss.

Christy was moving away as Billy turned to watch her. As usual, she could feel his eyes on her back.

She was disgusted by him. It was a view shared by the majority of Shillingham's inhabitants.

"Coffee, Iris. When the wench has time, that is."

"*I'll* bring it over if you find a table," replied Iris. Billy was always bad news.

65

"Just thought I'd pop round for a bit of service, know what I mean? Been working on those friggin' sheep all morning. Need something to drink. Need a bit of *service*, eh?"

Dennis and Bob were shuffling uncomfortably as Christy placed Linda's coffee on the table. Billy was close behind her now, pulling out a chair at their table, legs scraping the floor, turning it round to lean against the back-rest as he sat heavily down beside them. He scooped up the cup, smiling.

"All right, lads? Getting much?"

"That's Linda's coffee," put in Christy tightly. It was always the same whenever this oaf turned up. Dirty. Disgusting. Lecherous. Why hadn't Iris banned him from the shop?

"That's no way for a wench to behave, Christy," replied Billy, slobbering at the coffee. "The customer's always right. Right? And if I say that this is mine I must be right. Right?" He began to laugh. And, of course, Dennis and Bob laughed as well, because it was always safer to laugh at Billy's jokes. "Get another one for Linda. She can wait, can't she? Where is she, anyway?"

"Looking for another coffee shop now that you're here, I shouldn't wonder," replied Christy, moving away.

"That's no way to talk, Christy. Don't be a smart-arse. It's a nice arse, but don't get too smart with it. Might have to smack it."

"Yeah?" replied Christy, reaching the counter again. "And I might have to break your fingers."

Billy laughed again.

Len and Julie were moving their kids away from their table, pulling coats and jumpers onto small and unwilling arms and legs. Billy seemed to have that effect on people.

"Why do you let him in here?" hissed Christy to Iris. "He's

just an animal. He smells. He's dirty. And he's . . . well, he's just foul."

"He's one of God's children, just like us," replied Iris. "As long as he does what he's told, we can't refuse him business."

Christy sighed, pouring coffee. "The pub's open now. Why doesn't he go there? He just comes here to eye me up, you know. It's horrible."

Linda re-emerged from the toilets, dabbing at her skirt. Her flashing glance at Christy was quickly replaced by a look of unease when she saw that Billy Rifkin was sitting at the table. Christy finished pouring.

"Doesn't matter," said Linda hastily. "I've got to go now."

"What about . . . ?" began Iris.

"Doesn't matter. Really." And then, to Dennis and Bob: "Got to go. See you!" Moving quickly to the door as Billy began to wave her over with an exaggerated sweep of his arm, she called: "See you, Billy. Can't stay."

The door banged. The bell jangled. Linda was gone.

Christy looked down as the Haig kids pulled at her hands. Len and Julie were ready to go.

"See you later, Christy?" asked Graham.

Christy bent down and kissed him on the forehead, noticing Julie's frown. Len was pulling him away.

"Yes . . . sure . . . see you . . ."

Then the Haigs were gone, too, and that terrible lonely feeling was clogging Christy's throat, lodged in her gullet like unswallowed food. She fought it down and started collecting cups and saucers. She could not shut out the sound of Billy Rifkin's voice as she moved.

". . . so I just sat there and waited, see. Even though it's the middle of the night, you've gotta be quiet, otherwise the little bastards can suss where you are. Switched on the torch and just moved it around a bit. Never fails. Light from the torch reflects back from the rabbit's eyes, see? Like a pair of headlamps. Then they freeze . . . always do that . . . that's the best bit. That's when you squeeze one off." Billy was laughing. "Blow the top of the little bastard's head off! Got seven like that." More laughter. "Broke a tooth when I was eating the pie, afterwards. Did I tell you that? Should have known better. The little bastards are always full of shot, see."

Billy enjoyed killing animals although he did not have to sit up all night waiting for rabbits to emerge from their burrows: there was more than enough livestock on the farm which he worked with his father. He only wished that he could explain properly, without being misunderstood. There was something good about seeing a rabbit hop and twirl in the air after you'd hit it. Sometimes it seemed that he was seeing it in slow motion, just like those Sam Peckinpah films: the rabbit turning and whirling as a lazy, dark ribbon of blood swirled around its head. It was, well . . . yeah . . . *poetic*. But people did not understand that kind of poetry. He had once killed one of his father's sheep with an axe, just for the hell of it.

It had been like a ritual.

It was magic.

Poetry.

Christy reached across the table for an empty cup. Billy's grimy fist closed over her hand.

She pulled back, first in alarm, then in anger. She snapped her wrist back, twisting it away.

"Just being nice, Christy," said Billy. Bob and Dennis were silent, uncomfortable.

"Be nice with somebody else, Billy." Christy rubbed at her wrist as if it had been contaminated.

"Rather be nice with you." Again, that leering smile; the wet, gleaming eyes.

Christy leaned forward. "Let's not have any misunderstanding, Billy." Her voice was cool and calm. "I think you're a lecherous, disgusting animal. You're filthy, coarse and repulsive. The thought of being nice to you makes me feel physically ill."

Billy's eyes were cold and dead now, like marbles; the grin a frozen rictus. Bob and Dennis began to shuffle uneasily.

"And another thing . . . if you ever . . . *ever* . . . put your hands on me again, I'll report you to Sergeant Grover for assault. Do you get my drift, Billy? Is it sinking in?"

An eyelid twitched on Billy's face. Then he began to laugh: forced laughter, loud and unfunny. Bob and Dennis tried to smile. Billy's laughter died away. Christy still stood facing him, flushed with anger.

"Spunk," said Billy quietly. "That's what I like in a girl. Lots and lots of spunk."

Knowing very well what he was saying, Christy made a sound of disgust and turned away from the table, almost colliding with Iris who had come up behind her. Trying to avoid Iris's eyes, she headed for the room at the back. Billy was grinning again.

"Take that smile off your face, Billy," said Iris, eyes blazing. "Up until now I've always tolerated your bad behaviour. I know you've had your troubles, like everybody else. But if you make one more comment, or upset any of my customers again . . ." Unconsciously, Iris was waving a kitchen fork at Billy as she spoke.

Quietly, still grinning, Billy stood up.

"See ya," he said to Dennis and Bob. Blowing another exaggerated kiss at Iris, he walked slowly out of the shop.

The door crashed shut, bell ringing stridently. Iris gritted her teeth and turned back to the other two youths at the table.

"Nothing to do with us, Mrs. Wooler. Honest." Dennis was immediately defensive.

"We didn't ask him over," began Bob. "He just . . ."

Iris shook her head, ignoring their words. "Billy Rifkin is bad news. If you'll take my advice, you won't have anything more to do with him."

"We don't, Mrs. Wooler. We . . ."

"Don't give me that, Bob. I know fine well that you go out joyriding with him in that old banger of a car of his. Getting yourself drunk, tearing around those mountain lanes like nobody's business. Well, take my word for it, if you keep bad company—and Billy is bad company—then one day you'll be sorry for it."

"Mrs. Wooler, it's easy for you to say. But Billy's the kind of bloke who's difficult to avoid. If he wants you to do something, then . . ."

"You're big lads. Too big to be living in anybody's shadow. Avoid him."

Sheepishly, Dennis and Bob rose from their seats and wandered sulkily away to look for Linda. Iris watched them go, listening to Christy blowing her nose in the back room; blowing away the pent-up emotion. Iris had seen the way Billy Rifkin watched her. She had seen that dull, unhealthy glaze. There was nothing but trouble in those eyes. And yes, she had to admit, there were times when those eyes frightened even her. She had also seen the way Billy sometimes looked at the Haig kids, and that frightened her even more. There was a terrible hunger in those eyes. There were hidden depths that Iris did not care to think about for too long.

Pulling herself erect again and suddenly aware of the threatening way she was holding the kitchen fork, she thrust it into her apron and began clearing cups.

Chapter Thirteen

Frank had found the bottle of vodka in the ottoman by the time Christy arrived home that night. He had been searching for it for well over an hour and his temper had not as yet been soothed by the alcohol. That would take another couple of hours. He was slumped in an armchair, staring out of the window, when he heard the front door of the cottage open gently.

"That you, Christy?"

Quiet and resigned: "Yes."

"Out of luck again, eh?" laughed Frank ruefully. "I managed to find it, didn't I? You've used the ottoman before, you know. I'm surprised at you. Can't you find any new places?"

Christy sighed, entering the living-room. "I haven't even got my coat off yet and you're starting again." She threw the coat over the sofa, briefly taking in Frank's sprawled form in the armchair, eyes glazed, bottle cradled in his lap. He was right. She was running out of places to hide the bottles he brought home. Maybe she should just give up hiding them altogether and let him get on with it. Maybe things would be happier if she did that.

No. Things wouldn't be better. I've tried that before. He gets worse when the sorrow sets in and he loses control. I've got to keep on trying.

A gun battle was taking place on television; the Indians seemed to be having a bad time of it. She crossed the room and turned it down.

"Where've you been?" asked Frank, eyes still fixed on the screen.

Christy froze, her hand still on the control knob. She closed her eyes resignedly.

"I've been to work, Dad. That's where I always go."

"But you're late."

"By fifteen minutes, yes. There was extra work to do at the shop. I stayed behind to help Iris."

Frank made a derogatory sound: half-laugh, half snort of derision. Christy watched as an Indian somersaulted from a cliff onto a wagon.

"Good old Iris. What would we do without her, eh?" The sneer was almost too hard for Christy to take.

"Yes, Dad." She began to pick up newspapers, collecting discarded rubbish and empty tins. "Good old Iris. If it wasn't for Iris, I wouldn't be earning any money. And if we didn't have any money, we couldn't afford to eat." She stopped. Her father's shoulders were hunched, his hair awry, and he was cradling the vodka bottle like a baby. She had no intention of upbraiding him for getting drunk again. That only made things much worse. He ran a hand through his unruly hair, looking at her for the first time. He drank again, slowly.

"Go on," he said at last. "Say it, then."

"Say what?"

"You know what I mean. You know what happened yesterday. So let me have it, then. Come on. Let it go."

"What's the matter, Dad? What's eating you up all the time? It's just a piece of wood sticking out of the ground. They're going to move it carefully. They're going to . . ."

"They're going to rape our town, Christy! They're blind, ignorant idiots. They don't know what the hell they're doing. If they only knew . . ."

"If they only knew what, Dad? What? I'm sick to death of this. You go on and on about that gibbet as if it was the most important thing in the world. You're sitting in here . . . killing yourself!" *Oh no . . . no . . . I don't want to be saying this. But, oh God, I can't help it!* "You're drinking yourself to death. You've got no respect, you've got no *self*-respect. You're making laughingstocks of us both. We haven't got two pennies to rub together, debts up to the eyes . . . and all you can do is rage on about a bloody crossroads and a bloody bit of wood."

"I can't expect you to understand, Christy. I can't expect anyone to understand. I'm the only one who knows what's going on. I'm the only one who knows what would happen if . . ."

"If what, Dad? God in heaven, I'm sick to death of your riddles. You talk in circles all the time. You never give straight answers any more. You get drunk and we fight while both of our lives are just . . . running away down the drain. Can't you see that?"

Frank pulled himself clumsily to his feet, screwing the cap back on the bottle and throwing it onto the chair; he was swaying on his feet. This evening, he looked genuinely pathetic; only a shadow of the towering, strapping, brave man who had been her father. The tears which had been threatening to engulf Christy all day were very close now.

"Nobody can understand," slurred Frank. "Nobody would even listen if I told them what might happen."

The tears were coming now. Christy could not stop them. They were choking her voice as she spoke. "What's going on, Dad? What's the matter with you? What's between us?"

"I can't tell you that, Christy. But maybe, when you're older . . . you'll learn . . . you'll find out."

"Older? What are you *talking* about?"

It was too much for Christy to take again. When he was like this she could never get any sense out of him. The night would be spent arguing, or painfully avoiding arguments.

"Have . . . you . . . eaten?" The words were a desperate attempt to restore normality, but they came out like broken glass, tearing her vocal cords, choking her with tears.

"I want nothing." Frank slumped back in the chair again, grabbing for the bottle.

In seconds, Christy had snatched her coat from the sofa and left the room. Frank never heard the front door slam.

Chapter Fourteen

Somehow, Michael was not surprised to see Christy standing on the threshold when he answered the door. The dogs had already told him of her approach. They were pushing against her legs with obvious pleasure when he opened it. She looked up from them, smiling. And then Michael saw that she had been crying. In that instant, he was able to imagine most of what had happened as a result of her father's unscheduled appearance at the village hall. Christy's smile was brittle and he knew that it was important to react properly.

"Christy! I see my guard dogs have been letting me down again."

"Hello, Michael. Can I come in?"

Michael held the door wide. The dogs barged in and Christy followed slowly behind. He was glad that she was here; ashamed of his selfishness, but still glad. The very fact that she had chosen to knock on his door was a pleasure. Outside, the sun had almost vanished behind the mountain range; amber shadows stretched lazily over the fields and hedgerows.

A log fire was burning in the large grate, pervading the room with warm light: an inner companion to the beautiful light outside. The interior of the cottage was just as Christy had imagined it. She stood in the centre of the room looking round. The brittle, wistful smile was still on her face, and Michael found himself thinking, again selfishly: *God, how I want to change that smile; how I want it to be the way I've seen it before.*

"I'm not disturbing you, am I?" asked Christy.

"So what's to disturb? Like you said before, I need company. I'm too isolated."

The smile flickered.

Careful, Lambton. That's dangerous territory.

"Come on, Christy. Sit down."

Christy settled down on the sofa. Dutch and Mac moved in close immediately; Dutch acting coy in his usual sham manner by sticking his head on her knee and Mac lying at her feet, as if they were both somehow trying to prove a point. Christy began to stroke Dutch. The brittle expression was now more than he could bear.

Oh, to hell with! She needs help and I can't give it by playing games.

75

"What's wrong?"

"I'm sorry . . . I didn't have anybody to talk to. I just needed to get away from home for a bit."

Michael moved to the drinks cabinet. Christy was looking down at Dutch, still stroking his ears, and seemed more like a vulnerable little girl than ever before. She nodded when he asked if she would like some wine.

"I know about your father, Christy. I know it must be hard for you."

"Yes. It is. But he's all I've got. Michael . . . ?"

Michael brought her glass over. "Yes?"

"It's okay. You don't have to think of nice things to say. You don't even have to listen to me pouring out my heart. I just needed to get away and have some company."

He handed her the glass. "I understand. And you can have my company any time you like. You may not know this, but you've made me realise some important things about myself recently. I've a lot to thank you for." The smile was not so brittle now: some of the confidence had returned. "But we *can* talk about it if you want . . ."

"No, Michael. I don't need to now. Just company. That's all I need."

Michael waved his arm at the comfortable surroundings. "It's all yours."

Christy slid from the sofa, smiling; on hands and knees she made for the record cabinet and opened the door. "Let's see what else you have in here. What do writers listen to apart from Dire Straits?"

"Golden oldies, mostly. Want something to eat? I was just going to make supper."

Christy looked up. The old smile was back in all its glory. "Yes . . . yes . . . I think I would like something."

"Good!" beamed Michael. "Let's have a party."

Chapter Fifteen

Billy Rifkin swore at the brambles which had raked his hand as he squirmed forward to the rim of the hill. He cursed the long grass in front of him, which impeded his view of Split Crow Farm below. He flattened it savagely with the flat of one hand. He wriggled forward again on his elbows until he could see the landholding clearly, then he cursed at not being half an hour earlier than he had intended.

After leaving the coffee shop (*the stuff they serve in there is shit; wouldn't feed it to the pigs*), he had wandered back to the farm. As usual, his father had set him a schedule for the day and he had got down to it with a vengeance. With any luck, he would be able to get it all finished in time. Once the sheds had been washed out, he would head back to Shillingham. He would stop just outside the village, beside the crossroads, and wait for Christy coming home from work. He had timed her before. Six-thirty. That was the usual time.

He would wait for her there, and then walk back along the path with her. He had some questions to ask. Like . . . *How can you turn me down when you know I want you? I could be good to you, Christy. I can be nice. But I can be hard, as well. I don't want you screwing around with anybody else. I've always kept my distance. I've always respected you . . . never tried anything on directly.* And then came the memory of Christy dragging her hand away from him in the coffee shop, and of the things she had said. The look in her eyes that said he was dirt and that he should not touch. Billy's patience had been sorely tried by that look. He had been biding his time, which was unlike him. If he saw something that he wanted, he just reached out and took it. He had not done that with Christy. But after today? Well, after today he had intended to walk back with her, talk to her, reason with her. Give her another chance to take back the things she had said and the way that she had looked at him. If she did, everything would be all right. If she refused, if she gave him some more of the same . . . well, it was a long walk back to Christy's farm. There were not many people walking along there at this time of evening. There were lots of places where he could take her and convince her. Places where no one could hear. Places where he could prove to her just how much of a man he could be.

But messing out those sheds had taken longer than he had expected. He could have made a shorter job of it, but the old man himself had come into the barn after a while, smoking one of those cheap cigars, watching him and smiling. And Billy had been forced to do a thorough job under that watchful eye (*never pays me more than a pittance. I'm just slave labour, that's all. One day, one day, one day, I'll . . .*). As a result, he was an hour later than he had expected. He had run all the way down to the crossroads. Maybe she was working late. Maybe he would meet her on the road. But there was no sign of her. Maybe there was a chance. He had rounded the bend leading down past Split Crow and had seen the familiar scarlet flash of her coat. His mouth was dry now, heart hammering. But his anticipation had turned to rage when she turned down towards the farm fence. He had halted in his tracks, breath wheezing, as Christy began to climb the fence and the weirdo's two dogs came racing across to meet her. Shaking with anger, he had watched as she walked towards the house, playing with the dogs. There was an animal sound in his throat as he marched, stiff-legged, towards the gnarled tree on his right. He turned back once to see that Christy had reached the front door. She was knocking (*Bitch! Bitch! Bitch!*) and now the door was opening. She stepped inside. Billy punched the tree; once, twice, three times—until the blood seeped from the ragged gashes on his knuckles. He wanted to rip the bark off the tree in the same way that he would rip the bark off that bitch and her weirdo writer friend.

But that had been an hour and a half ago. Billy's red heat had now subsided to a slow, poisonous burn. He could wait. He was good at waiting. For an hour and a half, he had watched. And he knew just what was going on in there. He could see it happening now. He could see what she was letting him do to her, he could see what she was doing to him. And he promised himself that when she came out and started for home, he was going to give her something that she would never forget. After that, he was going to go down there to the loony's place and he was going to make sure that he could never do anything to a woman ever again. He had done it to pigs before. With that shithead, it would be just like another farm job. A lot of squealing, and not a little blood.

Billy could see a light in the window. Occasionally, a shadow would move past it. He began pulling out chunks of grass in front of him. It was like pulling hair out of someone's scalp. The sensation helped to calm him, helped him prevent that slow burn from becoming white-hot again.

But that light in the window was beginning to infuriate him. Even though he could imagine what was going on, that light seemed to be mocking him. It was drawing him forward: *Come and see what's going on in here, Billy. Come and look . . . then you'll really know . . .*

"You'll come out soon, Christy. I know you will," he muttered under his breath. "You'll come out when you've had enough. And then I'll show you what you've been missing . . ."

Chapter Sixteen

"So . . . that's about it," said Christy, staring down at the wine in her glass. "Mother was killed by a car right in the centre of Shillingham while she was shopping. A couple of tourists, out for a joyride in the country. Poor people. It wasn't anybody's fault, really. She never recovered from her coma. And Dad went steadily downhill after that. I often think that the fact they were tourists might have something to do with Dad's reaction to the road development scheme and the removal of the gibbet at the crossroads. More tourists and all that."

After some good music and more wine, Christy had begun to talk after all. Michael had listened carefully, not pushing the conversation, not trying to help. Just listening. And he could tell that she was feeling better for it.

"Dad buried things inside himself. And it didn't do him any good. Do you know . . . ? I think that sometimes we all bury things deep down, things we should deal with straight away, as soon as they happen. It's no use burying them, really, because they just stay there festering. Sooner or later they're going to come back. They're going to rebound on us and make things worse."

"You're talking about the story of my life, Christy." Michael laughed, crossed the room and poured more wine into Christy's glass. Topping up his own, he returned to his seat. "So your dad . . . ?"

"What do you mean? The story of your life?"

"Nothing. Really. Your dad . . . ?"

"No, Michael. I'd like to know."

Michael swallowed a false excuse to change the subject. Christy had been talking for over an hour now, pouring out her heart to a relative stranger. But there had been nothing odd about that. It was honest, direct and . . . well . . . flattering. She was genuinely interested. The request was not being made by an inquisitive child: it was being made by a strangely mature young person.

"I know what it's like to have tragedy in your life," he said at last. "Like you, I was an only child." He swirled the wine in his glass. "When I was nine years old, my parents were killed in a railway accident. The three of us were returning on the King's Cross line to Newcastle. We'd been on holiday. The train was derailed—no one knows how. I came out of it alive, but my parents were killed. I don't remember too much about it, to be honest. Shortly afterwards, I became a Barnardo's boy. There weren't any other relations, you see."

"I feel so guilty, Michael," said Christy quietly. "I've been sitting here bending your ear for ages about my . . ."

"You needed to talk, Christy."

"And I think you do, too."

Michael smiled. "You're right."

There was a pause. Not an uncomfortable silence, but

81

somehow very *natural*. A log cracked in the grate, sending a shower of sparks up the chimney. The mellow warmth and colour of the room matched the mellow taste of the wine. Dutch stretched and yawned on the carpet.

"I think that I was aware, even before my parents' death," continued Michael, "of an inherent vulnerability inside me. I developed a protective 'shell' against the outside world. It served me well in a lonely existence. I became a bookworm, burying myself in fantasy worlds, creating my own fantasy worlds. That's how the writing really began, I suppose. I went to a teacher training college and did pretty well, managed to find a good teaching job almost straight away, but always keeping my writing as a sideline. When my writing career really did take off, I gave up teaching to write full time. That's when my problems started . . ."

Now, Michael was speaking about things he had thought he would never put into words again; things that had only been spoken to a psychiatrist a lifetime ago.

"You told me that you read the blurb on one of my books in the supermarket. Well, you've also guessed from the blurb that my books have done pretty well."

Christy screwed her eyes shut, trying to recall a line of the blurb from *Beyond Me*. " 'Lambton sees the true fear inside mens' hearts.' Something like that, isn't it?"

"Near enough . . . I took my work seriously, Christy. As it turns out, I took it too seriously. The critics raved about my analysis of fear . . . if that doesn't sound too grand . . . and the human condition. I'd spent four years analysing and debating the nature of fear. I was a lecturer in literature during that time and it was an area that became a kind of speciality to me. That experience and analysis were all incorporated into my first novel. They say that there's a novel in all men and women who deal with the spoken word.

Beyond Me was my first novel, and it really took off. The second and third novels were written in a shorter period of time, concentrating on specific areas of fear and—again, if you'll pardon the pretension—subconscious dread. I was always interested in the fear response—the flight or fight syndrome. I'd come to regard it as the prime motivation of human behaviour."

"What about survival? Isn't that a prime motivation?"

"Yes. But I'd argued that survival in itself was a development of the fear response. Up to that time, I was in control of my work and my materials. I was working long hours, of course. Too long . . . I was drinking a great deal to give me a 'lift' when I was physically and emotionally worn out. And all the time, the expectations of my readers and my critics were driving me to dig deep into the collective unconscious, dredging out more conclusions on the nature of fear. My perfectionism and drive wouldn't allow me to produce anything substandard.

"And then I came to write *The Borderland*." Michael paused to drink some wine. His mouth had suddenly become very dry.

"I wanted it to be my masterpiece, containing elements of all that had gone before, but really digging deep into how and why people have fear. I worked eighteen hours a day to meet a publishing deadline. My drinking escalated. I began to dredge my own subconscious, began to identify closely with aspects of the characters and their responses in the novel. Although I couldn't see it, I was losing my objectivity, losing control. I wasn't using the material any more—the material was using me. The book became a bestseller. It *was* my masterpiece. The film of the book made me a fortune. It bought me this place. But I'd pushed myself too hard and too far. I'd dredged up things from my own subconscious; things which should have stayed down there and should never have seen the light of day. The accumulated, suppressed fears and neuroses of a lifetime— my lifetime—were released. So it's like you've just said: those things which I hadn't confronted, those things which I had buried deep down inside, were suddenly released on me."

"Pandora's Box," said Christy quietly.

"Exactly. They were released and they . . . took over. I had a nervous breakdown."

Another instant playback: *A man on a stretcher being carried to an ambulance, crying like a baby.*

"I'd lost control. My own fear attacked me, wrecked me. I couldn't function. Reality and fantasy were fused together for a while. I was haunted by . . . an absolute terror . . . something I couldn't rationalise. Although there was actually no specific thing to fear, that was the strange thing— it was everything and nothing—it was the fear of fear itself. And it swamped me day and night: the feeling that something terrible was going to happen at any second. I didn't know what it was, but it was terrifying and it could only end in madness, death or worse. Sometimes, in the sanatorium, I think I wanted to die rather than have that fear any more. They pumped me so full of drugs that I was existing in a twilight world.

"I was in there for six months. And when I discharged myself, it seemed that the fear had gone; it seemed to have been resolved by the therapy. Everything seemed okay— until I tried to write again. Just the thought of sitting at a typewriter made me break out in a cold sweat. I could feel the old fear resurfacing, threatening to drag me back under. I couldn't rationalise it. Every time I tried to start something, it was as if my subconscious told me: 'Here Be Dragons.' I was finished.

"After a few months, it seemed as if my 'success' was haunting me. I couldn't function in interviews any more; couldn't give lectures on my work; couldn't meet my publishers to discuss future projects. It was just too much. So . . . I bought this place. That was two years ago, and I'm still haunted by what happened to me."

"So you'll never write again?" asked Christy.

"No. I don't think I'll ever be able to do that. I'm afraid that the old fear will return. I've felt like . . . a dead man . . . for over two years. My emotions have been dead. I didn't want to bring them back to life again, in case the fear came back with them."

"Who said: 'The only thing we have to fear is fear itself?' "

"President Roosevelt, wasn't it?"

"Could be . . . You need people, Michael. All this isolation isn't good for you."

Michael smiled. "Point acknowledged. And I've got you to thank for that."

"You will be able to write again. I'm sure of it."

"No. I don't think so."

"We'll see. Let me work on it."

"You've got your hands full, Christy. You've got your own troubles to work out."

"So? You can help me, as well, can't you?"

They both laughed, and Michael was astonished to find that he had opened his heart so freely and readily to this young girl. His laughter reflected that astonishment; he felt no shame, no embarrassment . . . and no fear. *No fear, Michael! No fear!* This young girl—with her own horrendous problems—was working some kind of miracle for him. At last, he said: "We weren't going to talk about our problems, remember?"

They laughed again as Dutch and Mac prowled to the windows.

"Have we bored them, do you think?" asked Christy, sipping her wine, eyes sparkling.

"Probably." Michael went to the front door and opened it. The dogs glided silently past him and out into the night. "They've probably scented a rabbit."

Christy watched him steadily over the rim of her glass as he returned to his seat.

"You've sickened yourself, Michael. You've been thinking, living and breathing pessimism. No one can do that as intensely as you say and come through it without cracking up—or worse. Iris would have a quote for this. She's got one for every occasion. How about, 'That which I greatly feared has come upon me?' Isaiah, I think. No . . . She would probably say: 'A man is what his thoughts are every day.' "

"Marcus Aurelius."

"Really? I never knew that Iris was so well read. Anyway . . . it's true."

"You think a lot of Iris, don't you?"

"Yes . . . I do. Since the accident, she's been the closest thing to a mother to me. And as for you, Michael, you've got yourself into a mental rut. You need to crowd out all those black thoughts with optimistic ones."

"How do I go about that?"

"I'll help you. Optimism has been my forte for a long time now."

"You make me feel ashamed, Christy. I'm twice your age and I should be wiser for it. I've brought my own problems on myself, in a sense. You've had all kinds of awful trouble

which you couldn't avoid . . . but you've managed to deal
with it."

"You'll pull through, Michael. I know you will."

"For the first time—for the *very* first time—I think you
might be right."

The perfect moment was broken by the full-throated
barking of Dutch and Mac, somewhere outside in the night.
Michael groaned and moved back to the door, opening it.

"Dutch! Mac! Come on in here!"

The noise continued unabated. Michael shifted uneasily:
there was an element of savagery in their barking which
suggested that they really had unearthed a rabbit or a fox.

"Dutch! Mac!"

The two dogs emerged from the surrounding blackness
into the rectangle of orange light shining from the farmhouse door. They were putting on a show for Michael, strut-
ting in the light, heads erect, chests out, growling low and
constantly turning back to the mysterious object hidden in
the darkness, which had drawn their attention.

"Come on, you two! In!"

Reluctantly, the dogs glided inside. Michael squinted
into the blackness, but could see nothing. When he returned to the warmth and comfort of the living-room, Dutch
and Mac were curled round Christy's feet in front of the
fire. Christy was lying back on the sofa, proffering her
empty glass, eyes shining in the firelight, flowing hair ebony
black. Michael could not remember when he had last felt
so good.

He closed the door.

Chapter Seventeen

Billy Rifkin scrambled over the Split Crow fence, nursing his arm. Scrabbling through the gorse, he fought his way back up to the track. His mind was filled with a black rage. How could he have known that those dogs would still be prowling around at this time of night? The light in the window had proved too great a lure. Even though, in his mind's eye, he could see what was happening in there, he still could not resist the impulse to get closer . . . to look through that window . . . to really *see*. But he had hardly cleared the fence before the first dog had spotted him. It had come silently out of the dark, fastening on his arm, its teeth tearing through his jacket. He had been bitten before on the farm, but this bastard knew what it was doing. Just when he was aiming a punch at its head, the other one had hit him from behind, taking his jacket pocket clean off. Fortunately, the weirdo himself had appeared and called the dogs in. He could not have seen him in the dark.

He was going to pay! Really pay!

And Christy would watch while Billy made him pay. Before he did it to her.

He scrambled back through the night, down the track towards home, all thoughts of lying in wait forgotten. His new plan would be better . . . much better.

Chapter Eighteen

For over an hour, Frank had been cursing and swearing at Christy. She was late again! She knew that he expected her home at a certain time every night. She knew it! But she was late again, and he was seething with rage. And then he remembered that she *had* come home. They had had a fight and Christy had walked out again.

She was ungrateful! Bloody ungrateful . . .

And then, corking the bottle of cheap wine that he had found in the garage, the tears suddenly rose to his eyes, welling up from a still lucid part of his soul.

"No, she isn't ungrateful," he slurred aloud. "How can she be? She doesn't know what it's all about. She doesn't know what's ahead of her—because I haven't told her."

The tears were forcibly subdued. Frank stood swaying in the garage. It was time again.

Staggering back to the kitchen, he rummaged through the drawers until he found a biscuit tin. Emptying the contents on the bench, he began hunting for the material he needed.

"Earth," he said aloud when he found the half-loaf of bread and placed it in the tin.

"Sea." A tin of pilchards which had been in the cupboard, unopened, for months now.

"Fire." A piece of coal from the scuttle in the kitchen.

He jammed the lid back on the tin, and turned unsteadily to look out of the garage window into the night. It was waiting out there for him.

Clutching the biscuit tin tightly to his chest like the bitter burden it was, he staggered out into the darkness, leaving the garage door to swing creaking on its hinges. A wind had arisen as he reeled down to the path. It searched his body inquisitively as he moved, ruffling through his hair like a dark lover. It found nothing there. It tugged at his trouser legs and jacket, pulling out his shirttail. Finally, pulling and flapping at his sleeves, it reached the tin box clasped to his chest but could find no ingress. Frank could not afford to release that box. It was too important.

"All right, all right. I'm coming."

Tattered trees and fences swung at him as he walked. A pock-marked moon grinned behind a shredded gauze curtain of clouds. Grass clutched at his legs, curling round his ankles, wanting to bring him down. He kicked out at it angrily. The wind hissed back at him in displeasure from the trees.

Half an hour later, he had reached his destination.

It was still there, waiting for him. It was always waiting for him. He was bound to it.

The gibbet.

He halted, swaying to the tempo of the wind, staring up at the weathered wood. It was creaking in the wind and to Frank that creaking seemed to be like low, mocking laughter.

Here-again . . . Back-again . . . Come-to-me . . . Give-to-me . . .

He moved forward, still clutching the tin. Before and above him, the gibbet seemed to pierce the grinning moon. The mocking creak of ancient wood was too much for him. Images flashed before him: of heartbroken lost years; of wasted life; of Christy, her eyes filled with tears. And, of course, the Secret.

90

That damned, bloody Secret! The thing that's ruined my life! And Christy's!

Dark clouds roiled angrily in the night sky behind the gibbet.

Come-to-me . . . Give-to-me . . .

And then, in a torrent: "You damned bastard! You've taken everything away from me. Everything good! First my wife, and now my daughter!"

He wrestled angrily with the biscuit tin, pulling it out from under his jacket. Steadying himself, he drew back his hand and flung the tin full at the gibbet. The tin clattered and bounced away from the base of the wooden beam, spilling out its contents onto the ground.

"Take it and be damned!"

Something dark growled overhead in the clouds—perhaps a storm on its way. The moon glared from behind its veil, bathing Frank in stark-white, skeletal light.

"Everything!" shouted Frank again, whirling in disgust from the crossroads gibbet and shambling away into the darkness. "You've taken away everything I ever had."

Chapter Nineteen

At Split Crow Farm, talk of fear and insecurity turned gently to means of overcoming those fears and insecurities. Sophisticated reflections, held in reserve by each as individual secrets, were now revealed as common experience. Laughter chased shadows. Comfort and security from the night chased away bitter yesterdays and ominous tomorrows.

And at last, when they touched, that touch proved to be the most special thing that either had experienced. It surprised them both in its intensity; brought back emotion and feeling that they had both presumed dead. Their mutual loneliness combined became a new and vibrant force, banishing loneliness.

Suddenly, Michael was much less the lonely, isolated and impotent man that he had assumed.

And Christy—far from being a girl—was much more a woman than both had realised.

Like two lonely roads to unknown destinations, they had met at a crossroads and, far from continuing in separate directions, had made their new destinations as one.

On Split Crow Lane, waiting in the night, the gibbet creaked and swayed in lonely vigil.

Another, completely different crossroads, awaited them both.

Chapter Twenty

Blood-dark rage burned with feverish intensity behind Billy's eyes as he reached the west field, the boundary of his father's property. He swung over the gate, catching his leg in the darkness and falling heavily onto the arm which had been savaged by Lambton's dog. The grass was soft and the pain minimal; but the further indignity made something burst and blossom in Billy's heart as he pulled himself up, spitting fury at the night sky and kicking savagely at the fence.

Bastard! I'll kill you! I'll kill her! Both of you! Bastard Lambton, I'll make you pay, really pay for what you've done . . .

Each word had a special new meaning. It burned with an intensity and power that he had never felt before. The badness inside that had been eating at him since Christy had gone down to Split Crow Farm had become so bad that now . . . now, it was beginning to feel *good!* He wondered at this as he walked across the west field, uncaring of the freshly ploughed furrows which threatened to topple him to the ground again at any second. The badness was changing, burning itself into something really pure. Something really good.

It was arousing him.

He was like a raging furnace inside as he reached the first barn and turned the corner into the Rifkins' litter-strewn farmyard. His dad was inside, probably watching television and safely out of the way. Now, the new feeling was showing him just how he could get what he wanted and also get his revenge. It was a short-term revenge, but it would do for the time being. His mouth was dry as he reached the pig shed and swung over the fence. The shed was well out of the way; his father would not hear a thing. Just like the time he had axed that runt to death and the old man had not even noticed.

The sow was grubbing at the fence rail as he approached.

You bitch, Christy! You could have had me, but you'd rather be fucked by a weirdo, wouldn't you? Wouldn't you? Well, when you've had your fun, I'm going to have mine. And you're going to wish you'd never been born.

Billy licked his lips.

93

The sow looked up at him enquiringly as he fumbled at his trouser buttons.

"Here, Christy! Come over here to Daddy! Come on, Christy . . . come and see what Daddy's got, you bitch . . ."

Billy moved forward.

Chapter Twenty-one

It was more excited than it had ever been since its committal to limbo. Its fevered dreams were filled with enraptured images of revenge. Still comatose and drifting in its fathomless sleep, it was nonetheless aware that interconnecting and opposing forces in the external world had never been so favourable for release. Images of gratification ebbed and flowed in the tides of its poisonous sleep. It gloried in the screaming faces of men and women which it recognised from its past existence, and it pictured new faces in the blood-smeared, mutilated masks which it would eventually give them on release. It savoured the sounds of death and the dying, of torture beyond imagining—and revenge. It could smell and taste the blood even now; a foul wine that replenished and further excited its sleeping core.

And now, out of its evil and fractured sleep, it found another desire, which it could and would fulfil upon release. It was a desire that stirred and excited it even more. A desire which could and would extend not only to those who had imprisoned it, but to all humankind. It was the desire to create. And it had the ability to be a creator.

It would create a new fear, a new living terror for the

species which it hated and detested above all.
It would create a living Hell on earth.
In longing and expectation—
It waited.

Part Two
The Awakening

Chapter One

The bulldozer snorted angrily into life, pushing before it a mound of pebbled earth as it gouged a furrow seven feet wide. Tommy Harrison, gaffer in charge of Harrison Construction, sidestepped a renegade boulder and climbed the Split Crow bank to look down on the crossroads.

Split Crow Lane had been cordoned off and temporary traffic lights placed in the centre of the roads leading to Shillingham, dead ahead, and to the outer valley on the left. It was a waste of time, really, since traffic was very limited—only one argumentative old bugger in a battered pick-up van since nine o'clock that morning. Tommy had briefed his workmen, a team of seven, earlier in the week about the removal job, and they had made a good, concerned show for the Environment officials who had fussed and buzzed around the gibbet all day. No one knew how deep the gibbet stake was buried, not even the DOE "experts." Tommy had privately reckoned on eight feet or so, but his lads had dug a small trench around the base of the gibbet (under strict supervision, of course) down to twelve feet, and had then stood back for a time while the bloody archaeologists decided what to do next. Concern about a gnarled willow tree, twenty feet away up the hill, and the possibility that its roots could be entwined around the stake, had resulted in Tommy ordering his bulldozer driver (under strict supervision, of course) to clear away the mound on which the tree stood, together with the tree itself. Even as he watched, the bulldozer lowered its blade again and jammed it into the base of the tree. The bulldozer tracks spun, found purchase in the soil, and the tree began to keel over with a sighing, cracking sound. Roots sprang in soil-covered, tattered ribbons from the ground, snaking through the earth . . . but stopping ten feet from the gibbet itself.

Tommy was decidedly pissed off. He had successfully managed to keep his temper under control all morning, but it was a hard battle and each fresh hassle caused by the Environment men was weakening his control. First of all, the whole bloody job had been fixed from the beginning. Tommy had heard of "jobs" like this before and knew for a fact that, normally, the Environment people would not let a contractor anywhere near an "historical artefact" like Shillingham's gibbet. They would have their own squad of wallahs picking and digging at the thing. Like everybody else in the village, he knew of the road scheme—and welcomed it—but he also knew that the contract for removal (under strict supervision, of course) had been given to him deliberately because he was a local lad. It was a public relations ploy to take the heat away; keeping the local yokels happy. Number one: he did not like being manipulated. Number two: the money was crap.

If he had not needed the cash quickly (which he did), he would have told the daft sods fussing away down there in their tweed jackets to sod off.

From where he stood, Tommy could see the head man down below—Elphick—walking briskly to the Datsun which was parked on a nearby grass verge, sticking his head in the driver's window to converse with the driver—Mrs.-Bloody-Garvanter of the Rinsed-Hair-and-Bloody-Historical-Society. So far, she had stayed in her car, nodding sagely and wisely at each development. Tommy hoped that it would stay that way. Things were hard enough without that bucket of lard sticking her nose in.

Elphick headed back to the crowd around the gibbet workings and Tommy watched the animated debate which ensued dissolve into a crowd of heads anxiously scanning the site for a missing person—him. Tommy thrust his hands deeply into his pockets, feigned a nonchalant examination of the bulldozer as it finally snorted to a halt with the ruined willow tree imbedded in its blade, and descended slowly and casually to the site once more.

"Ah . . . there you are, Tommy," said Elphick as he joined the group.

Yes, here I am, you arrogant little snot!

"We've had a chat and we think your lads should continue digging. The tree's obviously not a problem."

"How deep *are* these things usually, then?" asked Tommy, walking past Elphick to peer down into the twelve-foot trench surrounding the stake.

"Not as deep as this, I would say." Laughter. Forced, tight and condescending. As in: *Let's get on with it, Tommy!* "How deep would you guess yourself?"

Tommy looked up, fixing the man wearing the thin moustache and the thin, disposable smile with as steady a gaze as he was able. "Me, *myself*? Well, Mr. Elphick, speaking as *me myself*, the building contractor, as opposed to *me myself* the archae-bloody-ologist, I'd say that's for you to know, innit? I'm just the hired hand, remember? I'm the guy who waits to be told what to do while certain people fart about."

The thin-faced man's disposable smile, already fragile, vanished.

"Just dig, Tommy, if you don't mind. And might I say that . . ."

"Okay, Andy!" shouted Tommy, moving to the roped rail and shouting to one of two labourers in overalls who were leaning on their spades nearby. "You and Eric keep digging until you hit Australia."

Also pissed off and sharing Tommy's opinion of Environment officials and archaeologists, Andy and Eric slipped under the rope and dropped into the trench, carrying their spades.

Tommy leaned on the rope, looking down and trying to conceal his disgust, as the two workmen continued to dig. Elphick looked on in approval, occasionally turning to acknowledge a satisfied nod from the omnipresent Mrs. Garvanter in her stationary Datsun. The gibbet loomed implacably overhead.

"The reinforcement of the wood seems particularly interesting," said Elphick at last to his colleagues, to break the silence. "It was obviously built to last . . ."

"Leave it alone!"

All heads turned as one at the strident shout from the bank of soil on Split Crow Lane. A dishevelled figure was standing silhouetted against the skyline, swaying from side to side. He was instantly recognisable. An empty whisky bottle rattled to the foot of the mound.

102

"Oh, bloody hell," moaned Tommy.

"Warwick . . ." sighed Elphick under his breath.

Exasperation turned rapidly to fear when it became apparent what Frank had with him, and which he was now hoisting to his shoulder.

It was a shotgun.

"Move away from there, Elphick! Leave it where it is!" Frank sighted unsteadily along the barrel, struggling to retain his balance on the sliding soil.

"Mr. Warwick! Please, don't do anything rash!" Elphick moved forward, face suddenly beaded with sweat, hands held out imploringly, aware that Tommy was ducking under the rope ready to jump down into the trench. "There's no need for violence. Please . . . put the gun down . . ."

THOKKK!

Elphick saw the flash of smoke and cried out involuntarily. Arms outstretched to ward off the approaching shot, he heard the windscreen of the bulldozer disintegrate with a hissing crash even before the actual sound of the shot reached his ears. The combination of terror and relief robbed his legs of all feeling and he collapsed to the ground. Figures were running in all directions; he was only dimly aware of Mrs. Garvanter's frenzied attempts to start her car, as Warwick began an unsteady descent of the mound, moving in their direction.

"I told you! I told you not to interfere!"

Please, God, whimpered Elphick, *make him go away . . . He's mad . . . make him go . . .*

THOKKK!

MAKE HIM GO AWAY!

The second shot ricocheted, screaming from the blade of the bulldozer.

Elphick scrambled away to one side. On his right, Mrs.

Garvanter had made another donkey-start. The Datsun coughed and jumped forward as her foot slipped from the clutch. If he could only get to the car before Warwick reloaded . . .

A third shot slashed harmlessly into the air.

Oh God, please don't let him kill me!

On all fours, Elphick scuttled across the deserted site. Mrs. Garvanter's car roared into life. The fourth shot slammed directly into the Datsun's radiator, sending the emblem on the bonnet whirling away into the air; water gushed from the radiator grille. The car coughed and died. Elphick turned to see Warwick striding purposefully forward, shotgun breach open, the L-shaped iron hanging over his forearm as he fumbled in his pocket for more shells. Elphick opened his mouth to scream for help, but the words never came. For something impossible was happening. Mouth still open, his gaze was drawn to the roots of the overturned willow tree now lying behind the gibbet. Warwick was just drawing level with the tree, and Elphick thought that the shock of the attack must have unhinged his mind. Warwick could not see it—but the roots of the tree were *alive*.

They were moving. Wriggling and twisting like snakes. One root was squirming across the ground towards them, like some kind of tattered boa constrictor, curling and contorting.

"I told you!" said Warwick, jamming a fresh shell into the breach. "You can't say I didn't warn you!"

"Roots . . ." said Elphick weakly, holding up an ineffectual hand, as the coiling root suddenly whipped forward to strike at Warwick. Elphick yelled in alarm, throwing himself out of the way. The root wound itself with uncanny accuracy around Warwick's ankle. He shouted once, harshly, and fell headlong. The shotgun rattled from his grasp. Instantly, it seemed, one of the workmen appeared from nowhere and flung himself on top of Warwick. In a second, he was joined by another, who kicked the shotgun aside with one foot and then kicked Warwick in the ribs with the other.

Elphick clambered shakily to his feet as people began to appear from their hiding places. Mrs. Garvanter was weeping behind the wheel of her car, mascara streaming in black rivulets over her rouged cheeks. Elphick opened the car door and tried his best to soothe her.

Tommy was now standing beside Warwick, who was still pinioned to the ground, cursing hoarsely. Tommy joined in the vindictive oaths.

"You could have killed someone, you stupid bastard! You bloody maniac!"

Elphick looked back at the tree.

The roots were unmoving . . . which they must always have been, of course. They were nowhere near Warwick. *It was shock, that's all. I was seeing things*.

He turned his attention back to Mrs. Garvanter.

His white-faced colleagues were approaching now, as Tommy ordered one of his workmates to telephone Sergeant Grover from the site hut. Frank's shouts had been reduced to a drunken burbling, but Tommy's string of oaths continued unabated.

"Dreadful . . . dreadful . . ." moaned the corpulent Mrs. Garvanter.

Elphick tried an awkward "there-there" pat on her broad, meaty shoulders, which somehow did not work. "You'll be all right, Mrs. Garvanter. Sergeant Grover will be here soon. He'll see to everything . . ."

"He . . . tried . . . to . . . to . . . *shoot me!*" bawled Mrs. Garvanter, burying her face in a handkerchief. Elphick straightened up, clearing his throat, unsure how to handle things. A workman was sprinting past him from the direction of the gibbet, straight towards Tommy. Something in the young man's manner drew Elphick's attention as he began talking excitedly to his boss. Elphick could not hear what was being said and could see nothing wrong with the excavation when the young man pointed excitedly back at the gibbet.

He watched Tommy draw in a deep breath, and then:

"Whaaaat!" he roared at last.

The gibbet, thought Elphick in alarm. *Something's happened to the gibbet!*

Suddenly, the two workmen were hauling Warwick to his feet, and everyone else was running past Elphick towards the gibbet. He could only watch, ill-equipped for any fresh shocks, with Mrs. Garvanter still bawling in his ear, as Tommy marched stiff-legged towards him. The man grabbed his arm in a painful grip and hissed directly into his face.

"You and your fucking gibbet, Elphick. First that stupid bastard. Now *this*!"

"What? What?" mumbled Elphick ineffectually as he was frog-marched to the excavation site. When they reached the rope barrier, Tommy forced him to look down.

The trench around the gibbet stake had caved in.

They were looking into a black and apparently bottomless gaping hole which had opened around the base of the gibbet.

"It's caved in, Elphick," hissed Tommy, jabbing a finger at the yawning fissure.

"And one of my lads is down there!"

Chapter Two

Andy Hudson squirmed round, clawed his way from a mound of suffocating soil and rolled over, retching and choking. There was dirt in his mouth, his nostrils and his eyes. He coughed it out, trying to remember where he was and just what in bloody hell was going on.

Rubbing the soil from his eyes, he remembered that Tommy had been pissed off at the Environment men all day and—after a lot of farting about—had ordered Eric and himself to begin digging in the trench again. Then that maniac Warwick had appeared out of nowhere like Wyatt Earp or something, and had started taking potshots at them. Andy and Eric had climbed out to see what the commotion was about, but in the split-second when Warwick had blown out the bulldozer windscreen, Andy had figured out that the safest place to be was back in the trench. He had jumped over the rope barrier and landed heavily. Then it seemed as if the world had caved in.

Caved in!

He wriggled over onto his back and squinted upwards in alarm. Dust still swirled and the dirt in his eyes impeded his vision, but he could make out daylight about thirty feet or so above. Hastily, he checked himself for injury. His hip hurt where he had landed, but there did not appear to be any breaks, thank God. His head hurt like mad (*Concussion?* he wondered), but he was in one piece. He wondered if Warwick had chased everyone away, and tried to shout, but his voice came out in a choking bark. He climbed to his feet and looked round, his eyes gradually becoming accustomed to the dark.

He was in a cave of sorts, with roughly hewn stone walls, about fifty feet in circumference from what he could tell in the gloom. The floor was littered with boulders and debris from the cave-in. How the hell he had avoided a cracked skull in that fall, with all that muck coming down on him, he did not know. But he thanked his lucky star.

He saw the dark, tapering bulk before him which reached upwards towards the patch of daylight overhead, and moved forwards to examine it more closely.

It was the gibbet stake.

Bloody hell! it must be fifty feet long, if it's an inch.

Looking up, he could see that the cave funnelled upwards into a kind of chute through the earth to ground level. The base of the gibbet was implanted in the cave in which he stood, but the stake rose up through the funnel to the ground above. There were metal bracings at ten foot intervals around the stake itself, like the spokes of a wheel with the gibbet at the centre. The corroded, rusted spokes were imbedded in the chimney sides, apparently to keep it upright. Wondering, Andy moved forward to the foot of the gibbet.

Now, he could see that the gibbet was not imbedded in a mound of earth and boulders, as he had originally supposed in the dark. It was rooted in what looked like a stone, coffin-shaped box with roughly hewn sides; as if it had been carved from rock. Andy reached out to the box, squinted upwards again at the distant sunlight, and then looked down into the box. It was filled with a chalk-white substance and, at the centre, where the stake entered, there was a shrivelled black something that looked like . . .

Andy's eyes traversed the length of that shrivelled object

until he was looking directly down at the head of the rectangular, stone container.

He recoiled in horror, the hair standing up on the back of his neck, a pulse of sheer terror shooting down his back.

Slowly, he moved back to the box and peered inside again, mouth opened in awe.

The stone container *was* a coffin!

The black mass, half-buried in the white stuff, was a shrivelled corpse. A skull-like countenance grinned up at Andy from the head of the coffin, black-parchment skin stretched taut across the face, the eye sockets and gaping mouth filled with the crumbling white powder. A black, skeletal claw protruded from the white stuff, as if beckoning. The gibbet stake had been plunged through the centre of the corpse's chest, the tapering shaft almost two feet in circumference.

Andy looked up again, now knowing that the spiral spokes anchoring the shaft to the funnelled walls had been fixed there to keep it firmly in place and to prevent the corpse from being crushed. But why the hell would anyone go to such bother? Bloody weird. He looked down again.

"Ugly bugger, aren't you?"

The corpse was obviously old, very old indeed. Andy remembered that one of the Environment guys had said that the gibbet had been there since the 1600s. So the body had obviously been down here all that time, too. *Some engineering feat for the 1600s,* he thought. And then a shadow from above fell across him.

"You down there, Andy? You okay?" It was Tommy.

"Yeah, I'm okay. Don't know how, though. It's bloody deep down here."

"Are you sure you're all right, lad?" echoed Tommy's

voice from the skylight opening. "It must be a thirty-foot drop down there."

"I'm okay, really. But the fella down here with me doesn't look too good."

"What?"

"There's a coffin down here with a body in it. And this bloody gibbet goes straight through it."

"Right!" said Tommy with a ring of finality. "We'll have you out of there in two minutes, Andy. *And* this bloody gibbet!" His head vanished from view.

Chapter Three

"What do you mean, 'And the gibbet?'" asked Elphick, striding forward, his authoritative air suddenly returning as Tommy moved quickly to his workmen and began issuing instructions. Three men began to haul rope and tackle from the back of a lorry.

"I've had enough of you," replied the contractor at last. "Giving me a public relations piss-all job. Screwing me and my lads around all day. This bastard here tries to blow somebody's head off . . ." Tommy stabbed a finger at Warwick, ". . . and now Andy's fallen into that bloody pit. Well, I'm getting my lad out of there. And then the gibbet's coming out, Elphick. Like it or not. The whole bloody thing!"

"You'll do no such thing, Mr. Harrison! This relic is far too valuable to . . ."

"Sod you, and the gibbet!" Tommy seized Elphick by the collar, pulling the official's face close to his own. "I've had enough. You try to stop me and I'll bury you down there."

Elphick spluttered helplessly, his colleagues standing back as Tommy's workmen moved in, ropes slung over their shoulders, like makeshift mountaineers. Tommy pushed Elphick roughly aside and moved to the rope barrier, shouting down: "Stand back from the pit, Andy. We're coming down."

Elphick's helpless rage somehow failed to galvanise his colleagues as preparations for the descent were made. They merely watched as ropes were secured and dropped into the pit, and then two men began gradually to lower themselves into the chasm. But when Tommy and one of the other men erected a metallic harness and pulley around the gibbet and began fixing a protective brace around the shaft in readiness for hauling it out of the pit, Elphick could not restrain himself any longer.

"You can't do that! It's too deep! The shaft will snap if it keels over . . . Sergeant Grover will be here shortly for Warwick! I'll see to it that the full force of the law . . ."

"*You'll* suffer in a second, Elphick!" Tommy walked two threatening steps towards Elphick, stabbing his finger again. Elphick shut up immediately. "This winch can extract and elevate the shaft for a good thirty feet, enough to keep it upright before levering it out. Unless you want to lose teeth, you'll keep your trap shut until Andy's back up and the gibbet's out of that bloody hole."

A distant voice echoed from the pit.

"We've got him, Tommy. He's okay. But he says he wants to stay here and make sure it comes out straight."

"He can't," hissed one of the Environment men quietly, risking Tommy's wrath. "If there's another cave-in, he'll be buried alive."

"There won't be another cave-in," replied Tommy, equally quietly, "It's a man-made, reinforced aperture and

111

the shaft is well clear of the hole." He moved to the pit, cupped his hands and shouted down. "Okay, Andy! Step back out of the way! The lads are going to knock those spokes out from the cave wall. Let's do it, lads!"

Elphick turned to look anxiously for any sign of a police car but could see nothing.

The sound of hammering echoed back to them from the pit as the corroded metal spokes were beaten out.

"You're destroying an archaeological treasure," muttered Elphick. "You . . . ignorant . . ."

The sounds of hammering seemed to awaken Frank Warwick from his stupor. He looked around in puzzlement, found himself held by two burly workmen, and then realised what was happening.

"You can't do this! You don't know what you're doing!"

"Shut him up," growled Tommy. "Gag him and tie him down if you have to, but shut him up."

An elbow in the ribs took the breath out of Frank. He doubled over, gasping, as the hammering stopped and the two workmen emerged from the pit on their rope harnesses, swinging safely to one side away from the chasm.

"Bloody hell, Tommy," said one of them, dusting himself off. "There's a coffin down there with a skeleton in it."

"Yeah, I know."

"A body!" Elphick moved forward, stammering. A look from Tommy stopped him cold, lips trembling, body shaking with rage. Another priceless find, about to be ruined forever!

"Start it up!"

The winch growled into life, great steel gears clanking, cogged teeth rasping as the chains tightened on the braces, which were padded to prevent them from cutting into the ancient, reinforced wood.

Groaning, the gibbet began to rise.

Chapter Four

Andy moved back from the stone sarcophagus as his work-mates began knocking out the ancient spokes. Rusty debris cascaded down into the pit, filling the air with heavy, dark brown powder.

His eyes now fully adjusted to the gloom, he could make out his surroundings with greater ease. The cave floor was littered with moss-covered boulders, the walls running with brackish water and slime. His first guess, that the cave was about fifty feet in circumference, was about right, but he knew from the rock-hewn walls that it was not a natural cave. This cave had been hacked out of the earth by living hands many, many years ago. The roof was about eight feet overhead; small stalactites had formed, dripping and green, like rotting teeth. Overall, it was not particularly spectacular, not like the caves you saw on television. This one was just dank, dark and creepy; not the place to hold a garden party. Why the hell anyone should go to so much bother was beyond him. All this . . . just to bury some guy in a stone coffin, and then plant a bloody great gibbet on top of him. *Maybe they had a lot of time on their hands in those days. Or maybe they just didn't want this guy to get out of his box.*

Standing back against the cave wall when Tommy shouted down to him, Andy touched the stone and felt cold slime on his fingers. "Yaaacchh . . . shit!" He wiped it on his overalls, looking back at the shaft of sunlight which pierced the cave's darkness from the funnel overhead. The

113

sound of the winch reached his ears, low and growling. The gibbet stake started to rise.

"Well done, Tommy. I bet you really gave it to Elphick."

After two feet, Andy could see that the actual wooden shaft, stained white by the stuff in the coffin, had ended. But protruding downwards from the centre of the flat base of the shaft was what looked like a corroded, cylindrical pole; almost eight inches in diameter. Two feet more, and a wicked-looking point came into view. He could see that it was a metal spike.

The shaft and spike moved slowly upwards above the coffin, swaying gently as the winch quieted for a few seconds. Then the overhead gears rasped again, and the gibbet stake continued its ascent, passing from sight into the chimney of the pit.

Andy moved slowly forwards, wiping his hands again on his overalls and smiling broadly. What a hell of a story to tell the lads in the pub tonight. That maniac Warwick and his shotgun. Falling into a pit and finding the body in the coffin. Watching as the stake was hauled out. He could live on free pints of beer for the rest of his life while he told this story. He crossed the slime-covered floor and moved to the sarcophagus. He squinted up into the sunlit chimney and saw the swaying gibbet on its way to the surface.

And then he looked down at the corpse.

And began to scream.

Chapter Five

Andy was still screaming when Tommy and his two work-mates descended into the pit in alarm. At first, Tommy could not see a thing, but he could tell where Andy was from the sound of his hoarse voice.

"Andy! What the hell's wrong?"

He felt his way past the coffin, squinting into the darkness. A huddled form was cowering against the farthest wall. He stumbled towards him.

"Are you hurt? Are you . . . ?"

Andy started to make baby noises and crawled further away from him. He was terrified, and now Tommy could see his glassy, staring eyes.

"It's me, Andy. Tommy. What the hell happened?"

But Andy continued to make the baby sounds. Behind him, Tommy became aware that the other two men were shuffling uneasily. He did not blame them. There was something very wrong with Andy. He was acting as if . . . as if . . . he had lost his mind. Something had terrified him . . . *was* terrifying him. "It's all right, lad. All right. We're going to take you back upstairs now. You've had a bad fall, had a nasty shock. Everything's going to be okay."

Andy began to cry as Tommy moved to touch him. He flinched away, hugging the slime-covered rock, eyes fixed on the stone sarcophagus. It took the three of them to prise him away from the wall. Eyes glaring, he continued to utter hoarse, terror-filled cries as they began to drag him back towards the chimney. Something about his insane behaviour and the noises he was making triggered off a deep fear inside Tommy, and he could tell that his two workmen were feeling the same way. Andy began to dig his heels into the moss-covered ground as they approached the coffin. They dragged him, struggling violently, to its base, tying his arms to his sides and lashing him into the rope harness.

Tommy glanced into the sarcophagus as his two men finished roping Andy in. The blackened, decayed corpse stared sightlessly upwards at the shaft of light and the aperture above.

What in hell happened down here?

He shouted up to his men on the rim of the pit, and they began to haul Andy's struggling, whining body towards the surface.

He looked at the corpse again and began to climb.

The bad feeling inside was not going to go away.

Above ground, Frank Warwick had found his voice again and lunged forward as they hauled Andy from the pit opening. "I told you! I told you to leave it where it was! But you wouldn't listen . . ." His two captors moved forward, pinioning his arms. Andy was screaming again as they began to loosen the harness: long, wordless yells of fear. Elphick stood frozen, unable to participate in this hideous cacophony.

Tommy appeared on the rim of the pit. "Shut up, Warwick! Shut up! The whole bloody world has gone crazy."

"You don't know what you've done! None of you!"

One of the workmen forced Frank to his knees, shoving a calloused hand across his mouth, and silenced him.

Tommy knelt down beside Andy and began to shake him violently. "What happened down there, Andy? What happened? What the *hell's* the matter with you?"

Andy's eyes seemed to focus on Tommy for the first time.

He was gasping for air, chest heaving with exertion. He grabbed at Tommy, clutching his lapel.

"It's . . . it . . ."

"What, Andy? *WHAT?*"

"It . . . *looked at me. It LOOKED at me!*"

And then Andy began to laugh.

The laughter was worse than the screaming.

It was the best moment of the day for Tommy when he looked up to see Sergeant Grover's Land-Rover turning into the crossroads site.

Chapter Six

I'm free! Free, free, free, free . . . I'MMMMMMMMMMMMM FREEEEEEEEEEE!!!

Michael felt it deep inside. A dark feeling. He was standing in the kitchen, cutting a salad. Christy was coming over later for supper. And the black moods which had been kept at bay after their first shared love weeks before, now seemed to be threatening him again. Was that terrible depression coming back? No . . . somehow it was much more than that. The same kind of feeling, yes, but deeper. Deeper and darker. The knife trembled in his hands, the blade slipped and stabbed into his thumb. Wincing, he held the wound to his mouth. The knife dropped to the kitchen bench, a dark globule of blood on the bright blade.

The milk bottle fell from Christy's nerveless fingers, shattering on the tiled floor at the back of the coffee shop. She felt dizzy. The ground was rearing up at her as she clutched at the fridge door, holding it to steady herself. There was a horrible singing noise in her ears, like the sounds you hear underwater. Her stomach was cramped, like a period pain. Had something happened to Dad? No, she did not believe in premonitions. She had stood up too quickly, that was all. It would pass.

Karen felt it first, but Graham was only seconds behind her in awareness. They both rushed to the bedroom window, leaving a scattered trail of brightly coloured Legos behind them, their joint castle-building enterprise forgotten.

"Did you feel it?" asked Graham in awe.

"Yes." Karen stared out of the window but could see nothing. Just the usual trees, the front lawn and the road that led into the village.

"Wowwww!" exclaimed Graham, not understanding but conscious of something momentous in the air.

But Karen was not awed. She was frightened. And she knew where that feeling had come from and what it would lead to.

I dared it to come out! I dared it! And it's coming . . . It's coming!

She grabbed Graham in a hug, wanting to hold him there forever. She would protect him. He was her brother. The gibbet could not have him. Graham struggled to escape from the embrace, moaning that he did not like sissy stuff. He continued to gape out of the window, expecting to see something, but not knowing what that something was.

You won't have him! Not ever!

Iris felt the chill and looked up. There was an ugly black cloud in the sky overhead. Until then, it had been a day of bright blue skies, without a cloud in sight. Now that cloud had come straight out of nowhere and blotted out the sun. She continued to clear the table by the window, still feeling that chill down her spine. The cloud would pass and the sun would come out again. No matter how bad things were in this world—and they could be bad—the sun always came out again. Didn't it?

Billy Rifkin threw the hayfork into the stack and felt that dark, *spreading* feeling inside him again. It was just like the feeling he had experienced on the night that Christy had made out with that writer freak from Split Crow Farm. It was good. Really good. And it made him realise that he had not been kidding himself after all. After that first time— the first feeling—he had not proceeded with his intention to get even with them both, because the feeling had told him to wait. Something else was going to happen, some- thing that would give him . . . he could think of no word to describe it but *power*. And it would not be ordinary power. No, sir. It would be a power to give him anything he wanted; power to get even in a big, big way that he would never have believed possible. The dark, spreading feeling was like rich, intoxicating wine. It flowed and expanded inside him. The great time he had been promised was just about to start. Wiping the sweat from his face, he looked out towards Shillingham, and smiled. It was a broad smile. And it was also dark. To Billy, it seemed that a very special new friend had said hello. And he knew that it was a friend who would keep promises.

In Shillingham Hospital, with eyes staring and glazed, Andy Hudson, who had been taken there following the incident at the crossroads site, punched a fist through the window of his room, wrenched out a jagged spear of glass and stabbed it firmly and repeatedly into his eyes until the shard pierced his brain, killing him instantly.

Chapter Seven

When Sergeant Grover's Land-Rover pulled to a halt outside the farmhouse, Christy's sick feeling returned with a vengeance. It had never really gone away since its first onslaught in the coffee shop that afternoon; and she wondered if, after all, she did not really believe in premonitions. Particularly when she saw Grover's set face and watched as, thinking himself unobserved, he sighed deeply and punched the steering wheel before climbing out of the car. Christy opened the door at the same time as Grover slammed the Land-Rover door shut and moved purposefully across the yard towards her. His head was down. He sighed again.

He was a big man; well over six feet tall. He had left his police cap and jacket in the car as usual; his shirt sleeves were rolled up to reveal strong brown arms. His hair was sandy blond, with thick eyebrows. Christy herself had once described him cornily as "craggy," and it was a description which fitted him perfectly. A too-gentle voice nevertheless carried considerable conviction and strength. Christy always liked the easy way he had of walking, but the purpose in that walk today said everything as he approached.

"Christy," he said, gently and simply.

"It's Dad, isn't it?" She had known something had happened when she had come home to an empty house.

Grover was gazing out over the fields as he replied, as if he did not want to look at her just yet; did not want to hurt her. "Yes. It's Frank."

"He's not . . ."

"No, no, no! He's all right. A little drunk, that's all. But he's done something really bad this time. We've got him in the station lock-up. You'd better come down with me."

"I knew something like this would happen. It's that bloody crossroads again, isn't it?"

"Yep. 'Fraid so. He opened up on the contractor with a shotgun."

"Oh, my God! Is anyone . . . ?"

"No. But someone could have been, Christy. Up until now he's been a lucky man, and got away with a lot. You know that. But this time . . . well this time I'm afraid he's going to have to face some serious charges."

"I'll lock up. Just give me a minute."

As Christy bustled inside to find the keys, Grover thought: *It had to happen. She's right. Maybe if I'd handled him firmly from the beginning, instead of letting him get away with it, this wouldn't have happened. But the poor lass has been through so much. So has he. They need all the breaks. Well, it's finally come . . .*

"Ready," said Christy at last. Grover could see the tears held at bay in her eyes.

They climbed into the car and drove down towards the village.

On the way, Grover told her of all that had happened back at the crossroads. Her father had been overpowered and the shotgun had been taken from him. A bulldozer and Mrs. Garvanter's car had been damaged. He was sure that Frank had not been aiming the gun deliberately at anyone, he was just trying to scare them off. But no one could be certain of that, and Mrs. Garvanter was definitely pressing charges for assault with a deadly weapon. There had been an accident at the site, a cave-in. There had been a quarrel between the contractor and the Environment officials present. (Grover was not surprised at that development. He had expected Tommy's patience to snap.) The gibbet had been removed from the site despite their protests and it now looked as if Tommy would be charged with something-or-other, when the Environment people sorted themselves out. They had found a body in the pit beneath the gibbet, and the excitement of the find had temporarily overcome the desire to have Tommy locked behind bars. The sarcophagus containing the body had also been removed (Grover noticed that Elphick and his colleagues had not complained about *that!*); and Andy Hudson had been removed from that pit crying and raving like a madman. He had fallen in there and his nerves had been shattered by the experience. An ambulance had taken him off to Shillingham Hospital where, no doubt, he would be sedated and looked after. All in all, it had been one hell of an afternoon, and Grover could not believe that Christy's father was going to come out of it unscathed.

Christy listened to it all, hands clasped in her lap, biting her lips. Grover was watching her out of the corner of his eye all the way. The girl had guts; she deserved better luck than this. It made him feel a little happier after all that he had not been as hard on Frank as he had wanted in the early days.

"Thanks," she said at last as the Land-Rover bounced down Split Crow Lane. "Thanks for coming out here to collect me. Thanks for not just ringing me up to tell me."

"Okay, Christy. Okay . . ."

As Split Crow Farm came into view, Christy remembered that she was due to see Michael that evening. Now, of all times, she did not want to be alone.

"Can we stop here to pick someone up?"

"Lambton?"

"Please."

"All right, Christy." Grover had heard the gossip in the village. He wondered if Frank's sudden descent into uncontrolled anger had something to do with it.

The Land-Rover swerved into the main gateway and down to the farmhouse. Michael had heard the car's approach and locked the dogs inside. He walked out to meet them. Christy was out of the car and running towards him even before Grover had stopped. Michael caught her in a full embrace. Grover looked behind him, checking out nothing in particular as Christy dissolved into tears.

Three minutes later, the Land-Rover and its three occupants were on their way to Shillingham.

Chapter Eight

Apart from the blue sign hanging outside, Shillingham's police station could have been any one of a variety of official buildings: a village hall, a council office, a wholesaler's. The bland brick building gave no clue to its true identity. Set on the northern outskirts of the village, in a street between a Co-operative store and an empty grassed space which the local businessmen hoped would eventually become a car park for the thousands of tourists that the motorway would bring, the police station had always preserved a discreet anonymity. Law-breaking in Shil-lingham was usually a matter of minor offences. Something like the incident today would be a talking point with the villagers for the next fifty years or so. Even though the station was well away from the village centre, Grover still took the Land-Rover round the back way, just in case any eager sightseers were hanging around. He did not want to make things too painful for Christy.

George Frankham, one of Grover's constables, had seen the Land-Rover approaching and was waiting on the rear fire escape when they pulled into the car park. The Land-Rover squealed to a halt.

"I'll wait here, Christy," said Michael. Christy nodded and climbed out. Frankham held the door open for her as she ascended the fire escape. Grover remained in the driving seat. When Christy had disappeared inside the station, he turned back to Michael in the rear.

"You're obviously very friendly with Christy."

Michael was careful. Wary and careful. "That's right."

Grover cleared his throat, looking out of the window in a way that, to Michael, seemed just a little too nonchalant. "This business at the crossroads. Frank and the shotgun, I mean. Has that got anything to do with you and her?"

"No, Sergeant. Nothing. Frank doesn't know anything about us."

"You're sure? Perhaps Christy told him?"

"You know what Frank's like. I don't have to tell you. There's no way in the world Christy would tell him."

"Maybe. We'll see."

"Are you trying to imply that this business is *our* fault?"

"No, I'm not. I just want to get a full picture, that's all." Grover moved to open the Land-Rover door and then paused. Later, he would have no idea why he should have said the things he was now about to say. It was almost as if he was an actor, and had suddenly remembered some very important lines that had to be spoken next. It was uncanny. In a curious kind of way, he actually liked this strange bloke who wrote novels and lived in splendid isolation up at Split Crow. Perhaps that was the reason. Or perhaps he was imagining that if Lambton's motives towards Christy were honourable, then he would be able to give her the kind of happiness that she had been missing for so many years—making up for her dad, and all that. Or maybe he empathised with this strange new "loner." Grover was a kind of loner himself. It was the copper's lot, after all. Whatever the reason, he found himself leaning back and saying:

"Christy told you they found an old body under that gibbet?"

"Yes."

"A very old body. Sent the Environment people into a real ecstasy. Well . . . after Tommy's mob heaved it out of the ground, they took everything back to the Storehouse. To get it out of the weather, so to speak. Just in case some kind of . . . I don't know . . . deterioration, I suppose, set in. Elphick's there with it now. Maybe you should pop over and see. You might be able to help. You write spooky stories and things, don't you . . . ?"

"Psychological novels," replied Michael calmly.

"Yeah, that's what I mean. You should go over there. You could help him out, or maybe it'll give you an idea."

"I don't know. Christy might need me when she comes back . . ."

"She's going to be at least half an hour, Lambton. Go on over there. It's the last building on the corner. Say I sent you." *Now why the hell did I say all that?*

Michael looked back at the fire escape. Without really giving it too much thought, his mind still on Christy and the effect that this latest little escapade might have on her, he climbed out of the Land-Rover with Grover.

"Last building on the corner," repeated Grover. "If Christy gets finished before you're back, I'll bring her over in the car. Okay?"

Michael nodded and walked away, head down and brooding.

Grover ran nimbly up the fire escape, taking the steps two at a time.

Chapter Nine

"Hello, Dad," said Christy, clutching the cell bars before her. The cell was small, with a single bed; just like those silly old-fashioned cells you saw on TV Westerns. Not like an English cell at all, really. A barred window above the bed cast slanting orange light into the room, which spilled over her father.

Frank was sitting on the bed, with his hands to his face, when Christy came in. Frankham had retreated to a respectable distance; he knew Christy and her father. Frank looked up when she walked in. He groaned aloud, stood up awkwardly and came over to her, taking her fingers in his through the bars.

"I'm so sorry, Christy. I'm really so sorry. But I had to stop them."

"A shotgun, Dad? Why did you have to use a shotgun? They're going to charge you, you know that?"

"I know it. But I wasn't trying to hit anybody. I *didn't* hit anybody."

"That's not the point, Dad. Why? Why?"

"It didn't make any difference, anyway. They took the gibbet out. And it's too late to do anything about it. They took it out. And they found *it*."

Christy could smell the whisky on his breath, but there was something different about her father now. He seemed sadder, resigned. As if everything had been knocked out of him; as if all the bad stuff that had been torturing him for so long had been knocked out of him. He was looking tired, but he was in control. Sober, restrained and in control. It seemed like years (*God, it* is *years*) since she had seen him so in control. But the sadness in his voice and in his eyes was almost too much to bear.

"I could never do it before, Christy." He gripped her fingers tightly through the bars. "But maybe I can give you proper answers to your questions now. What I feared most has come to pass. *And things are going to get very, very bad now*. I don't know whether what I have to tell you will breach the Covenant . . ."

"Covenant?"

"Just listen, Christy. I don't know if it will breach the Covenant. But I'm going to have to tell you Shillingham's Secret. And the reasons for so much unhappiness. I'm going to tell you the *Secret*. Because very soon now, things will begin to happen. And we haven't got much time."

Christy listened.

Chapter Ten

The Storehouse was a red brick building not dissimilar to the police station. Its gables were worn and weathered and it looked as if it had also served a variety of purposes over the years. A relatively new brass plaque on the front gate bore testimony to the source of the contributions which had given it a new lease of life.

Financially supported by the
Garvanter Historical Society

"No unauthorised personnel in here," said Elphick tightly when Michael entered.

"I'm authorised," said Michael, surprised somehow to hear his own voice. "By Sergeant Grover."

Elphick sighed, hating to be disturbed, but too intent on his work to ask further questions. He was at the far end of a low-ceilinged room, busily engaged in examining what looked like a rectangular stone slab, raised on metal trestles at waist-high level. He was wearing a white dust jacket, as were his two nervously excited colleagues who looked up in something approaching alarm when Michael came in. Elphick waved backwards at Michael without taking his eyes from his work. The two other men returned to their work on the object which occupied most of the Storeroom floor behind Elphick. "All right, but don't disturb us. And close the door."

Michael obeyed. The room was a large rectangle and he

supposed that it had once been a barn of some sort. A single light bulb gave the only stark illumination, directly above the stone slab. He looked down at the two technicians and what they were working on, instantly recognising the immense, mud-stained and weathered object lying on muddy tarpaulin sheets.

The gibbet.

But it's over fifty feet long!

He walked forward, studying the ancient wood. In places, the reinforced timber had cracked, and he could see traces of rusted metal beneath. At the end of the gibbet, nearest to where Elphick worked, the wood ended in a thick, corroded spike, about four feet long.

"What do you want exactly?" asked Elphick at last.

"Grover thought I might help. I'm . . . a writer . . . of sorts."

Elphick whirled round. "Not a journalist, I hope!"

"No. I specialise in . . . folklore, I suppose you could say. As I said, Grover thought I might be able to help."

Elphick returned to his work. "Yes, I'm sure. But we do have our own experts, you know. They'll be on their way over here tomorrow. No . . . the only thing I want to say to the press relates to the outrageous behaviour of the contractors involved in the operation . . ."

"As I said, I'm not from the press . . ."

". . . They may have retrieved the material without damage, but they haven't heard the last of this. That site should have been left untouched until such time as our archaeologists could examine it. Who knows what valuable material has been destroyed in the process?"

Michael turned round and saw the sarcophagus properly for the first time.

He moved closer, and seemed to see everything at once.

He saw the horribly blackened and contorted skeleton; the grinning skull; the gaping eye sockets, and the mouth opened hideously in mid-scream, filled with crumbling white powder. He saw the clutching hand, and the crumbling white powder which filled the coffin and in which the corpse was half-submerged. And he saw the gaping hole in the corpse's chest. He looked back at the white-stained spike and knew what had made the hole.

The gash in his thumb, caused by the kitchen knife that afternoon, began to throb steadily. He stood back, feeling slightly giddy and wondering if another anxiety attack was coming. Elphick was taking tissue from the corpse's face with tweezers, carefully placing it in a sterile glass dish.

"What's the stuff in the coffin?" asked Michael. "The white stuff."

Elphick turned, eyes gleaming in excitement. "It's remarkable. Really remarkable."

"Yes, but what is it?"

"Salt!" exclaimed Elphick, almost proudly. "Ordinary, plain salt. It's preserved the corpse to a remarkable degree. And I wouldn't be surprised if the high saline count at the crossroads site isn't in some way connected with this . . . shall we say . . . ritualistic find."

He returned to the coffin again and busied himself once more with the tweezers. "The metal spike was taken from the corpse's chest when the gibbet was lifted. I don't quite know how it was done, but it seems as if the spike was driven into the body first, and then the gibbet was erected around the coffin and the spike. The spike must have been slotted into the base of the shaft. The gibbet stake itself was supported so as not to crush the body below. Very strange. Why should they go to such elaborate lengths? Driving a spike through the body and then carefully erecting the stake over the spike so as not to crush the body."

"Maybe they thought he was a vampyre."

Elphick laughed. "That's a *wooden* stake, isn't it? And why should they want to preserve him in all this salt? Anyway, this is all far too elaborate. Something we've never come across before . . ."

"How long has he been down there?"

"1620, I should say. That's when the gibbet was erected."

Michael did not like what he was feeling. He could not rationalise it, or understand it, but he did not like it. It had to do with the gaping hole in the corpse's chest. He rubbed his hand across his mouth and tasted salt. Recoiling in horror, he hastily wiped it away. Elphick continued with his work, pulling out a steel tape measure. The two men on the floor remained engrossed in their own task. Michael walked away. He checked his watch, and decided to go back to the police station to wait for Christy.

The three men in white dust jackets never noticed him leave.

Chapter Eleven

"I want you to listen," said Frank, fingers still interlocked with Christy's through the iron bars. "It won't be easy for you. The way things have been these past few years, you might even think I've lost my mind. I wouldn't blame you. But it's important—*vitally* important—that you do believe me."

Again, Christy was struck by how different her father seemed: sad, resigned, but so much more in control than her father of old.

"I'm sorry for the way I've been, Christy. But I'm a . . . weak . . . man. I've had a special burden to bear for a long time. And it's just been too much for me, even more so after your mother was killed . . ." Frank paused, swallowing the emotion which threatened to clog his throat. "Something happened here in Shillingham. Many years ago—in fact, hundreds of years ago. Something very bad. Something evil. My ancestors . . . *your* ancestors, Christy . . . were responsible for putting an end to that evil. We stopped it. But to our shame, although the power to kill it was with us, we were too afraid to use it. We stopped the evil, but we couldn't kill it. So we buried the evil . . . the most evil thing in the world . . . and our shame was buried with it. We buried it at the crossroads. Buried and dormant. And now, it's been found again.

"The evil had a name. It was called the Wyrm."

Her father's grip felt ice-cold, colder even than the iron bars of the cell through which their fingers entwined. The word itself seemed to make Frank afraid, and that fear communicated itself instantly to Christy.

"It first came to Shillingham in the seventeenth century, and it almost killed everyone here. It hated mankind, it hated everything that lived. And it had powers to destroy and corrupt. Terrible, terrible *powers*.

"There's a book, Christy. It's called *The Book of the Wyrm*. I've hidden it at home, under the floorboards in the kitchen. It's a very old book, handed down from father to first-born son since that time. It tells what happened and how to fight the Wyrm. Our family has been the Keepers of the Secret . . ."

"Dad, I don't know what . . ."

"Listen to me, Christy! It's important that you listen!" Frank drew breath and continued: "I got the Book from your grandfather on my twenty-first birthday. He got it from his father on his twenty-first birthday . . . and so on, back down the line. Father to first-born son; father to first-born son. Our family—the Warwicks—were instrumental in sending the Wyrm to limbo. So we became the Keepers of the Secret, the special knowledge. There was a *unique* rapport between father and son. But you're my *daughter*, Christy. The covenant was specific—father to first-born son. And for the first time since 1620, there was no son to hand the Secret to. Don't you see? It's a terrible responsibility, Christy. I love you so much. But after your mother died and there couldn't be any more children . . ."

Frank paused, again swallowing his emotion. Christy tried to make sense of what he was saying, and could not.

"The responsibility for the Secret is heavy, Christy. There are *dreams*. Dreams and emotions which are hard to handle. I began drinking. I couldn't possibly marry another woman. Not after your mother. Now I know that the breaking of the Covenant—the breaking of the Ritual—resulted in the unearthing of the gibbet. But I'm hoping that somehow, in some way, you can assume responsibility for the Secret if I'm killed . . ."

"Killed, Dad?"

"Listen! I'm hoping that the Covenant will be fulfilled by my passing the Secret to you as *first-born*—even though you're my daughter, not my son. But the words of the Ritual are important . . . it's so very important to adhere to the words . . . I just hope that . . ."

"Dad! Stop it! This all sounds insane! You're in very big

133

trouble with the police and we've got to do something about that. How can I . . . ?"

Christy stopped. There was a look of sad reproach in her father's eyes that she had not seen and had missed since she was a child. A look which had always stilled her misbehaviour. It stilled her now.

"Christy," continued Frank quietly, "something terrible has happened. The crossroads have been violated and the gibbet removed. The thing our family has feared most has happened. The Wyrm has returned. And it's up to *me* . . . hopefully, us . . . to stop the horror before it begins. I've been stupid. I did a stupid thing and now I'm locked in here. You have to go back home and get the Book. Bring it here to me. Now that the Wyrm's loose, the Book may enlighten men in a way that it's never done before. It was created for that purpose."

"We've got to see about . . . your . . . bail . . ." said Christy weakly, her words dwindling to nothing as Frank went on.

"This is the very thing I've feared for so long. Now it's happened, I've been confined—helpless to stop it. I want you to go and get the Book. Bring it here quickly, Christy. The Wyrm has *scented* me. We may not have much time. Bring it."

Christy stood motionless, staring at her father. She stepped back, breaking their grasp through the bars.

"I . . . don't . . ."

"Now, Christy! Now!"

She was running down the cell corridor into the police station. The door banged behind her and, in a dream, she was standing listening to Sergeant Grover. She seemed curiously distanced as the policeman began to tell her that charges were to be pressed and the possibility of bail in the circumstances was remote. She watched his lips move, heard the sounds. Unable to act, not really comprehending and feeling that awful sick feeling inside, she saw his expression change to concern. She could see that he had noticed her strange detachment. She heard him say: "Are you all right?" And then she heard her own reply: "I'm okay. This is all a bit much, that's all." But she could only think of the extraordinary things her father had said and wonder if, despite his new-found self-control, he had not finally gone insane after all. Tears were choking the back of her throat as Grover continued. She heard him offer her a lift home, and heard herself decline. Now Grover was telling her that Michael was at the Storehouse, and not to worry, because they'd make sure that her father was comfortable.

Still dazed, still absorbed by thoughts of her father and the strange Book under the kitchen floorboards, she left the police station by the main entrance.

Grover watched her go and thought: *Why do the innocent ones always have to suffer? Sometimes the world just isn't fair. Why her?*

Chapter Twelve

Michael saw Christy leave the police station and turned to meet her as he made his way back from the Storehouse. It must have been bad for her: her eyes were downcast, she was chewing her lip and seemed mentally to be a million miles away. And she looked as if she had the worries of the world on her shoulders. Her black hair was flowing in the early evening breeze and Michael could not remember her ever looking more beautiful. She did not see him until they were almost face to face.

Her eyes were brimming with tears. Michael moved instinctively to her, but she flinched away. "I've got to go home and get something for Dad, Michael. Something he needs."

"I'll come with you."

"No . . . thanks. I'd really rather walk up there and back by myself. I need some time. I don't want to be . . . cold . . . with you. But I need the time. Can you see that?"

"Yes, Christy, I understand." He took her hand and squeezed it gently. "Look . . . I'll go and have a pint in the Dun Cow back there. When you've come back, perhaps I can . . ."

"Yes, Michael. Thanks. That's what I want."

Christy turned and headed for Split Crow Lane.

Michael recognised the pain from old times. He had felt that kind of agony himself and the need to have time alone. It was a temporary measure, he knew, to deaden the hurt. Their mutual loneliness had been combined and dissolved, but they still needed time. He thought ruefully of Frank and his latest escapade; it had threatened their happiness. But he would help. He would help Christy, and he would help Frank if he could. They would pull through.

He headed for the pub, glancing back only once to see Christy's distant figure turning a bend in the road, casting a long shadow before vanishing from sight.

The sun was setting.

All shadows were lengthening.

Night was beginning to fall on Shillingham.

A new and terrible night—the Night of the Wyrm.

Chapter Thirteen

Elphick's colleagues had long since returned to their rooms in the Dun Cow. The events of the day had eventually taken their toll. But Elphick himself remained just as enthusiastic, despite everything that had happened. The sun was going down, but not on his excitement. He was still working on the coffin and its occupant when Jack Ray, general odd-job man about Shillingham and caretaker of the Store-house for the Garvanter Historical Society, shuffled into the room.

"Still here, then?"

"Obviously." Elphick continued with his work, his attitude towards this simpleton just as brusque and conde-scending as his attitude towards that rather obvious journalist fellow earlier on. Jack grunted, wishing that Frank Warwick had been a better shot, and shuffled round the room, checking the windows. Maybe the bars had been put on the windows to keep loonies like this away from decent people. From time to time he glanced back at the gibbet on the floor, feeling bloody peculiar. He had played beside that gibbet when he was a kid; had passed by it on his way to work practically every day of his adult life. Now it was lying muddy and naked on a tarpaulin sheet like some gigantic bloody tooth, pulled from its socket. It seemed somehow unnatural lying *there* like that. It had always been a part of Shillingham; always been there come rain or shine. Maybe Frank Warwick had a point, even if he had rather overplayed his hand. Jack remembered standing by the gibbet once and hearing some kind of voice in his head, saying: *Come and play with me.* It had really spooked him. He had run away home to his mother, just like the impressionable little kid he was. He had never heard that voice again, but the memory of it had stayed with him all these years.

Funny thing, he thought. He shuddered, feeling a sudden icy chill.

He closed a window, sniffed loudly, and turned back to Elphick.

"Gotta lock up, mister."

"What?"

"It's late." Jack raised a hand and twisted his fingers in imitation of turning a key. "I've got to lock the place up."

"I'm not one hundred percent satisfied with the security in this building, I must say." Elphick turned sharply, appraising for the first time this runt of a man in his shabby top-coat. There were *stains* on his lapel, for goodness sake.

"Yeah?"

"Yes. I've had a look round this afternoon and I can't say I'm entirely satisfied. There is a great deal of valuable material in here . . ."

"Bollocks."

". . . and I would like to think that it was more secure. Is there any way you can guarantee that there will be no opportunist theft? Can you give the place a thorough examination?"

"Opportunist theft, eh?"

"Yes."

Jack fished in his pocket. He had met blokes like this before and there was only one way to deal with them. "I'm paid fifteen quid a week to look after this place. It's got two Chubb locks front and back, with bars on the windows.

If you feel strongly about it . . ." Jack threw his key ring at Elphick, who recoiled in alarm. The keys rebounded from his chest and clattered on the cold stone floor like a set of dentures. ". . . *you* can check the security arrangements and bloody well lock the place up yourself. I'll be in the bar of the Dun Cow—where you're staying if you recall. Bring them back to me there when you're locked up."

Indignant rage and enforced dignity crowded out the pain of Jack's rheumatism as he marched, straight-backed, out of the room. Slamming the door gave him the best "buzz" he had had in a fortnight.

Elphick picked up the keys in disgust, sighing heavily. "Really," he groaned. He spent the next fifteen minutes checking the Storehouse's security. He was right. It was abysmal.

Chapter Fourteen

The tiredness was creeping up on him. Yawning, Elphick looked down at the gibbet on the floor. Fascinating. There was so much to learn about this strange business. He moved to the sink at the far side of the room and began to wash his hands. He was aware that he was hungry now; he had hardly eaten anything all day. And what a day! The prospect of a good meal at the Dun Cow (if such a thing was possible) and a comfortable bed cheered him. He looked up through the fly-stained window. The sun was sinking below the rim of the valley. He watched as the last rays of light died and night settled on Shillingham.

Something moved behind him.

Elphick turned round, curiously. He was certain that he had heard a slight, scratching noise. He listened. Nothing. Just the gibbet lying on the tarpaulin and the sarcophagus on its trestles and . . . soil on the floor at the base of the coffin. It had not been there before. He walked slowly towards the coffin, drying his hands on a cloth. Why did he feel so strange?

Overhead, the light bulb flickered briefly. Elphick stopped, looking up. The flickering disturbed him but he was damned if he knew why. He moved forward, reached the coffin. Why was he reluctant to look inside again? Just what in hell was wrong with him? His mouth was suddenly dry. He could feel sweat prickling at the base of his neck. His heart rate had increased. He braced himself. This was ridiculous. Obviously, it had been a very trying day in more ways than one. He was overtired. He needed food and a good night's rest, that was all.

But why am I suddenly frightened to look into the coffin again?

Elphick knew what was wrong. Despite attempts to rationalise everything that had happened to him that day, he could not get the image of that young man who had fallen into the pit out of his mind. The way he had begun to scream down there had been hideous; even more so when they brought him above ground, his nerves obviously shattered by his experience. Particularly, Elphick could not get those words he had uttered out of his system: *It looked at me! God help me; it looked at me!*

Swallowing hard and cursing himself for an overtired fool, he stepped forward, braced his hands on the coffin and looked inside.

"No . . . I don't believe it."

The coffin was empty.

The corpse had gone, leaving only a human-shaped imprint in the crumbling white salt where it had lain. He retreated slowly, refusing to believe what he had seen. It was not possible. He rubbed his eyes, stepped forward again and looked once more. The coffin was empty. The blackened corpse had gone.

Elphick stumbled away in confusion. Overhead, the lightbulb flickered again. He had only been gone from the coffin for fifteen minutes or so while he had checked the building's security. It was not possible that someone could have come in and taken the body without his knowledge. It was simply impossible. Soil crunched underfoot, and he looked down again to see that there was more salt and soil on the floor.

Something moved on his left.

The caretaker! That's who it had to be. He had come back to laugh at his joke. Elphick spun round to face the idiot.

"You fool! You have no right to . . ."

Then he saw what was standing beside him and would have screamed but could not. His voice had frozen in his throat.

It reached out.

A gnarled and blackened hand fastened on his face.

Chapter Fifteen

The Wyrm fed.

Now that it was free, the hunger had returned. This would be the first. It sensed that this pitiful animal was not one of the things directly responsible for its imprisonment, but had been instrumental in its release. It made no difference. It was food.

It was hungry.

First, it took his eyes.

The man stood frozen, juddering in agony, as his life-blood spewed forth. The Wyrm took it eagerly. It shredded his clothes and fed directly from the man itself. Then it took the genitals, gorged itself on the lifeblood which erupted from his manhood and then opened the rib cage to take the vital organs. And all the time, the man stood, frozen by the Wyrm's power. It fed well. But it was aware that it could not allow its own greed to betray it. There was much to be done. It could not let its existence be known at this stage. Later, of course. But now . . .

The Wyrm gave its instructions. The still-living puppet, which now no longer had a mind of its own, shuffled across the room to the gas heating system. It turned on the gas taps and stood back.

Fifteen minutes later, it took the blood-sodden box of matches from its tattered coat pocket and, one by one, began to strike the matches.

Chapter Sixteen

"How was it?" asked Michael.

Grover picked up his pint of beer from the bar and turned to him. "I was a little worried. She looked . . ."

"Shocked?"

"Yeah."

"I *knew* I should have stayed with her."

"No, you did the right thing. She'll need you later."

The locals had been talking about the events of the day when Michael walked into the pub. They had looked him over for trouble, found none and, lowering their voices, had continued their conversation. Michael's relationship with Christy was now well known and the locals, in a major acceptance in Shillingham's terms, had accommodated his presence in the Dun Cow for the occasional pint of beer. However, when the off-duty Sergeant Grover walked in, all furtive gossip ceased. Grover was aware of it and joined Michael at the bar: two loners together.

Jack Ray entered, spitting fury at Elphick. He spotted Grover at the bar and decided to spend some of his "fifteen quid a week" drowning his anger in whisky.

"Will Frank . . . ?" began Michael.

And then the pub windows exploded inwards, showering everyone in glass.

The lights were snuffed out, plunging the room into darkness as a great roaring blast of deafening sound filled the bar. Jack Ray tumbled heavily to the floor. Pint glasses skidded, crashing in foam from the bar. The two tables nearest the windows were blown over, glasses shattering. The glass mosaic above the bar cracked and fell apart in cascading shards as the barman dived for cover. The room itself was shaking as Michael grabbed for support at the bar pumps. Grover was plunging to the shattered window frames as the ear-splitting crash became a muffled roaring sound. Michael turned to see orange tongues of flame leaping into the air beyond the jagged gap of the window. Cursing and groaning, customers began to pull themselves to their feet.

Michael picked his way over the glass-littered floor to join Grover. Deep inside, a horrible sick feeling was re-emerging; the same gut feeling he had experienced earlier that day when his hand had slipped and the kitchen knife had gashed his thumb. It was as if this hideous roaring of destruction was the second phase of some terrible enactment. Grover was staring out into the night through the broken windows. At last, Michael could see what had happened outside.

The Storehouse had exploded.

The roof had been blown apart and had caved in. Great roaring blossoms of flame spouted from the shattered windows. Clouds of sparks were falling now; burning beams and woodwork littering the grassed area between the pub and the Storehouse.

"My God," said a small voice at Michael's shoulder. It was Jack Ray. "Elphick was still in there when I left."

Grover exchanged a glance with Michael, grunted, and turned quickly back to the other customers in the pub, checking on injuries. No one was badly hurt, just a few cuts and scrapes. Quickly pulling open the pub door, he was out and running towards the Storehouse. Michael followed.

Chapter Seventeen

Christy whirled on the rise of Split Crow Lane which overlooked Shillingham. The night was suddenly alive with flame down by the Dun Cow. She watched blazing girders from the Storehouse roof crashing to the ground in showers of sparks and flame. Brickwork and masonry crumbled; black oily smoke began to gush into the night sky. The interior of the Storehouse had become a crackling inferno. Knowing instinctively that both Michael and her father were safe—but also that it was only for a short time—she turned and began to run for home, raven hair flying behind her.

Bad things are going to happen, Christy, her father had said. *And things will get worse.*

She kept on running.

Billy Rifkin had just arrived and was standing at the northwest corner of the Dun Cow, talking to Dennis and Bob, when the Storehouse blew up.

The force of the blast threw Billy against his "friends" and they all sprawled in each other's arms. Billy could feel the breath of terror on his neck and yanked himself round to gaze in awe at the blazing inferno before him. He snatched at a spark which landed on his cheek, stood up and walked slowly forward in a daze, silhouetted by the roaring orange flame.

He turned back to Dennis and Bob. Bob had been hit

145

by a spar of wood and was slumped against the pub wall, holding his head in his hands. Dennis was bent over double, retching.

Billy began to laugh.

"Did you see that? Did you see *that?* What a bloody bang, eh? What a *blaze?*" And then the contents of the Storehouse came to Billy's mind. The irony was wonderful. His laughter began to build to a peak. "Oh, man! All that work . . . all that bother about the bloody gibbet. And it's just ashes now, man. Just . . . ashes!" Something else occurred to him. Something stupendous. Something so awe-inspiring that he sank to his knees in wonder, his soul flooded with the fantastic possibilities.

"Hey . . . maybe . . . hey . . ."

More wooden beams cracked and crashed inwards. An orange cloud of flame belched gratefully skywards. The night was raining sparks.

"Maybe . . . *someone's burning alive in there, lads.*"

It was wonderful.

Black, billowing clouds undulated overhead, blossoming upwards into the night sky. Even though Billy's eyes were tear-blurred by the smoke, he fancied he could see a face in those clouds; the same way that you could sometimes see a face on the surface of the moon. But this face was not remotely human. This was a dark, evil, gloating and rapacious face with blood-red eyes of sparks and with ravening fire in its throat.

To Billy, it was a friendly face.

Chapter Eighteen

It walked through the inferno.

The initial blast had all but destroyed the ravaged, blackened shell which had been its host for so many centuries. Within seconds, the raging flame had consumed the last traces of the decayed frame. And, as it walked free from that shell, it was aware that the gibbet which had been the main instrument of its imprisonment for so long was now destroyed. The fire warmed the mad, corrupted soul of the Wyrm. It could sense the terror of those who watched the conflagration—and revelled in it. It gloried in the terror—the real terror—to come. Within that staring crowd it also sensed something else—something special—something that could be used. It was a small, pitiful yet promising reflection of the smallest part of itself. It was evil. A small spark of evil. That evil was watching and rejoicing. And aware.

The Wyrm emerged from the rear of the Storehouse, away from human eyes. The night beckoned. It followed, and was swallowed by darkness. Free at last, it walked the night.

It killed as it walked, rejoicing.

Grass withered, trees absorbed its poison and began to die, animals beneath the ground curled up and slept forever. Its breath was the stench of contagion; its very presence an anathema to life.

It stopped, sensing something new, something important. The night air was carrying the scent of the most important one that it had to find. It rejoiced! The Keeper of the Book was near, so very near. As the major threat to its new exis-

147

tence and its main quest before the Great Plan, the Wyrm's initial task was now so much easier. It did not have to hunt. He was here! He was near! It scented again, turned and moved.

Towards the Keeper.

The Keeper of the Book.

Chapter Nineteen

Frank heard the roar of the blast, felt the walls of his cell shake and leaped to his feet, tugging at the bars.

"What happened? What is it, George?"

"Shut up, Frank!"

Frank heard the commotion as George Frankham ran to the main office windows; then he dashed to the barred window of his cell, craning his neck to see. The night sky was glowing orange-black but he could not see what had happened. *Fire!* he thought, when he heard the muffled roaring and saw sparks sailing on the night air. *Something's burning!*

He twisted to the right and saw the cemetery. The erupting fire-shadows from somewhere behind the police station elongated and shortened the shadows of the weatherbeaten crosses and gravestones. The ragged shrouds of trees beyond seemed to loom and heave threateningly as if trying to respond to this firework show.

Christine, he whispered, thinking of his wife lying out there in the cold earth. *Christine, why did it have to happen to us? Why does this have to be my lot?*

He hurled himself at the bars.

"George? What's happening?"

But George was gone. The roaring and the flame and the undulating shadows had taken him away.

"George! George!"

Frank flung himself away from the bars. It had started, just as he had always been told. All this time, all these years, and now the responsibility had come down to him.

Why me? Why?

He lashed out at the bars, his knuckles ringing on the iron. The blow echoed in the close confines of the cell.

Hurry, Christy . . . hurry . . . bring the Book.

He sank to his knees, hugging his bleeding fist. He raised the torn knuckles to his mouth and sucked, kissing the hurt away as his mother had kissed the hurt away, as he had kissed the hurt away from Christy's pains when she had been a child. It was an ordinary human reaction, but it brought back to him the memory of basic human emotions which had been denied him for so long because of the damned Secret.

"Everything!" he yelled again. "*Everything!* You've taken everything away from me. How to be ordinary. How to live a normal life. How to be a good husband and a good father. You damned . . . damned . . ." He paused, gasping for breath. He grasped the bars before him and hauled himself to his feet, speaking slowly and methodically. "You . . . won't stop me. You . . . won't win . . . Even if I die, you won't win. I know I'm weak. I KNOW IT! But you won't beat me and mine. Not ever . . . *never!*"

He turned back to the window of his cell. The night was still stained orange. But his soul was stained a deep, deep blue.

"I wish things had been different, Christy," he said to the night. "But it was out of my hands. The Secret required strength and I was weak. It required a *man*, and I was less than that; so much less when your mother was killed. With her, I was strong. I was really strong. Without her . . . I failed you. And I'm so sorry."

Somewhere, beyond the window, something roared and split; cracked and belched an angry flame. It brought Frank back to his surroundings. "Hurry, Christy. Hurry back. It's our only chance. Our only . . ."

Frank.

He heard the voice. He recognised it of old, but he did not believe it. His mind had been full of phantoms and phantom voices for so long now that he could not trust his own senses.

Frank, it said again, in that familiar, oh so familiar, loving voice. And this time he could not ignore it as a phantom.

He twisted sideways, again craning his neck to peer out of the window. The voice was coming from the cemetery. It was where his wife had been buried, rather than in the old graveyard at the parish church, high up the valley.

I love you, Frank. Why did you leave me?

"I never left you, Christine!" shouted Frank. "Oh, Christine, I never left you. *You* left me!"

Frank, said the voice again. And the sound of that voice pierced him to his soul. It filled him with joy because he had thought that he would never hear it saying his name again. Oh, God, he wanted her back.

She was there.

Now.

Standing amidst the gravestones, in that beautiful lilac-blue dress he loved so much. She was the woman he had loved beyond life.

He pushed forward against the window bars, his heart bursting.

"Christine!"

She moved quickly forward. She was lost. She was tired and hungry. And she loved Frank so very, very much. She could see him now through the bars of his cell.

"Christine . . ."

How could he have been so stupid? She had died. She was buried out there. But the depth of his sorrow and his feeling for her were bound to bring her back. He should have known. Nothing could keep them apart. Nothing.

He jumped down from the window, searched frantically, and then snatched up a small wooden stool. Leaping back, crying with joy, he beat against the glass. It cracked, splintered and then shattered outwards. He threw the stool aside and thrust his arms out through the jagged gap into the night. He felt biting pain as the glass slashed his skin. Blood began running over his hands, but he did not care.

"Christine?"

She was still there.

His cell was more than three stories from the ground, but it in no way surprised him to see her face only two feet from his own. He loved her and wanted her.

She wanted him.

Kiss me, Frank.

"Oh, God . . ."

He yearned forwards through the bars of the window.

She moved towards him, arms held wide to receive his embrace.

They loved.

Chapter Twenty

PC George Frankham re-entered the police station, leaping up the stairs three at a time. Seconds after the initial blast he had been outside on the village green. People were staggering out of the Dun Cow, which had taken the brunt of the explosion. He had spotted Sergeant Grover running towards the blazing Storehouse and intercepted him.

"Get the fire tender over, George!" the sergeant had shouted. "And get Ben Lightfoot out of bed. We'll need him."

George had run full pelt back to the station. He would telephone from there; even though the sound of the blast must have been heard throughout Shillingham and the fire engine would automatically be on its way.

In the station at last, he grabbed for the telephone and rang the fire station. He was right. They *were* on their way. He replaced the receiver and stood back, running his hand through his hair. What the hell was happening in Shillingham? First that business down at the crossroads and now all hell had exploded in the Storehouse. What was going to happen next?

And then he heard the sounds.

Greedy, gulping, *hungry* sounds. And they were coming from Frank's cell.

"What you doing, Frank?"

The noises continued unabated.

George moved quickly to the glass window overlooking the cell corridor. He could see that Frank was standing on the bunk with his back to him. He seemed to be shivering and juddering. Then George saw the broken glass on the floor. Cursing, he grabbed the cell keys from the desk drawer, burst through the door and stormed down the corridor to Frank's cell. His view was still obscured but he could see that Frank's arms were thrust through the bars of the window. The crazy bastard had smashed the glass! He was not shivering anymore and the noises had stopped. Frank simply stood, stiff-legged, on the bed as George shouted:

"Get down from there, Frank! Come on!"

When no response or movement was forthcoming, George roughly opened the cell doors and strode angrily inside.

"Come on! Come down!"

He yanked at Frank's shoulder.

Frank's rigid body, bloodied arms still outstretched, swung backwards from the window. George jumped aside in horror as Frank fell backwards, full-length on the floor, with a great wet slap.

"Oh, my God . . ."

He was dead.

Something had torn out his eyes. But in death, Frank was still smiling up at George; and those ghastly bloodied sockets gaped at the policeman like portals into Hell. George's hand flew to his mouth as he pressed back against the bars.

Something moved at the window.

Smoke, thought George, still fighting to keep down his gorge. *Smoke from the fire.* Creeping tendrils were even now curling through the jagged gap of the window.

But now he could see that it was not fog, and he knew that he was face to face with what had killed Frank.

The Wyrm slid hungrily and quickly into the cell.

George began to scream. It slid into his throat. His screaming ended.

Long, agonising seconds later, so did his life.

Chapter Twenty-one

Christy kept on running.

Her breathing came in racked sobs as she pounded along Split Crow Lane; the evening air raked her throat and tangled in her hair. There was no time to rationalise; no time to question what she was doing.

Bring the Book, he had said. And that was just what she was going to do. *Quickly, before it's too late*. The Storehouse had exploded and, somehow, Christy knew that it all had to do with her father's fear. The fire and the smoke and the crossroads and her father were all part of the same chain.

She caught at a tree and rested against the rough bark, sucking in air. Now she had an image of Michael's face, of that pained expression when she had told him she wanted to be alone. She knew that she had hurt him. She pushed away from the tree and started to run again.

He's okay. He's safe. He was in the Dun Cow. When Dad has the Book, I'll find him again. How could I explain to you, Michael? How could I explain what I'm doing now—running and running—hunting for some damned book? How could I explain when I don't even know what I'm doing myself?

She struggled on.

Chapter Twenty-two

Billy cast a glance back over his shoulder to see if anyone had spotted him as he worked on the car door.

"Leave it, Billy!" hissed a scared Dennis from the shadows.

"Yeah, come on," said Bob. "We don't need to do this."

"Shut up, you yellow gits!" rejoined Billy, twisting the master key deeper into the car lock. Beyond them lay the stark silhouette of the Dun Cow, surrounded by the orange glow of the hidden, burning Storehouse. Billy twisted round as the fire engine's siren blasted from somewhere nearby, grinned and heaved at the lock. The car door sprang open. Everyone was too busy with the fire to notice what he was doing.

"Come on, then. Who's for a joyride?"

"I don't think we should," said Linda hesitantly. "What if we get caught?"

"What if the sky pisses whisky and we all get drunk? *Come on!*"

Three shapes flitted reluctantly through the shadows as Billy climbed into the Citroën's front seat. He did not know who the car belonged to, but he suspected that it might be one of the Environment men. Chuckling again at the destruction of the gibbet, he twisted the key in the ignition. The car coughed into life. He leaned over and opened the passenger door. Bob was about to climb in.

"Not you in the front! Linda!"

Bob sheepishly climbed into the back with Dennis as Linda joined Billy in the front.

The burning Storehouse and the prospect of what might have happened inside had been too exciting for Billy. He needed to . . . to *run*. And the idea of a joyride through Shillingham's lanes, pushing the car way over the speed limit, had been too much of a temptation. The other spineless wimps had been easy to influence when he had decided to nick one of the cars behind the Dun Cow. So what if they lost paintwork, or bumpers, or crumpled the bodywork—or even pranged the bloody thing? It wasn't his car, after all. He leaned over and squeezed Linda's knee. She had learned not to shrink away.

The car took a hairpin bend with a screech of tyres and Billy whooped with joy. He laughed at the moans from the back seat, fumbled in his pocket and found the half-bottle of whisky. He tossed it backwards over his shoulder and heard the *clunk* and "Ow!" as it connected with a skull.

"Try some of that for Dutch courage."

Trees loomed and reared in the headlights. The car swerved again and a chunk of fence tore into the bumper. Metal shrieked from the rear of the car.

"Bloody hell, Billy!"

The car skidded. Billy wrestled with the wheel and got it under control again.

Dennis unscrewed the whisky bottle cap, swallowed and grimaced, passing the bottle to Bob. If his father found out what Billy had done—what they had done—he would skin him alive. Dennis saw the look on Bob's face: the flickering eyes, the enforced bonhomie. He also recognised the look of fear. Just what the hell were they doing here, anyway? They had talked about this only last night, in Sean's shop. They had all agreed that Iris Wooler had given good advice.

They should give Billy Rifkin a wide berth. But Billy had told them to meet him tonight, and they had all dutifully turned up. Only Sean had kept away, and Dennis envied him his guts.

The car screeched and jolted. Twigs raked at the windscreen and Billy whooped again.

"Pass the bottle! Gotta keep the driver happy!"

Bob handed it back.

"Any of you two got AIDS?" Billy laughed, gulping down the liquid and handing the bottle to Linda. Beyond, the headlights picked out an empty lane.

"I don't like whisky . . ."

"Drink it!"

Linda drank.

"That's it, Linda. That's the way to do it . . ."

"Look out, Billy!"

There was something ahead, standing in the middle of the road, suddenly illuminated by the headlights. In the split-second before the car reached it, Billy had a sudden and vivid impression that he was looking again at the clouds that had billowed from the roof of the Storehouse. He had a flashing glimpse of roiling black smoke, of eyes like fire in a hellpit, and a maw filled with thunder and lightning. And then he swerved hard left to avoid whatever it was that stood undulating in the road, unconcerned at their approach.

"Billllleeeeee!"

The car crashed through a hedgerow; the windscreen cobwebbed. Linda clawed at Billy's hair as the car careered on through a barbed-wire fence, the burrs biting and ripping fiercely at the bodywork. Bob began to scream in a high falsetto as the car slewed sideways into a tree. The windscreen imploded. A side window flew out and Dennis followed it in a tangle of limbs as the car heaved over. It bounced twice, rolled again and came to rest on its roof, steam gushing from the radiator.

Coughing and choking on petrol fumes, Billy crawled forward on his elbows through broken glass. He tasted grass, felt it on his face and kept on crawling. His neck hurt and a sick headache, like a hangover only worse, threatened to make him throw up at any second. He had no idea where he was or what had happened. There was a pain in his head and his hands were cut, that was all he knew. He rolled over onto his back, feeling cold night air. His vision was blurred. He rubbed a bloodied hand over his eyes and looked back.

Battered and torn, the car lay upside down in a field. One of the headlights was still working; a shaft of light illuminated the wreckage. There was glass all around, and the car had acquired a tangled corset of rusted barbed wire. One of the doors lay several feet away. The air stank of petrol: the tank must have ruptured. At last Billy remembered what had happened.

Something in the road. Like smoke . . . like . . .

And then he saw it coming through the gap in the hedge where the car had plunged from the road. He rubbed his eyes again: he must still be concussed, because no matter how hard he tried, he still could not identify the thing that had caused the crash. It swirled over the grass towards the car like a pillar of twisting fog. Twenty feet from the rear of the vehicle, it stopped. Billy sat up in the long grass and squinted, trying to see it better.

It was tall, maybe fifteen feet or so. Sometimes it looked man-shaped and then, suddenly, just when he thought he had it in focus at last—it was just a twisting column of grey-black smoke. Sometimes it was that face, the face in the firecloud. Then it was not. It roiled and twisted; changing and shifting. Now there were lots of faces in there, and now there weren't.

It was the smash. I'm concussed. I can't see straight.

It moved again, towards the car.

Billy squinted at it, then heard the sounds of moaning off to his right.

The thing stopped. It had heard the noise, too. Billy watched it glide like fog chased by wind towards the noise.

It was Dennis, about thirty feet away. Billy saw him struggling groggily to his feet, holding his head. He must have been thrown out of the car. Billy stood up as well, watching as Dennis, unaware of the approaching cloud-pillar, began to call out.

"Billy . . . Billy . . . I'm hurt . . ."

Now Dennis could see the thing and he began to move uncertainly away.

Billy stood spellbound as the changing, twisting *thing* swept down around Dennis in a shrouding fog-like mantle.

Dizziness engulfed Billy and he sank to his knees, bent over and stared at the ground. He could see double now. He rubbed his eyes again and became aware of the screaming.

It was Dennis.

He tried to look back to where the fog-pillar had descended on him, but his eyes just would not focus. Only impressions registered. Impressions of that strange undulating mass and its changing faces. It seemed *preoccupied*. Now Billy seemed to see fleeting images of Dennis within the cloud, as if he was being picked up and examined. His legs protruded from the mass, six feet above the ground, kicking and squirming. Now the legs were gone as Dennis was turned over and Billy could see one of his arms and his wildly thrashing head. And all the time, Dennis was screaming, screaming, screaming.

Billy could not be sure, but now it seemed that the thing was holding Dennis upside down by the legs, like a rag doll. There was a ripping sound. Dennis's sreams reached a new, horrifying pitch . . . and then abruptly ceased.

The thing had ripped him in half.

It threw the two pieces to one side and the bloodied meat vanished into the long grass. Billy felt fear and horror curdling in the pit of his stomach. He turned and, unable to run yet, shambled towards the car for safety. The thing, undulating and moving and with all its faces now aware of his presence, drifted quickly towards him like a haze of poisonous marsh gas.

Billy could not speak. He had just seen Dennis torn apart like a doll.

He became aware of moaning from within the car. Linda and Bob were still alive. Linda was crying for her mother and Bob was just groaning. He reached the car at last, turned round to look back and saw that the thing was almost on top of him. Crying out, he lost his balance and fell heavily. He coughed and choked; the air round the car still reeked of petrol.

"Please don't . . . please don't kill me." He started to cry; great blubbering noises that he had not made since he was a child. He knew that the thing which had killed Dennis was the thing he had seen in the Storehouse. No one else had seen it, but he had recognised its presence. He held his hand up in hopeless defence, waiting for the unholy, shifting mass to pick him up the way it had picked Dennis up. But nothing happened. He looked back again, sobbing; half-expecting to wake up and realise that he had imagined everything since the fire.

The thing was still there, six feet away, swirling and coiling like smoke. Billy knew that it was watching him. He suppressed his sobbing, but could not hide his fear. Inside the car, Linda was crying now. Bob was silent—perhaps he had died.

Hello, Billy.

There was no real sound. The voice had spoken inside his head. It was a velvet sound, not like a voice at all, really. Billy struggled to a sitting position. Even from where he lay, at such close range, he still could not see the thing properly. It refused to focus.

"Hello," he said.

You know me, don't you?

"I've . . . I've seen you . . . before."

I can give you everything you've ever wanted. I can give you the girl called Christy. I can give you everything.

How the hell did it know about her?

You'd like that, wouldn't you?

"Yeah . . . yeah, I'd like that."

We can be friends, Billy. Good friends.

"Friends?"

You've got to prove yourself to me. Three times, Billy. Prove yourself to me three times and I'll give it all to you. You can have everything.

"Three times?"

Billy did not hear the sound in his head, but he knew that it was saying *yes*. He struggled to a kneeling position, shielding his eyes and peering into the living cloud. Something inside told him that this was the moment; the moment he had been waiting for all his life. He had dreamed about it. Now it was here: the chance to get even, to have everything that had been denied him. The voice had been telling the truth. He had seen this thing's power, could feel its strength, and *knew* that it was not lying. He pulled himself erect.

Three times, it had said.

Nodding, he moved away from the thing and round the side of the car. Somewhere inside, Linda was still crying. Smiling, eyes still fixed on the undulating mass and knowing that it was watching for his decision, he fumbled inside his coat pocket. He remembered what had happened at the Storehouse, and how he had felt then. Smiling still, he found what he was looking for, took it out and held it up before the thing, as if for approval. Again, he could not hear that voice, but he knew that it approved, knew that it was saying *yes*.

The air reeked of petrol.

He opened the box of matches, took one out and struck it roughly.

The match flared.

He was sure that the thing was smiling. He smiled again.

And threw the match at the pool of spreading petrol around the car.

Linda's crying was drowned by the sudden roar. A lake of fire swarmed around the bodywork of the car. The blast of heat sent Billy sprawling as clouds of oily black smoke wreathed the wreck. Orange blossoms of flame devoured the interior of the car in the same way that they had devoured the Storehouse and, this time, Billy *knew* that someone was burning alive in there. He wished he could hear the screaming. He smiled again, turning to look for the thing's approval.

It was gone.

But Billy knew that it approved. He seemed to sense that approval, and to sense the voice again, saying: *That's fine, Billy. You have shown what you can do. You must prove yourself three times more. Then you'll have your reward.*

He looked up at the roaring black smoke, expecting to see the thing's faces in there, but saw only night sky and roiling thick clouds. The thing had gone, but it would be back. And he knew that Shillingham would suffer at last for everything that it had done to him. He laughed wildly, swung his arms wide and embraced the night.

Three times. And he would have everything.

Chapter Twenty-three

It swept through the night, tasting the darkness and revelling in what was to come. There was pain and death and fire in the air. Good things. It scented the life that it hated, abundant life to be extinguished. It scented the prospect of agony and retribution. It scented despair. It scented great things. It scented . . .

HER!!

Enraged, it tried to find the direction of that scent. It had killed the Keeper of the Secret. But the Keeper's pig-spawn still existed and was intent on unearthing the Book. Filled with an unholy fury, it sniffed at the night air again, scented the direction and moved quickly, hungrily and furiously towards her through the night.

Chapter Twenty-four

Christy hurled aside the milk crate and stamped in frustration. *Underneath the kitchen floor*, Dad had said.

"But where, Dad? Where?"

Breathless and with lungs aching, she had finally reached home and gone straight into the kitchen without pausing for breath. She had been over every square inch of the rough wooden floor but could find no loose boards, no tell-tale signs of compartments containing stupid bloody books. She had good experience of finding her father's little hidey-holes containing half-bottles of whisky and gin, knew every single place that Dad could find to stash his latest supply. But she could find nothing now. She kicked the crate across the floor and resumed the search.

"Why the hell am I doing this, Dad? Why is it so important?"

Maybe under the fridge? She bumped the fridge away from its niche under the bench and examined the boards beneath. Nothing.

"How do I know this isn't another of your lunatic obsessions? What if it's just a fantasy? Why aren't I getting you a solicitor, instead of doing this?"

Because of that look on his face. And the way he talked to me. And—somehow—because of that terrible explosion and fire back in Shillingham.

Maybe that cracked floorboard beside the outside door. The one that cracked when Dad dropped the kitchen bench and oh, how Mam had laughed at that . . . Swallowing hard,

Christy tried to lift the cracked floorboard and found that it was wedged tight. She dug her fingernails into the crack itself and tried to lift. Nothing. It was a cracked board, that was all. There was nothing under there.

"Oh, God, Dad!"

She slumped cross-legged on the kitchen floor, sobbing in rage and frustration. It was hopeless. She had searched the house over and over, and she still had not found the book.

"Because there *is* no book!"

There is a Book, Christy.

But where? Where?

Something knocked on the front door.

Puzzled, Christy pulled herself to her feet again and went quickly into the hallway, looking at her watch. She had been searching all night; it was almost five-thirty. Who could this be?

It must be Michael. He's come to look for me when I didn't turn up again.

Another, solitary knock. It was louder this time and had an impatient tone to it.

"Michael?"

There was no answer. Just another knock. But this time it was a heavy blow, as if the sound of her voice had excited whoever it was on the other side. For no apparent reason, Christy suddenly felt very claustrophobic in the close confines of that narrow hallway. The floral wallpaper, the prints of the Lake District with awesome, stormy mountains and rain-lashed trees, the sound of her footsteps on the carpet as she finally drew level with the door, seemed to increase the sensation. Why did she feel so uneasy?

"Michael?" she called again, reaching for the doorknob.

This time, the blow from the other side was so heavy that

the hinges creaked in protest. Christy jumped back in alarm. Another blow. And then another. Until the hammering on the other side echoed and reverberated in the hallway and the door seemed to be groaning under the strain. It was as if someone was hitting the door with a sledgehammer. It was an old, solid, weatherbeaten door but it was feeling the strain.

"What do you want?"

The hammering became a pile-driving series of terrifying blows. Christy bit into her clenched fist, feeling real fear for the first time. She began to back away down the corridor.

"Go away! Leave me alone!"

A panel in the door cracked apart and Christy cried out as wisps of curling smoke or steam began to creep through the rent. She could see pulsating light through that crack. And now she knew that something utterly evil and inhuman was on the other side of the door.

The pounding increased. She turned to run, and cried out in alarm again when the door suddenly burst inwards with a splintering crash and slammed against the wall. Nothing human could make the door burst in like that. Feeling terror breathing on her neck, she ran into the living-room and slammed the door behind her. Just before the door shut, she had an impression of something coming through the front door; a hazy vision of billowing smoke— and of something within the smoke which was large and black and utterly horrifying. It had turned towards her as the door slammed. Quickly, she ran into the middle of the room and started towards the window which led into the garden. Something slithered on the hallway carpet towards the living-room door. Christy stopped. The prospect of climbing out of the window and running outside into the

166

night was far too terrifying. Once out of the house she would somehow be more vulnerable. She turned back, grabbed the edge of the sofa with both hands and pushed it hard against the door, just as something heavy bumped against it from the other side. She held it firmly there as the pressure increased from the other side and the door began to bulge inwards.

"Go away! Leave me alone!"

Chrissssstyyy! said a voice like death from the hallway. And Christy felt fear such as she had never known before. She screamed as a terrifying blow to the door punched out a wooden panel. It bounced onto the carpet.

But now the light and the smoke were somehow gone as if there had never been anything there at all. Breathing heavily, Christy looked round frantically.

Am I dreaming? Shall I wake up and find everything back to normal?

She strained to see into the hall. There was no sign of anything there at all. Through the missing panel she could see down the hallway and past the shattered front door, out into the night. The door was swinging on its hinges, groaning and squeaking in the night wind.

She looked round and felt her heart leap in her throat.

Curling, billowing clouds were forming outside the living-room window from the garden. Slow, roiling, poisonous clouds; as if some terrible night smog had suddenly descended from nowhere. And she could hear the unmistakable sounds of some large animal *breathing*. The smoke curled and spread against the glass panes. And Christy knew, as she pulled the sofa frantically away from the door, that this terrible, terrible thing from the night was playing with her. The sofa bumped away from the door. She glanced back, in time to see the smoke *rearing* backwards and then *plunging* at the window. Glass shattered, wood splintered; and the terrible black cloud was foaming into the room as Christy ran round the sofa and back into the hallway.

It wants me out of the house!

She raced back down the hallway and into the kitchen, slamming the door behind her and throwing the bolt. She could not run forever; it must get to her eventually. Crying with fear, she ran into the centre of the small room, looking for something—anything—with which she could defend herself. She could see nothing. She backed against the far wall, waiting. Sounds of destruction echoed through to her. The thing, wherever in hell it had come from, was tearing the living-room apart. She heard the furniture being ripped to pieces, cabinets and glasses shattering.

"Stop it! Please, stop it!" She sank to her knees.

She could hear it now, moving away. She held her breath. Was it coming down the hallway towards the kitchen? Or was it really going away? Was it standing there silent, waiting for her to move? Long, agonising seconds passed. Christy could hear her heart hammering, taste the fear in her mouth. But there was no sound. She rose to her feet, listening. She moved towards the kitchen door slowly, hesitantly. Could it be on the other side, waiting for her? She placed her ear against the wood panelling. Still nothing. She backed away again, too afraid to open the door. It could get her easily, she knew. Anything that could tear open a door and explode through windows like that could easily get to her here in the kitchen. She would be far better to . . .

And then she heard the sounds on the kitchen roof. Groaning, settling sounds as if some great pressure was being exerted from above. She looked up frantically. The kitchen was an extension, built years ago. There was nothing above it. Nothing except . . .

Except the thing!

She ran for the kitchen door again, but was too late.

Overhead, the kitchen ceiling suddenly split apart. The lights went out instantaneously. Beams of wood crashed downwards. A splintered beam banged heavily against the door, spinning Christy round and knocking her back into the kitchen as plaster dust swirled and a great chunk of masonry hit the ground beside her. She rolled into a tight ball, spinning away beneath the beam which blocked the door as great chunks of masonry, plaster and splintered wood tumbled down. Night air flooded into the ruined kitchen. A great roaring noise from overhead told her, in the confusion and the dust and the crashing timber, that the thing was coming in to get her. A spar of wood whirled down and caught her a glancing blow on the side of the head. The world spun away from her in confusion.

The thing descended.

It clawed among the rubble for the pigspawn.

Chapter Twenty-five

And then it reared away shrieking.

It scrambled from the rubble and detritus of destruction in alarm, sensing that danger was near. Confused, it emerged into the night air above the ruined kitchen and scented the air again. There was danger, but where? It scanned the night, hunting for this source of unease and finding nothing. Beneath it, the Wyrm was aware that the girl was senseless, awaiting its vengeance. But it could not return to the task until this impending danger was resolved. It whirled again, and then scented the direction of the danger.

It was on the horizon.

A faint, creeping orange line.

Dawn.

A new day was dawning.

It rose from the rubble, snarling at the creeping light which was invading the earth. Very soon, the sun would be rising over the horizon. The night was at an end. It looked down again to where the pigspawn lay.

Soon. I'll be back again. You are the last of your line. You cannot stop me. But I can wreak my vengeance upon you in more suitable circumstances. Soon . . .

It fled, scenting the air again for a place in which it could shelter during daylight hours. Instinctively, it knew that such a place must exist in Shillingham. But how far away was it? And would it be able to get there before day dawned?

Orange light was seeping over the horizon now; a poison to its corrupted soul. It fled like a dark wind, hunting.

It found what it was looking for at last. And not as far away as it had feared.

It swept into its place of sanctuary just as day swarmed over the countryside. It was a place of welcome; a place of retreat until night was ready to engulf the land again. It was a place to rest. A place to savour the vengeance which it would visit on Shillingham soon. A place to hide from the sun.

It was a place among the dead.

Chapter Twenty-six

The fire tenders had soon coped with the fire, even though the Storehouse had been rapidly consumed by the flames. Michael had stood watching as the last remnants of roof gave in, just before the firemen had positioned themselves to pump water into the gutted building. An ambulance from the hospital had soon turned up to take care of those people who had been hurt inside the Dun Cow. But as Sergeant Grover had surmised, there were no bad injuries—cuts from flying glass and bruises from falls, that was all. Michael had stood with Grover, watching and feeling helpless, the sergeant as impotent as he was.

He had seen PC Frankham approaching from the police station, then dashing back to telephone unnecessarily for the fire brigade. They had arrived almost immediately; but Frankham had not come back—much to Grover's annoyance and disapproval.

When the fire had been put out and Grover had become caught up in the necessary police procedures to find out what had happened, Michael had found it politic to leave. He had waited for Christy to come back, as she had said she would; but there was no sign of her. He wondered if the new life he thought he had discovered with her was over before it had even started. He appreciated that she might need time to get over the business involving her father, just as she had said to him earlier that evening, but damn it all, he only wanted to help her. Why did she have to freeze him out like that? He considered what to do.

Should he follow her home and find out what was happening? If she had been going home to get something for her father, surely she would have been back by now. Perhaps it had been a ruse to get away. Maybe she simply did not want his company. Feeling heavy inside, Michael walked back through the night to Split Crow Farm.

The dogs sensed his despondency when he arrived and avoided him. Tonight, he could have done with their attempts to cheer him up, but they would not oblige. He also sensed that they were somehow expecting Christy to be there and were severely disappointed that she had not turned up with him.

Michael poured himself a drink, stoked the fire and sat back in his armchair, reviewing the day. What a hell of a day it had been. First Frank, and then that Environment guy being blown up in the Storehouse. He had always thought Shillingham to be a sleepy village. Sean had been right. The motorway was on its way and all hell seemed to have broken loose as a result.

Morose and depressed, he went over to the telephone and dialled Christy's number. But all he could see was the look on her face as she had said: *I need time, Michael. Time to be alone.*

He replaced the receiver, looking down at Mac. The dog whined and moved closer to the fire.

"You and me both, pal."

Two whiskies later, Michael was dozing in front of the fire. One more, and he had fallen into a troubled sleep.

In his dream, he experienced something he hoped he would never experience again. As an objective observer, outside his body, he was again looking at himself as he was

*strapped into a stretcher and carried towards an ambulance.
His head was twisting wildly from side to side. He could still
feel the mental agony, even though he was not inside that
tortured body.*

"I'm dead. Leave me alone. I'm dead . . . I'M DEAD!"

*And suddenly, it was not himself on that stretcher. It was
Christy.*

*Blank, faceless men in black uniforms were pushing the
stretcher into the ambulance as she cried out over and over
again! "I'm dead! Dead! Dead!" Michael pushed forward
through a writhing sea of hands clutching at his body, holding him back. Christy's agony was his agony, and he had to
save her. One of the ambulancemen leered back at him,
smiling cruelly. He recognised the face now. It was Frank
Warwick, and he was laughing wildly at Michael's helpless
attempts, as he slid her away from reach into the vehicle.
Michael lashed out at that face, but could not reach.*

"Christy!"

"Dead! Dead! Dead! Dead!"

Michael was suddenly awake, bathed in sweat. The fire had
almost gone out; glowing red embers lit up the room.
Something had woken him. A noise. But he could not be
sure what it had been. He jerked to his feet, rubbing his
face.

"What . . . ?"

Dutch and Mac barked and Michael realised that they
had woken him.

Someone was knocking at the door.

The dogs barked again.

Michael looked at his watch. It was just after six o'clock.

He moved sluggishly towards the door as the dogs prowled uneasily around his feet.

He opened the door.

Christy was leaning against the doorframe. Her clothes were torn, her face smeared in blood and dirt.

Chapter Twenty-seven

"Michael . . ." She held out a hand and then fell forward. Michael caught her as she fell, the dogs barking excitedly.

"Mac! Dutch! Get down!"

The dogs obediently slid to the carpet in front of the fire. Michael felt panic rising inside.

The dream's not over! This can't be happening!

He carried her gently to the sofa, her full weight leaning against him.

"Easy, Christy. Easy. Where are you hurt? What happened? Who did this to you?"

She was mumbling now, eyes closed and feverish. She seemed to be on the verge of sleep. He hurried quickly from the room, dampened a cloth under the kitchen tap and, returning, washed the blood and grime from her face. There was a cut above one eyebrow.

"Oh, God, Christy. What happened?"

Had she been attacked?

He went quickly to the telephone, found the number of the police station from the notepad on the bureau, and dialled. He checked his watch again. Six-fifteen. Would anyone be there . . . ?

"Shillingham police. Grover here," said the voice at the other end of the line.

"Thank God you're there. I didn't think . . ."

"Lambton?"

"Yes."

"Where's Christy Warwick? Is she with you?"

"Yes, she's here. And she's in a bad way. She needs a doctor." Michael had sensed the tension in Grover's voice.

"What the hell is going on?"

"I'll be there in fifteen minutes. I'll bring Doctor Stark with me."

"What . . . ?"

"Just wait! I'll be there!"

Chapter Twenty-eight

The tension was still reflected on Grover's face when he arrived shortly afterwards at Split Crow Farm. The dogs went wild when the Land-Rover screeched to a halt outside, so much so that Michael was forced to lock them in the kitchen. Even so, their barking did not waken Christy and Michael was desperately worried when he let Grover and the doctor into the living-room. Small, slight, balding and with—curiously—National Health spectacles, Dr. Stark went straight to Christy on the sofa, opening a Gladstone bag. Grover silenced Michael's questions with a wave of the hand until the doctor had examined her.

"She's not badly hurt," said Stark at last. "Just cuts and bruises. No broken bones or internal injuries. She may be slightly concussed."

"What happened?" asked Grover.

"I don't know," Michael replied. "I tried to ring her earlier at home. There was no reply. She'd gone over there in the evening to get something for her father . . ."

"I tried to get through to her, too."

". . . She came here in a state of collapse shortly before I called you. Doctor, has she been . . . ?"

"Assaulted? I can't say until she's been fully examined."

"What a bloody night!" Grover ran a hand through his sandy hair.

"What's happened, Grover?" Michael asked. There was an unspoken *something* in the air. He had to know what it was. Grover just stood, looking at him, as if deliberating whether to speak or not.

"It's Frank, isn't it?" said Michael. "Something's happened."

"Yes," groaned the sergeant, looking back to Christy. "It's Frank."

"He's dead."

"Yes. He was murdered in his cell last night. And so was George Frankham—the guy I sent to telephone for the fire brigade when the Storehouse went up. Both murdered."

"Murdered? Oh no, Christy . . . How?"

"God knows. Dr. Stark isn't sure. It must have happened some time between eleven and four this morning, the doctor says. In all the confusion of the fire, anybody could have gotten in there. Listen, Lambton . . ." Grover steadied his gaze deliberately at Michael. "Christy's going to need you now more than ever."

"I know."

Grover turned away to the window, braced his hands on the sill and looked out into the dawn.

"Nice quiet place, Shillingham. I've lived here all my life

and, apart from the odd road accident—poor Christy's mother included—farm accident or punch-up in the Dun Cow, life's been very easy, very quiet." He turned back to Michael. "And then, in one day and night, Frank turns a shotgun on a bunch of people doing their job and is locked up, the Storehouse blows up killing a government man— an important government man. A poor guy loses his mind and kills himself. Two men are murdered in my own police station—one of them a policeman and a close friend. Three stupid kids kill themselves in a joyriding accident— and now a young girl is attacked. Tell me this, Lambton: are they cramming everything into one night to make up for thirty-five quiet years?"

Christy began to moan. Michael moved quickly to her side as she attempted to sit up.

"What happened, Christy?"

"Were you raped, Christy?" asked Stark, rather too bluntly.

"Raped? No . . . Up at the farm. Something tried to get in . . ." And then, in dawning horrified memory: "*Something* tried to kill me, Michael! It broke into the house, tore out the kitchen roof. It nearly crushed me. I got away. I didn't have anywhere to go, Michael! I couldn't find Dad's Book! I couldn't . . ."

"Take it easy, Christy." Grover came forward. "What do you mean, 'something'? You mean someone?"

". . . Dad . . ." There was a desolation in Christy's voice now as she saw Grover for the first time. Michael could also see that desolation in her eyes.

"Someone tried to break into the house, you said . . ." Grover tried uncomfortably to continue with his line of questioning.

"It's Dad, isn't it? Something's happened, because I couldn't find the Book."

"Your dad's dead, Christy," said Michael softly, holding her.

Christy searched Michael's eyes, found the truth there and looked back at Grover. The sergeant nodded and lowered his head.

"I thought so," said Christy in a little girl's voice. Turning to Michael, she said: "I've got to go to sleep now, Michael."

"Christy," began Grover again. "What happened at the farmhouse?"

"No!" interrupted Stark, rising from the sofa. "Can't you see she's in shock? I'll give her something. No more questions until she's rested, okay?"

Grover turned back to the window. "What the hell is going on in Shillingham?" He did not like the sound of that word: "hell"; it seemed to carry a heavy connotation.

"Can she stay here?" Stark asked Michael unnecessarily, but feeling professionally obliged to do so.

"This is her home now," replied Michael.

"I'm driving up to the farmhouse, Doctor," said Grover at last, reaching for Michael's telephone. Michael nodded assent. "I'll drop you off afterwards. But I'll need a full medical report on Christy tomorrow."

Stark rubbed a hand across his face. "It's been one hell of a night." Again, that word: *hell*.

Grover rang the police station, told them where he was, reported on Christy and asked two men to meet him at the Warwick place as soon as possible.

Chapter Twenty-nine

An hour later, Grover was standing amidst the ruins of the Warwicks' kitchen, looking up at the morning sky and wondering when, if ever, he would see his bed again. His men had sifted through the wreckage, surveying the destruction and commenting that the house appeared to have been bombed. The living-room window and wall were completely blown in: glass, rubble and wood littered the carpet. The front door looked as if it had been ripped apart; and nothing short of a bomb blast could have demolished the kitchen in that way.

A gas explosion? thought Grover. *Leakage from a Calor gas cylinder? Bloody funny damage for that. The cylinders in the outhouse were intact. Whatever happened, Christy was lucky to have come out alive.*

He stepped through the shattered kitchen door. Beyond the vale, he could see the chimneys and rooftops of Shillingham. That feeling of uneasiness was creeping over him; a feeling that he had never experienced before in his entire career as a policeman. The horrifying explosion and death of Elphick had been bad, but he was trained to deal with that. Discovering the bodies of Frank and George had been worse . . . much worse. And watching Dr. Stark as he performed an examination of the bodies had been a hideous, "out-of-body" experience. He had found difficulty in looking at those terrible, eyeless corpses.

"What killed them?" he had asked at last.

Stark had shrugged. "I'll have to carry out a full post-mortem to find that out. Apart from the eyes, there's no other evidence of injury. One thing's certain—they've both suffered major blood loss."

And that was when the eeriness had hit Grover.

"Where's the blood gone, Doctor? There's not a drop of it in the cell."

Now, standing in the ruined kitchen of the Warwick farmhouse, he lit a cigarette with a trembling hand. His initial fury at realising, after several telephone calls, that a special CID squad and forensic experts were moving in that day, effectively to take the investigation out of his own hands on his own patch, had now abated. Let the bastards sort it out, if they could. There was something going on here—something he could not understand—and for the first time in his life, he was happy to have someone else take charge. He would organise a preliminary report on the Christy Warwick incident and then he had to sleep. Weariness was creeping over him now, eating its way into his bones.

Just like that damned, sick, eerie feeling.

And deep inside him, deep in that part of all people which refuses to accept rationalisation, Grover wished that they had just left that bloody crossroads gibbet where it was.

Hiding from the day with the dead, in the darkness below ground which it knew so well, the Wyrm continued to feed and grow strong. In perpetual night, it began its plans to build the web. Shillingham would be the cocoon, and after that cocoon had been consumed amidst the death, blood and carnage of its vengeance, it would emerge fully, forever.

Chapter Thirty

"My name's Pemberton, Miss Warwick," said the man in the business suit as he eased himself up from the chair normally occupied by Grover. The sergeant stood against the far wall, arms folded, watching. "I've taken charge of the investigation into your father's death. I'm afraid this next part isn't easy, but it has to be done."

Christy sat in front of Pemberton/Grover's desk. Michael was beside her, holding her hand.

"I understand," she said, again in the too quiet voice that had been worrying Michael since morning. She stood up and moved towards the door which Pemberton had opened on their left. Beyond lay the body of her father, and the task of formal identification.

"I'm coming, too," said Michael firmly, standing up beside her. There was something about Pemberton that he disliked. It was quite obvious that Grover had been put to one side in this business, but Pemberton's manner was too brusque, too roughly delivered for Michael's taste. He looked at Grover for support. Grover nodded and lowered his eyes.

Pemberton grunted and held the door wide. Christy and Michael passed through. Two bodies had been laid out in preparation for the trip to the morgue.

"I'm sorry," said Pemberton again, sounding as if that was the last thing in the world he felt. He strode briskly to the white-sheeted form on the trestle table, lifted the cloth and looked back at Christy. Michael felt her grip tighten on his hand, felt her body lean against his as she approached the table. She was moving forward but still shrinking away from the horror of it all. Michael gritted his teeth, hung on to her and steered her towards the table.

The doctor had worked on the body to make it more "presentable." But the eyelids on Frank's face had gone. The cotton wadding in the empty sockets looked obscene.

"Is this your father?"

". . . yes . . ."

Again, that voice. Too quiet.

"Thank you."

Michael helped her out of the room, back into the main office. Grover was still standing where they had left him, head down and apparently absorbed in some internal problem.

"Christy," said Michael, holding up her face to look deeply into her eyes. The loneliness was there again, the hurt and the pain that he thought they had banished together. "Christy . . ." And now it was brimming over, the anguish was surfacing for the first time. Michael saw it rising inside her like some dark and bitter flood; it ebbed and rushed to the surface, spilling over from those beautiful dark eyes. She flung herself at him. He embraced her tightly and the agony came out of her in racked, despairing sobs. Michael was crying, too, not giving a damn for the embarrassment of Pemberton and his two blue-suited cronies, as they cleared their throats, sipped at their coffee or looked out of the windows. Grover came forward, placing a hand on each of their shoulders, and steered them towards an interview room. He gently opened the door and led them inside.

Hours later, it seemed, the anguish in Christy evened out.

It could never leave her completely, but the breaking of the dam inside had got rid of the destructive, mind-numbing debilitation. Michael stroked her hair, crooning words of love into her ear. At last, he opened the interview room door. Pemberton was waiting.

"I'll have to ask you further questions about last night. You appreciate that, don't you, Miss Warwick?"

Christy swallowed hard. "I understand. It's all right."

"Mr. Lambton. This is something that Miss Warwick will have to do herself."

"Yes, okay. I'll go outside for a few minutes, Christy. But I'll be here when you've finished."

Michael knew what Christy would tell Pemberton. Although still in that terrible daze, she had told him what had happened up at the house. Her memory was vague, retaining only a series of impressions; nothing that could possibly be of any use at all. Recollections of clouds descending on the house, of something that called her name and broke down the door. Of something that had literally crushed the kitchen roof above her. A shapeless, formless *something*. Maybe a little more would emerge; perhaps she would remember more specifically what had happened now that her grief had finally come out. Somehow, Michael thought not.

Pemberton pushed past Michael into the interview room and closed the door behind him. The other police officers in the outer office—blue-suited and uniformed—continued with what they were doing as Michael walked to the main doors and pushed through them. There was no sign of Grover now.

Outside, there was still the smell of smoke in the air. It was a fine, clear day. Michael walked down the steps into the forecourt and saw the little figure of a woman bustling quickly towards the police station from the direction of the Dun Cow. He recognised her immediately: it was Iris Wooler, Christy's boss at the coffee shop. She began to talk when she was still twenty feet away.

"How is she? Is she badly hurt? No one thinks to tell me anything. I'm just allowed to find out by word of mouth and then to worry myself sick. Well?"

"She's okay, Mrs. Wooler . . ."

"Iris, please. None of that 'Mrs. Wooler' nonsense."

"She got the bad part out of her system, but it's still a hell of a shock."

"Don't understate, young man. But what happened at the house?"

"She's not really sure. It's all a little mixed up in her mind. Someone tried to break in and attack her. But she's all right. She wasn't hurt."

"I've a good mind to go in there and . . . and . . . well, I don't know what I'd do. But I'd sort something out. They tell me that they've brought in outside police and taken everything out of Sergeant Grover's hands."

"That's right."

"No, it's not right. He's a fine man. If anyone can sort out this terrible business, it's Harry Grover. I've known him all his life. What's going on in there now?"

"They're questioning Christy about last night."

"And you'll stay with her?"

"Of course."

"Walk back with me. I want to tell you something."

Slowly, they began to stroll back towards the Dun Cow and the still smoking, cordoned-off Storehouse ruin.

Iris levelled a steady gaze at Michael as they walked. He could see her out of the corner of his eye. She was assessing him, she wanted to say something but was chewing it over first. Michael looked the other way and allowed her to gather her thoughts. After two full minutes, she reached up, grabbed him by the shoulder and brought him to a stop.

"Christy's always needed love, as long as I can remember. No one's needed it more than her. She got it, to be sure, when she was a child. But when her mother died, Frank went to pieces. You know all about that, of course. From Christy, I expect. She had to become the head of the household after that. She gave Frank more love than he ever deserved, because he was incapable of giving it back. Do you *love* her?"

It was impossible for Michael to react any other way than with honesty.

"Yes, I do."

"I'm not just talking about the kind of 'love' people feel by . . ." Iris struggled for the words, ". . . physical attraction. I'm not talking about that at all. I'm talking about wanting to give your life and everything in you to make that person happy."

"I know what you mean, Iris. You don't have to spell anything out for me. I'm a grown man, and she's not a girl—she's a mature woman. We're in love with each other in exactly the way that you would want it."

"Good," said Iris. "Good. Because if you're not being straight with me, Michael-Lambton-the-writer-man, you'll have me to answer to. I'm going to tell you something now, something that I want to trust you with and which I never want you to tell Christy."

"Don't tell me anything. You don't have to . . ."

"I've got a feeling that you're right for Christy. That you'll be able to give her the happiness she really deserves. I wanted to give her that happiness, Michael. I wanted to take that tragedy away from her life. Two years ago, I offered to marry Frank Warwick."

They continued walking again. Michael was astounded.

"It was for Christy's sake. I wanted to help her. But Frank turned me down . . . He turned me down because he said I 'wasn't of child-bearing age and couldn't produce a son'—which gives you a fair idea of how Frank's mind was operating. So . . . I tried . . . but I wasn't able to help her in the way I thought best. So now it's down to you. You *will* give her that kind of love, won't you, Michael?"

"Yes, Iris. I will."

Iris nodded. Tears were in her eyes. She brushed them away angrily. "Good, good. Well . . . give Christy my love, tell her not to bother with the shop until she's feeling better. And tell her I'll be coming to see her very soon, provided I can get past your two lions, that is."

"So the grapevine has told you that she's living with me now."

Again, that level gaze. "I'm old-fashioned. But I'm not stupid. I think it's the right thing." Iris turned and bustled busily back in the direction she had come from.

"Iris been reading you the riot act?" asked a voice from behind.

Michael turned to see Grover approaching from the direction of the police station.

"You could say that. I was getting a more aggressive version of the speech you gave me before about looking after Christy."

"Sorry. Shillingham's a pretty tight-knit society. You should know that by now."

"Does Pemberton have to be so bloody-minded?" Michael sounded off. He had wanted to say something for hours.

"There've been seven deaths during the same night—two of them almost certainly murder. Not to mention the attack on Christy by something that can tear a wall out and knock down a kitchen ceiling. He's got a job to do. He's got to be—as you say—bloody-minded. Literally. Even though . . ."

"Even though what?"

". . . even though he's going about it rather differently than I might." And then, quickly diverting the conversation: "Look, Lambton. You write books about . . . *weird* things . . . don't you?"

"It depends on what you mean by 'weird.' I've written books on fear and the nature of things that frighten people."

"Inexplicable things? Things that . . . well, I mean . . . *bloody hell!* I mean supernatural things."

"Yes. What are you getting at?"

"Doesn't it seem strange to you that on the day that the gibbet was removed from Split Crow Lane, all hell's broken loose in Shillingham? And the very fella who was freaking out about removing the bloody thing is murdered on the same night that the fella examining what was found underneath the bloody thing is burned to death. Nothing happens in Shillingham until the day the gibbet is yanked. And then . . . seven deaths!"

"You're thinking that something supernatural is going on?"

"I don't know what to bloody think. But something's eating at my mind. Something that says there's more of a pattern to everything that's happened than I . . . or anyone else . . . can see. It's a little voice inside me, and it won't go away no matter what I tell it. What about this business Christy was telling me her father had told her. The 'some-

thing' that was buried down there at the crossroads site—
and the Book?" Grover gestured to Michael that they should
walk on towards the Storehouse.

"You're wondering if Frank wasn't so crazy after all?"

"Maybe. I don't get the bit about 'worms.' "

"That's W-Y-R-M, I think. The Northumbrian accent gives
it away."

"And what the hell's a wyrm?"

"It's a mediaeval description of an ancient, evil force.
Literally, a serpent or 'dragon.' "

"What? You mean scales and fiery breath and damsels
in distress? Frank must really have been off his rocker."

"No. That's a colourful description from legend. A
dragon or a wyrm could be any evil force—anything inexplicable. There's a high incidence in legend of wyrms in
the North East and the Borders. Even your pub, the Dun
Cow, is named after an ancient Northumberland monster."

"So maybe we've got a wyrm running around loose."

Michael laughed. "I doubt it. It could be that, generations
ago, Christy's family buried someone down there at the
crossroads, believing him to be evil—or believing him to
be a 'wyrm'—on the assumption that the crossroads would
keep him down there below ground forever."

"How's that?"

"A suicide, or person feared to be a vampyre was buried
at crossroads with a stake through the heart so that if he
ever came back to life to plague the living, he wouldn't
know which road to take and would effectively remain
there forever. The practice was forbidden by law in 1823."

"A vampyre," said Grover, blankly. (*"Where's the blood
gone, Stark? There's not a drop of it in the cell."*)

"Maybe that's what they thought the corpse was. That
would explain the shaft that pierced the body in the sar-

cophagus. Films and books about vampyres all suggest that a stake through the body of a vampyre was to destroy the heart. That's not the case. The idea of the stake was to pin the vampyre down in its coffin and keep it there so that it couldn't get out again. The crossroads site seems to indicate a fear of vampyrism."

They had reached the crumbled exterior of the Storehouse wall facing the Dun Cow. CID operatives were still sifting through the cordoned-off remains. A crowd of onlookers had gathered to watch.

"Well, the whole bloody lot's burned to ashes now," continued Grover. "Corpse, wooden shaft . . . and that poor bugger Elphick."

"Sergeant," called a police constable from within the ruin.

Grover moved away from Michael to the ruined wall. The constable whispered something in his ear.

Michael scanned the charred, carbon-deep floor of the Storehouse. Everything had burned through to the soil underneath. Beneath the rubble and blackened beams, he could see the shattered sarcophagus.

Grover returned, grim-faced.

"Well, that's two murders, three accidental deaths . . . and *two* suicides."

"Suicide?"

"Elphick. They found the gas taps turned full on. All of them."

"But why in hell would he do that?" asked Michael in astonishment. "He seemed okay to me when I left him. He was really absorbed in his work."

"Why in hell, indeed?" asked Grover. Again, that word. *Hell*.

They walked back to the station.

Chapter Thirty-one

Karen and Graham stood at the junction of Split Crow Lane, holding hands and looking across to the site where the gibbet had been. Karen's worst fears had been realised. She had dared the gibbet to come out—and it had come.

For days, Graham had been eager to go back to the crossroads, but Karen had managed to keep him away. Now, after all the fuss and confusion of the gibbet's removal, she had summoned up her courage to go back and *see*. What she had seen had frightened her deeply.

The actual ground where the shaft of the gibbet had stood was now cordoned off by a wooden safety barrier with bright orange tape pinned to it at regular intervals and with "Warning" signs to keep well away. The ground had been chewed up by tractor treads and the old gnarled tree which used to disturb her had been torn out and taken away. Karen remembered how she had called the gibbet "Dead Wood."

But the wood wasn't dead. It had come out of the ground when she had dared it. And it was hiding somewhere now, away from the day; waiting for the night-time so that it could come out again and go hunting for them.

Graham tugged excitedly at her hand and she allowed herself to be pulled across the open space towards the site. When they reached the safety barrier, she hung on to Graham, preventing him from climbing over. Beyond the barrier yawned a gaping pit. To Karen, it seemed that if she were to drop a stone into that pit, it would not stop until it had reached the centre of the earth—the place where nightmares lived. But her own particular nightmare had come out of that hell-hole into the real world.

"The voice," said Graham at last, craning his neck to look over the barrier and into the depths.

"What about the voice?" asked Karen.

"It isn't here any more."

"Come on, let's go."

She had come. Now, she knew. She dragged her protesting brother away from the site up Split Crow Lane, up towards the high parts of the valley, looking down into the cradle where Shillingham lay. It was still early afternoon, but dark clouds were moving in from the west; rolling to obscure the sun.

"Why's it going dark?" asked Graham as they walked.

"Night-time's coming early," replied Karen.

"But that just happens in the winter, Dad says. When it's cold and raining and snowing and stuff."

"I think winter's coming early to Shillingham, Graham."

"Great."

They had reached the summit of Split Crow Lane, where the dried mud and stone gave way to a gravelled drive leading into the cemetery of St. Peter's Church. No birds sang in the silent trees; a single shaft of brilliant sunlight pierced a black cloud overhead, shining like a spotlight on the church tower. They stopped at the fence of the cemetery, looking out at the ranks of gravestones marching upwards to the church itself.

"Listen," said Graham, cocking his head to one side, eyes alight. "Listen."

No bird sang in the sky overhead.

Karen felt a familiar, terrible chill creeping over her skin. Graham rushed to the cemetery fence, searching. In sudden excitement, he pointed. Karen looked and saw a hunched figure fifty feet away, sitting in the long grass beside a gravestone. He was chewing a stalk of grass and had seen them now, because he was glaring at them hatefully for the intrusion. Karen recognised who it was.

It was Billy Rifkin.

"There!" said Graham. "The voice is under the ground over there. And it's talking to *him!*"

Billy reached up, grabbed the edge of the gravestone and hauled himself to his feet.

"Hi, kids. Come on over. See what Uncle Billy's got for you."

Karen pulled Graham away from the fence, feeling something bad inside which she could not explain. She began to drag him back the way they had come. Graham tried to dig his heels into the gravel to prevent her; but Karen was wise to that old trick—he had tried it before. She kicked at his calf, the tension went out of one leg, and she hauled him back into the middle of the road.

"Whatchadoin'," Karen? Stop it. Billy wants us . . ."

"It's time to go," replied Karen firmly.

Billy shouted, one hand cupped to the side of his face. "Don't go, kids. Come and see what I've got for you."

"Come on, Karen. Let's see . . ."

"No!"

Karen dragged him away.

"It's not fair!" blurted Graham. "I found that voice, not him. He just wants it for himself. He wants to keep the magic. It's not *fair!*"

"The voice isn't for you," replied Karen as calmly as she could. "It's not . . . not . . . a right thing. Mum and Dad would be really angry if they knew about it."

"It's got nothing to do with them! Nothing . . ."

Still protesting, and with the brewing prospect of tears in his eyes, Graham was gradually dragged down Split Crow Lane. Karen was the kind of sister who did not question the existence of the voice, as grown-ups would do. She knew its unhealthiness by instinct. It was the voice from the gibbet; the voice of the hanged man who talked in her dreams, and who came down from the gibbet to take her. The voice of the night. The voice which she only heard in dreams, because she was too old to hear it during the day, unlike Graham. She reaffirmed her vow to protect her brother, hit him on the ear when he started snivelling again, and hauled him home.

Chapter Thirty-two

Billy watched them go, first in disappointment and then in satisfaction. He had been sitting there in the long grass all day, and they had been the first intruders on his commune. He grinned, plucked a fresh stalk of grass and jammed it into his teeth before slumping down beside the gravestone again. Cocking his head to one side in a listening attitude, he was able to take up where he had left off. The voice from the ground continued to speak.

And you'll be able to do it to her any way you want because that's what she will want and she'll do your favourite thing Billy you can make her cry when she's doing it and that'll be okay too because that's what she'll want just like you've always known you can make her cry and you can even kill Billy yes kill just like you showed me and it won't matter 'cause you can if you want to all you have to do is

*prove yourself another three times Billy three times that's all
the car was easy wasn't it? Yes of course it was easy three
times that's all tonight do it tonight three times tonight . . .*

"Prove myself three times," said Billy looking up at the
sky. Dark, boiling clouds had smothered the sun. They
seemed to be alive, curling and twisting above the Shillingham valley like giant wraiths on their way to some kind
of extraterrestrial gathering.

*Three times Billy start tonight three times tonight anything
you want everything you want tonight tonight tonight . . .*

"Tonight," said Billy.

He smiled.

Chapter Thirty-three

Christy and Michael stood in the ruins of the kitchen. Most
of the rubble had been cleared away from the floor and a
tarpaulin sheet had been fixed over the gaping rent in the
roof.

"A thunderbolt," said Christy softly in disbelief. "How can
they believe that? The sky was clear that night."

"What else is there to believe?" asked Michael. "You
were very confused yourself, you admitted it."

"How does a thunderbolt explain the front door and the
windows being smashed in as well as the kitchen. How
does it explain that voice calling my name?"

"A fireball? Three separate strikes? Maybe it only
sounded like your name. It's possible."

Christy looked at him, tightly. Michael held up his hands
in defence.

"I'm stating their view," he said, "not mine. It's the easiest explanation. And at this moment, they're looking for answers to all kinds of bloody strange questions. They're bound to go for the easy answers."

"What do *you* believe, Michael?"

Michael pushed a beam to one side with his foot, took Christy's hand and led her into the hallway. "I believe you. I believe that things are happening in Shillingham with a very definite intent and purpose. Dangerous things. And I'm not the only only who believes that. Sergeant Grover told me as much today, even though he isn't in charge of operations now and his word counts for very little. I believe that something did try to kill you. The same something—or someone, I should say—who killed your father, PC Frankham, Elphick and perhaps those friends of yours who were joyriding in the car. It all hinges on the crossroads. I believe all these things—and hearing myself say them I sound crazy—but, God help me, I do believe them."

They reached the living-room. Workmen had boarded up the shattered window frame to keep out the weather, but the carpet was still littered with broken glass. The curtains hung in ragged shrouds, like broken bats' wings. Michael had brought a holdall for Christy to collect any personal belongings. There had been surprisingly little to collect.

"I'm frightened," said Christy.

"So am I. But I don't know what I'm frightened of."

Christy looked round the room and had difficulty recognising it. Vaguely, it resembled some place that she had once shared with her father. Now, it was like a stranger's house. It was certainly not her home—if it had ever been

that. Her only home now was on Split Crow Lane, with
Michael, and with two dogs called Mac and Dutch.

"Let's go," said Michael, lifting the holdall.

Quickly, they left the empty house.

Chapter Thirty-four

"So what are you trying to tell me?" asked Pemberton.

Doctor Stark took a deep breath and tried to control his
temper. Far from being regarded as "one of the team," Pemberton and his cronies were treating him as if he was under
some sort of suspicion because of his findings.

"I'm not *trying* to tell you anything," he said. "What I *am*
telling you is that Frank Warwick and PC Frankham died
from shock and severe blood loss. Those are my findings."

"So?"

"So what?"

"So what could be the cause of that?"

"I really have no idea. Apart from the blood loss, there's
also evidence of a general and severe loss of body fluids
generally. The corpses have, as you can see, a significantly
shrunken aspect. Apart from the eyes, there are no external
injuries, so my presumption is, pending a coroner's inquiry,
that somehow the blood was drawn from the eyes by some
means of suction. But just exactly what kind of suction is
beyond me."

"I don't believe in vampyres, Stark. They go for the neck,
or so I'm informed by Hammer Films."

"I don't believe in them either."

What about a wyrm? thought Grover from the corner.

Chapter Thirty-five

Billy strode through the farmyard, scattering chickens. He was smiling as he walked. He had not felt this good in years.

"Three times," he hummed to himself. "Three times."

The bitter thoughts of Christy and the weirdo writer were easy to live with now. Those thoughts had been eating at his insides, like a cancer, while he planned and thought about how he could get even. Now, he did not have to worry about that, because it would all be resolved very soon. If only . . . if only . . .

"Where the sodding hell have you been?"

Billy stopped and looked up. His father was standing in front of him, dressed in stained overalls; he had spent the afternoon under the car. The damn thing had clapped out again last week, and Billy had promised under threat to help his father this afternoon. Billy's father was a smaller, shrunken version of his son. The family resemblance was remarked upon in Shillingham—like father, like son. People gave as wide a berth as possible to dealings with Joe Rifkin, as they did to Billy. Years of experience with the father had shown that the bad trait in the family ran deep. Mrs. Rifkin had died young, and it was the popular opinion that she had been lucky. A lifetime with the Rifkins would be a daunting experience for anyone.

Now, Joe Rifkin's face was crimson with rage and smeared with oil and grease. Billy stood looking at him.

"Well?" asked his father.

"I . . . forgot . . . Dad."

"Forgot?" Joe strode forward, wiping his hands on a rag, limping badly because his arthritis had been giving him bloody gyp under that car in the barn; particularly bad gyp because his no-account son had not been there to help him. Joe delivered an uphand, backhand slap with the cloth that jerked Billy's head to one side and left a greasy smear on his cheek. Billy stepped back before the blow, saying nothing. As he moved his head to look back at his father, Joe saw the cut across his hairline and the dried blood in his hair.

"Been in another punch-up, haven't you? I wondered where the hell you got to last night. Now I know. Been fighting again, haven't *you*?" Joe delivered another stinging slap.

"Can you hear it?" asked Billy, looking back at his father, another smear on his face.

"What?"

"Can't you hear it? It's burrowing underneath us."

"What the shit are you talking about, you . . ." *Slap!* ". . . stupid bugger? You're pissed again, aren't you? Spend all your time getting tanked up and leaving all the frigging jobs for your old man, eh?"

"No . . . of course you can't hear it."

Slap!

Billy reeled this time, caught off-balance, and sat heavily in a pile of pig muck.

Joe laughed, wiping his hands again. "That's the only way I've ever been able to get through to you, you little turd. The only thing you understand. Look at you . . . a little turd in a pile of turds. Best place for you." He turned and walked back towards the farmhouse. It was nearly time to eat.

He kicked open the cottage door, threw his rag on the floor and went into the kitchen. As usual, the place was a mess; but that did not bother him. Cleaning up was women's work and there had been no women's work done at the Rifkin place since his wife's heart had given out—literally and metaphorically. He pulled open the freezer lid, took out one of the pre-frozen chicken dinners he had made for himself, crossed to the microwave and threw it inside, twisting the dial and leaving a series of smears to join the others on the glass face plate. He remembered how much Billy had enjoyed killing that batch of chickens. Moving to the sink, he gave his hands a cursory wash over a sink full of dirty crockery.

Little bastard, he thought. *Always skiving, always sloping off to the village and putting himself about. What kind of a son is he, anyway? How the hell can I even be sure he's my son? Norma could have gone with someone else, couldn't she? We were having a bad time round about then. So he looks like me a bit! So what? He looks more like her. So it could be a coincidence, couldn't it?*

He heard a clattering of cans from the barn.

"Get your arse out of there, Billy!"

He wiped his hands on a towel, checked on the chicken dinner and picked up the *Mayfair* magazine from the kitchen bench. Taking a can of lager from the refrigerator, he sat down at the pine table in the centre of the room and pulled the tab. He drank straight from the can, aware, without looking up from his magazine, that Billy was standing in the doorway.

"Come on in or bugger off, Billy. But stop cluttering up the doorway."

Billy remained motionless.

Joe took another drink.

"Well . . . ?" He looked up.

Billy was standing, straight and erect, in the doorway. He was smiling. And he was holding a can of petrol in both hands.

"What are you playing at, you little bastard?"

Billy stepped forward into the kitchen, smiling. He began to unscrew the cap from the can and now Joe could smell the petrol.

"You're still pissed, aren't you? Wasting the good money I pay you for the little work you get around to doing . . ."

The rusted tin cap clattered to the floor. Grinning, Billy quickly took another step forward, jerking the can at his father. A gout of petrol erupted from the can, arching through the air and directly onto Joe's head and shoulders.

"*You . . . little . . . bastard . . .*"

Coughing and gagging, Joe leaped to his feet, overturning his chair and the pine table. The can jerked again, soaking his chest and stomach. The petrol was in his eyes and mouth as he blundered towards Billy in a blind fury. But Billy was gone as he clutched at the doorframe. Joe heard laughter behind him and plunged back into the kitchen, clawing at the air. Another wave of petrol surged and foamed on his back. He whirled, still not understanding, as he rubbed the petrol from his eyes enough to see that Billy had dodged round him and was back in the doorway.

Then he saw Billy's grin.

And the burning match in Billy's hand.

Finally, he understood.

"The first time," said Billy.

Joe started to scream.

Later, emerging from the blackened and smouldering kitchen, Billy stood in the open air and looked up at the

200

sky. The clouds had thickened and blackened. They were rushing from the east and west now, a meteorological anomaly, to gather round and hem in the Shillingham valley. Billy heard the sound of thunder, suddenly realising that it came, not from the sky, but from underground. He looked down, feeling the reverberations beneath his feet.

He smiled.

The Wyrm was burrowing.

Its time was near.

Chapter Thirty-six

Christy sipped at her wine, staring out of Michael's cottage window across the darkening landscape that now seemed so alien.

"But I do want to talk about it," she said.

Michael pushed Mac's head from his lap and got up from the sofa, stretching. He moved across to her and put his arm round her waist.

"It's too early, Christy. Are you sure? It may not be good for you."

"Dad said that, hundreds of years ago, something evil existed in Shillingham. Something that my ancestors were responsible for burying . . ."

"The body at the crossroads."

"It must have been. He said that they didn't have the . . . the courage . . . to kill it. I don't know what he meant by that, but he said that they could only stop it; they couldn't kill it. He said that it was the most evil thing in the world."

"I've no doubt that they believed that."

"But he said it was buried and *dormant*. Could it . . . could it be . . . ?"

"What are you trying to say?"

"What if Dad wasn't off his head? What if that body was a . . . *Wyrm*. Really. What if we've dug up something that's evil? Evil and *alive*, Michael."

"Christy . . ."

"You weren't there. You didn't see his face or hear him speaking. For the first time in years, he was in control. He wasn't rambling. He wasn't. He told me that each Keeper of the Secret was a son, but I was a daughter—the last Warwick. That's what was cracking him up. Don't you see? He told me that the Ritual of passing on the Secret might not work on me because I'm a girl, but perhaps it might because I'm a first-born child. But he couldn't be sure. He *knew* that things were going to happen, Michael. He knew that he would die if I didn't find that *Book of the Wyrm*. It was the only thing that could save him, he said—the only thing that could save us. I didn't find it—and he died."

"Christy . . ."

"I want to go back to the house, Michael. We've got to find that Book."

The clouds overhead now seemed much lower than before, entirely covering the sun. On all sides, fog was creeping over the rim of the mountains, down towards Shillingham, rising to meet the clouds as they descended. Together, they seemed to be forming a barrier against the outside world.

Chapter Thirty-seven

Iris looked up from the counter with a smile on her face as the coffee shop door jangled. The smile faded.

"Hello, Iris," said Billy Rifkin. "Am I barred, or do I get a cup of coffee?"

Iris poured coffee while Billy perched on the counter, examining the customers.

"Bad news about Bob and Dennis and Linda, wasn't it?" he said, banging down a fistful of change. Iris flashed him a sabre-edged look. Billy picked up his cup. "Taking that car was just asking for trouble. None of 'em could drive, you know. That Bob always did have a wild streak. I bet it was him. I told him to curb himself more than once." Billy sipped at his coffee as Iris began to wash dishes. "Where's Christy?" he asked.

"If it's any of your business, I've given her some time off."

"Oh yeah, her dad. Funny business, that. Where's she staying? Still with that writer freak?"

Iris carefully polished a cup and replaced it behind the counter. "Why do I think you had something to do with that stolen car and those poor kids getting killed?" she asked in a quiet voice.

"I don't know. Why do you, Iris?"

"It's a little voice inside me that won't go away."

"Well you should make it go away, Iris. Because little voices like that can get you into serious trouble with the law. I was working on the farm with my dad last night. If he heard you saying things like that about me, he'd get all burned up."

"Stay away from Christy, Billy. Stay away from her and from Michael Lambton."

"Stop fiddling with your cup!" came a loud female voice from the table beside the far window. Billy looked towards the sound.

"Heyyyy, kids!" He moved quickly away from the counter with his cup.

Karen looked up in alarm as Billy approached their table. Graham had spilled his cup of orange juice now and Mum was really fed up with him. Dad was in another of his silent moods and was staring out of the window into the street. Somehow, her mother and father always seemed at a distance. As if they were grown-ups in charge of someone else's children; as if their real parents had been stolen by the gypsies years ago and these two grown-ups had been forced into service to care for them. What Karen needed now, after the strange encounter she and Graham had had with Billy in the cemetery, was protection. That's what grown-ups were supposed to give. But Karen could sense no protection, and had no confidence in her parents' ability to protect them from Billy as he pulled up a seat and sat down, banging his cup on their table as if he was staking a claim. Karen watched as Mum looked at him in distaste at his intrusion and Dad just looked out of the window.

"Where you been hiding the kids?" Billy asked Karen's mother.

Julie smiled. It was the sourest smile that Karen had ever seen her deliver. Graham seemed pleased to see Billy.

"I thought you might have stayed to play with me today," continued Billy, looking at Graham.

"They haven't been hiding us!" exclaimed Graham

cheerily. And then, remembering how Karen had dragged him away from the cemetery: "It was Karen who wouldn't play. I wanted to stay. But she made me go."

"That right, Karen?" Billy turned his smile on her, and to Karen it seemed that the smile had been carved out of ice.

"We had to go home, for tea."

"Having your tea here, though, aren't you?"

"Drink up, kids," said Len as if he had suddenly come out of a dream. "We have to go now, Billy." They were the first words he had said since entering the coffee shop more than forty minutes earlier.

"Of course you do," said Billy. "Kids gotta get their beddy-byes. Right, Karen?"

Karen looked hard at Billy, trying to find out what was going on behind those eyes. She could see nothing but ice.

"Right, Billy!" said Graham. "I'll play any time you want to, even if Karen doesn't."

Mum! Dad! screamed Karen in her mind. *Aren't you supposed to say something now? Aren't you supposed to protect us?*

Julie picked up her coat, not listening to Billy. Len grunted and rose from his chair, grabbing Graham by the arm and pulling him roughly to his feet.

Say something to him, Mum. Tell him to leave us alone. Tell him . . .

Iris was suddenly standing beside Billy. She was looking directly at Karen and from that look Karen knew that she had heard everything Billy had said.

"Iris . . ." pleaded Karen. She did not have to say any more, because she could tell by Iris's eyes that she understood in a way that her father and mother never could.

"I want to talk to you, Billy," said Iris, still looking at Karen. There was reassurance in those eyes.

205

Stephen Laws

"Sure, Iris," said Billy, turning, a deeper ice in his eyes.

"Come on, Karen." And now Karen was being dragged out of her chair by her mother. "Thank you, Iris." A perfunctory acknowledgement of the tea and cakes.

Karen's last impression as she left the shop was of Billy standing up, towering over Iris. But Iris did not seem dwarfed by that daunting jerkin-clad figure. She was standing there, small and slight, a flowered apron covering her pink blouse and tweed skirt, just like the grandmother Karen had always wanted but had apparently never been given. And there was a silent power in Iris as she looked up; a power that was more than a match for Billy Rifkin. It was a sight that Karen was to recall many times in the horrifying hours to follow.

"Yeah, what?" asked Billy at last.

"Over here," said Iris, leading him past the other customers and back to the counter.

"What?" asked Billy again, the coldness in his eyes now replaced by a sarcastic mirth.

"I'm on to you, Billy."

"Yeah?"

"Yeah. I can't prove it, but I know that you had something to do with that car crash. I can see the cut on your head. And I also want you to leave those kids alone."

"Why don't you fuck off, you scumbag?"

Iris ignored him. "Your custom's no longer welcome here, Billy. In fact it's never been welcome, but with so many people disliking you and with everyone against you, I thought it my Christian duty not to turn you out. There was a time when I actually felt sorry for you."

"Why don't you just die, Iris?"

"Yes, I felt sorry for you. But I don't feel sorry for you any

206

more. There's a bad streak that runs deep in you, Billy. And I can't feel sorry for you because you enjoy that bad streak. You revel in it and you poison everyone who comes into contact with you. So be careful, Billy. Because I'm on to you, and I'll do everything I can to stop whatever it is that you're up to."

"You're the one who should be careful, Iris. I can play grown-up games as well as kids' games. Maybe I'll pay a visit to you rather than the kids."

"Get out of here, Billy," said Iris in a quiet voice. "Go anywhere near those kids again and I'm going straight to Sergeant Grover. Get out of here and don't come back."

Grinning, Billy turned and headed for the door. Iris watched him go, feeling waves of revulsion. At the door, he turned and looked back. "You're going to be sorry, Iris. Sorry for all the things you've said about me. I'm going to make *everyone* sorry. You'll see. It's going to happen soon. Much sooner than you think." He unzipped his fly quickly, wagging an obscene tongue at Iris.

"Get out, Billy. And mind what I said."

The door crashed and Billy was gone.

Chapter Thirty-eight

Another shop doorbell jangled. Another face looked up from the counter and another smile faded.

"Hello, Billy," said Sean dejectedly.

"Hiya, Sean! How's my pal? How's the comic shop business?"

"I don't run a comic shop. I deal in specialist magazines, books and art."

"Course you do, Sean. Course you do. But don't get sarcastic with me, eh?"

Sean saw the ice in Billy's eyes and felt sick. Panic was rising in his gorge. And then he heard himself say: "How did it happen, Billy? How did that car crash?"

"Dunno. I wasn't there."

"But you told us all to turn up at the Dun Cow. That car was stolen from the Dun Cow." *What the hell am I saying? He'll kill me for sure!*

Billy moved forward until their faces were only inches apart.

"I had nothing to do with that car. I turned up, yeah. Had a couple of pints and then went home after the Storehouse went up. Got hit by a piece of glass, see?" He pointed to the ragged cut on his forehead. "The others pinched that car. Stupid buggers. None of 'em could drive. You know that."

"I . . . didn't . . . turn up. Sorry . . . about that."

"No need to be sorry, kidder. Just as well you didn't. Or you could have ended up like they did."

"God, Billy, the whole business has shaken me up. I was talking to them only a few days ago. Now they're gone . . ."

"Yeah. Sad, isn't it? You got those magazines I wanted?"

"First that business up at the crossroads, then the Storehouse going up and killing that fella; then the car . . ."

"You got those magazines?"

Sean vanished behind his counter, rummaging through boxes. His mind was racing, as it always did when Billy was about. Billy was bad news, and since last night he had been dreading seeing him again. He found the magazines. They were obscene and lurid, cheaply produced magazines depicting the "best" moments from banned video nasties. The magazines themselves had been condemned by other mainstream periodicals in the genre as "carnographic." Sean bounced back, and handed them over.

"On account?" asked Billy.

"Yeah. Sure." Sean had not been paid a penny for over six months.

"Hey, Sean." Billy looked at his watch. "I've got an idea. It's nearly six o'clock; you're not going to do any more business today. What do you say we shut up shop and go for a spin? I've got my dad's car outside and a bottle of whisky in the back seat."

"I'd like that, Billy. I really would. But I can't leave the shop. I've got to . . ."

"Balls! No one else is coming today. Listen, we could finish that bottle up at the crossroads. Get stoned. I've got a little bit of smack in the dashboard—you know how much you like that—and we could see that off in no time at all. It would be great."

Please, God, no. The last thing I want to do is go out with Billy Rifkin.

Sean heard himself say: "Okay, then. Let's go."

Although it was still daytime elsewhere in the Border country, night was falling early on Shillingham. The clouds now completely blackened the sky, the sun only occasionally shining through a rent in the dark canopy. The fog on the outskirts of the village, to east and west, was steadily thickening as the battered Ford clattered and groaned from the village on its way to Split Crow Lane. Sean had finished a good fifth of the bottle, glad of Billy's prompting to do so, and now the warmth of the alcohol in his stomach had chased away the apprehension. Smoking one of Billy's weeds, he felt good and was on his way to feeling great. Maybe Billy Rifkin wasn't such a bad guy after all. Particularly so, when Billy eventually said:

"You know, Sean, I've always liked you. You're good company. You're not a wanker. You've a nice little business there, doing fine. A lot of people didn't think you would make it. But you did and you are."

"Thanks, Billy."

"I really mean it. We've got to make the best of ourselves. Look at Dennis and Bob and Linda, the poor sods. Their whole life in front of them and—bang!—they're gone. Just like that."

"Awful, Billy. Just awful." Sean swigged again from the bottle and took another snort on the joint.

"They were lucky in a way, though. They didn't suffer. It must all have happened very fast. That's what I want. When I do go, I want to go in a big way. I don't want to hang around on my deathbed somewhere, just wasting away." Sean passed the bottle. Billy took a drink and went on: "I remember this film I saw years ago . . . what the hell was it . . . ? This girl and this guy could make you explode just by *thinking* about you. Remember that?"

"*The Fury*," replied Sean, taking another drag, "directed by Brian De Palma."

"That's the one. Fella blew to pieces at the end . . ."

"John Cassavetes."

"That's the guy, yeah. Just exploded all over the place like a bag of mincemeat. Now that's how I wanna go. *Bang!* You know? Nothing slow. Fast, with lotsa noise. Splatter other people while I'm going. How about you, Sean? How would you want to go?"

Sean laughed drunkenly. The memory of the car accident seemed a million miles away. "Never thought about it. Stamped on by Godzilla maybe? No. Maybe riding down on an atom bomb like in *Dr. Strangelove*."

"No, I mean—*really*," said Billy, smiling.

"Okay, then," replied Sean, searching his mind for something ridiculous to match his frame of mind. "I'd go for . . . being flayed alive. Then, salt rubbed all over my body. Then . . ." Sean belched and laughed. ". . . then hung up in a burlap sack." He laughed again, loudly, and took another drag. The car jerked into a ditch and bounced out of it again.

"Flayed? What's flayed?"

"Never heard of that? It's where you strip the skin off an animal.

"Oh, yeah. I've done that at the farm before. And then you'd want salt rubbed in, yeah?"

Sean laughed. "Yep. Imagine the agony."

"Yeah," said Billy. "The second time."

"What?"

"Nothing," replied Billy, smiling again. The car jolted and bounced onto Split Crow Lane under the darkening sky.

Chapter Thirty-nine

Three-quarters of an hour later, Iris emerged from the coffee shop and turned to lock the door behind her. It was mid-August, but it could have been November; there was a cold chill in the air. Glancing up at the hostile sky and then beyond to the fog bank at the foot of the valley, she ducked quickly into the lane at the side of the shop. Minutes later, her battered Fiat trundled out of the market-place and headed for home.

The recent disturbing events were racing through her mind, making her feel quite ill. All these deaths, the terrible accidents and, worse still, her forebodings about the changes for the worse in Billy Rifkin; and her instinct that somehow all these things were connected. She had tried to give Billy the benefit of the doubt, she really had. But then his conversation with the kids seemed to have justified the fears she had held for a long time. Iris considered that life had been kind to her, or at least relatively kind. Her experience of Shillingham was one of warmth, sunshine and helpful people. But now the clouds overhead and the bank of gathering fog seemed to militate against those memories. Wasn't it strange that there should be clouds *and* fog? One or the other, surely, but not both. How was that possible?

And then Iris thought of Christy, and Billy's unhealthy interest; of the things he had said. Billy was dangerous—very dangerous—of that she was sure. Her mind suddenly made up, she swerved onto the stretch of road that would take her to Split Crow Lane. Now, more than anything, she wanted to see Christy; to talk to her and reassure herself that she was all right. How could she warn her about Billy Rifkin? Despite the obscenities, his threat was vague—she could not explain precisely why she was so disturbed by his words—but the threat was nevertheless substantial in her mind. She would work out what to say to Christy when she got to Split Crow Farm. The crossroads loomed up ahead, the orange road signs reflecting back from the wooden safety barrier surrounding the pit where the gibbet used to stand. Iris drove straight on past the site workings wishing that, after all, they had left that gibbet where it had been. So many bad things had happened since it had been moved yesterday. As the car passed, her eye caught something hanging from a cross-bar on the barrier. In itself, it seemed insignificant, but for some reason she could not get it out of her mind.

It was a large, dripping canvas sack.

Shrugging off that uneasy feeling, she pushed the car into top gear and continued on up the lane towards Split Crow Farm. She remembered her conversation with Frank Warwick two years ago. She could recall the exact words.

"I think we should be married, Frank. It would be for the best."

"What are you talking about, woman? I hardly know you. You hardly know me."

"I know Christy. And I know what she needs—what you need. It would be for the best."

"Oh yeah? You think you know what I need? Well you know nothing, Iris. Nothing at all. If you knew what I really needed, you would probably run away screaming."

"Tell me, Frank. Tell me about it. Tell me what's wrong."

"You could never understand, Iris. Never."

"But I need to know. Don't you understand, Frank? I want to make you a happy man."

"Happy? I don't know what you've been drinking, but I could do with some of it."

"Don't laugh at me, Frank. Say anything you like, but don't laugh at me. Don't imagine for one second that you've got a monopoly on loneliness or misery, because you haven't. You think I'm just a stupid old woman. Well, I'm not. If you'll let me I can give you strength. Real strength."

"Well, thank you, Iris. Thank you for riding in on your shining white charger and saving my day. You must think

*I'm bloody stupid. Christy works at your place. I know it.
You're bosom buddies by now, I expect. Sharing heart to
heart conversations, no doubt. I expect she tells you all about
her home life and vice versa. I suppose you feel sorry for
her . . ."*

"Sorry? Sorry!?" Iris remembered how she had slammed
her fist down on his mahogany table and sprained her
hand. Only her pride had stopped her from wearing a sling
in the days to follow. *"Don't you understand what I'm saying?"*

"I understand. But why, Iris? Really. Why?"

"Because I . . ."

"Yes?"

"I . . ."

*"You're not of child-bearing age, Iris. If you were, it might
be a different matter."*

End of conversation. Iris jerked back to the present again
as the car trundled on its way to Split Crow Farm. Something was bothering her. Something at the back of her
mind.

A large, dripping canvas sack.

She had been disturbed by the look in Billy's eyes when
he talked to the kids. And she was also disturbed by . . .
by . . .

That dripping canvas sack.

She slammed on the brakes and the car crunched to a
halt. She had to go back. Executing a shaky three-point
turn, she rammed her foot on the accelerator and drove
furiously back to the crossroads.

Chapter Forty

Karen knew that she was supposed to be big and strong in order to protect her brother, but everything had gone wrong tonight and she was finding great difficulty in keeping her own tears at bay.

She lay in bed, watching the dark, scudding clouds through the bedroom window, and fought down her tears and her fury.

Graham had been touchy all day, but their most recent encounter with Billy Rifkin in Iris's coffee shop had made him insufferably irritable. Mum and Dad were already not speaking: she could tell that much by the silence over the tea table. Graham had begun whining when they returned home because he had not been allowed to watch *The A Team* on television, and that in turn had sparked off a furious row between Mum and Dad, resulting in Karen and Graham being bundled off to bed at seven o'clock.

Karen bit her lip and listened to Graham snivelling in the bed by the window. She was angry with him for precipitating the row which had led to their enforced early night; but the more he cried, the more she felt like crying, too. She tried concentrating on the posters which adorned the bedroom walls: "He-Man" (for Graham), "She-Ra" (for Karen), a poster of the Ewoks from *Caravan of Courage* and Rupert the Bear.

Something scratched against the bedroom window. Karen turned her head to look. A tree branch, perhaps? Graham had not noticed, and was still snivelling. She looked back at Rupert the Bear again and tried to project herself into his world.

Another scratch.

Karen sat up in bed, and now Graham was sitting upright, too, his tears subsiding.

This time, they both saw the small pebble bounce against the window pane. Someone was down there, trying to attract their attention. Graham clambered out of bed and leaned against the windowsill. Karen came up quickly beside him and together they stared outside into the darkness.

A tall figure was standing on the lawn, beside the bird bath. He was gazing earnestly up at the window and beckoned when he saw the children looking out.

"It's Billy," hissed Graham. "He's come to play."

"In the middle of the night?" asked Karen.

"It's not the middle of the night, stupid. We were sent to bed early. It just looks like night because of the clouds. I *want* to play!"

Although it was dark, Karen could sense that Billy was smiling. That smile was invisible but real; a part of the night itself. Now, he was whistling softly, beckoning again for them to come down and join him. He was whistling: "Who's afraid of the Big, Bad Wolf?"

"What does he want?" she asked again. "What's he doing out there?"

"I told you. He wants us to go out and play."

Karen shrank back from the window as Billy moved forward, beckoning again. *"Come on, kids. Come on down."*

"What's he *doing?*"

Billy moved back to the bird bath and picked up something which had been propped there, invisible until that moment.

It was a pitchfork.

216

Holding it in both hands, he looked up again, still whistling.

A slab of orange light spilled over his figure as someone downstairs drew the living-room curtains. Karen was right; Billy was smiling. And she did not like the way he was smiling at all, or the way the orange light reflected in his eyes. Now she could hear her mother downstairs saying: "What is it, Len? Who's out there?"

And then her father, answering: "It's Billy Rifkin. What the hell . . . ?"

"Hiiiii . . ." said Billy.

Now he was walking forward, out of Karen's sight, towards the source of the light. She suddenly became aware that she was gripping Graham tightly by the arm. Downstairs, the front door opened and Karen heard mumbled voices: her father and mother. And Billy's quiet voice answering their questions.

"You're hurting my arm!" hissed Graham. "Leave me alone. I want to go downstairs and see Billy!"

"No!" said Karen. "Stay here. I don't want you to . . ."

And then someone screamed downstairs.

Karen pulled Graham close to her in terror. There was no way of telling who had screamed. Something crashed to the floor. There were the sounds of a struggle, a distant cursing and grunting. And then a dull, heavy *thumping* sound. Something else crashed, something made of glass. A man shouted—but Karen could not tell whether the voice belonged to her father or to Billy. The shout was abruptly cut off by that horrible *thumping* sound. It seemed to go on forever.

"Karen, what's . . . ?" whimpered Graham.

"Stay still and keep quiet!"

Downstairs, everything was quiet now. Karen could feel

her heart pounding; could feel Graham close to her, rigid with fear. They strained to listen for any sound. And then they heard it: a steady, muffled tread.

Someone was coming upstairs.

The sound of whistling drifted up the stairs to them; Karen hugged Graham tighter to her.

Who's afraid of the ... Big ... Bad ... Wolf? Hah, hah, hah ... not me ...

Breaking free of the paralysing terror, Karen jumped from Graham's bed, ran across the room and locked the door, backing quickly away from it.

The footsteps reached the landing outside. The whistling seemed to be mocking them.

"We've got to get out!" Karen ran back to the bed and tugged at the window sash. Graham was helping her now as the door handle began stealthily to turn.

"Come on out, kids," said the voice from behind the door. "Come on out to play. I know you're in there."

The window squeaked open as the door handle began to shake vigorously. The voice was different now: no longer sly or mocking, but full of threat: "Open the door, Graham! Come on out, you little bastards! *Come and see what Daddy's got!*" The door rattled as the man on the other side applied his shoulder.

Karen yanked the window open and grabbed Graham's wrist.

"We've got to jump to the branch!" she hissed, pointing at the elm tree limb, three feet from the window ledge.

"I don't know if I can!"

"You've got to! You go first! You've got ..."

Something howled in anger behind them and Karen turned to see the pitchfork tines stab through the panel of the door, sending splinters whirling into the room.

"Quick! *Quick!* QUICK!"

Karen flung Graham from his perch on the windowsill. He caught the limb with both arms, hugged it, swung round and started to clamber downwards. Karen climbed onto the sill as the bedroom door suddenly burst inwards with an echoing crash. Behind her, she was aware of something hurtling across the carpet towards her. And then she jumped—as something clawed at her nightdress, tearing a strip of fabric from her shoulder, raking her arm. But now the tree was rushing at her and Karen gave a short, barking cough as she landed astride the tree limb and the breath was knocked from her body. Without looking back, she started down as quickly as she could.

"Gentle Jesus, meek and mild . . . gentle Jesus, meek and mild . . ."

She could see Graham on the ground, waving frantically at her as she scrambled downwards. Twigs raked her face, her arms and legs, snagging in her hair. And from above, she was aware of a frenzied commotion: a clattering and banging on the stairs as if someone had fallen down them in his effort to get to them. Karen jumped the remaining six feet, landing beside Graham. Instinctively, she grabbed his arm again to stop him from running back into the house. It seemed quiet in there now, as if the monster had fallen and knocked himself out. She dragged Graham away.

"But I want to go in!" he protested. "I want Mum and Dad."

"No! You can't go in there . . ." *Gentle Jesus, meek and mild.* "You can't!"

They began to run across the lawn to the drive.

"Why . . . can't . . . I . . . ?" panted Graham.

"Keep *running!*"

Behind them, something screamed again. A scream that branded a red-hot poker of fear on her back as she turned to see the devil, with his pitchfork raised high, leaping from the door towards them. She turned back, yanked at Graham and yelled: "Run! Run! Run!" The shrieking thing charged after them across the lawn.

They ran into the driveway, the gravel biting into the flesh of their bare feet. Graham was running as fast as he could, but he was still too slow. Karen turned to lift him, her foot caught in the trailing hem of her nightdress and she fell heavily onto the sharp gravel. Graham tangled in her legs and sprawled headlong, gravel skinning his knees and the palms of his hands. Karen rolled round and then recoiled as the manic, grinning white face of Billy Rifkin reared above them. He whooped like a wild animal and raised the pitchfork high above his head.

But now the whooping had become the sound of a car horn blaring stridently and Billy was suddenly brightly illuminated by headlights. Karen rolled over, dragging Graham with her, as Billy half-turned in alarm to the source of the noise and light, pitchfork still held high. She heard a screeching and the loud hiss of sprayed gravel as something huge and fast exploded between them and Billy.

"Noooooo!" Billy howled.

And then there was a loud *crump* as Billy was smashed onto the bonnet of the car. It scooped him up and flung him out of sight like a broken doll as the car brakes were jammed on.

Karen fainted.

Dimly, she was aware of a car door being flung open beside her; then of strong yet gentle arms scooping her up and carrying her to the back seat of the car. She seemed

to fall asleep, and then became aware of Graham's unconscious form being laid gently beside her. She could smell
a familiar fragrance and knew the owner of that perfume.
It was Iris. She slept again, aware that Iris had gone inside
the house. When she woke again, they were driving
through the "night."

"Iris?"

"Just sleep, love. You're all right now."

"Have Mummy and Daddy gone to heaven?"

"Yes, Karen."

"And where's Billy Rifkin?"

"Gone. Vanished. Don't worry, love. He's probably gone
to the other place. He won't hurt you again."

Karen slept.

Chapter Forty-one

Grover stopped his Land-Rover on the high valley road and
climbed out. He had never seen anything like it in his life.

The rolling fog blocked the road in front of him and
stretched away on the left and right like some great grey
curtain walling in the valley—just as if someone had created a barrier to seal in the village. Overhead, the black
scudding clouds had mingled with the rising fog barrier.
Together they formed an enormous, ragged dome over
Shillingham. Grover went to meet the fog wall. To him, it
seemed almost "material," rather than a mist vapour.

Now he was standing beside the huddled forms which
had first made him stop the car. There were eight of them.

221

He knelt down and examined one of the dead sheep. There were no signs of violence, no blood or wounds. But it felt icy cold to the touch.

As if it froze to death, he thought.

He examined each of the sheep in turn. Not a mark on any of them, but all with that icy touch of death. There were birds lying around, too. Dead pigeons and sparrows littered the grass at the base of the fog wall. This was bloody stupid! In ordinary fog, you could still see ahead of you, even if only a few feet. But this fog began six feet from where he was standing and was so thick that it was impossible to see beyond it. What the hell kind of fog was it? He picked up a rock and threw it into the miasma. The rock was instantly swallowed up from sight. Why did that make him feel so uneasy?

Cursing himself for a fool, he strode forward and stepped into the fog.

Instantly he felt as if he was suffocating. The grey vapour swamped his head, tasting poisonous, burning and *thick* in his throat and nostrils. Ahead, he could see nothing; only a vast, grey plain. The fog burned his eyes. Coughing and retching, he staggered backwards into the fresh air, eyes streaming. Kneeling, he coughed out the dead smell and taste for a full two minutes before he felt better.

Now he knew what had killed the sheep and the birds. It was the fog, whatever in hell it was or wherever in hell it had come from. He had read about acid rain and factory emissions. Maybe the birdbrains had just offloaded more of their nuclear shit on the countryside.

The sound of crackling static drew his attention to the Land-Rover. He walked quickly back to the vehicle, leaned in through the driver's window and lifted the short-wave receiver.

"Rover seven. Grover here."

"Sarge? It's Adams here. Pemberton doesn't know that I'm ringing you, but I don't give a shit what he thinks, anyway."

"Why? What's happened?"

"Billy Rifkin's gone nuts. He's killed Julie and Len Haig. Iris Wooler managed to save the kids. She's here with them now."

"Christ . . ."

"And there's something else."

"Yeah."

"Frank Warwick and George Frankham."

"They're dead. I know."

"But their bodies are gone. They've been stolen from the mortuary."

Crawling through the darkness with both legs badly smashed, Billy cried like the child he had once been. Tearing at each handful of grass, grabbing at every tangled bush, he hauled himself off the roadway into the gulley which ran alongside the kids' place. Down amidst the dank, dark mess, no one could see him—not that bitch Iris, whose face he had seen stark white in the driving seat just before the car hit him. Billy had also seen a look in her face just before the impact: a look of knowledge. She knew what he was doing and what he had done.

Crawling through the muck and slime which soaked and infiltrated his shattered legs with malignant filth, he tried to get away as far as possible. When he heard the car door slam and the engine start again, he knew that he had lost her. Grinning even through his excruciating pain, he crawled hand over hand up the gulley bank, scrabbling across the road, dragging legs broken in a dozen places

223

and leaving a trail of slime and blood. He could feel something on its way. Something was coming to him. It smelt like approaching death. But Billy had to fight it! He had been given a promise.

He had to get to the crossroads. He would crawl all the way if necessary. He had fulfilled his promise three times, hadn't he? Now he could claim from the voice what was rightfully his. So the kids had got away? So what? He had got their parents, right? With his father and Sean, that made three. Crying and weeping, laughing and gurgling, he hauled himself through a hedge and up a grassed embankment.

Again, a nightmare ascent; he lay gasping for breath, the pain eating into his legs like a living cancer. "Three times . . . three times . . ."

"THREE TIMES," said a strange croaking voice from above.

Billy looked up and recognised the face looking down. There was a smile on that face. A hint of promise. In real life, he could never stand looking at the old bastard, the drunken bum, even if he had been Christy's father. But now the Wyrm was in him and everything was okay. The tall, spectral figure turned, smiled and pointed in the direction of the crossroads. Billy crawled on. Smiling again, a smile of teeth and death and madness and no eyes, the scarecrow figure lurched away into the darkness.

Billy crawled onwards.

Chapter Forty-two

Michael helped Christy on with her coat, looking outside as he buttoned his parka. "It's starting to rain."

"We *must* go and find that Book. I know it's there."

"If you say so."

"Dad said so."

The dogs had brought their own leads in their teeth from the bench and were eager to get started. Soon, everyone was kitted out and ready for their journey into Shillingham's night. The lights of the village wavered distant and fragile off to their left.

"I feel safe," said Christy.

"Yeah, they're good dogs. And they seem to like you."

"I don't mean the dogs. I mean I feel safe with you."

They pulled close and started the ascent to Split Crow Lane and the deserted Warwick farm.

Chapter Forty-three

Billy forced himself halfway through a fence and stuck there, rain lashing at his face. He twisted and felt barbed wire snare in his arm.

"Damn it!" He yanked, leaving a piece of white flesh twitching from a spike; kicked, squirmed and pushed himself upwards. Turning his head and looking down, he saw the crossroads site, the traffic barriers and the Pit.

His howl of triumph became a gargled mixture of rain, saliva, blood and pain. He rolled down the slope, lifeless legs slip-slapping in the mud and water. The impetus carried him to the foot of the slope. Even from there, he could see that the contents of the tarpaulin sack had been disgorged onto the ground. A pink, gelatinous mass was being washed clean by the rain. Billy smiled and called as he clambered towards the Pit on his elbows.

"I'm back, see? I'm back . . . just . . . like I promised."

The rain hissed angrily and splattered on the barriers and mud surrounding the Pit.

"You . . . promised . . . me . . . Three times, you said. Three times. And that's what I did."

He reached the Pit edge, ignoring the glistening pile of flesh at his shoulder. "Three times!" he shrieked into the Pit, agony racking his mind and body. The words echoed back above the hiss of the rain. "I've done it like you said! Three times. You don't have to hide any more: it's nighttime. You can come out now! Come out and give me what you promised!"

Something stirred deep within the Pit.

Billy froze, mouth open and filling with rain.

Silence.

And then, another heaving sound from deep inside the Pit.

"Yes, that's it!" chuckled Billy. "Come on out! Come out and give me what you promised." The ground beneath him heaved and he laughed aloud, ignoring the agony in his legs. A wave of noxious green gas began to spill up over the rim of the Pit. Billy coughed and wheezed, hiding his face in the mud until the worst had passed.

He looked up.

The Wyrm swarmed out of the Pit before him in a column of glutinous, swirling light and shadow; a massive pillar of energy that was neither entirely solid nor ethereal; but was nevertheless a *force*—an ancient, evil, primal force. It reared up above the Pit like some gigantic, glowing serpent. Billy recognised it as the same thing that he had seen at the car smash. It had been smaller then, much smaller. But this thing was . . . was . . .

"Bloody *gi-normous!*" hissed Billy in wonder, looking up.

Twisting and turning, writhing within itself, displaying its own unholy internal workings, the Wyrm represented no single thing ever seen on earth. But as Billy looked he could see dozens of vague things within its towering, squirming bulk. He could see half-formed faces shouting obscenities, twisted animal and human limbs—most of them decomposed—dozens of blank, emotionless eyes; a heaving, twisting mass of formless tissue: the Wyrm.

"You promised me," said Billy in a little voice.

PROMISED? said a voice in his head.

"Yeah. Look." Billy prodded the red pink mess on the rim of the Pit. It began to slide down the slope towards the bulk of the Wyrm in the Pit. "He was the second. My father was the first—you know that. And the kids' parents were . . ."

Three times, Billy, said the voice. *Ah, yes. And now you want your reward?*

"Yeah. But first you gotta heal my legs. I'm smashed up pretty bad but you can fix that, can't you?"

Yes, I can do that.

A transparent, oozing tendril descended from the bulk of the Wyrm towering over him. When it was hanging over his head, and he was beginning to feel afraid, the voice

227

inside his head said: *Reach up, Billy. Reach up and put it in your mouth.*

". . . My mouth . . . ?"

All will be well. You will be healed. And you will have everything you wanted.

"*Everything?*"

Everything.

Hesitantly, Billy leaned up and took the tapering tentacle in his hand. It was cold, covered in soil, and felt like some gigantic earthworm. The tip of the tendril was gaping wide like a mouth.

"You mean like this . . . ?"

And then the tendril whiplashed in his hands and sprang at his face. Recoiling in alarm, Billy could not prevent the slimed tentacle from shooting into his gaping mouth, squirming deep and filling his throat, burrowing like a ravenous worm into the pit of his stomach. Billy heaved and retched, grasping at the tentacle, to no avail. His eyes starting from his head, he rolled onto his back, juddering in agony. The exterior of the tentacle was now suffused with a purple-black liquid as *something* was pumped directly from the amorphous mass in the Pit directly into Billy's ravaged body.

For me, Billy, said the voice. *For me.*

The tube withdrew from Billy's swollen throat, spilling black liquid on his chin and chest. A look of horror came to his face as the tentacle retracted slowly.

"You . . . promised," he choked.

And so I did.

Billy suddenly arched in pain, looking back at his fractured legs in the rain. They were twitching and moving; no . . . they were being somehow *manipulated*, restored. They were being reset, reorganised and healed. Billy howled in pain as the manipulation grew faster. It spread to his torso and Billy could feel things going on in there, terrible, painful things that were healing him. There was no gentleness, only a voracious will that the healing be done quickly. Billy shrieked long and loud as bones were set, fractures mended, torn cartilage knitted together.

At last the pain subsided and, exhausted, he let the cool rain play on his face.

"You've healed me?" he croaked.

Yes, you can have your every wish now, Billy. But there is one codicil we did not discuss.

Billy stood up shakily, feeling his legs. They were strong and healthy. Better than they had ever been before. "Every damn thing I want!" he shouted at the top of his voice.

But for the codicil. Because what you want is what I want. We are now two flesh together, Billy. You're my first Chosen Flesh, my first Embodied, my Vanguard. So you will do my will. I will take my flesh from your form to begin the vengeance that I have promised. You will do as I say.

"Hey, wait a minute. You said . . ."

Flesh of my Flesh, Billy. You will walk in me and I in you.

"You said I could have everything."

The towering-Wyrm-thing-voice laughed. A hideous, echoing sound that seemed to emanate from deep within the Pit.

Everything I want! hissed the voice that was not a voice.

Billy whirled, holding his fists in the air.

"You promised!"

And promises are always kept, Billy. You're mine to mould now.

Billy felt it first in his hands. The fingers began to curl inwards towards the palms and he could not stop them. Then the agonising, stretching feeling in his forearms and

229

shoulders, reaching into his gut and bowels; as if everything in there was being reorganised or torn apart again.

"No . . . no . . . you promised . . . you healed me . . ."

Forces were at work within Billy and he could only gasp in agony as they made him kneel in the mud, crying out in pain at the stretching and rending in his limbs. He beat his hands against his face and chest. And then he held them before him and watched in horror and fascination as the fingers merged and squirmed into contorted black stumps, like plasticine or dripping mud. Something was moulding both hands into unrecognisable, swollen shapes. They were like spatulate claws now, with no fingers; the spatulas were curving inwards to form oval *muzzles*. His hands were turning . . . turning into *something*.

An eye opened on his left hand. And then another blinked open slowly, sleepily. Hooded, cowled eyes, burning red. Now, where the compacted fingertips had become a muzzle, the black flesh ripped open to reveal jaws, full of jagged teeth. Billy held up his other hand and saw that the process was also taking place there. Screaming in terror, agony and fear, he raised his mutating hands to the black sky.

"Dogs!" he yelled. *"Bloody dogs! My hands are fucking dogs my hands . . ."*

The emerging, contorting, canine heads were snarling and snapping savagely at him. He held them away, crying in fear. They began snarling at each other as they squirmed free and more of the devil dogs' bodies began to squeeze out painfully from the ragged shirt sleeves of Billy Rifkin's arms. Collapsing in the mud, he watched the hideous creatures sloughing off the skin of his arms, growling as they emerged. He almost fainted, and when he looked up again it was to see clawed rear legs breaking free. The things had grown during their birthing pangs to animals almost twice the size of Doberman pinschers. The two hellish black animals bounded through the darkness to the Pit barrier and the Wyrm.

"My hands!" whimpered Billy, looking at his tattered sleeves.

You gave me flesh, Billy. I return flesh to you.

And then his hands were whole again.

Now I give you something else. Something to remember.

A tendril snapped from the Pit and ripped away the front of Billy's shirt. The flesh of his chest seemed to have become transparent. He looked down at the swarming, roiling material which had been pumped into him and smiled. He was One with the Wyrm. He had been chosen because of his deeds. He was happy.

And then Billy, the boy who had loved his father and suffered the beatings; the boy who had always been misunderstood; the boy who had needed love more than anyone in Shillingham and who had come to this confrontation with an ancient terror, gave in at last and died.

The new Billy, Billy/Wyrm, Wyrm/Billy, became an absolute Oneness with the Evil from before time began. The Hellhounds, eyes blazing red, prowled back to him with their heads lowered, shaking ectoplasm from their backs. They licked his hands in obedience as the rearing, ephemeral thing in the Pit shrank in upon itself like a collapsing cloud. With eyes of an opaque green, Billy watched it disappear below ground. The Hellhounds darted from his side and fell upon the pink gelatinous mass which had fallen from the sack. Voraciously, they began to tear it apart, devouring great gobbets of flesh. Billy turned to look up at the sky. The huge dome of fog and cloud was complete: the Shillingham valley was shut off from the world.

Part Three
The Book of the Wyrm

Chapter One

The Warwick farmhouse loomed ahead as Michael and Christy climbed Split Crow Lane in darkness. Mac and Dutch prowled in the undergrowth behind them. They had been uneasy all night and Michael could not understand why. Perhaps it was the strange weather, the black storm clouds and the rolling fog barrier around the village? He found a gnarled root and used it as a walking stick as they climbed, fingering the torch in his pocket.

"You tried your best last time, Christy. What makes you think you'll find it this time—if it exists?"

Christy was pushing on slightly ahead as she answered: "The Book exists. It's in the kitchen somewhere, like Dad said."

Michael resisted the urge to say: *Maybe whatever broke in and attacked you was trying to prevent you from finding it.* It was that little voice inside, the voice that had whispered his secret fears across the years.

They reached the house. Christy struggled with her key in the makeshift door. It juddered open.

"It's like someone else's house now," she said.

"I know."

Michael heard Mac growling and turned to look back. Both dogs were prowling uneasily back and forth in the drive. Their hackles were raised. Dutch was showing his teeth.

"Come on, you two!" called Michael. But the dogs refused to come any closer to the house. "Bloody weather. Well, you can both stay out here, then." Michael turned up his collar and followed Christy through the front door. She switched on the hall light.

"Well, at least the electricity's still working."

She walked down the hallway to the kitchen door. "We'll have to rig something up for the kitchen, though . . ."

Outside, the dogs growled again.

Michael restrained Christy by placing a hand on her shoulder. "What's that?"

"It's the dogs," she replied.

"No, not that. The other noise. In the kitchen."

Christy stopped and listened, looking back quizzically at Michael; she could hear nothing.

"No, listen," he said. "I think there's someone in there."

This time they both heard the noise: the sound of something large being moved; of creaking wood and a spray of rattling rubble and plaster. Michael moved past Christy, listening at the door. Christy pushed his shoulder, prompting him into action. He shoved open the door.

It was very dark in there. Overhead the canvas which had replaced the roof rattled and furled in the wind. Debris littered the floor: wooden beams, jumbles of electrical wiring, chunks of broken plaster, ruined furniture, splintered shelving and cabinets.

And there was a man in the middle of the kitchen.

He was rummaging amidst the debris, pulling up planks from the shattered floor; a wild, dishevelled silhouette, grunting like an animal in frustration. Rummaging in the dirt beneath the floorboards, the figure gave a small cry of triumph and lifted out a dull, square object.

Michael took the torch from his pocket and shone it directly on the figure.

"Who the hell are you?"

The figure froze and then whirled towards them so that the torch beam illuminated its face.

Michael shrank back. Christy gave an involuntary cry.

The face was stark white, the lips drawn back from stained teeth in a frozen snarl. The hair was wild and matted. And the face had no eyes, only gaping blood-encrusted gaps stuffed with wads of cotton. It was an inhuman face from hell. But it was a recognisable face nonetheless.

"Welcome home," said Christy Warwick's dead father.

"Frank?" asked Michael in awe.

The ragged figure stepped forward and for the first time Michael could see the post mortem incision in its chest. It grinned again and took another step towards them, raising one withered arm in their direction.

"Come and see," it said. *"Come and see what I've got for you both."*

And then it hissed like some venomous snake and lunged forward.

Suddenly, Mac and Dutch had pushed between their legs. Hackles raised, growling low in their throats, the dogs slid into the room and stood between them, legs braced for action, lips curled back from bared fangs. The thing that had been Frank Warwick halted, raging as it surveyed the animals, hissing sibilantly. And then Frank took another step forward. Dutch bounded two feet into the kitchen, barking. Frank stopped.

"Oh my God, Michael," sobbed Christy. "It can't be Dad. He's dead."

"No, it's not your dad!" snapped Michael. "Look at it. It's something else using his body."

"Then what am I, Michael?" gurgled the thing without eyes, cocking its head to one side. The fact that it spoke Michael's name utterly horrified him. He shone the torch up and down the full length of the thing as Christy clung to his shoulder. Frank was wearing a mortuary shroud, white and flapping about his body. The blue-black stitch-work of the post mortem incision was hideously apparent.

"You talked of your fear, Michael. While you lay with my daughter, you talked of the deepest fears within you. The fears which had almost killed you."

"That's not your father talking, Christy. Don't listen to it."

"The Writer and his Philosophy of Fear. How very civilised. No such thing as the supernatural? Well, let me be your teacher, children. And you, Michael . . . " The thing laughed; a sick, unholy sound. *"I will show you what real fear is."*

Frank hissed again, a sound like death, and jerked towards them with one clawed arm outstretched.

Michael and Christy recoiled, just as Dutch bolted forward aggressively, flying directly at Frank, jaws wide and roaring. The dog went straight for Frank's throat. A metal box, tucked under one of his arms, clattered to the ground. Frank staggered backwards, clasping Dutch round the ruff of his neck, keeping the jaws from his face. Smoke seemed to seep from his grip as they whirled in a crazy dance. Dutch whimpered and was suddenly flung heavily away

238

across the kitchen like a stuffed toy. Mac flew past Michael, darting and snapping at the thing's legs as it began to hiss and roar in rage. The palms of its hands were smoking as it attempted to grab the second dog.

Michael looked down, saw the splintered spar of wood and grabbed it like a spear. Frank roared again, an inhuman, abominable sound, and lunged towards him, arms outspread, hands smoking sulphurously. Michael stepped forward and stabbed the jagged edge into Frank's midriff, knocking him back. Dutch had rejoined the attack with Mac, growling low and darting at the thing's legs, dodging with Mac the sudden lunges of those horribly steaming and dangerous hands. Frank swung towards Michael again. Michael stabbed outwards and Frank staggered on some rubble, grabbing the splintered edge of the wooden beam in both hands. In horror, Michael could see that the wood where Frank held it was blistering in the heat.

"Fear like you've never known, Lambton!" hissed the Frank-thing. *"This I promise you."*

"Run, Christy!" shouted Michael over his shoulder. But Christy was no longer behind him. She had ducked around the milling figures and now Michael could see her retrieving the metal box which Frank had dropped in the rubble. "Christy, for God's sake get back!" Frank had seen her; he swung at Mac who leaped to one side, then lunged to take Christy where she knelt. Christy jumped backwards but there was no way she could avoid those hideous hands. Mac was suddenly a blur of motion, flying through the air, landing on Frank's back; the impetus flung the thing down into the rubble. Christy screamed, scrambled to her feet and away from danger. Frank and Mac thrashed in the rubble, the dog avoiding his raking hands instinctively. The dog retreated again and Frank, hissing like a cobra, began to rise.

Michael ran forward, raised the spar like a sledgehammer and swung it in a slicing arc at Frank's head. Christy screamed again as the spar connected with Frank's throat, sending him reeling. Dutch savaged another leg and backed away. Michael grabbed Christy and pulled her to him, still holding the beam threateningly. He could see that the mane of Dutch's neck, where Frank had grabbed him, was still smoking. The fur had been scorched.

Frank rose slowly, straight and erect, a feral snarl on his face; watching them with those ragged no-eyes. Michael could sense something now and was dreadfully afraid. The thing was drawing power from somewhere as it rose. It was somehow much more powerful than it had been before; much more powerful and deadly. Frank's eyes were ragged pits into Hell; pits that could see right into their souls.

They began to back away as the Frank thing advanced steadily.

Mac and Dutch moved forward.

"No, lads! Off!"

Reluctantly, the dogs inched backwards with them to the kitchen door.

Suddenly, Frank lunged again, roaring. Michael stabbed at him and the spar shattered on his chest. The thing seized the remnant, snapped it to pieces and, grinning, threw them disdainfully away. Michael pushed Christy behind them as Frank's smouldering claws swooped towards his neck. He felt Hell breathe in his face, his will suddenly sapped by those terrible, gory eye sockets. Behind him, Christy screamed again.

Michael saw approaching death in those no-eyes.

The Ultimate Fear.

"Get out of the way!" yelled a familiar voice at Michael's right and then something knocked his paralysed body to one side as a dark figure blundered into the kitchen. Frank opened his mouth, hissed in rage and came on. Then Michael saw the twin barrels of a shotgun emerge into view. The smoking claws were reaching for them as someone pulled both triggers.

The shotgun barrel exploded in roaring orange flame, rending the darkness. Frank was suddenly gone. The dogs began barking excitedly at the sound of the blast and Michael turned to see that Grover was standing there, holding the shotgun at hip height, barrels smoking. Two police constables were behind him, wide-eyed and incredulous. Michael looked back at the kitchen: the blast had thrown Frank clean across the room, leaving him sprawled on a pile of rubble.

"I just don't believe it . . ." said Grover.

And then Frank began to clamber to his feet again, making that same malicious growling sound in his throat. His chest was shredded, the marks of the mortuary incision expunged.

"Both barrels?" Michael heard Grover ask.

Frank raised his head and came on again, growling.

Grover jerked his head backwards. "Roy! Keith!"

The kitchen was suddenly a firing range as both constables opened up with their shotguns. The blasts echoed and rang as Frank's mangled body was hurled and pitched against the walls. Grover jammed two fresh shells into the breech of his own gun, his face a mask of horror as Frank clambered to his feet yet again.

"You will die," said the thing as it rose. *"Every one. I am only a part of the whole and you cannot stop me."* It cocked its head in a mocking gesture at Michael. *"Are you fright-*

241

ened, Michael? Is this the beginning of real fear?" The thing laughed. *"You haven't yet begun to learn."*

Grover raised his gun and fired again. The shot punctured a clear hole in Frank's body; but his ravaged expression remained unchanged.

"It is just the beginning," hissed the Frank-thing. "Just the beginning." And then it began to laugh again; a liquid gurgling that sounded like blood in its lungs. Michael flinched back to protect Christy as Frank suddenly spun and raced for the far kitchen wall. Smouldering arms outstretched, he hit the ravaged boards with terrifying strength. They shattered outwards into the night. Plaster dust whirled, another roof beam crashed to the floor.

Frank Warwick, or what had once been Frank Warwick, vanished into the night.

Five frightened faces exchanged glances, looking at the heavy-duty twelve-bore shotguns as if they had been toys. Michael saw Christy's expression and comforted her immediately.

"It wasn't your father, Christy. He's dead. Whatever it was, it wasn't Frank."

Chapter Two

"So what the hell was it?" stormed Pemberton, banging his executive pen on Grover's appropriated desk. Despite the darkness outside, the clock on the wall indicated that it was early afternoon.

"It *looked* like Frank," replied Grover calmly, taking up his usual position, half-seated on the general office desk in the midst of the police station confusion. "But it wasn't him. At least, it was his body . . . but there was something else inside it, making it move around. He spoke with a different voice . . ."

"It was an evil voice," interjected Christy. "Not my father's voice at all."

"And you shot him?"

"Seven times, in all."

"With no effect?"

"None at all. It ripped him up badly . . . I'm sorry Christy . . . but it didn't stop him or slow him down."

The two police constables who had been with Grover—Roy Wallace and Keith Jones—nodded sheepishly from their corners.

Pemberton drank his coffee, walked the length of the office and back, deep in thought. He rounded on Grover. "What the hell were you doing up at the Warwick place with two of *my* constables?"

"I had a feeling that something bad was going to happen."

"Who authorised that? Did I?"

"No, but . . ."

"No, but nothing. You went up there of your own volition, without authorisation, and what's more you took firearms."

"Just as well we did. Without them . . ."

"That's not the point."

"Look, Pemberton, don't give me any more of this! There's something bad happening here and we're just running around in circles. Dead bodies all over the place, suicides, murders, those poor kids, people who should be dead but decide to go walkies. You got my report about that fog boundary surrounding the village."

Pemberton lifted a piece of paper from Grover's desk. "Radioactive waste. Acid rain. Some kind of atomic fallout. Leakage from a chemical plant."

"Have you been up there yet? There are dead birds and sheep lying about all over the place on the mountain road. They can't get through. It's killing them. And, for all I know, it might be killing people, too."

"I won't have you talking to me like that, Grover. You're out of line. I'm in charge. I know that this is your patch, but I'm the one in charge."

"Okay. So tell me what to do."

"I want you to organise search parties for Frank Warwick, PC Frankham and Billy Rifkin. They must be outside some-where . . ."

"Discreet search parties? Or can we take guns?"

"You take guns. As for the fog barrier, we haven't had any civilian reports yet, but I'm taking my team up the mountain road right now with some of the Environment people. Whatever it is, we do think it's responsible for the radio interference we've been getting."

"Interference? Haven't you been getting calls from all over Shillingham? No telephone contact with anyone out-side the valley, lines all dead. We can't get through to any-one in the outside world at all by radio. That's some interference. Expected deliveries by road into Shillingham aren't coming through. People are leaving through the fog and not coming back. No one's coming into or getting out of this valley through the fog."

"So what is it? A nuclear war? Nuclear fallout? You think everybody's dead out there?"

"That fog's not natural. We have to organise the people in Shillingham. Tell them to keep indoors, away from the fog. Check on the farmers further up the valley to see if they're okay. Bring in those people who are closest to the fog. We're talking about a twenty-mile radius."

There was a look of suffused rage in Pemberton's eyes at the attitude of the man he had been sent to supersede. Tightly, he said: "You're doing a lot of talking, Grover. But I'm in charge, in case you've forgotten. I'll take a look at this fog with the specialists. If it's dangerous, I'll radio in and you can organise the Council and begin moving the inhabitants in. If not, I'm going on to Kilgar."

"You're not running out are you?"

"I could have your job for that!"

"Then listen to me. That fog is death. I went in there. Two more minutes and I'd have been dead. You're not going to make it to Kilgar, even with the car windows rolled up."

"I'm driving up to the mountain road and, if it's okay, on to Kilgar. It's only five miles over the mountain and we can have access to their resources there. The fog—if it *is* dangerous—won't stretch that far. I want you to take charge till I get back. Find Warwick and Frankham and Billy Rifkin, Grover." Pemberton rose from the desk as Grover moved away.

"And, Grover?"

The sergeant turned back.

"I don't believe in zombies, premature burial or bizarre fucked-up situations in small rural towns. Okay?"

"If you say so," replied Grover.

Pemberton left with his back-up men.

Chapter Three

Michael, Christy and Iris Wooler had seen and heard the exchange from the interview room: its large glass window gave a good view of the entire police station. They watched as Pemberton and his men left and Grover began to issue instructions for the search party to the assembled officers. Three radio calls later, Grover and the two policemen who had accompanied him to the Warwick house the night before, entered the interview room, followed by a nervous Dr. Stark, cleaning and recleaning his spectacles.

"You heard all that, I suppose?" asked Grover.

Michael nodded. "Just what the hell is going on?"

"That word again," said Grover. "*Hell*. Why does it keep cropping up?"

"How are the children?" asked Iris.

"Sedated and in Shillingham Hospital," replied Dr. Stark. "They'll be fine." He stopped cleaning his spectacles and looked at Michael. "Mr. Lambton, I've examined your dog ... Dutch ... and ..." He cleared his throat. "Well, he's fine, but extremely dehydrated. He gobbled up two pints of water. You say that ... Frank ... grabbed his ruff?"

"Yes."

"Well, there are two clear handprints around the animal's throat, burned into the fur like a brand. It's as if blood and moisture were drawn from the dog by Frank's hands. I believe it's the manner by which Frank and PC Frankham met their deaths. Massive blood loss and dehydration."

"Sarge?" asked Keith Jones hesitantly. "Was that really Frank Warwick or . . . or what?"

Grover looked at Michael.

"No, it wasn't," replied Michael. "Frank is dead. Something was inside him, possessing him, I think . . ." He paused.

"Go on," said Grover. "I know what you're going to say, but you may as well say it anyway."

"I think he was possessed by the thing that was dug out of the crossroads. An ancient, evil thing called a Wyrm."

"Dad . . . *it* . . . was after this," said Christy, and Grover looked at the rusty-hinged box on her lap. "He told me about it before he . . . died. It was hidden under the floorboards in the kitchen. It was too deep for me when I first looked, that's why I couldn't find it."

"What is it?"

Christy opened the crumbling box and lifted out a thick and battered book, also hinged on the sides. It looked like an old family Bible, heavily embossed, scrolled and bound in black leather. She traced the ornately tooled antique gold lettering on the cover:

THE BOOK OF THE WYRM

She opened the book and read from the first page . . .

Chapter Four

Pemberton was running away.

He had tried to rationalise it all, had tried to convince himself that the necessary investigations were being carried out in the most efficient manner; that all avenues were being explored and that his instatement at Shillingham to supersede Sergeant Grover and his six constables was completely effective. He had tried to maintain this attitude as the deaths had increased. The Environment man burning to death had been one thing, but then there was the car smash, the suicide, the pitchforking of two people, that terrible *something* in the sack at the crossroads, two men with their eyes torn out in the very police station in which investigations were based—both bodies vanishing; one turning up like a zombie and surviving direct shotgun blasts like something out of a horror film. And then there was the attack on Christy Warwick by something that was most definitely not lightning and which had the power to tear a kitchen apart. Now, the claustrophobic screen of fog and cloud closing in on the village, affecting the villagers themselves. Doors were staying firmly closed, people were remaining indoors, as if they knew that something was about to happen . . . that something *was* happening.

Pemberton gripped the wheel of his car and checked the rear-view mirror; the party of dazed Environment officials who had until now remained closeted in the Dun Cow awaiting instructions . . . *any* instructions . . . was following close behind.

He had rationalised everything. Yet still he knew, deep inside, that he was running away. Something was happenning in Shillingham; something beyond his experience with which he was not equipped to deal. If the fog was poisonous—and on that score he had no cause to disagree with Grover—then he was going to roll those car windows up and make a dash for Kilgar; get out of the Shillingham valley and back to civilisation where he could put things in their proper perspective. He knew that he was not alone in this instinct. He could sense the same feeling among his colleagues in the car with him and in the car behind. They, too, wanted to get away from Shillingham; away from the terror which had suddenly descended. They wanted to leave the Shillingham people to deal with their own problems.

Pemberton looked back as the car climbed the mountain road. The entire valley seemed to be sealed in by fog and cloud. It was three in the afternoon somewhere in the outside world, but in Shillingham it was the Dead of Blackest Night. A night without a moon. They would be reaching the fog on the mountain road any minute now. No one in Pemberton's car seemed inclined to speak as they drove onwards. The headlights picked out the rough road ahead, the car turned a bend—and suddenly the fog wall was there. It stretched up the sheer cliffside on their left into impenetrable blackness, over the road before them, and veered down the steep grassed slope on their right across meadowland in a vast, grey, roiling barrier, curving away parallel to the mountain wall on the other side of the valley.

And then Pemberton saw the dead animals lying in the road at the base of the unmoving fog: sheep, foxes and rabbits, in a scattered line stretching down the valley side. He slowed the car as they drew level. Grover had been right: the fog seemed almost solid and unmoving in composition, not natural at all, holding its position like a permanent barrier. As he watched, a bird plummeted from the sky and hit the cliff-face on their left in an explosion of feathers.

He stopped the car. Behind, the car carrying the Environment men did likewise. They climbed out into the chill air. Anderson, one of the men from the Ministry, approached Pemberton.

"What now?"

Pemberton looked at the fog, not knowing what on earth they were going to do.

"The sheep. Perhaps we . . ."

"Look at that!" said someone behind him, and they all stared into the fog at the object which had appeared there.

A man was walking slowly and steadily down the road towards them, out of the fog. The indistinct silhouette began to grow clearer as it approached.

"You see!" said Pemberton, smiling. "The stuff isn't poisonous. It *can't* be poisonous."

The figure emerged spectrally from the fog, smiled, and stopped. Its hands were clasped in front of it. Pemberton recognised the face from police photo-files shown to him by Grover back at the station.

It was Billy Rifkin.

"Welcome," he said, holding his hands wide; and somehow it seemed that his voice had an echoing effect, even in the dull, flat atmosphere created by the fog.

Pemberton stepped forward, cleared his throat and said, inadequately: "You're under arrest, Rifkin."

"Am I?" smiled Billy.

The air seemed thick now. Pemberton felt something acidic biting at the back of his throat and then someone shouted: "The fog's *moving!* Look at it! It's moving!"

Tendrils of fog were sweeping towards them. The immovable barrier was now closing in on them.

And there was something else in that fog now: two indistinct figures emerging on either side of Billy Rifkin. Large, canine shapes; but much too large for dogs; more the size of pumas, surely. Pemberton saw glowing red, hellish eyes in the fog, and glinting teeth. He began to back away, coughing at the poisonous tendrils which reached out like tentacles towards the two cars.

Billy raised his hands and Pemberton, still backing away, could hear those hideous shapes at his side growling like low thunder, as he suddenly shouted: *"Ten times ten thousand agonies will I visit on you who sought to kill me but were too weak! I will taste the blood of Shillingham, taste its terror and eat its heart!"*

And then the shapes at either side of Billy lunged towards them out of the fog.

Pemberton turned and ran for his car. He could feel the sudden terror which had descended on the men. Something in Billy Rifkin's voice, something in the movement of the fog and in the deadly and terrifying speed of those horrible dark shapes had communicated instantly to all.

I've got to get to the car! Pemberton screamed in his mind, desperate breath choking in his throat as he blundered back to the vehicle. Somewhere at his left, a horrifying black shape hurtled through the air, collided with one of the Environment men and knocked him to the ground. There was a deafening growl, a ripping, a scream; and a gout of blood sprayed on Pemberton's back. He reached the car door as someone else's scream turned to a liquid gargling, wrenched it open and dived inside. As he slammed the door, one of his own men—Collins—was clambering frantically into the back. Pemberton turned on the ignition and gunned the car into life as Collins shrieked from the back seat: "For God's sake, let's get out of here!"

The car coughed as another of Pemberton's staff slammed onto the bonnet and clawed at the passenger door. His eyes were wide, staring at something Pemberton could not see as he screamed: *"Don't let it . . . !"* And then a vast black shape with eyes like lanterns hit the bonnet of the car, rocking it on its suspension. The man was suddenly swept screaming from view. Pemberton drove straight ahead at the fog. Billy Rifkin had gone. Behind, he could hear the Environment people trying to get their car started. He could hear the engine coughing and dying, coughing and dying as he floored the accelerator and plunged into the fog. There was more screaming from somewhere behind, followed by an immense crash, as if the car had been turned on its side and was now rolling across the road and down the slope.

"Inspector . . ." said Collins from the back seat, his eyes stricken with fear.

Pemberton looked at him in the rear-view mirror.

"Something's following us! For God's sake, speed up. *It's running right behind us! Faster, Inspector! For God's sake GO FASTER!"*

The man turned to look out of the rear window, just as something large and black loomed at the glass. The car rocked again. Pemberton fought to retain control of the steering wheel; and then the rear window shattered explosively as an abominable Hellhound's head crashed into the car. Collins screamed just before the jaws descended over his head. The black mass with the glowing red lantern eyes twisted its head and lunged sideways.

Collins was decapitated.

The body lurched over the front seat, arms jerking, blood spraying. Pemberton screamed, jammed into top gear and the hideous jaws were gone from the rear window.

"Please, God. Please, God. Please, God . . ."

Fog was flowing into the car from the shattered window. He could not see the road ahead, but plunged on regardless of the steep slope at his right. The headlights were virtually useless.

"Please, God. Please, God. Please, God . . ."

Somehow, he was now losing speed. Something juddered under the car and it lurched to one side, slamming him against the door. He sensed rather than saw that the car was sliding into a hole. The rear wheels were roaring, making no contact with the ground. He began to scream again, fighting for the door handle.

And then the floor of the car suddenly punched upwards beneath his feet. He looked down in terror, still yanking at the door handle as he saw four shining protuberances, like the fingers of a great fist, like the jaws of a great snake, protruding through the steel and rubber flooring. Something beneath the car had seized it in a death grip and was dragging it down. Pemberton tried to open the door, but soil was tightly packed against it now as the car slid further and further into the pit. The sides of the car began to buckle, the engine still racing and wheels spinning.

Still screaming, Pemberton was dragged down to an even blacker night than the night which had descended over Shillingham.

Chapter Five

THE BOOK OF THE WYRM

I, John Frederick Warwick, being Head of Familie Warwick, do most solomnently declar and avouch on this sixth day of November in the Year of Our Lord 1620 that the factes here attested are true factes to be most earnestly recmended by those so Chosen to Read.

Thou, who readst this, a Warwick and Head of Familie to Be, hast now assumed a great Responsibilitie for a great Secrete. This Secrete must be passed from Head of Familie to Head of Familie—man to man—since the Great Horrore in Shillingham was visited upon us, God Save Us From Sinne. The Secrete involvs Ritualls most knowingly and soberly undertaken since the great Abomination which fell upon us is it self so subject to Words of Rituall. Thou alone must Bear the Book and keep its Secrete until time cometh to passe on, ever in the happenstance that the Wyrm might one day Return. For herein are contained the Secretes & Potions & Ritualls so painfully discerned which are to be used to combat the Evil Ones most Evil Wayes. With Gods Will, these may be used to prevent it from ending what it began during the monthe of October in our own home of Shillingham, which is so sorely afflicted at this time of riting and with so many soules gone from us forever. At the proper time this Book must be entrusted by the Elder in all earnestie and carefully into the care of the next Warwick House Leader at the age of one and twenty and thereafter until the Day of Our

Lords Judgement if it be His Will that the Wyrm shall remain where we have left it. The task of recording the loathesome Horrores hath been my burden as Elder and Presente House Leader. My eldest sonne—the new House Leader within these one and sixteen years to come—will take the Burden when his time is come.

In every village of God Fearing and hard working folk there might as happens be that One Person of ill repute who shuns the communitie by virtu of the aires and vapours of a mind preoccupied with selfish and evil designes. Such a man as was one Will Baylisse, a landowner of such manner whose squanderings of wealth by desirousnesse of flesh & bad manner & attitude towards the ordinary peeple of Shillingham did result in his companie ben shunned by all decent folk. Many were known to have observed his strange behaviore & walking alone at darkest hours of night speaking aloud to the vapours of the night and conversing perchance with elementalls of which all decent persons should beware.

Be it known that in the monthe of July of this year here attested, Baylisse was partaking of work on the bank of the Shillingham River for to further the securities of certain properties pertaining to him self which rested thereon. This after much reluctance on behalf of any to work with the man as aforesaid of his countenance and manner. During such work, an accident did happen beneath the beames of a boathouse, the pressures bearing upon said beames causing they to burst and fall, throwing boathouse and sundries into River and all those working upon it [Thank God our Father that all such were saved from death or injurie]. The Falling did result upon the discoverie of one large and graven coffin being found in a pagan place beneath the ground. In disturbance, the buriall coffin was sundered and reliable persons have attested that inside the vessell werte found to be the ancient and unhallowed remains of some creature which resembled neither man nor beast. Baylisse drove all away from the scene. The boathouse fell to ruin, never to be rebuilt. Our Very Reverend Father Harold Falter was him self turned away from the House of Baylisse upon becoming alearned that Baylisse had taken to a protection of this most Odious Discoverie. The Fathers protection and guidance was treated with a scorn which enraged all.

On the August of the same year, after Baylisse had kept privvy to him self and no other, John Thompson farm la- bourer did come upon Baylisse walking the river bank and in high spirit perchance with strong drink. On this time, he did merrilie divulge to said John Thompson that he had made Acquaintance & Pact with a haint *which was now in concordance with him, seeming as it did to regard him as benefactour for freeing it from its imprisonment for centuries without number. Baylisse at once went on to tell John Thompson [who has averrd and sworne many times on our Holy Bible] that the haint which had inhabited the coffin was a Wyrm—the last of an ancient breed once numerous upon our world. Of old, the ignorante had called such as these Dragones, Ogres, Vampyres or Werewolvren. These haints were not of our worlde, but of other worldes beyond the starres. Further, that our own world—this Earth—was a crossroads in the starres; a veritable Hunting Ground for many such as they being Hunters, travelling here to feed upon that which Men possessed . . . their lives, their flesh, their blood and soules were meate and drinke to these Odi- ous Ones.*

But the presence of these hostile to menfolk on our world was dependant upon the alignments of the starres in the courses of our heavenly universe. They were ever a change. In dayes when the alignments were of good favoure, our Earth was assuaged by many Deities & Atrocities & Cratures able to ride the starres to our Earth, which was their most favorite Hunting Ground. But as the starres changed in their courses & changed over many centuries without number, the pathwayes to our worlde were lesse definit and hid. The Abominable Ones could not find us. Only those few wise enough to read the Changes were able to find us. As had the Haint of Baylisse many centuries agone which in the stead of emerging wholesome and afresh for food had mistaken its path and become buried until the river bank had fallen to reveal its presence.

And now Baylisse made it known to John Thompson that for its freedom it could give him power beyond belief, if he would but prove him self to It three times. Since its imprisonment, it had grown in strength a tenfold. Baylisse enjoined Thompson to accompany him to his dwelling place but Thompson, fearing that Baylisses designes were upon his person, fled and held his peace from the Elders, being too affeared.

Three atrocities were committed in the valley shortly thereafter, but Baylisse him self appeared above suspicion and those in authoritie were powerlesse to indicte him upon charge. But Thompson him self knew of the perpetrator in his heart. Still he witheld, but kept watch upon Baylisses movement for fear of his owne life. Hearing screams from the House of Baylisse on the night of the thrd atrocitie, Thompson observed terrible occurrences of such horror which cannot be divulged *but could now avouch to the Elders that it was the Wyrm that had taken possession of the flesh of Will Baylisse and although Will Baylisse walked . . .*

it was not he . . . but the Wyrm, which bare his flesh as a
cloak. It had embodied within him. And the two dogs which
Baylisse had kept as constant hunting companions were
also tainted with the same evil . . .

Chapter Six

PC Robby Taylor had never handled a shotgun in his life
and in normal circumstances would have felt ridiculous
stalking through the gorse bushes like some kind of Texas
Ranger. But he did not feel ridiculous tonight. *Tonight?* It
should still be bloody daytime but it might as well have
been midnight. He had not been with Grover and his other
two mates when they had come across Frank Warwick in
his mortuary shroud; but he had listened to their white-
faced accounts. Seven gunshot blasts and he had just
walked away. Now, in the dark meadows to the west of
Shillingham and with the fog barrier at his back, Robby
wondered just what the hell he would do if he came across
Frank Warwick or George Frankham. Billy Rifkin was another matter altogether; at least he was alive. And the way
Robby felt at present, Billy could have both barrels point
blank, no bother at all.

Robby stood in it before he saw it.

It was a dead sheep. And it had been mangled pretty
badly. The eyes were gone. Robby jumped back in alarm,
uttering a cry of disgust, and then called for his mates.
When no reply was forthcoming, he wiped his Wellington
boots on the grass and carried on.

He saw the second sheep well in advance, and steered

round it. Ahead of him, in a clearing, was another—and someone was bending over it. Glad of company at last in this blasted darkness, Robby strode forward.

"Enough mutton to last a year lying around here," he said.

And then the figure stood up.

Robby felt his heart freeze and his hands weld to the metal of the gun he was holding. Slowly, he raised it as the figure turned to face him.

"Hello, Robby," said the blood-smeared, eyeless face of PC George Frankham.

Surprisingly, Robby heard himself say: ". . . Hello . . ." And then, calling in the darkness in fear and alarm: "Keith! Roy! Over here!"

"Don't be frightened," said George, smiling. There was blood on his hands and mouth. Sheep's blood. *"Come here and see what I've got for you."*

Robby raised the shotgun higher. George began to walk towards him, slowly.

"Everything's all right now that you've found me, Robby. Really. It's cold out here. Come on. Take me back. Warm me." George was holding his hand out as he walked slowly towards him.

"Keep back, George. Don't come any closer."

"Come on. Don't be frightened. Keep me warm."

Robby was hypnotised by that terrible bloody face. He seemed unable to move as George reached out and took hold of the shotgun barrel.

"Don't be frightened . . ."

Robby pulled the trigger. The shotgun bucked in his hands, roaring in the night, tearing a great hole in George's chest.

George grinned.

"*Don't be frightened,*" he said again. "*Warm me.*"

Robby's shotgun fell to the grass. And as George reached to take his trembling hand, Robby, unable to move, could see that George's hands were smoking sulphurously.

When their hands touched and George was warmed, Robby's agony began.

Chapter Seven

Then Baylisse was to be seen in the highe places of the valley walking with his two dogs, now of ferocious aspect and size and with eyes that glowed like hell fire. All who did so encounter Baylisse fled and shunned him at once as he was wont to call after them or to laugh in a most dredful manner. Then the Terrour began. The Demon Dogs stalked the valley, foule consorts of the Wyrm, bent on evil destruction. And began then the sicknesse to spread throughout the district. Afirst, sheep and livestock found torn and sundered and without eyes. All landowners did suffer much losse but were sore afraid to challenge Baylisse. And then in Abomination were Jack Telfer and his familie of eight innocentes taken in a same manner. Dead & Drawn of Bloode and with eyes as plucked by Ravens. Most contagious and evil did this Odious Disease then spread. And the elders among us remembered the stories of old of those that were called Vampyres and lived upon the blood of the living. Jack Telfer and his familie did walk, taking more for their Undead Familie. The Elders amongst us who had not forgotten the Olde Wayes remembered and had the knowledge to oppose such forces. The Decree was given that the Taint must be contained to the

*valley of Shillingham and not allowed unchecked to spread
therefrom. According, every ounce of salt was procured from
every House and every Farm. And a ring of Salt—of which
the Devil him self is greatly ascairt—was placed around the
village. This ancient enemie of the Devil sealed the Evil
Wyrm and its consort Hellhounds and they could not break
out of the village. Those among us who remained, hunted
out and destroyed with the salt those poor wretches who
had become infected of this disease in Death and put their
soules to rest. Ordinary weapons were of no accord in this
respect. And we learned to our cost that aught to be touched
by a Vampyre, whther by mouthe or hand or arm or leg, then
would its victim be drained of their life. Musket balls were
loaded with salt. All were destroyed, including those of us
who had fallen victim during the search. Most terrifying of
all—the Wyrms Familiars, the Devil Dogs, were tracked and
destroyed at great cost. At their wont, they could appear and
disappear at will and the cost to us was of many lives, of
many hale and strong men ripped assunder. Rvd Falter himself [God Blesse and Preserve Him] destroyed both Abominable creatures by thrusting the image of the blessed Crucifix
into the midst of these shape-changing forms . . ."*

Chapter Eight

The telephone rang and Christy almost dropped the Book.

Grover wiped his face with a handkerchief and lifted the
receiver. No one spoke.

"It's for you," he said at last, pointing the receiver at Dr.
Stark. The doctor had been cleaning and recleaning his

spectacles throughout and now moved quickly to the telephone. Christy remained quiet while he answered.

"Robby Taylor? Oh yes, I thought you were on search patrol."

More silence, while Stark listened.

Finally, he said: "All right, I've got your address. I'll be straight across."

"PC Taylor?" asked Grover when the doctor had replaced the receiver.

"He's had an accident out on the search party. I'd better get over there and see what's the matter. Arm injury or something. Frankly . . . I don't think I'm going to be able to listen to any more of this gobbledegook. All very quaint and Olde Worlde . . ."

"Don't you recognise the similarities between what happened then and what's happening now?" asked Michael.

Stark replaced his spectacles on the bridge of his nose, took his coat from the stand and made as if to say something. Words failed him.

"I'll be back," he said at last, and left. Christy turned back to the Book.

"Shall I go on?"

Michael nodded.

Chapter Nine

But Most Terrible of All to be faced—the Wyrm it self. Taking refuge in the Village and unable for to destroy the salt barrier that we had created, it emerged in all its Horrour to take Vengeance. We who were left did flee from the village into the mountains round about the valley what time the Wyrm in its rage and in the earthley form of Will Baylisse and in still Other & More Horrendous Formes did destroy our village with flames and furie.

In the mountains our Father Falter did recall to us a man who had once been a Holy Man and who now lived as an hermit in the wild places. We knew of this man but had shunned him as it was known that he was the subject of fits and visitations. Now, to our shame, as the Wyrm destroyed Shillingham, and all within it, we implored him with the help of Our Holy Father to commune with the spirits which visited him in an attempt to destroy the Wyrm. Below us, we could see Shillingham—our beautiful Shillingham—burning.

The Old Man took upon him a trance and by the Grace of God discoverd the form of Rituall which former human opposers of the Wyrms kind had used to subdue it. In Dayes Long Gone, the power of Words was very powerful indeed and the conjuration of Wordes of Great Importance. The Rituall to overcome the Wyrm was in Two Partes. The First Part to act verily as a Lure to the Beast. Upon utterance of the First Part of the Rituall, the Wyrm must perforce return to the place of its emergence upon our world. There would it be dormant for a brief period only. The Second and Greater Part of the Rituall was thus . . . to prepare a metall made of man, a pike, or shaft which hath been bathed in the monthly blood of ten virgins. And then to Confronte the Great Beast in its Den and to impale said Monstrous Abomination with the shaft. At the point of impalement, and this Be the Most Terrible of All, the wielder of the spike must be prepared to put an ende to his olde life, and only in the shedding of his blood could the Wyrm truly be destroyed for ever. Should this latter part of the Rituall be not afollowed, then still would the Wyrm live and be free again . . .

Chapter Ten

Garth Tidyman kicked his television set. Growling, he hit the top of it with his fist, but after banging the side of the box again, he decided to give up. Ever since that bloody fog had descended, the television and radio had refused to operate. He was good with his hands, but not good enough to know what to do with all those bloody internal wires and valves. He was not much of a man for reading, so after a hard day's work, and with no wife, what the hell else was there to do?

Still grumbling, he went to fetch a beer. The horses were whinnying in the stable out at the back. Normally, he would have ignored them; but there was something about the noise which suggested that they were genuinely alarmed. Crossing to the back door, he picked up the torch from its rusted hanger on the shelf and nudged the door open. The stable was directly across the farmyard and now he could hear the horses kicking and plunging. Cursing, he picked up a sharp hoe and began to walk across the yard, breaking into a run when the horses started screaming in fear.

Before he could reach the barn, both doors suddenly burst open and one of his horses galloped out at full speed. Garth dodged in its path, trying to catch it, but it passed straight on, nostrils flaring.

"What the bloody hell . . . ?"

He stormed straight into the stable with his torch held

high. His other horse was still in its stall, but lying in the straw thrashing frantically. There was a movement on its left and Garth swung the torch over. At first, he thought that the horse had injured itself; he could see its head, squirming from side to side. But there was also something else. Something huge and black on top of the horse. Something that raked and savaged the stricken animal with blood-red claws. Something like a huge dog, but which could not possibly be a dog. Nothing so big could be a dog . . .

The Hellhound looked up, jaws dripping. The torchlight was reflected back from those hideous glowing eyes. It snarled and turned from the mutilated horse in Garth's direction.

"No . . ."

The animal slithered towards him in a stalking motion. Screaming, Garth dropped the hoe and torch and ran back towards the farmhouse. His feet pounded on the cobblestones. He could hear the rasp of the thing's breath behind him, the scrape of scythe-like claws. If only he could get to the door. Something slashed at his back. Garth felt his shirt rip apart and the agony of a deep furrow being carved between his shoulder blades. The farmhouse door loomed before him. He flung himself breathlessly through, whirled and slammed it shut. Throwing the bolt and standing back, he suddenly remembered with terror that his telephone, as well as his television, was not working. He looked round frantically for some way of protecting himself.

He was still looking when the door burst inwards, knocking him to the floor. The thing which stood astride the door tore and ripped at the wood until it reached the meat underneath.

Chapter Eleven

Doctor Stark's car pulled up in the driveway outside Robby Thompson's house. There were no lights on in the windows. He climbed out and locked the car door.

Remembering the name of Robby's wife, he called: "Sheila? Robby?" His voice had a hollow, unnatural sound. Turning up his collar at the chill in the air, he walked up to the front porch, calling again.

"Sheila? Robby?"

There was no answer. He climbed the steps, looking out across the darkened meadow beyond to the crawling fog on the valley side. Turning back again, he was suddenly startled by the sight of Sheila's shadowed face looking out at him from the screen door. She was smiling. But he could not see her eyes.

"Hello, Doctor."

He climbed the remaining steps as Sheila's face vanished into the darkness of the house. A power cut? Inside, as he passed through the screen door, only blackness.

"Problems with the lights, Sheila?"

No answer.

"Where are you?"

Still no answer.

"Where's young Robby, then? What can we do for him?"

"It's what we can do for you, Doctor," said a voice behind him. Alarmed, Stark turned to see another white, spectral face. It was Robby. And he was smiling, too. His wife's face joined him in the dark.

"What seems . . . ?" And then Robby and his wife raised their smouldering, sulphurous hands before him, stepping forward.

They had no eyes.

Stark turned and blundered towards the screen door. But something was blocking his way.

"Something for the doctor," said George Frankham, through blood-encrusted teeth.

Stark screamed.

Very soon, he was ready to make house calls.

Chapter Twelve

The First Stage of the Rituall Was Enacted and the correcte wordes were spoken. The Ravaging of Shillingham did cease as we watched from the mountains and the Olde Man gave unto us assurance that the Wyrm had returned to its place of emergence, bound by the very power of the Wordes uttered. We decended again to the ruins of our homes, being particular of the Old Mans Words that the Wyrm would remain dormant for a short time onely. In the ruins of Patrick Shars blacksmithe did we forge a metall spike to the requirement. In chaste and Holy Rituall did the menfolk withdraw while the blood of ten virgins was taken by our Father and anointed upon the spike. The Deed completed, we returned to the river bank whence the Wyrm had first emerged upon us. The Pagan place had been sealed by Baylisse, but in no short time, we had broken down the barriers thus erected and there in that most Foule & Hideous Place did we discover the coffin. And within that coffin, did find the bloated and possessed Will Baylisse himself; corrupt and filled with the essence of the Wyrm. The Spike was prepared and with great strength driven and hammered into that Most Vile Pressence as it lay abloated with the lives of so many in its keeping. I, John Warwick, the Magistrate and Zachary Mirdstone were the wielders of spike and hammer. But still did the Hideous Thing live on, smiling at us even though still dormant. None of us, no not one had the courage to fulfill the Second Part of the Rituall, by giving of our owne life to secure the Death of the Wyrm. The Sun had fallen low in the sky and we were avised that the Wyrm would soon be free from its bounds to the First Part of the Rituall. We removed the coffin and took it to the crossroads at Split Crowe Lane. The crossroads gibbet was removed and a pit was dug beneath of great depth. Another hewn stone coffin was prepared and the bodie of Baylisse, the Living Wyrm, layd within. And then, in accord with what we had learnd and seen with our own eyes, was the coffin filled with salt—the Devils Bane. The coffin was lowerd into the Pit, a large wooden shaft having been prepared, all survivours of Shillingham working with all strengthe. This shaft was refitted to the gibbet and the base of the shaft enjoined to the spike in the Hideous Abomination within the coffin. Using hoists and pulleyes, the gibbet shaft was fitted to the spike and the shaft anchored with great care and severitie to the sides of the Pit. The Old Man, now Blessed by Our Holy Father, had avised us that the Wyrm would be bound by the same fate of emerging suicides and vampyres buried at crossroads to remain there unknowing which road to take and remaining for ever trapped there so long as the crossroads should remain unviolated and offerings of Earth and Sea and Fire be given on every second Sabbath eve. The Pit was filled and the Unholy Wyrm was left there, God Willing, for ever. We *had failed. The Second Stage of the Rituall had not been completed and the Wyrm remained undestroyed. But although not destroyed, it would be sealed for ever in the Pit, as long as the gibbet and the spike were never removed. Bound by our strategie, the Wyrm must staye there.*

Chapter Thirteen

Mrs. Garvanter sipped at her Ovaltine, put her book down on the bedside table and reached for the bottle of iron tablets. She took two. So much had happened in Shillingham in so little time; it was too much for her nerves. Frank Warwick! He had been the reason for the distress which had driven her to her sick-bed. All that disturbance at the public meetings about the removal of the crossroads. All that personal abuse just because she was a good fund organiser and able to do something to preserve a little of Shillingham's heritage. They were not going to destroy the gibbet, just remove it, treat it scientifically and restore it for display in a proper museum.

And then that business down at the crossroads site itself had been the final straw. The man had gone absolutely berserk with a *gun* of all things. He had tried to shoot her! One of the most outstanding ladies in Shillingham's social circle! It had come as no surprise that Warwick had somehow subsequently died in mysterious circumstances. Whatever had happened, he had clearly brought it upon himself . . .

Something scratched at the french windows.

Mrs. Garvanter listened and heard the sound again.

Minutes previously, she had let her poodle out into the garden to do its business, but Pinto did not usually come back so quickly. She eased her bulk out of the bed and crossed the plush pile carpet to the french windows. She pulled a curtain to one side and looked out into the darkness. She had puzzled about that darkness earlier but had sensibly attributed it to an eclipse or something.

There was nothing to be seen outside.

"Pinto!" she called to the dog. But there was no response.

Something dark moved on her left.

Mrs. Garvanter turned, smiling.

Her smile became a grimace when the spectral white face of Frank Warwick stepped into the light. He was holding the limp poodle in smoking hands.

And then the grimace of fear became a scream as something huge and black, with blood-red eyes and flashing teeth, crashed bodily through the french windows, hurling her back into the bedroom.

Chapter Fourteen

But three families remained. All Others were dead and the village of Shillingham sorely damaged. To avoid being shunned by decent Christian folk, the Elders of each Familie averred to keep the Secrete of our encounter with the Wyrm. We loved our homes, even though great Terrour had Visited there, and were of a Mind to Rebuild again. Moreover, there would be a need we knew, to keep watch over the Buriall Place of the Wyrm and ensure that None should so tamper with the site as to allow for its Release. The Wielder of the

Spike, I, John Warwick, was chosen as the Keeper of the Secrete and in accordance have I committed all that happened to The Book of the Wyrm. *This Book and Secrete shall pass to my sonne Joseph and henceforth to all Heads of Household down the years for ever.*

Now all that remains is to give the Rituall to be employed in all earnestnesse should the Abomination ever emerge upon us again. And the words are thus. [Remembering at All Times that the Words are Rituall & that the Wyrm is bound by powers we do not understand to obey this Rituall.]

FIRST To draw the Wyrm to the place of its emergence, the following wordes must be spoken: Narlatonep ad minesrale por verminus necroplenet naa hadlagorg.

SECOND The Wielder of the Spike which hath been bathed in the blood of ten virgins must saye these wordes in the Wyrm's presence: Omini Chraston Perdolchey ad Iminis Vermini. *And at that moment of saying, The Wielder must strike first the blow that will ende his olde life, and as that blood is shed, then must be deliver the Death Blow to the Wyrm, which bound by the Rituall of Wordes must perish.*

Where we failed in our fear, may God preserve those whose task it may be in yrs to come to face the Abomination and by Faith and Courage overcome it.

God Deliver us from the Wyrm.

Chapter Fifteen

Christy closed the Book, resting her hand on the ancient bindings.

"Well, what do we make of that?" she asked.

"We've seen what happened to your father, Christy," said Michael. "I think we have to take the whole thing seriously if we're going to come out of this alive." He looked at Grover for his reaction.

"It's a nightmare," the sergeant replied. "And I wish I wasn't living it, but I agree with you."

"Poor Dad." Christy stroked the Book. "All those years. Now I know why he wanted a son so much instead of me. All his agonising and raging about the crossroads gibbet. And he was right! All the time he was right. Now he's dead . . . part of the Wyrm."

Michael looked at the two white-faced constables. They were standing uneasily in the corner of the interview room, unsure where to look. He turned to Grover.

"What now?" he asked.

"Well, if we assume that this is all *real*—the deaths, Frank and George Frankham, Elphick—and don't spend any time arguing about the whys and wherefores, we've got to take the warnings seriously and get people in Shillingham organised. If it's not too late. Frank and the others are out there somewhere—and even Billy Rifkin, for all we know—spreading this *plague* just as it happened before. How far can it spread before we . . . ?" Grover paused for a second, stared at the telephone and then ran a hand through his hair in that familiar gesture of unease. "I don't know why, but I've got a bad feeling about that last telephone call for Dr. Stark."

His words hung heavily and brooding in the air.

He strode to the telephone, dialled and waited.

Eventually, there was a click at the other end of the line as someone picked up the receiver.

"Robby?" asked Grover.

"I'm waiting for you, Sergeant," said a voice thick with blood at the other end. *"Come and warm me."*

Grover slammed the receiver down.

"It's spreading," he said.

Iris had been sitting quietly, wringing her hands in her lap. She spoke now.

"Billy Rifkin."

Everyone turned to look at her, waiting for her to continue. At last, she said: "I don't know why, but I can sense that he has something to do with it. That Book said the Wyrm 'embodied' in the man called Will Baylisse. I think it's done exactly the same thing in Billy."

"How the hell do we start preparing for this thing?" asked Grover, fear and doubt eating at his soul. "A salt barrier around the town?"

"There's already a barrier around the town," said Michael. "Don't you see? The people of Shillingham once sealed it in. Now it's sealed *us* in. We can't get out . . ."

"What was that?" Christy was on her feet, looking down at the floorboards. "I thought I felt something."

Outside, in the Land-Rover parked in the police station forecourt, Dutch and Mac began to bark frantically. Michael again experienced that sudden sick feeling of fear that he had experienced when the Frank-thing had attacked them back at the cottage. The air was electric with an imminent *something*.

"*Something's happening*," he said, moving to Christy.

They became aware that something large and unseen was padding up the stone steps leading to the station entrance. It began to prowl around the front of the station, snuffling at the windows. Mac and Dutch continued to bark hysterically and now it became apparent that there was more than one thing out there. Michael and Grover exchanged glances. "Something's out there, Grover. It wants to get in."

"Roy! Keith! Lock the doors and windows!"

The Sergeant and his constables quickly moved round the room, checking locks and latches and closing window blinds. Grover had a glimpse of unnaturally large, glowing red eyes in the darkness outside just before he pulled down the last blind.

"What the hell . . . ?"

Heavy, padded footsteps sounded back and forth in the station porch, like lions stalking back and forth in their cages.

"What about the back?" hissed Michael, pointing to the cell corridor.

"It's locked," replied Keith.

Something growled and clawed at the outer door. Steam began to curl underneath the door as Grover backed away.

"What the hell *are* they?" asked Roy.

Again, in her quiet voice, Iris answered: "God protect us, I think they're what's mentioned in that horrible Book. I think they're Hellhounds."

Another low and menacing growl, this time from beside a window. Grover knew that any large animal intent on

getting to them would certainly not be stopped by that fragile glass.

"Shotguns!" he hissed, and was joined by Michael and
the two constables at a large glass cabinet in the far corner
of the room. He fumbled with some keys and the case
rattled open.

Something scratched at one of the windows, long and
squealing; a single claw on glass.

Grover gave a gun to each man and began handing out
boxes of cartridges. Somewhere in Michael's mind was a
crazy, unbidden thought. They were the besieged cowboys, handing out firearms while the Indians crouched outside, waiting to attack. But they were not cowboys, they
were ordinary, everyday people in an, until now, ordinary
sleepy village in the Border country. And what prowled
and clawed outside was infinitely worse and more hellish
than any Apache.

"Michael," said Christy as he came over to her, snapping
open the shotgun breech and jamming in two shells. "I can
feel something else. Something beneath . . ."

Iris screamed, jumping away from her seat as one of the
windows suddenly exploded inwards; shards of glass sliced
through the air. Large, inhuman claws raked at the window
sills and tangled in the plastic windowblinds.

Michael and Grover fired simultaneously, shredding the
blinds. The claws appeared unharmed, raking and scrabbling in a frenzy, tearing out chunks of masonry as the two
constables also opened fire. Glowing eyes and red breath
reflected in the blazing bursts of flame from the guns. Michael and Grover prepared to fire again.

And then the floorboards erupted beneath their feet in
a sudden bulking heave of rending, splintering wood and
exploding timber. The lights went out and the air was filled

with a black howling and shrieking as the police station floor caved in.

Grover tumbled backwards over his desk, his gun discharging into the ceiling. Michael was lifted and flung headlong against a filing cabinet; he lay there stunned as the sounds of exploding hell and chaos rang in his ears.

He pulled himself up, coughing and retching in the dust-filled atmosphere. Fanning the air with his hand, he saw what had happened. There was a gaping hole in the centre of the floor as if something huge had burrowed up beneath them and burst through the floorboards. Iris was holding her head, standing dangerously close to the splintered edge of the hole. Michael moved forward, but Christy was there before him, grabbing Iris by the arm and guiding her over to the far corner, away from the ragged hole and shattered windows. The raking claws had withdrawn from the windowblinds. Silence had fallen and dust swirled choking in the throat of the pit before them.

"Grover!" called Michael.

"I'm here!" The sergeant emerged from behind his overturned desk, limping. And then, shouting for the others: "Keith! Roy!"

Roy, his uniform torn, scrambled from the rim of the pit, helping a plaster-powdered Keith to his feet. As they moved, Roy suddenly pointed down into the hole.

Something had moved in the depths.

Now they could all see some kind of light down there, a swirling, purple light. And even as they watched, pressed up hard against the wall, the coiling, phosphorescent light was rising from the pit.

Something was coming up.

A shifting, insubstantial column of blue-black smoke was rising. But this was more than smoke. It was alive. Contorting, writhing and squirming, yet still indistinct, the pillar of undulating substance blossomed and rose from the jagged hole, lighting the interior of the ruined police station. A bulging spherical shape began to emerge from the top of the column, which now reared fifteen feet into the station. The shape contorted, wriggled and features gradually became apparent: an evil, grinning face; bloated, repellant and, although now inhuman, instantly recognisable nevertheless.

"Billy Rifkin," whispered Christy.

The face began to laugh; wild, ringing peals of derisory laughter.

" 'For God did not give us the spirit of fear, but of peace and love and of a sound mind,' " quoted Iris.

The thing laughed again, its face shifting and blurring like rippling clay, oozing and reforming into its original shape.

"Oh, my God . . ." Keith swung up his shotgun in disgust and fired. The shot punctured the torso of the swirling shape, which was instantly refilled by more twisting ectoplasm. The Billy-thing laughed again.

"*Once,*" said the Wyrm, "*this village sought to destroy me. And, pathetic creatures though they were, it was in their power to do so. But their hearts were weak and their fear of me was great—as it is with you. Now, I will have Vengeance. Once, they sealed me within this village with an accursed substance. And now, I have sealed this village from the outside world with a power of my own. I have created a barrier which cannot be breached.*"

"Maybe Pemberton and the others got through . . ." whispered Grover to Michael.

The Wyrm laughed again; a malignant, deeply hostile noise.

"You believe you have a saviour, Prefect?" said the thing. *"Here, let me show you the fruits of his endeavours."*

Something gobbled and squirmed in the twisting mass of the Wyrm; an obscene orifice emerged, puckered and *spat!*

Christy leaped aside with a shriek as something flew outwards and rolled bouncing to their feet.

"Behold your saviour," said the Wyrm.

"Oh, my God!" said Christy, standing back.

Pemberton's severed and eyeless head lay at their feet, teeth clenched.

"And now," continued the abomination, *"I will bring Hell on Earth here to Shillingham. The means of my returning from this Feeding Ground have changed and gone during my centuries of imprisonment. Therefore I must stay. And in retribution I will make a Hell here of my own. All will die. Fear and Death will be my Cup of Vengeance. And when you have all supped of that Cup, then I will emerge from my cocoon in Shillingham. For then, my strength will have no limits and I will spread beyond my barrier to turn your entire World into my Hell. I have told you this because I want your fear and terror to be all the greater and my Cup of Vengeance will be all the Sweeter."*

The Wyrm was silent now, the blue, swirling, inchoate mass shifting and coiling in the centre of the pit. At the apex, Billy's swollen head contorted into another grin; there was movement at the side of the mass and a half-formed, spectral arm emerged slowly. It pointed to the outer doors.

"Now . . . leave . . ." said the Wyrm. *"Leave and await the ultimate Terror—my Blood Children."*

Cautiously, throat dry with fear, Grover moved round to the left and the others followed, picking their way over broken furniture. The hideous Billy-Wyrm eyes followed them all the way.

"Those things outside," whispered Roy. "How do we know they're not waiting for us?"

"We don't," replied Michael.

They reached the outer doors. Grover unlocked them and stepped carefully outside. The shattered window blinds rattled in the night air. But there was no sign of the things that had been stalking around the police station. As they moved quickly down the stone staircase and into the forecourt where the two police Land-Rovers were parked, Michael noticed that the brickwork of the station walls and the heavy wooden door bore deep scratch marks. The car on the right contained Dutch and Mac in the fold-down, still barking and howling with all their strength.

"We've got to get to . . ." began Grover as they moved.

And then something sounding like a pride of lions bellowed in rage behind them. They spun round as two hideously black and deadly forms slithered round the sides of the building to converge at the top of the station steps. The glowing blue light through the opened doors silhouetted the gigantic canine forms sitting motionless, like the megalithic statues of some obscene and forgotten museum; red eyes blazing, steam rising around their heads.

Behind the hounds, a familiar revolting voice, the Master of the Hellhounds, hissed: *"Something to remember me by!"* And, with guttural snarlings, the two Hellhounds leaped down the steps towards them.

The first Beast sprang at Grover. He ducked, pulling Iris to the ground as the animal flew over him. It landed on the first car roof, scrabbling for purchase before rebounding to the other side of the car. The second Hellhound slid like some gigantic puma down the steps and off to the right towards Michael, Christy and Keith as Roy dashed across the intervening gap between the two cars to Grover and Iris, juggling frantically with the keys of the Land-Rover. Grover and Iris joined him just as the first Beast came over the hood of the Land-Rover at them. Grover levelled the shotgun and fired at the creature. The impact flung it away, its claws tearing ragged gashes in the hood as it went.

The second animal pounced at Michael.

"Look out, Michael!" screamed Christy. Michael turned, firing both barrels at the Hellhound. The Beast twisted caterwauling in the air and was flung back to the station steps. Keith had the car doors open now and pushed Michael and Christy into the back of the Land-Rover. He looked back, shotgun crooked in one arm to see where the thing had gone as the other Land-Rover roared out of the forecourt. The Hellhound that had attacked Grover was loping hellishly straight across the forecourt in his direction, eyes glaring, jaws slavering. Half-in, half-out of the car, Keith twisted the shotgun in the crook of his arm and fired straight into the thing's face. It reared on its hind legs, clawing backwards.

"Let's get out of here, *now!*" shouted Michael from the back seat, above the enraged sounds of Mac and Dutch.

And then something hit the roof of the car, rocking the suspension. Through the rear window Christy caught a glimpse of the second Hellhound bounding across the roof. In the front seat, Keith screamed as an outstretched claw hooked over the rim of the driver's door and plunged into his eye sockets, gripping deep. The shotgun discharged again and Keith, screaming in agony, was hauled kicking from his seat and up over the rim of the car.

"Michael, help him!"

"It's too late!"

Keith was gone, dragged backwards out of his seat and onto the car roof, legs kicking spasmodically, his screams silenced. The thing was feeding; blood ran down the windscreen in rivulets.

"There's nothing we can do!" Michael leaped from the back into the driving seat, slammed the door and turned the ignition keys, stamping on the accelerator. The Land-Rover screeched out of the forecourt, Dutch and Mac howling wildly. Christy twisted round to see the Hellhound flailing from the roof of the car with Keith's head in its jaws, his body bouncing on the tarmac. As the Land-Rover screeched away, she watched as the other Hellhound ran to join its companion. Together, they dismembered Keith's body.

Grim-faced, Michael was watching through the rearview mirror as they raced away. He heard Christy's gasp as the Devil Dogs bounded up the police station steps and back through the door into the source of the swirling blue light.

Just ahead, Grover's Land-Rover skidded and veered crazily past the Dun Cow. Michael looked ahead and swerved wide as well when he saw what Grover had been trying to avoid. Three people had emerged from the pub and had staggered into the Land-Rover's path, arms waving. Michael just had time to see their stark, white faces and terrible bloody eye sockets before he flashed past. Behind them, something crashed.

"Michael!" cried Christy. "The police station!"

Looking through the rearview mirror again, he saw the police station roof caving in. The walls were crumbling and disintegrating inwards towards the pulsing blue light. With a great roar, masonry and timber was splitting and cracking, tumbling in upon itself. As he watched, he had a hideous mental image of some gigantic trapdoor spider pulling its prey down into its underground nest. A great cloud of dust and debris obscured the building.

But the devastation was not confined to the police station.

Ahead, Michael saw Grover waving to the left, warning him to avoid the road into the village centre and turn off up the mountain road.

"Oh, my God . . ." Now he could see why.

The spire on the council offices was toppling into the village square, the walls of the building itself shaking and cracking, emitting clouds of dust. With a great crash, the spire demolished the war memorial and pulverised several cars in the square. The building's stained glass windows exploded as the roof and walls began to cave inwards. People were running through the market square as shop windows shattered, chimneys toppled and crumbling roofs shook off their slates. All around was the nightmare earthquake sound of destruction as the two Land-Rovers roared up the mountain road away from the village. Michael could feel the tremors beneath the car and fought to maintain control of the steering wheel.

Christy's eyes were riveted on the village as they climbed. The roofs of every building in sight—shops, houses and office buildings—were crumbling and collapsing, burying people beneath the rubble as they ran. Somewhere deep within the village something exploded, sending a mushroom ball of oily orange flame into the air. The cobbled streets were undulating and heaving beneath the feet of scrambling villagers as if something was moving beneath them. Flame roared and spread as the supermarket blew apart. Clouds of dust and flame belched skywards.

"It's been *tunnelling*," said Michael from the front seat.

"Under the village. The foundations of everything in the
village are caving in . . ."

Christy fought down the urge for tears as she looked back
again. Even from here, she could hear the screaming above
the sounds of crashing, roaring masonry, splintering timber
and exploding gas mains. Water mains were erupting from
the streets, pumping up jets of water. She saw a car bounce
crazily through the air like a child's toy and then explode
like a bomb. All was flame and belching smoke down in
Shillingham as the two cars turned a bend in the mountain
road and the village was momentarily lost to sight. The
dogs had been strangely quiet after the attack of the Hellhounds. Christy suddenly realised that her knuckles were
bleeding. She had been punching *The Book of the Wyrm*,
which was clamped tightly in her lap.

Chapter Sixteen

They stood together watching from a pockmarked knoll off
the mountain road as Shillingham underwent its death
throes. The explosions had ceased now, and although no
details of the village could be seen other than the occasional skeletal finger of brickwork or crumbled wall
through the flames and belching smoke, they knew that no
building had been left standing. The orange-yellow flames
of destruction were reflected in the roiling black clouds
overhead.

The Land-Rovers were parked together, twenty feet away
from the fog wall. They had driven as far as possible and
could go no further. Dutch and Mac prowled around the

cars, grunting their own warnings at the barrier itself, know-ing instinctively of its threat, nudging the dead birds and rodents which lay scattered at its perimeter.

"All those people," said Iris.

White-faced, Grover grunted and turned away, heading for the fog barrier behind the Land-Rovers.

Looking down on Shillingham, Roy said: "What the hell kind of thing can *do* that, for Christ's sake?"

"God and Christ are the only ones who can help us," said Iris quietly. "Don't take their names in vain, Roy."

"There may still be people alive," said Michael. "In the farms and the cottages on the mountain slopes and the outskirts."

"If they haven't been . . ." Christy struggled to find the word, ". . . *contaminated* by the Wyrm yet. Turned into those horrible . . . things. Or killed by those Devil Dogs."

Behind them, Grover suddenly cried out in pain.

They turned quickly to see him staggering back from the fog wall, clutching his right hand. Michael ran to him.

"It's okay, okay," said Grover, rubbing his hand. The fin-gers were blue and discoloured. To Michael, it looked like frostbite.

"What happened?"

"I reached out and *touched* the fog wall. I don't believe it, but the bloody thing is solid, like ice."

Michael looked at the fog barrier; grey, unyielding and, yes, looking somehow like a solid mass. He stooped, picked up a stone and pitched it at the wall.

The stone struck the barrier and bounced off.

Stunned, Michael exchanged a glance with Grover and leaned against the Land-Rover hood.

"It's a cocoon," said Grover. "Just like that thing said. It's sealed off the entire Shillingham valley in a bloody impenetrable cocoon."

"What the hell are we going to do?"

"That word again," said Grover. "And now I know why it kept cropping up. *That's* hell, down there." He pointed to Shillingham. "Just like the Wyrm said."

He rubbed his hand again, joining Michael to lean against the Land-Rover.

"And I'll tell you what we're going to do. We're going to fight back. We're going to use Christy's Book. And, somehow . . . we're going to fight back."

Chapter Seventeen

The Land-Rovers turned into the small drive of the farm they had passed on their way up the mountain road. It had looked deserted then and looked even more so now, when they climbed out and moved towards the main gate. Michael kept the dogs firmly at heel as they walked; they were both clearly wary of the place. There was no sign of life—animal or human or *inhuman*—as Christy opened the gate and they crossed a cobbled forecourt to the main building.

"This is Garth Tidyman's place," said Grover, holding his shotgun defensively, even though he had seen its lack of effect so far on anything that had threatened them.

On their left, they could see a ramshackle barn. The doors were open, but they were disinclined to venture inside.

"Look." Christy pointed to the cobblestone yard between the barn and the farmhouse. Even in the unnatural darkness created by the Wyrm, it was still possible to see that there were pools of dark red and partly congealed blood on the cobblestones.

The front door of the cottage had been burst in, hinges torn from the surrounding brickwork, and then apparently ripped apart. *It's been clawed to pieces*, thought Christy as Roy and Grover kicked the shattered remnants of the door aside and entered the cottage cautiously.

"Come on," beckoned Grover to the others. "But be careful where you stand. There's blood all over the place."

Inside, the living-room was small. Table, chairs, sofa and television set all somehow looked ridiculously normal.

"We'd better check the rooms in case any of those *things* are around," said Michael.

Roy pushed the kitchen door aside with his foot and walked in, shotgun ready. Grover checked the main bedroom while Michael looked inside the second bedroom. The farmhouse was empty. When Michael returned to the living-room, Iris was holding Christy in a comforting, motherly embrace. It somehow looked the most natural reaction he had ever seen. Grover had joined Roy in the kitchen. Michael patted both women on the shoulder before moving into the kitchen to find them rummaging through cupboards and drawers.

"What are you doing?"

"Rock salt," replied Grover, sweeping a shelf of condiments to the floor. "We're looking for rock salt."

"What the hell for?"

"You heard what was written in that Book of Christy's. Salt is one way of protecting yourself against these horrors, like that old guy said."

"But how . . . ?" began Michael.

"There's some ordinary salt here," said Roy, holding up a salt box and cellar.

"That's no good. We need rock salt. Crystals." Grover turned back to Michael. "I've got an idea, Lambton. It may help, God willing. Better start looking yourself."

For five minutes, they pulled out every drawer and the contents of every cupboard before Grover himself found a small sack of ordinary rock salt on the kitchen floor, wedged between potato and turnip sacks.

"This is it. Now, let's see if it works."

Christy suddenly burst into the kitchen, breathless.

"Michael! Sergeant Grover! Someone's coming up the mountain road."

They followed Christy out into the yard and walked across to the Land-Rovers. Dutch and Mac ran ahead, growling. Michael called them back. Below and beyond, Shillingham was still burning, lighting up the dome of thick black cloud overhead and the dense grey barrier behind. The occasional flare of flame silhouetted the three silent figures staggering slowly up the mountain road towards them.

Christy moved forward, beckoning. "They're survivors. We've got to help . . ."

Michael caught her arm. "No, they're not. They're . . ."

". . . a part of the Wyrm," Grover completed. "They're infected. Look at them."

And now Christy could see the terrible blank white faces and the gouged red eye sockets. She could see the hands smoking sulphurously as they moved ever nearer.

"They've seen us," said Iris.

"Inside! Quick!" Grover bundled them back into the cottage, darting into the kitchen to retrieve the bag of rock salt and a small pair of pliers from one of the drawers.

Michael and Roy upended the living-room table and jammed it into the shattered doorway. The spectral figures—two men and a woman—were slowly turning towards the farmhouse from the mountain road.

Grover opened the breech of his shotgun, took out the two shells inside and another from his pocket and dropped the weapon on the floor. Opening the bag of rock salt, he scattered its contents onto the small telephone table beside the sofa, retrieved the pliers from his pocket and prised off the crimped ends from the tops of the shells.

"What the hell are you doing, Sarge?" asked Roy, raising his shotgun over the edge of the upturned table towards the approaching figures outside. They were staggering closer. "I'm doing what the Book says!" Grover removed the shot from the shells, took several pinches of the rock salt grains and poured them into the resulting cavity, pushing the substance firmly down with his finger. "It said salt was the means of killing these things."

"Then hurry up!" exclaimed Roy. "Because they're almost into the drive and they know where we are!" In fear, he swung his shotgun up and fired. Christy cupped her ears at the terrible blast.

One of the approaching men staggered aside, regained his balance and came on.

Grover recapped the shells carefully with the pliers, pinching down the crimped ends again.

"Hurry up!" shouted Christy as Michael raised his shotgun and fired at the woman. The noise was ear-shattering in the close confines of the cottage living-room.

The woman took the blast directly across the torso. Michael saw the scattered shot mutilate her patterned dress. But she still came on.

Grover jammed the shells into the breech of his gun and

shouldered his way to the barricaded door-frame. He snapped the gun shut and aimed as the three figures reached the Land-Rovers, staggered round them and clawed through the farm gate towards the cottage.

"Shoot, for God's sake!" exclaimed Roy.

"I can't. Not yet." Grover's voice was firm and low. "It has to be short range or the heat of the blast on the shell will incinerate the rock crystal before it reaches the target. That's why ordinary salt wasn't any good."

"I hope you're right," said Michael, as one of the men raised his smoking hands and staggered grinning across the farmyard towards them.

When the man was only twenty feet away from the cottage door, Grover slowly squeezed the trigger. The shotgun barrel blazed orange flame and hit the man squarely in the torso. His shirt flew apart. The effect was instantaneous. The thing screeched, hugging its middle. It staggered, raising its terrible eyeless face to them in the darkness, and howled; an inhuman, bellowing sound of pain. Dropping to its knees, the thing coughed blood and keeled over to one side, lying still. The other two figures had remained motionless throughout.

"Good for *you*, Sergeant Grover!" exclaimed Iris, slapping his shoulder. And now Grover had swung the shotgun to his left over the edge of the table and fired again. Christy looked away in horror as the woman's head disintegrated and the decapitated, twitching body was flung back into the mud. It was dead.

The remaining man was backing away now, raising a ragged arm and pointing at them as Grover ejected the spent shells and rammed his remaining salt-loaded cartridge into the shotgun.

An inhuman voice issued from the mouth of the thing

as it retreated; it was a voice they had heard before: the Voice of the Wyrm.

"You have only killed two parts of me, you fools! But there are many parts to my whole. You will all die! All of you!"

"Shoot the damned thing!" exclaimed Roy.

"It's too late," replied Grover. "It's out of range. The shell wouldn't have any effect."

"I grow stronger by the moment!" howled the thing as it retreated into the darkness down the mountain road. *"You will sup my Cup of Vengeance as have the others. You will sup . . ."*

It vanished into the night.

"Give me your cartridge boxes," said Grover. "I've got work to do on those shells. No telling how many of those things are wandering around in the dark." He took the cartridge boxes from Michael and Roy, emptying them with his own onto the telephone table. He took out the pliers and began work again.

"What are we going to do now?" asked Christy.

"Well, I don't know what Grover thinks," said Michael. "But it might be an idea to drive round the valley rim checking out the 'fog' barrier. It might not be as impenetrable as the thing wants us to think."

"You think so?" said Grover, without looking up from his work as he prised open another cartridge, jamming salt crystals into the casing.

"What other alternative do you suggest?"

"No, don't get me wrong. I think it's the best idea at the moment. There may be a chance. But I think that deep down you feel the same way as me—that the barrier *is* impenetrable. And that sooner or later we're going to have to use that Book and face the thing head on."

Roy looked back from the barricaded door in alarm.

"You mean going back down into Shillingham?"

"It may be our only chance," said Michael. "We'd better face the fact."

"Just the five of us . . . against *that!*"

Iris took Roy by the arm and fixed him with an intent look that Christy recognised of old. "We're not alone. This thing is evil and we're fighting it. The very fact that we're fighting it means we have God on our side."

"God may well have abandoned Shillingham, Iris," said Grover, still working. "We're not in the real world any more. We're in Hell. A Hell of the Wyrm's own making, as it said."

"Are you speaking as a Christian or an atheist?" asked Iris.

Grover looked up. "As an agnostic."

His words had been automatic. They were now followed by a thoughtful, puzzled expression as Iris continued.

"All you've seen, all you've experienced . . . and you're still agnostic."

"I've seen death and horror and things that are inhuman and abnormal; men and women who should be dead but aren't; things that . . . if the Book is right . . . aren't even from this world. A thing that uses us as food. Does that prove that there's a God, Iris? If it does, then I've seen little evidence of His work in this valley."

"You've seen greater powers at work. Powers that transcend the natural . . . *supernatural* powers. But they're evil powers, Sergeant. Powers of a very great and hideous Evil. The earth, the universe, the heavens couldn't exist if there wasn't any balance to that kind of power, don't you see that? There must be *other* powers. Powers that work to the ultimate Good, powers that would oppose the thing that we're faced with now."

"You're quite a philosopher," said Grover.

"It's more than philosophy, Sergeant. It's a faith. And calling on that Higher Power is the only thing that will stop this . . . this Wyrm, and get us out of the valley safely."

"Then pray for us, Iris. Pray very hard. We've got twenty-three cartridges loaded with salt and a battered old Book with Rituals to fight the Wyrm . . . as long as one of us is prepared to offer his or her own life in the process. We're going to need all the help we can get."

"Believe, Sergeant. Believe. 'According to your faith, be it unto you.' "

"Time to go," said Grover.

Chapter Eighteen

The Land-Rovers crawled slowly back down the mountain road, headlights picking out the rutted track littered with dead birds, rabbits and other wildlife which had come into contact with the fog barrier. The barrier itself glowed dull and grey on their right; rearing high into the sky, joining with the swirling black clouds overhead. Grover had taken the lead, with Roy and Iris in his Land-Rover. Michael and Christy followed behind in the second, with the two dogs in the back. Dutch had acquired a new colour to the ruff around his neck; a streaked white mantle where Frank Warwick had grabbed him round the throat. Christy ruffled the dog's mane as they continued their descent.

"Do you remember back at the house when Dad . . . that thing . . . attacked us?" she asked.

"Yes. Why?"

"It knew that you were a writer; knew about your preoccupation with 'fear.' And then it made that awful threat about showing you real fear."

"Yes, I remember that."

"How did it know that you were a writer? How did it know that you'd had a problem with fear?"

"I've been thinking about that. I think that the Wyrm must have a slight telepathic ability. It used that to scare me . . ."

"And did it scare you?"

"What do you think? But Christy . . ." Michael paused. "Something very strange has happened to me since this terrible business started. I told you that I'd been debilitated by fear after my breakdown, unable to write. Well, I'm able to write again, thanks to you. But since the horror began, that old fear has gone. Don't get me wrong. I'm just as terrified of this thing as you are. And all I want is for the nightmare to end and for us all to get away safely. But the old fear, the fear that was eating me up inside—the fear of my own making—has been displaced. It's stopped eating me. Because now we're faced with a real Fear that we have to face and physically overcome. It's a greater and more dangerous Fear than before, but even though I'm still afraid—for me and for you—I'm going to face it and fight it in a way that I wasn't able to fight that fear of my own making." Michael uttered a sound of disgust, and slapped the steering wheel. "I'm sorry, Christy. Talking about myself and my own selfish fears. I'm sorry. But I have to face and kill this thing, for more than one reason."

"We're fighting it together," said Christy.

The Land-Rovers had almost descended to the foot of the mountain road again when Grover's car, in the lead, screeched to a halt and Iris climbed out. Michael pulled in behind, rolling down the window as she ran to the car.

There was a strong smell of acrid smoke on the night air.

"Look! Over there!" Iris almost shouted. Michael and Christy followed her pointing finger across the shrouded valley to where the mountain road rose again past Split Crow Lane. On the left, Shillingham still burned, its skeletal, smoke-shrouded ruins erupting in orange-black clouds of devouring flame. But on the right, higher up the valley and beyond, they saw what had caused her so much excitement.

"The hospital!" exclaimed Christy.

The hospital building still appeared to be perfectly intact on the ridge almost overlooking the burning village. Beyond the environs of the village itself, it seemed to have missed the ravages of the Wyrm. Lights were clearly visible in some of the windows.

"The children!" said Iris. "Don't you see? Karen and Graham—and all the others in there. They might still be alive."

"If the *infection* hasn't reached there already," said Michael. "But you're right. We have to find out."

Iris rejoined Grover in the Land-Rover and the two cars continued at top speed down towards Split Crow crossroads.

Christy's attention was riveted on the crossroads site as they approached. The contractor's barrier was still there, surrounding the Pit where the Wyrm had first been unearthed. She thought of the mornings on her way to work when she had found her father's "offerings" at the foot of the gibbet. And then of the fresh, crisp mornings when she had walked past that place looking forward to passing Split Crow Farm and waving at the strange, new person who lived there. There had been a special magic to those times. And then, when Michael had emerged from his self-imposed shell, the prospect of a new, good life. A life with someone who could appreciate her for herself. Shillingham had no longer seemed such a prison to her. Now, it was a literal prison for them all, with the fog/ice barrier all around the valley and a ravaging horror within.

Michael kept an eye on the devastated village on their left as they drove, looking for any sign of life among the burning ruins. The dogs made low, rumbling noises in their throats. But the village seemed dead, the only movement being billowing flame and smoke. He had seen something like it before. He searched his memory as they passed and then found it. It looked like one of Gustav Doré's paintings of mediaeval Hell, or a literal Dante's Inferno. The Wyrm really had turned Shillingham into its own Hell.

They swept past the crossroads and the outskirts of the village, and took the mountain road towards the distant ridge where the hospital overlooked Shillingham.

Michael found himself continually looking in the rear-view mirror, as if expecting something to emerge from the blackened ruins of the village and follow them up towards the hospital. There *were* lights in some of the windows. Perhaps the Wyrm might see them at any time, turn from its ravaging of Shillingham and suddenly surge up the mountain road towards them, spreading its death and disease.

After what seemed an interminable drive, they reached the hospital grounds. Michael was aware that he was soaked in sweat as the Land-Rovers screeched through the wrought-iron gates and began the ascent of the long gravelled drive towards the main entrance. Some of the single-storied building's windows had been shattered, but the main entrance lights were still burning, as were some of the ward lights off to the side. Grover stopped at the main entrance. Michael pulled in behind him, conscious of a terrible weariness.

"It's so quiet," said Christy as they stopped.

In the other Land-Rover, unknown to Michael and Christy, Grover said: "Quiet as the grave."

They climbed out, looking back apprehensively at Shillingham. Michael walked over to Grover.

"We'll check out the hospital," said Grover, "and then carry on to examine the fog wall around the valley, as you said. There might be a break in it. Who knows?"

Michael walked back to the Land-Rover, opened the back door and released the dogs. Mac and Dutch began prowling the grounds, sniffing at the abnormal scents in the air.

"The dogs . . . ?" began Christy.

"They can scent it," said Michael. "I think they can scent the Wyrm. We should be glad they're here, I think."

They stood for three full minutes outside the main entrance, the dull yellow light silhouetting their figures, but no one emerged to greet them.

Eventually, Grover sighed. "Come on, we've *got* to go in."

Together, they climbed the steps, Michael and Christy keeping the dogs on a firm leash and watching their reactions as Roy opened the glass reception doors and they moved inside. The reception area was empty, and ahead of them a corridor stretched away, dimly lit, into the heart of the hospital.

"Surely someone would have seen us or be around somewhere," said Christy.

Dutch *gruffed* deep in his throat and strained towards the corridor.

Fighting his instinctive reluctance to break the uncanny silence, Grover stepped forward, levelled the shotgun at hip height, and called: "Hello! Anybody here?" His words echoed to nothingness down the corridor. The wall lights flickered and Grover wondered how he would react if they all suddenly went out.

They continued down the corridor, walking lightly, afraid of the clattering echoes of their steps on the linoleum-tiled floor. Michael and Roy checked the offices and wards on either side as they passed. They were all empty.

"It's like the bloody *Marie Celeste*," said Roy.

"There should be more than a hundred and fifty patients in here," continued Grover, licking his lips again as the corridor lights continued to flicker. "And all these beds are empty. Where would one hundred and fifty sick people go?"

Ahead, they could see the glass double doors leading into the main men's ward. Beyond, there seemed to be less illumination than in the corridor; only a dull, somehow mocking, yellow light shone back at them through the glass. Michael checked the dogs. They were still straining ahead, but now he wondered whether they were doing so because there was no threat from the Wyrm or whether they knew that it lay ahead and they were anxious to attack. Their instincts now seemed less comforting than they had when they first entered the building.

"I'm for going back," said Roy. "There's something about the place I don't like. It's all too . . . too bloody easy. Like a . . ."

". . . trap," finished Christy.

"But the children . . ." began Iris.

Angry at his fear, Grover kicked open the glass double doors and moved into the ward. Michael and Roy followed close behind. Iris held the doors while Christy struggled to restrain Mac on his lead.

"I knew it," said Grover.

"It's been here and taken everyone," said Michael. "They're probably all wandering around outside in the night somewhere."

The ward had been devastated. And the marks of that devastation were strikingly similar to the destruction wrought on the police station earlier that day. Something had erupted through the floor, scattering beds in all directions, and the beds now lay tangled and enmeshed amidst the surrounding debris. The floorboards had been ripped apart from below, jagged spikes still jutting from around the edges of the hole like broken teeth. The windows were shattered, and the smell of burning was overpowering. Smoke was also rising from the pit in the centre of the ward. There was a great black stain on the ceiling above the hole in the floor.

And then Grover saw the children.

"My God, Lambton. Look! I don't believe it."

Michael looked and could see nothing. Grover grabbed his arm and pointed as the others joined them.

On the far side of the gaping hole in the centre of the ward, sitting on a bed clasped in each other's arms, were Graham and Karen. They were dreadfully afraid and silent.

"Karen! Graham!" shouted Iris in joy, rushing forward. Michael stopped her.

"This is all too . . . too easy, Iris. We came here on the off-chance that the kids would still be alive. Everyone else is gone . . . probably dead . . . and they're sitting there, almost waiting for us."

"Like bait," said Grover.

"It's a trap, just like I said." Roy was turning from side to side as he walked, keeping his shotgun raised.

"Karen!" called Iris again.

"Help us, Iris," said Karen in a small voice. "They've been keeping us here . . ."

"And we want to go *home!*" wailed Graham, clinging tightly to his sister.

"They?" said Roy, and the word seemed to lodge in his throat like thick phlegm as a figure suddenly emerged from behind an upturned bed on the far side of the gaping pit, directly beside the children. The figure was dressed in pyjamas. It strode stiffly to the children's bed, turned from them and faced the others.

It had no eyes. Smoke curled from its fingertips.

"The children wanted you so much . . ." said the dead man, in the voice of the Wyrm.

". . . and you so wanted the children," said the same voice from the ragged mouth of a blood-soaked eyeless woman in a nightdress as she emerged from behind a cabinet on their right.

"I knew that you would have to come," continued the Wyrm, this time from a small boy in patterned pyjamas as he crawled from beneath a bed.

Michael turned to look back down the corridor.

From every room they had passed and had known to be empty, a dead patient was emerging, feet dragging, nightwear torn and bloody, eye sockets empty yet staring. They began shambling towards the ward, each body a part of the abominable Wyrm.

"I told you!" screamed Roy. "I knew it!" Whirling, he levelled his shotgun and fired twice in rapid succession down the corridor. Remnants of glass in the shattered window-frames crashed loose as three of the approaching vampyres fell backwards. A fourth clutched at its blasted arm and bounced from the wall against its oncoming companions before finally falling to the floor.

The Wyrm laughed. And its hideous laughter issued from the mouths of every dead thing that came towards them.

"The children!" screamed Iris.

The vampyre that had first spoken to them in that terrible voice was grinning and reaching across to take Karen's arm. Karen was shrinking away from it, clutching at Graham.

"Shoot it!" shouted Christy.

"I can't!" replied Grover. "I'll hit the kids."

Michael fumbled at the dogs' leads, releasing the clasps. "Mac! Dutch!" he snapped. "Get 'im!"

The two dogs raced across the ward floor. Mac hurtled over the pit, jaws clamping on the descending arm. Dutch came round the outside, leaped upwards and hit the thing squarely in the back. The vampyre and the two dogs flailed backwards away from the children in a blur of motion. Grover fired two precise shots at the woman and the child in the ward. The woman whirled backwards and crashed through a window. The boy rolled squirming back beneath the bed. Michael raced ahead towards the pit. The dogs had backed away from the thing now—Dutch had learned his lesson from the last time—and were feinting snarling lunges at the vampyre as it began to regain its feet.

"Run!" shouted Michael, aware that Christy was at his side. "Run!"

Karen and Graham leaped from the torn bed as the thing reached out again with that terrible smoking hand. Michael shouted: "No!" and pulled the trigger. The thing's arm blew off. Hugging its severed stump, it curled up and died for the second time. The children ran sobbing around the pit into Christy's arms as Roy fired another two rounds into the crowd shambling towards them down the corridor.

"Back off!" shouted Grover, jamming fresh shells into his shotgun. "Keep moving back. These shells aren't going to last forever."

Iris moved to help Christy with the children as Grover and Roy backed away from the ward doors towards Michael at the rim of the pit. Michael called the dogs to heel, jamming a fresh shell into his shotgun breech. Christy looked over her shoulder down the ward, away from the approaching horde. The way appeared clear.

"Come on," she said. "Let's move."

The shattered doors juddered open and the staggering crowd entered: old and young, male and female, some of the patients hobbling and trailing loosened bandages from their arms and legs, like some travesty of the old Mummy films with Lon Chaney.

"*You can . . .*" said a woman.

"*. . . never escape,*" said an old man.

Grover fired. Both the vampyres went down. Again that abominable laughter issuing from every one of the approaching things. Michael skirted the edge of the pit, nervously watching the broken windows for any sign of movement. Roy fired again. The glass doors blew apart. Several of the things groped at their faces, blasted with salt. Roy laughed; a dry, brittle sound, turned to Grover . . . and then screamed in agony.

Shocked, Grover recoiled. There was a look of mortal fear and pain in Roy's eyes as he stared at Grover. But nothing anywhere near seemed to be harming him. Slowly, Roy looked down and Grover followed his gaze. What he saw filled him with horror.

A smoking hand had appeared over the rim of the pit, groping at the edge to join the other hand—which had fastened on Roy's ankle. Smoke curled around his leg as the thing below began to drain his body. Horrified, Grover stepped quickly forward, raising his shotgun as a blood-streaked, eyeless face appeared over the rim.

"Look out, Sergeant Grover!" warned Iris.

Grover looked over his shoulder and saw a blur of motion behind him. He twisted to see a straggle-haired young woman, face a mask of blood, mouth wide and leering, rushing at him with her deadly hands outstretched. Grover dropped to his knee and fired. The blast halted the thing's advance, flinging it back towards its companions.

"*Sarge!*" screamed Roy, and the sergeant turned furiously back, in time to see his colleague tottering on the rim of the pit as a second white hand fastened on his leg. He made a grab as Roy tried to manipulate the shotgun downwards at the thing. He saw Roy's wild, frightened eyes and knew . . . knew that both of them *knew* it was too late.

Roy screamed and jerked sideways on the edge. Still clutching his shotgun, he fell twisting into the pit.

Grover ran to the edge, crying out Roy's name. He could see nothing but blackness. The thing had gone down with him.

The sound of Michael's shotgun brought him back to their immediate danger. He turned to see that two of the things had fallen to their knees, coughing blood. But the horde was close, much too close. They had to get out of the hospital. Grover ran to join the others as they moved quickly away down the ward towards another set of double glass doors leading to the next ward.

"Roy?" asked Michael grimly, eyes still fixed on the approaching, shambling vampyres.

"Gone," replied Grover.

"God protect us." Iris was crying now as they hurried on,

pointing ahead at the glass doors before them.

The doors were clattering open.

Another crowd of the undead things which had once been patients was pushing through to them from the next ward.

"They're behind us and in front of us." Karen pulled Graham to her. "They'll never let us out."

"Oh, my God . . ." said Grover as the further horde blundered towards them. He fired, both barrels. The glass doors blew apart and half a dozen of the things squirmed away in agony. Michael fired once while Grover frantically reloaded. A young intern flew away backwards.

"*All will die in Shillingham . . .*" said the voice of the Wyrm from a nurse.

". *. . none shall escape,*" continued an old man, trailing a drip bottle which dangled from his arm.

"*This is my Cup of Vengeance . . .*": a young girl, still clutching a teddy bear.

". *. . which the whole of your world will eventually taste*": a naked young man, fresh from surgery, his abdomen pinned open by surgical clamps.

They backed away from the new assault, halting when they saw how close the first horde of vampyres had approached.

"What are we . . . ?" asked Iris desperately.

And then Michael saw the store-room door just ahead on the right.

"Over there!"

Grover followed his glance, saw the door and bustled the others towards it. Firing two shots at two of the things which were nearing the door, Michael ran to it and wrenched at the handle. It was unlocked.

"Inside! Quick!"

They bundled quickly through the door into the store-room. The key was still in the lock on the other side. Grover fiercely slammed it shut as Michael twisted the key and pulled it out. The room was small, perhaps eight feet square, filled with shelves of arch-lever files and cardboard boxes. There was hardly room to move. But there was one possibility of escape: a small window, three feet square, above a filing cabinet. The fires of burning Shillingham reflected in the glass. Michael almost tripped over Dutch as Grover and he, having arrived at the same idea simultaneously, grabbed either side of the cabinet and began pushing it out of the way. The dogs were howling at the door now, while Iris and Christy, protectively sheltering the children, huddled in a corner, as the first assault on the store-room began. Dozens of smoking, sulphurous hands thundered on the wooden panels.

The store-room window was four feet from the ground. Grover pushed a smaller cabinet over onto its side to act as a "step" up while Michael finished pushing the larger cabinet out of the way.

Karen shrieked as a smoking, white hand punched a hole through the door and began groping at the woodwork. Mac leaped at it, snapping, removing a finger and spitting it out on the floor. It lay there, squirming. Another hand smashed through the door, and then another—and another.

Grover stepped up to the store-room window. Hefting the stock of his shotgun, he jabbed at the glass, shattering it outwards. He kept jabbing until all the glass had been removed.

The door hinges began to screech under the repeated attack from outside. A smouldering hand pulled out a section of panelling and a hissing white face appeared in the gap. Michael swung his shotgun stock backwards in the same motion as Grover, jabbing at the face.

"None shall escape . . ." it said.

". . . not one," said another hissing voice of the Wyrm from an invisible assailant beyond the door.

"Up!" snapped Grover, and Iris pushed Karen and Graham towards him. In one swift movement, he grabbed Graham and swung him up to the window. "Out!" And Graham was gone, scrambling through the gap. Michael continued to jab at the hissing faces and the terrible, smouldering hands, knowing that a shotgun blast would only serve to weaken or destroy the door altogether.

Karen was next and, as Grover seized her, she wrapped her arms around his neck and kissed him on the cheek.

"Thank you, Sergeant."

Grover looked at her—a split-second only—but her expression could never be forgotten.

Karen scrambled through the ragged gap.

"You next!" said Christy to Iris.

"No. You!" Iris returned.

"One of you!" shouted Grover. "Now!"

Christy shoved Iris into his arms. Grover grabbed her foot as she stepped upwards and heaved her to the window. Christy grabbed the other foot and pushed. Iris grunted and began to squirm through the broken window, Karen and Graham pulling at her arms.

With a resounding crash, the upper panelling of the door split apart. Hands clawed inwards, eyeless faces thrust forwards, shrieking and spitting. Michael recoiled, flipped the shotgun round and aimed high at the scrabbling, threatening mass of bodies. He pulled the trigger. The resultant blast blew the mass away from the gap in the door. He looked back. Iris's feet were vanishing through the window.

Mac growled low in his throat as another blood-streaked face appeared in the gap.

"*You will not . . .*" said the Wyrm.

Mac drew back on his haunches, growling . . . and then flew at the door.

"Mac! No!" shouted Michael.

But it was too late. Mac cleared the gap in the door, legs kicking as he fastened on the hissing face and scrabbled through to the other side.

"Mac! Mac!"

Michael heard the snarlings, growlings and hissings of a terrible struggle going on beyond the door. Grover grabbed Christy's arm and hauled her towards the window. Dutch made a dash for the door. Michael caught him by the collar, restraining him from his attempt to join Mac. Christy began squeezing out, Grover ignoring her sobbing entreaties to Michael to get out. Dutch was howling as the sounds of Mac's yelping reached their ears.

Mac was silent now. Gone.

And more faces were appearing at the gap in the door.

"You bastard!" Michael fired the shotgun from under the crook of his arm; the recoil hurled both himself and the dog backwards as two inhuman faces disintegrated. Christy was out and Grover had seized Dutch's collar, pulling the dog away as Michael dug into his pocket for more shells. There were three. The doorframe was beginning to splinter. He snapped open the breech and jammed two shells in as the door finally began to judder open. Outside, the Wyrm was laughing hideously in dozens of voices.

Grover heaved and Dutch streaked through the window, back legs kicking.

Michael fired once more, clearing the gap in the door of

vampyres, and was ready to fire again when Grover seized his collar and yanked him backwards.

"Your turn," said the Sergeant calmly.

"But . . ."

"Buts come later. Just get out!"

Iris and Christy had thrust their arms through the window. Michael pushed his shotgun upwards, Christy caught it and pulled it outside. And now Michael had leapt up to the window, launching himself from the filing cabinet "step" into the waiting arms. They dragged him clear into the night air; it was thick with the smell of dead and burning Shillingham.

Michael whirled back to the window, feet crunching on broken glass, as a shotgun blast reverberated from the store-room.

Grover's face was at the window now as he hurled his shotgun at them. His arms reached out for help. Michael grabbed them and hauled.

And then Grover hissed in pain, looking up into Michael's eyes.

I don't think so," he said plainly.

Two smoking, sulphurous hands appeared on either side of his head, curling inwards towards his face. They clamped over his eyes, pulling him back.

"*Oh, God, no!*" shouted Christy, rushing to grab one of Grover's arms.

"*Kill it!*" hissed Grover in agony as clouds of smoke began to wreathe his face and head. "Get away, Michael. And make . . . sure . . . you . . . KILL . . . IT!"

The hands yanked his head backwards. Grover was torn from their grasp, back into the store-room, amidst the frenzy of hissing, garbled voices which were all one voice: the Voice of the Wyrm.

Michael hesitated and then, knowing that Grover was beyond help, shouted: "Run!"

They ran through the unnatural night, round the side of the hospital. They kept clear of the windows, expecting the vampyric horde to emerge at any moment. But there was no sign of pursuit as they reached the gravel car park at the front of the building where the two Land-Rovers were parked. In moments, they had reached their own car. Iris pushed the children and Dutch into the back as Michael and Christy jumped into the front seats. Michael gunned the engine into life and began to reverse away from the hospital entrance.

Dutch barked, rearing on his hind legs and bracing his front legs on top of the front seats beside Christy. Christy looked up and saw.

There was a blur of motion behind the glass double doors of the hospital as something hurtled down the corridor in their direction: a black blur which suddenly hit the doors head-on and exploded through them like a projectile in a glittering cloud of shattered, whirling glass.

Michael looked up in alarm and the engine stalled as the Hellhound landed on the steps, shaking shards of glass from its hideous black mane like water as its hell-red eyes turned towards them. Black thunder rumbled in its throat, steam curled from its nostrils and maw as it watched them. Michael started the car again, cursing. He could see light glinting on the thing's demonic, dripping teeth. Dutch began to bark again, loud and challenging in the close confines of the Land-Rover.

The Devil Dog launched itself from the steps, gigantic and abominably fast.

Michael slammed the gears into first and twisted the

steering wheel to the right, aware that the huge black monster on their left was almost upon them.

"It's too late!" shouted Christy, twisting sideways in her seat as the thing launched itself through the air again, landing with a scrabbling crash on the hood of the car. Black and gigantic, its claws punctured the metal of the hood to find purchase. Its hellish head turned to glare, snarling at them through the windscreen—only inches away. There was death in its eyes, hideous red death, as it jerked forwards and impacted the windscreen with its jaws. Glass cobwebs streaked in all directions from the blow.

Michael slammed on the brakes, attempting to dislodge it. The Devil Dog's claws ripped great scars in the hood as it slid away. But now it was scrabbling forward again, lunging towards them, ready to shatter the windscreen and drag their bodies out into the night.

Michael raised the shotgun from his knees; face white, teeth gritted. He pulled the trigger—and the hammer fell on an empty chamber.

"Michael!" screamed Christy, as the ravening hellish jaws lunged at the cobwebbed windscreen.

The second barrel discharged in a roaring blast, blowing out the windscreen directly into the thing's gaping throat. The great beast reared backwards on the hood, front claws slashing at the air. A bellowing, screaming noise filled the air. Blood vomited from its mouth, but now the blood was smoke—thick, black, blossoming smoke. The thing seemed transparent, its body merging and blending with the cloud of poisonous smoke which erupted through the shattered windscreen and into the Land-Rover. It bellowed in agony again, its body hissing into a screaming dissolution of boiling black vapour. Michael dropped the shotgun across Christy's knees as they choked and gagged for air, floored the accelerator and the Land-Rover roared on through the poisonous cloud until it swirled away behind them.

They hurtled down the gravel drive.

Michael had a fleeting image of shapes emerging from the shattered hospital doors as the car screeched past the wrought-iron gates and turned left, following the mountain road away from the hospital, from Shillingham . . . and from Hell.

Chapter Nineteen

Three miles later, on the other side of the valley and with Shillingham still burning deep below on their left, the fog barrier remained as impenetrable as Michael had feared. They drove in shocked silence, anxious eyes looking for any break in the solid expanse of grey.

Grover was our strength, thought Michael. *Now that he's gone, what are we going to do?* He could not rid himself of that last horrifying image of Grover as those terrible hands had clamped on his face.

On their right, they passed St. Peter's Church. The fog barrier had fallen directly across it, so that the west door, windows and gables still protruded into the churchyard. The rest of the church remained hidden in a vast grey-white iceberg. Michael remembered Iris's conversation with Grover about the existence of a God.

If there is a God, the Sergeant had said, *then I've seen little evidence of His work in this valley*.

Beyond the church, the road wound round to their right.

There's no way out of this valley, thought Michael.

And then Christy said, in a very quiet voice:

"Stop the car, Michael."

There were people ahead, crowding the road. A milling throng of shambling figures like a host of refugees, young and old, blood-smeared and eyeless. Groping and reaching out towards them, the figures began to speak when they "saw" the Land-Rover. It was a wordless babble of noise; a wailing of souls tormented in Hell. But these citizens of Hell were the citizens of Shillingham.

Michael slammed on the brakes. The nearest of the figures was fifty feet away. The babble of sound from the host of vampyres filled the dead night air as he began to execute a frantic three-point turn.

"How many cartridges do we have left?" asked Christy.

Michael tugged frantically at the wheel. "How many are there in Grover's shotgun?"

Christy snapped open the breech on her lap. "One."

"That's how many we've got left."

The babble of noise had focused now into one voice. It was a voice which issued from all the undead mouths in a chanting roar as Michael swerved round to the left and the Land-Rover sped back the way they had come.

"All will die," said the voice of the Wyrm, *"and when all are dead, then will I emerge from my cocoon in Shillingham. Then will I extend my Hell to the rest of your world."*

The crowd vanished behind them. The night air whipped at their faces through the shattered windscreen as they drove.

"Will they get us, Mr. Lambton?" asked Graham.

"No," replied Michael, thinking of the single cartridge left in the shotgun and wondering if one shot could end two small, innocent lives. "They won't get us. I won't let them."

St Peter's churchyard flashed past them on the left.

"That's where I heard the voice from the ground talking to Billy Rifkin," said Graham. "But it wasn't a nice voice after all, was it, Karen?"

Karen hugged her brother close, unable to find any words. Dutch pushed forwards and licked her face, making her want to cry. But she was the oldest and she couldn't let her brother down by giving in to tears.

"Oh, my God . . ." Michael floored the brake and the Land-Rover screeched to a halt again.

"What?" asked Christy.

Michael pointed down the winding valley road which led back to the hospital and thence down past Shillingham.

Another crowd of milling, shambling figures was moving up the road towards them, perhaps two miles away. The flickering flames of Shillingham stained those figures bloodred as they advanced. Christy remembered the hospital and how they had been trapped in the ward between two shambling hordes of death. The same thing was happening again. No matter where they ran, there was nowhere to hide. The Wyrm was going to find them. There was nowhere else to go. The fog barrier stretched like a vast sheet of ice to the black clouds above; on their right, only the cliff-face sloping downwards into the valley below.

"There's nowhere else to go," she heard herself echo.

"Just one place," said Iris from the back seat. "The church. That's all we can do."

A perfect place to die, thought Michael. He turned the Land-Rover.

Minutes later, the churchyard loomed on their right again. The Land-Rover turned into the main gates, drove past the gravestones and up to the west door. A great grey cathedral of ice lay across the building. Stained glass windows depicting wistful saints looked out like sad eyes over the burning valley. Ragged shadows danced and wavered over the grey stone columns and porch as they climbed wearily out of the Land-Rover. Michael took the shotgun from Christy and returned Karen's shadow of a smile.

With a feeling of utter helplessness, he examined the solidified fog barrier around the church. It was as solid and unyielding as ever. Dutch prowled the drive, ears flattened and slinking low to the ground. The dog could sense the approaching horde.

Christy leaned against a gravestone, reading the inscription: *"Rest in Peace."* It seemed like a sick, mocking joke. Iris was suddenly at her side, placing a motherly hand on her shoulder and reading her mind again, as only Iris could.

"We're a family now, Christy." She pulled her close. "When we were all apart—you and Michael, the children . . . and me . . . we were all lost. Sad and lost. Missing something from our lives we could never find. Now that we're together, we're a *new* family. At least we'll die together that way. You know that we're going to die, don't you? There's no use believing anything else."

"I know it," said Christy.

"Love is stronger than anything, Christy. Stronger than life or death . . . stronger than the hideous thing that came out of the crossroads. And as long as you believe that . . ."

"Christy!"

They turned at the sound of Karen's voice.

The children were standing in the church porch. Graham had opened the door and was peering inside. Karen began waving frantically as Michael came hurrying to join the children. Christy and Iris followed suit.

313

Graham swung the door wide open as the adults reached the porch. "Look!"

Inside the darkened church, Christy saw rows of oak pews on the right and left of the main aisle. Beyond lay the choir stalls and the altar, draped with a red satin cloth. And beyond that, set into the furthest wall over eighty feet away, were two tall stained glass windows with a mansized silver cross standing on a ledge between them.

Sunlight was streaming through both windows in shafts of blazing yellow onto the church floor.

" 'And a little child shall lead them,' " said Iris and moved into the church.

"I don't believe it . . ." said Michael in awe, pushing past them and running ahead down the aisle, footsteps ringing and echoing on the marble floor.

Still puzzled, the events of the last few hours impeding her thoughts, Christy was asking: "What? *What?*" as Iris pushed them all inside the church.

Michael reached the far wall, spun round in front of the altar examining his surroundings, and raced back towards them, shouting as he came.

"Don't you see? The fog barrier has fallen over the church roof, but it can't penetrate *inside!* The barrier's at its thinnest here and *that* . . ." he pointed back at the high, sunlit windows, ". . . is the outside world. This church is like a tunnel through the barrier. And that's how we're going to get out."

Overhead, the roof beams of the church groaned and cracked as if in response to his words. Michael stopped and looked up. "But I don't know how long it will be before the barrier breaks through."

Outside, Dutch began to bark.

Iris swung back to the west door and saw the first congregating, shambling mass of the undead approaching the graveyard entrance. "They're coming . . ."

"Inside!" shouted Michael. "If the fog barrier couldn't break through into the church, maybe they can't get in here either." He called Dutch inside and slammed the door as Iris and Christy ushered the children away down the aisle towards the altar.

Running back with Dutch to join them, Michael looked round desperately for something they could use as a ladder to reach the stained glass windows. There was nothing. He thought of dragging out a pew and standing it up against the wall. But the pews were cemented in place, as was the altar table.

Christy saw the steps first. They led downwards on the left of the altar and ended at a great oak door studded with iron bolts and hinges.

"That's it!" Michael dropped his shotgun on the altar, jumped down the steps and threw himself at the door, yanking at the iron ring which served as a handle.

It was locked.

He kicked at the lock, pulling again. But the door remained firmly shut.

Overhead, something cracked in the rafters. Dust began to fall in grey, pattering shrouds. Dutch slid swiftly back down the aisle towards the west door, growling low in his throat.

"I need something to break the lock," said Michael grimly, returning to the altar. Iris and Christy began to look round. Michael picked up the shotgun and looked back at the lock. Would one shot . . . ?

Dutch began barking furiously. Something snapped in the rafters and a great chunk of masonry crashed from overhead into the pews.

"Oh no . . ." said Iris, and pushed the children behind her.

And then the west door exploded inwards, splintered and shattered, oak panels whirling apart at the great and intensely evil force outside. Christy shrieked and Michael sheltered her protectively as torn fragments of wood littered the interior of the church. Beyond, the Wyrm's undead vampyres shuffled and milled . . . but could not enter, as Michael had predicted.

But something infinitely more evil and powerful had suddenly burst through their ranks: the second and last of the Wyrm's Familiars.

The Hellhound leaped through the swirling dust and debris of the exploded door—and into the church. In one fluid, black movement it landed with a scrabbling of scythe-like claws on the marble floor. Its red hellfire eyes fixed on them; steam curled from its opening jaws and glinting white fangs as a low, rumbling growl echoed from its hideous maw. It moved towards them. Michael raised the shotgun.

Dutch lunged forward from the head of the aisle to meet the Hellhound; fur bristling, lips curled back threateningly. The Hellhound turned its head downwards slowly to meet what it considered to be an insignificant threat. Overhead, a wooden beam splintered and fell into the church, shattering more pews. Michael felt the floor shake as he steadied his aim and the Hellhound gathered itself to hurtle towards them.

Dutch snarled—and flew at the thing's throat.

The Hellhound's attack was diverted. It twisted to one side, shaking its head to loosen Dutch's grip around its neck. Dutch clung tightly as the thing shook him fiercely from side to side, crashing into the outermost pews. It bellowed in fury and snapped its great head upwards, its jaws catching Dutch's side and ripping open a long gash. Dutch was flung away across the pews. Michael aimed carefully at the Devil Dog and squeezed the trigger.

The stained glass windows in the side walls of the church imploded as another wooden beam and slab of masonry crashed down in a great cloud of dust. The impact shook the floor, Michael staggered . . . and the shotgun discharged its final shot into the front pews. The Hellhound bellowed again and came on down the aisle towards them. Michael could somehow sense that the thing was *smiling*. Iris was suddenly at his side, clutching a candlestick from the altar. She flung it at the approaching horror. The candlestick whirled end-over-end, bouncing harmlessly from the thing's snout as it advanced.

Michael pulled Iris back, cold fear eating at his soul, and then heard a familiar, throaty snarling from the pews behind the Hellhound. In a blur of motion, Dutch re-emerged, bounding from the edge of a seat in one lunging leap, landing precisely in the middle of the Devil Dog's back and sinking his jaws into the back of its head. Michael heard Graham yelling: "Go! Go! Go!" as the black horror reared to one side, crashing into the pews again, trying to shake its attacker off. The beast lunged and thrashed its head, scattering and splintering the wooden pews in all directions, but it could not loosen Dutch's grip. A huge cross-section of wooden beam collapsed into the portico at the front of the church; great cracks chased each other in a nightmare zig-zag through the walls and then Michael heard Christy shouting: "Look! Look!"

Michael turned round and followed the frenzied beck-onings of Christy and the children in the direction of the oak door. A great crack had fractured the wall beside the stairs and a sliver of daylight had appeared in the door jamb. Michael leaped back to the door. The gap between the door and the wall was two inches wide; he could smell the fresh, *clean* air beyond. The Hellhound still thrashed and lunged amidst the pews with Dutch on its back as Michael jammed the shotgun barrel into the gap and began twisting hard, using the weapon as a lever.

Realising what was about to happen, Christy pushed Iris and Karen hard to the floor, swept Graham up in her arms and flung herself against the wall as the Hellhound reared up from the aisle towards the altar. Bellowing like some great primaeval beast, it thrashed back and forth, crashing against the altar with terrifying impact. Michael crouched low in the stairwell as the beast crushed the altar into matchwood, still trying to shake Dutch loose. But Michael's dog would not be budged. The Hellhound's rear legs kicked and lashed backwards, gouging chunks out of the masonry. Overhead, another section of roof disintegrated under the terrible pressure above, and cascaded whirling and crashing into the church. The silver cross between the stained glass windows shook and swayed in its foundations. The Hellhound lunged forward, roaring, bracing its legs and shaking furiously. Dutch slid from its shoulders, kicking and clawing for purchase.

Iris saw the cross toppling from its perch and shouted: "Yes! Yes! Oh . . . *yes!*" And the base of the silver cross finally snapped as it fell forwards from above the shattered altar and plunged downwards. Dutch hit the marble floor on the instant that the cross plunged spear-like into the middle of the Hellhound's back. The Beast snapped its head up, jaws flying open in a great roaring bellow as the cross imbedded itself in the floor, skewering it there. The bellowing of agonised pain echoed throughout the church, the hellish red lights in its eyes going out as a great cloud of billowing black smoke gushed from its maw like an unearthly stream of spouting blood. It collapsed quivering, howled again . . . and then its body evaporated into a gushing cloud of black smoke. The smoke dissolved, and now the Hellhound was gone, leaving the crucifix still imbedded in the floor.

Michael was shouting wordless sounds of joy as he leaped to his feet again and leaned heavily on the shotgun butt. The lock shattered with a loud crack.

The door swung open.

Sunlight and air and freedom flooded in. Beyond, Michael could see grass and flowers; an ordinary, normal sight—but now somehow looking extraordinarily beautiful. "Here! Here! Here!" He was shouting as Christy bundled down the stairs and they tumbled outside into the clean fresh air of a summer morning. Michael turned, feeling the sun on his back, and saw Iris still at the top of the stairs; she was speechless with horror, pointing back into the church.

"Where's Karen?" He bounded back up the steps, pushed Iris behind him and saw what had so horrified her.

Karen had broken away and was kneeling beside Dutch, patting the badly wounded dog as it lay panting on the floor. Beyond her, at the shattered entrance, the Wyrm's vampyres were now shuffling into the church, their inability to enter somehow nullified by the power of the Wyrm.

Before Michael could react, Karen stood up and began moving forward down the aisle. Her face was set in a child's fury, looking at Dutch's blood on her hands as she walked; now glaring ahead at the advancing horde of the undead.

"Karen! No . . ." began Michael, and then was suddenly

319

immobilised from both speaking and moving as *something* . . . some great power . . . held him frozen to the spot.

Karen strode on, stiff-backed and unafraid, speaking in her fury; "Gentle Jesus meek and mild . . . Gentle Jesus meek and mild . . . Gentle Jesus *meek and mild*." There was a shining and ultimately terrifying power about her innocence as she walked towards the west door; a power which somehow made emotion catch at Michael's throat.

The vampyres in the porch were shrinking away from her.

". . . meek and mild . . . Gentle Jesus meek and . . ."

Moaning with one voice, the undead backed out of the porch into Hell again, milling and staggering in confusion. Michael was sweeping forward behind her, not knowing what he was going to do but somehow aware of what he *had* to do as he reached the cross imbedded in the floor and leaned against it, levering it out of the cracked marble. He looked up.

Karen was standing at the entrance. The vampyre horde had gone.

Cradling the cross in his arms, Michael rushed forward down the aisle, gently eased Karen from the doorway and jammed the cross into the doorframe, its edges digging into the wood. He turned back to Karen. She was no longer speaking but her lips were still moving, her eyes glazed with a faraway look. She was very, very beautiful. Michael swept her into his arms, kissed her and buried her face in his shoulder as he strode back through the littered church, keeping a close watch overhead for falling debris. Christy was standing beside the shattered altar and hurried forward to meet him. "What happened?"

Michael handed Karen to her. "I don't know. I don't think I'll ever know. But she scared them away."

They continued on up the aisle, Michael only stopping to scoop Dutch up in his arms before following Christy out into the sunlight.

Outside, in the pure air, they lay on the grass under a cloudless blue sky and breathed in the fragrance of the world. Inside the church, the roof continued to buckle and crack under the great weight of the fog barrier which stretched away before them, left and right like a huge ice wall.

"Where's Iris?" asked Christy in alarm.

Michael looked round. She was gone.

And so was *The Book of the Wyrm*.

Leaving the children on the grass, he sprinted back inside the church, with Christy behind him. What was happening now? Were they never to escape the horror? Inside the crumbling church, they saw Iris at the front portico, clutching the Book in her arms and ducking under the wedged cross out into the shadow-flickering Hell of the Shillingham valley.

"*Iris!* No!" cried Christy as they clambered warily back through the debris, pushing shattered wooden pews aside. Michael dodged backwards as a slab of plaster fell from overhead and shattered explosively before him. Iris had disappeared through the ragged doorframe into the night when they reached the porch at last. Something split apart above them just before Michael reached the cross and Christy grabbed his shirtsleeve, dragging him back.

"Look out, Michael!"

He staggered backwards as a tangle of wooden spars plunged down in front of them, crashing into the doorframe and barring the way ahead. The cross disappeared, buried under rubble.

They ran forward again, clambering through the jagged

321

wooden trellis, trying to reach the door. Michael pulled a spar aside and saw Iris standing just outside in the darkness, by the Land-Rover. She was looking back, *The Book of the Wyrm* clasped to her chest.

"Iris! Come back! What are you doing?"

They continued to claw at the tangled barrier as Iris came towards them and spoke.

"The Wyrm has to be stopped, Michael. Very soon now it's going to . . . to *erupt* from this cocoon it's made around Shillingham into the world. There are two Rituals in this Book. I'm going to say the Words of the first one and make it return to its place of emergence—just like the Book says. Then I'm going to face it with the Second Ritual."

Michael tore out another spar. "But you can't complete the Second Ritual, Iris! You don't have the . . . the . . ."

"I know . . ." Iris opened the Book and looked inside. "I don't have the spike . . . 'bathed in the monthly blood of ten virgins.' " She looked up again. "But I have my faith, Michael. The Second Ritual says that the destroyer of the Wyrm has to end his life. I'm an old woman. And I don't mind dying if it ends this horror. I'll willingly sacrifice my life for that. Maybe even a *part* of the Second Ritual will be enough to stop it. I have to try."

"You can't do it, Iris!" cried Christy, scrabbling at the wood and plaster, clouds of dust swirling around her head. "Come back . . ."

"It has to be done, Christy. But remember I love you."

"No, Iris! No!"

"God bless you."

And then, with utter horror, Michael saw the billowing black cloud of unearthly smoke swirling up on the other side of the Land-Rover. Poisonous, deadly and *alive*, the undulating black mass billowed over the roof towards her.

"Behind you, Iris! *Behind you!*"

Iris spun away from the Land-Rover, backing as the black cloud swarmed over the car, gathering and roiling before her in a shapeless mass of twisting fog tentacles.

"Come back, Iris!" Christy's hands were bleeding as she tore at the debris before her.

The shapeless black mass was acquiring a shape within itself now as it swirled and billowed. Features were emerging; abominable purple light glowed within. Iris stopped backing away and opened the Book.

"*Cunt . . . bitch . . . sow . . .*" said the face of Billy Rifkin.

Iris began to speak. "Narlatonep ad minesrale . . ."

A tentacle of smoke slashed out at Iris from within the black mass. Her hands flew up, the Book whirled from her hands into the drive and she was flung heavily to the ground. The Wyrm laughed; a hideous, mocking, inhuman sound. It surged forward, the face of Billy Rifkin leering and mocking.

"*Old bitch . . . sow . . .*"

The Wyrm swarmed over her, covering her body, leaving only her head visible. Within the black mass, Michael heard the first of those horrifying sounds.

The Wyrm was tearing her body apart.

"*Slowly, Iris . . . slowly . . . slowly . . . slowly . . .*"

Michael seized Christy and pulled her away, burying her sobbing face in his chest. "Don't look, Christy. Oh God . . . don't look . . ."

Beyond, the Wyrm was laughing. The hideous, wet ripping sounds filled the air. Michael could see Iris's face; lips firm and tight, hiding the terrible agony as she turned her head once to look in their direction. She was twenty feet away, but Michael could see that expression of endurance, agony and faith as she turned her head again to look up

323

into the seething, evil face of Billy Rifkin—the face of the Wyrm.

"Slowly, Iris . . . slowly . . ."

"I forgive you, Billy," she said.

The ripping sounds ceased. The newly acquired face of the Wyrm froze. The roiling of the black cloud slowed in its undulating, swirling movement.

"No . . ." said the voice within the cloud. *"You cannot forgive me."*

Michael became aware now of a low moaning, suddenly realising, as the sound increased in pitch and volume, that it was coming from the Wyrm. Iris's eyes were closed now and he knew that she was dead, but the moaning became a long, howling cry of pain, building to an ear-splitting scream of agony as the black cloud withdrew from her bloody and dismembered body.

Shrieking and howling, the black cloud swirled backwards over the Land-Rover; Billy Rifkin's face contorted in pain as it dissolved within the cloud to nothingness. The howling died away as the black cloud vanished into the night.

"What's happened, Michael?" sobbed Christy. "I don't understand it."

"I'm not sure, Christy. But somehow, Iris has hurt the Wyrm very badly. It's had to retreat."

"How, Michael? I don't understand."

"I don't know. But she's wounded it—and she may have given us some time."

"Time for what?"

"Time to kill it."

Chapter Twenty

"I'm going back," said Michael.

Karen and Graham were still on the outside with Dutch, under strict instructions to remain there. The debris obscuring the church door had been cleared. The overhead pressure on the roof had been weakened since Iris had forced the Wyrm to retreat, and no further debris had fallen. Michael had covered Iris's body with a sheet of tarpaulin from the back of the Land-Rover. Christy had watched, haggard and drawn, as he had retrieved *The Book of the Wyrm*. He had been silent for a long time, and she had been unable to find words herself until he had spoken.

"To kill yourself, Michael? To give your life the way that Iris was going to sacrifice herself? You can't do it. I won't let you."

"I'm not going to kill myself, Christy. But I think I may have found a way to use the Rituals and destroy the Wyrm. We can't allow it to be loose in the world."

"What way, Michael? You know what the Second Ritual requires. I'm the new Keeper of the Secret. Me. Not you. I'm a Warwick. The responsibility's mine. I'm going back, not you."

Michael thought of the prospects for their future life together if the Wyrm was not faced and was allowed to emerge from Shillingham. "We'll both go."

"Someone will have to die, Michael. And it's not going to be you."

"Neither of us is going to die. I promise you."

"What are you going to do?"

"I don't want to tell you yet. But there may be a way."

"We can't fulfil the Second Ritual. We don't have that . . . that spike . . . forged in the monthly blood of virgins. How do we get that?"

"We've already got it."

"Where?!"

"In the Storehouse ruins. The spike that was taken out of the Wyrm when the gibbet was removed. We're going to put it back."

"But the Storehouse was destroyed . . ."

"It's solid metal. It'll still be there."

"We don't *know* that, Michael! It could have been destroyed."

"It'll be there."

"But it's been used once. Will it work again?"

"I don't know. It's all we've got."

Christy moved forward, took Michael's hand and looked up into his eyes. For a long while, they stood there. Then she said: "Come on." She pulled him back to the church door.

Inside, she led him over the rubble-strewn floor, up the aisle and to the shattered altar. Sunlight still streamed through the stained glass windows and up the stairwell on the left.

"Do you believe what Iris said? About love?"

Michael stroked her hair. "I believe it."

"Then ask me to be your wife."

"What?"

"Here. Now. Ask me to be your wife. And if there is a God in this hellish valley, He'll hear."

Michael kissed her. Beyond them, light and sun and the

326

world of men and women. Behind them, all the terrors, torment and horror of Hell.

"Will you be my wife, Christy?"

"Yes. Will you be my husband?"

"Yes, I will." Michael embraced her again.

"Are we married, Michael? Do you believe it?"

"I've never believed in anything more."

They turned and looked back at the ruined porch of the church, and the crawling shadows beyond.

"It's time to go back now, isn't it?"

"Yes, Christy."

Chapter Twenty-one

As the Land-Rover roared back through the churchyard gates onto the mountain road, and the guttering fires of Shillingham came into view once more, under its pall of night, Christy clutched *The Book of the Wyrm* tightly in her lap and thought:

It's my responsibility, Michael. I know you're intending to kill yourself. But I'm not going to let you. If we have time before the Wyrm recovers—and if that spike is still there, only one more person is going to die. And that person is going to be the last Warwick.

As Michael drove, he could feel the hard object at his side, tucked secretly into his belt and under his shirt. He had found it in a toolbox in the back of the Land-Rover when he had been pulling out the tarpaulin to cover Iris's body. The edge of the object was razor sharp and he had quickly hidden it in his shirt when Christy had not been looking.

He thought of the sacrifice ahead and fingered the object as they drove.

It was a hand axe.

Chapter Twenty-two

Michael stopped the Land-Rover at Split Crow Lane, looking down to the burning, smoking ruins of Shillingham. Would the Wyrm re-emerge to stop them? He did not think so. The instinctive feeling that it was still in retreat and recovery had not left him. Steeling himself, he turned into the rutted, cracked road leading to the village, swerving past the ruins of the Dun Cow. He remembered standing at the bar with Grover when the windows had exploded. Had that really been only three days ago? It seemed to him that on that night his own private hell had been replaced with a more general and horrifying Hell. He gritted his teeth, remembering the task ahead and feeling again the hardness of the hatchet hidden in his shirt.

The road from the Dun Cow to the Storehouse had been destroyed, paving and cobblestones now a tumbled bed of shattered stone and fissured earth. Michael swerved onto the grass, looking ahead to the ruined shell of the Storehouse.

The Land-Rover stopped beside the ruin.

Please God, thought Christy, *let it be there*.

Michael vaulted over a blackened stone wall into the ashes and debris of the Storehouse, remembering that he had seen the Wyrm's sarcophagus under blackened beams. He shoved a carboned beam of wood to one side and saw the coffin, turned and trudged back through the ashes, mentally recalling his conversation with Elphick when he had walked the length of the gibbet which had lain on the floor.

"Where? Where?" asked Christy, scrabbling in the ashes.

"Ten . . . fifteen . . . twenty feet . . ." Michael waded through the rubble, furiously throwing detritus to either side of him as he walked.

"Where?"

"Here . . ." Michael stooped low, scattering ashes with his hands. Something caught his shin, tearing the flesh, but he did not care. His grasping hands found nothing but earth and ashes.

"Where, Michael? Where?"

"Here! It's *got* to be here!"

But there was nothing.

In a frenzy, he raised clouds of dust and ash as he rummaged in the ruins. He stumbled on, kicking and clawing.

Nothing.

He collapsed to his knees, sobbing. His knuckles were torn and bleeding. And now, everything was crowding in on him. Memories of fear—fear of his own making. Realities of fear—the terror of the Wyrm. Memories of insecurity and unease—realities of a new and happy future with Christy, now denied. Horrors exorcised, and of a new Horror unearthed. Memories of Grover and Iris—of innocent people killed. Michael raised his head to the undulating black mass of cloud which covered Shillingham and which soon threatened to explode into the world as the Wyrm emerged from the cocoon in all its horror.

"You stinking bastard, unholy bloody thing!" he

screamed, punching the night-black sky. "You won't win! You'll never win! As long as I'm alive you'll never win ... you ... you ..."

Christy plunged through the ruins, clasping Michael in a firm embrace as he knelt. Tears coursed down her grime-stained face. Michael lunged at the ash before him in rage. Christy pulled him back, covering his face in kisses. She turned back to look at the ashes and saw ... the black-ened, burned tip of something jutting from the ruins.

She dived forward, seizing the object, sobbing as she heaved it free.

It was the spike.

Burned and fused, corroded and pitted, it had crumbled to a three-foot length, its hollowed end powdering to ash. But it was the spike.

Christy turned, her joy dissolving when she remembered her task ahead.

Michael thrust forward, grabbing the spike like some kind of prize or trophy.

You won't, she thought. *I won't let you die. Never. It's my responsibility. My life.*

An end to life, thought Michael. *A small price to pay to end this thing forever ...*

Chapter Twenty-three

The Land-Rover was parked at Split Crow crossroads.

Michael stood at the safety barrier, looking down into the gaping black maw of the Pit. Christy was at his side, holding the guttering torch of wood and cloth that he had improvised. Their shadows leaped and lengthened in the smouldering shadows of Shillingham's Hell.

"Remember how it was?" Christy sobbed, looking back at the ruined village.

"Yes . . . but I don't want to," replied Michael.

He lashed the rope he had cut from the safety barrier to one of the wooden posts which had been planted by the workmen and threw it into the yawning aperture. He reached for *The Book of the Wyrm*.

"My responsibility, Michael," said Christy. "Mine. Not yours."

He nodded, took the torch from her and, cradling the shrunken, deteriorating spike under one arm, snatched up the rope and climbed over the makeshift barrier. The hand axe was still there in his shirt—a constant reminder. He dropped the torch into the hole, watching as it bounced to the boulder-strewn bottom. He had been through too much Hell and suffering to care about the dark unknown below him as he scrambled downwards into the Pit, feet kicking and scraping at the rough earthen sides of the chimney as he descended.

Twenty feet down, the darkness ended. Everything was lit by a poisonous, purple-blue. The Pit's sides were covered in a luminous glowing something as he descended, as if they had somehow been coated in the abnormal, unearthly slime of some great slug. He was aware that Christy was following him down the rope, *The Book of the Wyrm* still clutched firmly under one arm as she descended. He knew and blessed the fact that she was braver, more courageous than he had ever been in his life.

You're not going to die, Christy, he thought.

And then his legs kicked into empty space as he reached the cave below the Pit. Squirming and twisting, he finally reached the floor of the crossroads which had disgorged the horror upon Shillingham. Looking up, he saw Christy still descending. He stepped back, catching her waist and steadying her as she landed.

Beyond them, the hewn stone walls of the cave beckoned.

He picked up the torch and clambered forwards, Christy following close behind.

The Wyrm had been tunnelling, just as he had guessed. There were gaping black fissures in the cave on all sides, tunnels of darkness leading to Hell knows where. In the centre of the illuminated underground chamber, he jammed the torch into the cracked floor and turned back, reaching for *The Book of the Wyrm*. Christy flinched away.

"What are you going to do?"

"I'm going to read the First Ritual."

"And the Second Ritual? What about that?" She grabbed his torn shirt collar. "You're going to kill yourself, aren't you? You want to die and leave me."

"No, Christy. I'm not. Believe me. I'm not. Give me the Book."

She gave it to him. Michael opened it, turning back into the shadowed recesses of the Pit, still clutching the spike under his left armpit. It had crumbled a further ten inches, now only a blackened remnant of the spike which had once impaled the Wyrm.

Not you, Michael. Not you . . . Christy looked at the carved stone walls of the luminous cavern and considered the possibility of death by smashing her head against its jagged walls.

"Narlatonep ad minesrale por verminus necroplenet naa hadlagorg." Michael looked up from the book. "Okay, you bastard. Come back . . . come back . . ."

For a long moment, there was nothing.

And then, gradually, they became aware of a subterranean, rushing roar—like the approach of some underground train. The distant roar became a gradually increasing vibration within the chamber; an echoing, booming blast of *something* which approached at a terrible, unearthly velocity.

"It's working!" shouted Michael.

They watched the shadow-wavering tunnels on all sides, waiting for the Horror to erupt.

"Which tunnel?" asked Christy. "Which tunnel?"

The hewn stone wall on their left quivered under some terrible impact, cracking and splitting. Michael whirled, fighting to regain balance as the wall suddenly burst apart in a roaring crash of cascading stone and earth. A cloud of choking dust enveloped them.

Shrieking, the Wyrm erupted from its new tunnel into the cave.

Michael backed away, keeping Christy close.

"Oh, my God, Michael. My *God* . . ."

They looked in utter horror at the new incarnation of the Wyrm as the billowing dust cloud settled around it.

Abominable and evil, it crawled to the centre of the chamber, weaving and twisting from side to side, its horrifying bulk lit by the guttering torch.

The Wyrm had created its new body from the bodies of Shillingham's undead. Hundreds of torn, white corpses had been *compacted* together in a horrifying contorted, writhing mass of dead flesh. The Wyrm had become a vast and hideous coiling serpent the size of an elephant, its flesh composed of compressed and decomposing limbs. Faces of Shillingham's dead peered from the swollen bulk like individual eyes. It coiled and reared before them, like a gigantic cobra. Dead arms and legs flapped loose from the main bulk of the thing, as if beckoning. The knotted, contorted "head" turned to *look* down at them. A great hissing sound issued from the Horror.

It was waiting.

Michael opened the Book, stepping forward, fighting to keep his gorge down. The Wyrm was less than fifteen feet from them. There was not much time.

"You can't, Michael! I won't let you . . ." Christy tried to grab the Book.

"Stay back, Christy!" The look of fierce anger on his face halted her. He turned back to the Wyrm, intensely aware that the thing was gloating, knowing that it would soon be free and confident that he could not meet the Second Ritual.

Christy began to cry as Michael read from the Book again: "Omini Chraston Perdolchey ad Iminis Vermini."

He closed the Book and spoke directly to the thing. "You're bound by the Ritual of Words. The Words in this Book. The Words have Power and you must obey . . ."

"So do it, scribe," said a hideous, hissing voice which filled the chamber. *"Do it now. Why falter? My time is upon me. I will be free. You are too weak."*

"The spilling of blood!" shouted Michael, looking down at the spike beside his feet. "My life-blood! The ending of my olde life—that's what it says!" He pulled his shirt open, reached inside and found the hand axe. "You're bound by Words, the actual Words! Bound by the Words in this Book! And it says that 'the Wielder must strike first the blow that will end his olde life . . .' "

Christy saw the hand axe and screamed.

"I am bound," hissed the Wyrm. *"But you will not . . ."*

In one split-second, Michael thought of the fear and terror to which he had been prey as a writer, of the nervous breakdown, of *The Borderland*. He dropped to his knees in front of the hideous white thing, took the hatchet in his left hand and held it high. Frozen in horror, Christy could only watch as Michael raised his face to the Wyrm again.

"Bound by the Power of Words." *Please, God . . .* "You must accept my Words. You are bound to accept." Michael looked down again, at the right hand which had written his novels.

"I end my olde life!"

Teeth gritted, he gripped a boulder with his right hand and swung the hatchet down hard.

"Michael, no! Oh please, *no!*" screamed Christy.

The hatchet chopped savagely through his wrist into the boulder. Blood spouted from the stump of his arm. The severed hand flopped to the cave floor, fingers twitching. And then the pain came. Prepared for the act and for hideous pain, Michael was still unprepared for the agonising, mortal ferocity of that pain. He fell forward, dropping the hatchet and hugging his forearm as blood jetted over his shirt front.

"Michael, Michael, Michael . . ." Christy swept forward in horror as he began to claw at the cave floor for the spike.

"I've got to . . . kill it . . . Christy . . . the spike . . . I've got to . . ."

Above them, the Wyrm's head still hovered, silent.

"You're dying, Michael!"

". . . tourniquet . . . spike . . . I've got to . . ." Consciousness was slipping away from him as he fumbled for the spike, life-blood gushing from his arm. Delirium convulsed him. ". . . given up my *olde* life, Christy. Sacrificed it . . . like the Ritual says . . . must accept . . . token life-blood . . . hand . . ." Dimly, he was aware of Christy's face above him.

Time and meaning had vanished in a blazing red haze of pain and confusion. She was crying, holding the guttering torch beside her. She was looking at the torch and holding up the ruined stump of his arm as blood gushed over her, looking back at him again now and saying something about . . .

". . . the *only* way, Michael. I love you."

Christy thrust the torch flame under Michael's wrist, holding his arm fiercely in place. Pain crashed across his senses like a crimson tidal wave and consciousness left him.

The blood had stopped. Christy laid the arm gently across Michael's chest and stood up, eyes blazing. Weaving and twisting, the Wyrm remained silent. Its gloating had gone. Bound by the power of words, it waited.

"You're bound . . ." began Christy, retrieving the Book.

"But he cannot fulfil the Words," hissed the terrible voice of the Wyrm.

And now, it was coming to Christy, a series of fleeting images in her mind now all making sense. The Words. The ruined church. The spike. Iris's death. The ending of an olde life.

"We're man and wife," said Christy quietly.

"But he cannot fulfil the Words."

"In God's eyes we are one flesh. We're one. And his act is *my* act."

". . . *cannot* . . ."

"His hand is my hand. His words are my words."

Christy picked up the spike.

"You are a woman, not a man. You are not the Keeper of the Secret."

"The Words in the Book say nothing about the Keeper being a man. It says 'the Head of Household.' "

". . . *cannot* . . ."

336

"And ever since my mother died, *I've* been the Warwick Head of Household—because my father was incapable of it."

"CANNOT!"

And then Christy saw it within the mangled, compacted bodies which comprised the Wyrm's throat: a twisted, contorted face, mouthing obscenities. It was a hideously familiar face and, again, it screamed . . .

"CANNOT!"

. . . as she raised the spike in both hands like a spear and lunged forwards, ramming it deep into Billy Rifkin's screaming throat.

Black blood gushed in stinking jets from around the shaft as Christy held it there, thrusting deeper and shouting wordless sounds of hate and horror and fury at the thing. The blood soaked her face and body like black oil as she held the spike there. And then the Wyrm reeled away from her, shrieking and contorting, the spike buried deep within its obscene body.

Christy dragged Michael away as the howling, roaring Serpent writhed and coiled in agony. Its twisting coils reared upwards against the cave roof. Soil and boulders began to fall. It lashed sideways, unable to remove the spike, and Christy could see that the chamber walls were beginning to crumble.

"Get up, Michael! Get up! We can't go back the way we came, we have to use a tunnel. So you've *got to get up! Michael!*"

Bellowing and screaming like a primaeval beast, the Wyrm lashed upwards again; earth and boulders fell from overhead, crushing and pulverising the thing's obscene "flesh."

"We'll be buried, Michael. Get up! *Get up! GET UP!*"

In a dream, Michael was standing up. There was pain somewhere, but he could not identify where it was coming from. He was only aware that he was in a dark place which was shaking and roaring as Christy shouted meaningless words at him. In a dream, he allowed himself to be dragged into darkness, looking back hazily to see avalanching boulders and clouds of cascading earth plunging down onto something which bellowed and roared and twisted.

Darkness swallowed him as Christy dragged him fiercely onwards. Once again, time lost its meaning. Words echoed from somewhere inside his head as he staggered on.

The Power of Words . . . olde life . . . new life . . .

Sleeping, he kept moving.

Chapter Twenty-four

Light swarmed into his eyes.

Christy was dragging him up from darkness into the brightness of day. Staggering on loose soil, he allowed himself to be pulled forward.

"It's gone, Michael!" she shouted at him as they emerged from underground. "The fog barrier's gone!" The words were meaningless to him but dimly he was aware that they were standing on the rim of a rough, earthen hole, dimly he was aware that they were standing in the cemetery behind Shillingham's police station, where Christy's mother was buried. There was a smell of burning in his nostrils. He wondered if it had anything to do with the fact that his right hand was burning.

"It's dead," Christy said. Beneath her words, a distant

underground roaring of collapsing rock and earth. "Dead."

. . . *an olde life . . . dead . . .* echoed the words in Michael's head.

Much, much later . . . in a lighter and better dream, he thought that he could hear a dog barking and see two familiar children running joyfully towards him.

The death of an olde life, echoed the words. *The beginning of the new.*

Epilogue

"Do you know what fear is?" asked the white-haired man.

No. Perhaps not. But I could sense it in his question, feel its cold breath in my face and its cold hand on my shoulder. I could see its effects in the man's prematurely white hair. No shit. Honest. It must have been eighty degrees in that bar, but I swear I felt a shiver running through my body.

"I mean . . . real . . . *fear?*" he asked again.

He didn't wait for an answer. Not that I could have spoken just then, anyway.

"Well, I do. God help me, I do."

He did. I believed him.

He began to talk.

"I've seen it and faced it. And believe me when I say that . . ."

He stopped and looked out of the window again. And again, I could see the inner conflict reflected in his eyes. He wanted to tell me things, I could sense it. But something deep inside was holding him back. Had I finally lost him?

He turned back to me, reaching for his drink with the stump of his right hand. Seeing his error, he laughed reflectively and then said: "Look . . . you're a journalist. But you probably don't realise just how powerful words can be. Certain words. I want to tell you about what happened in Shillingham . . . but I can't. Because I made a pact. A pact of words. And the instant I tell you what really happened and commit my *words* to paper—then I become a writer again. And on the instant that happens, the pact will be broken and something bad . . . something very, very *bad* . . . could be reactivated."

"Have another drink . . ." I began. "There's no hassle. Take your time. Perhaps we can . . ."

He shook his head sadly, sighed and sat back. "I can't," he said. "I'm sorry . . . but I can't tell you anything."

I had lost him. Desperately I searched for ways of saving the situation. But I knew that it was hopeless. There was no point in continuing. Crestfallen, I sipped at my own drink and looked around the hotel bar. I had been so damned close. On the other side of the bar, I saw that his wife and two children had entered, and now she was smiling and waving at him. He saw them and waved back as they came over . . . and then he turned to me for the last time.

"It's all in the stars," he said. "Just pray that they never change."

I don't know what he meant, and I've thought about it ever since. It makes no sense to me at all, despite the conviction in his voice and the look on his face. But I believe it when he said he'd seen real Fear.

And even though I don't know why, I'll continue to pray that my stars don't change.